BROTHER OF THE KING CONSORT

Author's Note

Dear Readers,

I want to start by saying a huge thank you to everyone for how much love you've shown 'Queen of The Dome', the first book in this series. I never imagined that so many people would not only read the book but enjoy it.

For this reason, I've made the decision to expedite the release of 'Brother of The King Consort'. I couldn't wait any longer for you guys to read this book and have the opportunity to see a new side to the characters that weren't given as much attention in Book 1.

In regards to Book 1, I highly recommend that you read that one first. Not only does it have most of the world-building for the series, but there are multiple references, parallels, and character backstories that won't be appreciated or understood without the base knowledge from 'Queen of The Dome'.

Before you read though, here's a small disclaimer: The following book is heavily centered around two main characters, one of whom is deaf. While this piece of literature has been subject to a sensitivity screening, it falls under the genre of fantasy, and therefore, has very few scenes and plot points that can be applied to the life of a deaf person in the real world. Additionally, sign language is a huge component of this book, however, as this is completely fictional, all the dialogue that is held in sign language is not meant to be read or interpreted as ASL, BSL, LSF, etc. That is why you will see multiple words in their signed dialogue (in italics and inverted commas) that do not appear in many sign languages and would not make sense being signed. An aspect of the character's journey that may be transferrable to the real world is her overall experience regarding being born hearing and becoming deaf later in life. This book explores not only her personal experience, but it attempts to give an insight into how the people around her change and begin to treat her on a social level in hopes of bringing light to the very real stigmas and attitudes that deaf people deal with on a daily basis.

I'd like to offer my apologies if this is not the representation that you were looking forward to, but I do hope that you enjoy the book regardless, if you do decide to read on.

That being said, thank you again and please enjoy 'Brother of The King Consort' PS: Please read the CW/TW

- Amizah R

Content/Trigger Warning: this book contains strong language, graphic violence, sexually explicit scenes, and discreet references to sexism

Table of Contents

Prologue

"Like this."

Drake stood behind Cassian and bent down to adjust his hold on the slingshot. "You hold this part, tight as you can," he said as he held his hand over Cassian's. "And you use this hand to pull back. Try."

He stood back.

Cassian squinted his left eye, holding onto the frame as firmly as he could with his little hand. Pulling back the elastic, he let it rip.

The stone didn't go flying though.

It fell to the ground as the elastic slapped against his finger.

"Ow!" he cried.

His father rushed to his aid.

"Hey, hey, it's okay. That was a good try."

Cassian couldn't help the tears that welled in his eyes as he rubbed his hand.

"Let me see," Drake murmured.

He reluctantly held out his hand. Grasping his small hand in his palm, Drake blew gently on his red finger before giving it a soft rub.

"See, all better." He emphasized his point by pulling Cassian's fingers apart awkwardly and wiggling them around.

He released an amused giggle, pulling a smile from Drake.

"Good man." Drake patted Cassian on the back. "Want to try again?"

He nodded eagerly.

"Okay, here." He picked the slingshot back up and handed it to Cassian, standing next to him. "But this time, keep your hand lower, away from the 'V'."

Cassian followed his direction and pulled back the elastic to try again.

Then, in the blink of an eye, Cassian was no longer standing beside his father. He was facing him, head-on. And the slingshot wasn't a slingshot anymore.

It was a gun.

"Cassian, what are you doing?"

Cassian's small chest rose and fell as he mumbled his next words. "What I have to do..."

"Put the gun down."

He did no such thing.

"Cassian, please. I'm your father."

"Sorry, daddy."

BANG!

Chapter One

Cassian leaped halfway off the bed, chest heaving, drenched in sweat.

Again.

Again and again, he woke up like this. The nightmares had never stopped. They were all different but followed the same theme.

Drake's death.

It was inescapable.

He thought that moving away and changing his environment might make a difference, but he should've known better. He hadn't slept a straight night in the year before he left Old Dome territory, he was only fooling himself in thinking that he'd get a moment of reprieve six years later.

Cassian stretched out an arm to peak the curtains.

It was still dark outside.

He knew he wasn't going to be able to go back to sleep anytime soon, so he opted to do something productive instead.

Rolling out of bed, he padded over to his small drawer, picking up a roll of tape. Grabbing his headphones off the top, he made his way through the house and into the basement.

He lit a small candle on the mantle before putting his headphones on and quickly taping up his knuckles.

The headphones didn't even work, there was no electricity. Cassian just liked the way that they blocked out some of the noise. Noise like the rain he could hear pattering on the roof on the floor above.

He had to admit, the advanced hearing came in handy, but sometimes it was too much. Sometimes he wanted a break from the racket.

Even though he'd lit a candle, he closed his eyes as he stood in front of the punching bag. It was as close to sensory deprivation as he could get.

Pulling back his fist, he started with a few simple combos, just to warm up. As he gradually picked up the intensity, he reminded himself not to go too hard. After the way he'd just woken up, he wanted nothing more than to tear the bag into two, but he only had one and he wasn't eager to trek to the market in the heart of Terra to get another.

1-2

1-1-2

1-2-3-2

Squelch, squelch...

Cassian tore the headphones off his head and dove into a roll toward the mantle before blowing out the candle, all in less than five seconds.

Someone's outside.

While that might not have been unusual for most people, Cassian never had visitors. His small, secluded house, over a fortnight's walk from Terra, made sure of that. There was only one person in Terra who knew where he lived, and she knew not to show up unexpectedly.

Cassian toed off his shoes and started toward the stairs, swift and silent.

He'd spent years customizing his home to his exact specifications, and he knew it well. Even in the darkness, in the pitch-black room, he knew where the twists and turns were, the creaky floorboards, even where there was a slight incline or decline in the foundation.

Whoever was on their way had chosen the wrong house.

As he made it up onto the ground floor, he took a risk in whispering, "Echo."

She should've been asleep, but he wanted to make sure she was out of the way if there was going to be an intruder.

"Echo," he called again.

No answer.

Squelch, squelch, squelch...

Though dampened by the mud, he could still hear the footsteps getting closer, could feel the slight shake in the ground as they neared.

He huffed.

Echo was a smart girl, she'd be okay.

Cassian, his steps soft as clouds, darted to the front door and stood beside it, his back to the wall. He slid his hand above the door frame and felt around for his knife.

Got it.

Squelch, squelch, squelch...squelch.

He held his breath.

Maybe he was being paranoid. Maybe they were just passing by.

Knock, knock.

Cassian gave them no time to be surprised as he swung the door open and grabbed the figure standing in the night.

Pulling the stranger in, he threw them against the wall beside the door and brandished the knife against the intruder's throat before kicking the door shut with one foot.

He didn't hear anyone else, but he wasn't taking any chances. If so, a hostage would discourage them.

"Who are you?" he breathed harshly.

"What the fuck, Cass?!"

Devin?

"Who are you?" he asked again. He could never be too sure.

"Who do you think, asshole?"

Yeah, it's Devin.

That thought didn't comfort Cassian as much as it should have though.

Why is he here?

He released him before heading over to the fireplace.

"Cass? Where'd you go?"

Cassian ignored him and lit a match before placing it onto the short logs.

As Devin blinked, he glared at Cassian, squinting in the dim light. "If you're not gonna slice me up, can you put that shit away, you fucking psycho?"

Cassian looked down and realized that he was still holding his knife. He brushed past Devin and replaced it on top of the door frame.

As he turned, he watched as Devin's eyes fully took him in. "Woah. So that's what you've been doing out here all this time."

Cassian didn't pay him any mind. "Why are you here?"

Devin cocked his head back. "Hello, to you too."

When he only raised his brows, Devin's demeanor shifted. "I need your help."

"No."

Despite his history with Devin, he couldn't get involved. He didn't even want to think about the past, let alone walk right back into it.

"Cassian, it's serious."

"I don't doubt that. Answer's still no."

Devin's annoyance started to peak. "Do you really think Lia would've told me where you were if it weren't absolutely necessary?"

That got Cassian thinking.

He trusted Lia with his whole being. He knew that when he told her he planned to leave, she would object, but respect his wishes. He knew that she wouldn't have sent Devin if there was another viable option.

Gods give me strength...

"Talk," Cassian said, hoping that he wouldn't regret this.

"You might want to sit down."

Cassian's head was spinning.

When he left, he knew that things had changed, would change.

But not like this.

Primas.

What Devin explained made sense. It was just a lot for him to take in.

He was relatively new to the whole gifted thing in general, so this was basically uncharted territory for him.

Cassian didn't mean to be blunt when he asked, but he was still failing to make the connection. "What does this have to do with me?"

Devin didn't look offended. "It's Emori."

He nodded, urging him to continue.

"She's a prima. A God of Magic."

Cassian didn't give him a reaction, but he mentally choked. He didn't know Emori that well, but what Devin had just described didn't sound like her at all.

"How?"

Devin's knee bounced for a while. He seemed reluctant, but it was obvious that he knew he wouldn't get anywhere without giving Cassian the full story.

"When I was sixteen," he started. "I used to sneak around the edges of The Dome with some older kids. They would dare each other to see who would get the closest or who would touch the wall. I chickened out and they all made their fun." He sighed reminiscently, running a hand through his short locs. "But one night, I wanted to prove to myself that I could do it, so I snuck out and went to the very edge. I was about to touch it when a girl appeared, right in front of me. She was injured, real bad." His face tightened. "Her neck was cut open. I don't know how she was still alive, but she was gonna bleed out if I didn't do something...so I started digging."

"You dug?"

Devin nodded. "I wasn't sure if it would even work with it being magic and all, but something just told me to. I dug for almost an hour until the hole was big enough for me to crawl through and bring her in. I couldn't leave her after that so I took her home." He shrugged. "It was easy to hide her and sneak her food with all my siblings in the house. When she healed, she explained everything to me. She told me about our history, her people." Devin shook his head. "They were the ones that did that to her. Her friend turned her in for speaking against the crown. They slit her throat and threw her into the River Terra. She's been with me since that day and now..."

"Now what?" Cassian quickly asked, invested.

Devin looked like he was about to start panicking. "They took her, Cass."

Cassian frowned.

The primas?

"Who took her?"

"Your sister-in-law," he gritted out.

Wait. "What?"

Deianira took Emori?

This wasn't making any sense.

Devin's gaze bounced around the room as he blinked rapidly. "After what Lia found, I came clean. They would have never known what they were dealing with if I didn't tell them," he said, his voice gravelly, "and they took her in return." He sniffed and shook his head. "The girls are going crazy. I didn't know where else to go."

It still wasn't adding up. "Devin, took her where?"

"They've got her locked up in the palace. They won't even let me see her. Said they don't trust me not to bust her out."

“Would you?” Cassian responded.

From the way he’d seen Devin around Emori, he had a feeling that Deianira had the right idea.

“Hell yeah, I would. She shouldn't be in there!”

“Well...shouldn’t she?”

The look that Devin shot Cassian wasn’t an angry one. It was one full of hurt.

He narrowed his eyes. “Are you fucking serious, right now?”

“Devin, think about it for a second. You just described a terrifying species of monsters to me and then tell me your wife is one of them. What do you want me to think?”

He advanced menacingly. “You shouldn’t be thinking about it, you should trust me! She’s the mother of my children!”

Cassian dropped his head into his hands. This was why he didn’t like visitors.

Barring the nightmares, he’d been in a state of relative peace for six years and the second Devin walks through the door, there’s a new problem.

But as much as he wanted to distance himself, he felt for him.

Devin adored Emori. The same way that Cade adored Deianira.

Cassian couldn’t relate, but he understood.

Though he was young back then, there was no missing the way his mother doted on Drake. Even when her love wasn’t reciprocated.

“What do you want me to do?” Cassian asked. He should’ve started there.

Devin stared at him as he took a few breaths, calming himself. “Deianira said that her release is dependent on her cooperation and proof that she’s not going to be a danger to anyone in Terra.”

“Is she willing to cooperate?”

"Yes, but she can't speak to them. Not properly." Cassian immediately understood. "She won't talk to anyone but me, and I can't go near her until she's released."

"Then, how do you expect me to communicate with her?"

He flicked his eyes to Cassian nervously before speaking under his breath.

"Psionicism."

Cassian tensed.

He shouldn't know-

"Lia told me."

Oh, when I get my hands on her...

"What about Salem?" Cassian offered.

Devin ran his hands through his locs again. "They already tried. Emori has a higher threshold for things like this and she's not responding well. Salem's not powerful enough."

"And I am?"

"I don't know, but this was my last shot." He sighed before looking back up. "Lia seems to think you are."

When Cassian remained silent, Devin continued.

"It would make sense. You know, with the restoration. Cade can not only read emotions but manipulate them."

"I'm not Cade," Cassian responded defensively.

"I'm not saying you are. But you could be enhanced too. I didn't feel any different when I woke up."

Cassian tossed the idea around in his mind. It wouldn't be doing Devin a favor, it would be saving lives. Thousands of them. Information from Emori could prevent something catastrophic.

"Does anyone else know you're here?"

"No, only Lia."

Good. He could do this for them and come home, back to his life. Simple.

Cassian sighed and stood up to make his way to his room.

Devin sagged with relief. "Thank you."

"Yeah," he tossed over his shoulder.

"I'll go pull the truck around!" Devin called.

He heard the door open before a yelp filled the air.

"Gods!"

Cassian took a step out of his room to see what had caused Devin's reaction. When he saw her, he smiled for the first time tonight.

"Echo! Here, girl!"

Echo jumped off of Devin's chest and sprinted to Cassian at full speed.

He opened his arms as the ten-pound long-haired fur ball jumped at him.

"You were outside all this time?" he whispered, rubbing behind her ears.

"No, I'm fine. I'll help myself up. I get mowed down by fat cats all the time." Devin shook his head as he rose off of the ground and headed out the door.

Echo watched Cassian, fascinated, as he moved around the room, packing up his things.

When he finished, he picked up her bed from the corner of his room and held it under his arm as he made his way toward the door.

"Come on, Coco. We're going on a road trip."

Chapter Two

Salem paced across the room in front of the glass.

Why won't it work?

She'd never had an issue using her power on someone, and even though she knew that Emori was a prima, and hence, harder to manipulate, she couldn't help the feeling of uselessness that washed over her.

She didn't fail. It just never happened.

Success was what made her Salem.

She'd been in the room for hours now, and while there was nothing more she could do, she didn't want to leave the room and face Deianira and Cade to tell them that she'd achieved nothing.

So like she'd done eight times before, Salem tried again.

Emori...

Emori didn't move from her curled-up position.

Emori.

Still nothing.

Emori!

When Emori's head snapped up and her lips parted, Salem knew that she was right back to square one.

The glass shook, so did the floors.

It took a while, but when they settled, the lights in the room blinked three times.

Salem understood Deianira's message.

That's enough.

She reluctantly turned her back to the glass box and swiped her bracelet across the panel. She didn't look back as she walked out of the assessment room.

Deianira stood outside.

'It's okay,' she signed. *'You'll get it tomorrow.'*

Salem nodded even though she didn't believe it.

Bzz. Bzz.

She brought her bracelet closer to her face and read the message before turning to Deianira.

'Meeting in thirty. Devin's back.'

Devin parked the truck on the loading dock before walking with Cassian through the palace, Echo trailing behind them.

"Okay," Devin clapped his hands once they entered the east stairwell from the sub-level.

As they walked up the steps, memories came at Cassian from all directions.

The invasion.

Lockdown.

Sneaking through the sub-level.

Meeting Emori.

Cassian quickly shook them off as Devin started.

"She's told me a bit about Patriam but I'm sure there's a lot I don't know. If you can, ask her about Pola."

"What's Pola?" Cassian asked.

"Who's Pola?" he corrected. "Right now, I only know that she's running things in Patriam. They have a monarchy, just like we do, but you don't get elected or inherit the throne. You win it."

"How?"

"Combat trials. It's like a death match. Two individuals from each affinity, of prima blood, over the age of sixteen. They hold one every ten years and Pola's won the last five."

"You can re-enter the trials," Cassian noted.

"Yes. I don't know a lot about her. Only that she's crazy as shit. According to Emori, more and more people are taking a stand against her. That might have something to do with why they're making their way here. They could be seeking refuge."

"Deianira won't go for that." Cassian hadn't been able to get that image that Devin had shown him out of his head. "They might be against her, but they're still a danger to us."

"Not all of them," Devin protested. "Emori's been here for nearly ten years with no issue. They don't have to live that way."

Cassian wasn't so sure.

"I called a meeting on the way over here so they should all be waiting."

He paused. "They know I'm here?"

"No, but you'll have to see them at some point," he told Cassian softly.

He knew this. He just hadn't prepared himself to see them all again, especially Cade.

He wasn't afraid that his brother would condemn him for what he did to their father.

He was afraid he wouldn't. Afraid that after all this time, after everything that Cassian had done to him, he'd still forgive him. He didn't feel like he deserved his forgiveness.

In the year that Cassian had spent in the palace after the incident, everyone walked on eggshells around him. Treated him like he was fragile. He knew what he'd done and everyone pretending that it never happened did nothing to assuage his guilt.

In fact, it made it worse.

A little nudge on his leg pulled Cassian out of his head.

He leaned down and gave Echo a few firm pats before turning back to Devin.

"Let's get this over with."

Chapter Three

Salem stared at the happy couple as they waited for Devin.

Cade reached out and placed a hand on Deianira's swelling stomach as he said something to her. As Deianira's lips moved in response, she beamed up at him.

A lot of their interactions went like this.

If Salem really wanted to, she could have read them. But she knew that if they wanted her to know, they'd sign, so she took the hint and just observed them in their little bubble.

Despite the current circumstances, they were happy.

Truly happy.

Salem was glad that they were. She didn't necessarily enjoy Cade's presence as much as Deianira did, but she saw the way that he made her feel and that was enough for her.

She felt the slightest shake of the table beneath her flat palms. Turning to the door, she spotted Devin, strolling through the entrance, glaring at Deianira and Cade.

Deianira glared right back. "You are really starting to test my patience, Jacobs. Be mad if you like, but you have responsibilities, duties. You can't just up and leave whenever you feel like-"
Lia shot out of her seat. "Did you bring him?"
"Yeah," Devin responded, eyes still on the Queen, at the same time that Deianira and Cade asked, "Bring who?"
Devin said nothing, but he stepped aside.
Then Cassian Alden stepped through the doors of the council's study.

Cassian dragged his feet as he ambled over the threshold.
Instantly, his brother and sister-in-law left their seats. But strangely enough, Cassian wasn't looking at them.
The first set of eyes he found were Salem's. As she tilted her head, her gaze traveled up and down him with bored eyes.
Cassian's perusal was much less bored. It was contemplative.
She was different.
It wasn't her appearance that had changed.
It was her demeanor.
He could practically feel it the second he walked into the room.
Her head hung lower than usual, her eyes were slightly more dull, glum.
One of the things that had initially made an impression on Cassian was the way that she could look down at him when she barely

reached his chin. Salem could have been a hundred feet smaller and still be the tallest person in the room.

Not now though. She looked up at Cassian through those judgmental slits.

"Cass!" Lia ran over, interrupting his assessment.

Cassian opened his arms to receive Lia's embrace. He did miss her. But he was still annoyed at her. As she pulled back, he tugged on a loose curl at the back of her head.

"Ow!"

He gave her a knowing smirk, prompting an eye roll in response.

"Cassian?"

Finally remembering that they had company, he met Cade's eyes.

"Hey," he said as evenly as he could.

His brother stepped around the table and approached him slowly. He internally shrank. He had no idea what to expect.

Cade stepped up as Lia backed away and threw his arms around Cassian.

"It's good to have you back..."

He had to fight down his rising emotions. Cade didn't ask where he'd been or why he left. He was just happy to see him.

One thing that Cassian couldn't push down though was his guilt.

He wasn't back, technically. He wasn't planning to stay.

Cade stood back and looked at his brother. "You look good," he mumbled, his voice thick.

"Where have you been?" cut the icy voice.

He finally turned to Deianira.

"Away," he said with finality.

He didn't want to argue with Deianira, but he didn't want to talk about this with her either.

"Away?" she parroted with a disbelieving huff. "Is that a joke?"
"Deianira." His brother gave her a subtle head shake.
"No, Cade." She rounded the table, marching toward Cassian. "Have you any idea what you've put him through?" she asked, voice raised, as she gestured to his brother. "He looked for you. *We* looked for you. Gods, six years, Cassian."
He was barely listening to the words coming out of her mouth. Not when his gaze caught her stomach which was previously shielded by the table.
She's pregnant.
"You couldn't leave a goddamn note?!" she hissed.
Cassian kept his mouth shut. He had left a note.
For Lia.
He didn't want anyone else to know where he would be going and he trusted her not to tell the others. Now though, his guilt doubled. Maybe he could've tried to keep in touch. He couldn't just expect Lia to tell him every single thing that was happening in everybody's lives.
Deianira finally caught where his eyes had landed and paused.
"Oh yeah. Congrats. You're gonna be an uncle," she spat before she headed for the door.
Cade didn't wait to follow her out, giving him an apologetic head tilt.
When Cassian left the palace, the only thing on his mind was getting away, escaping the loop. He didn't stop to think about how his absence would affect the others, and in all honesty, he didn't think that it would. He also never thought about how much he'd be missing out on.
Cade's going to be a father.

He really messed up.
"That went better than expected."
Cassian cut Devin a glare at the same time as Lia.
"Hey, I thought she'd at least toss you around a little." At Cassian's straight face, Devin sighed. "We'll go get them. We still need to talk."
Cassian nodded to Lia and they both exited the room.
A chair scraping across the floor had his head turning back to the one person who hadn't spoken a word since his arrival.

Salem was stunned. And that didn't happen much.
One hundred and thirty-five years of life, a perfect memory, and a knack for probabilities didn't make surprises likely to happen.
The rush was quite refreshing.
It wasn't just his presence that surprised her though.
It was him. He looked so different.
From the broad shoulders that used to be more wiry, to his almost intimidating stature, to his buzzed hair, but more importantly, the look in his eyes. The eyes that had found Salem's the second he entered the room.
When things started to fire off, Salem remained seated. By the way that Deianira snarled at Cassian, she had an idea of what was happening.

Her Queen didn't like being blindsided. She liked people hurting Cade even less.

Cassian's disappearance did a number on Cade for quite a while. He tortured himself, thought that it was his fault, thought that he hadn't given Cassian enough to want to stay. Deianira hated it.

Evidently, she hated his unexpected arrival even more.

As Devin and Eulalia left the room, Salem took that as her cue to leave too. No one had told her what was going on exactly, but she doubted that Cassian would want her lurking in the room after that display.

Pushing her chair back, she stood.

She tried to avert her eyes as she walked by him, but surprising her again, Cassian blocked her path.

She hesitantly looked up at him in question.

'How far along is she?'

Salem blinked.

He was signing.

While she wasn't one to complain, no one had signed once since the whole altercation began and she couldn't help but feel a little out of the loop.

Cassian's signing was a little rusty, but she was just grateful that someone was communicating with her.

'Six months.'

Cassian's eyes narrowed at her, but she had the feeling that it didn't have anything to do with her answer.

'And they're healthy?'

'As far as Mikhael can tell, yes.'

He nodded awkwardly.

'And you?' he asked, watching her face closely.

'What about me?'

'Are you okay?'

Oh.

Salem subtly glanced down at herself, wondering what caused his concern.

'I'm okay,' she responded with furrowed brows.

As Cassian's head tilted at her, the room brightened slightly.

She turned to the door as Cade walked back in, his hand on Deianira's lower back. Lia and Devin followed as Deianira took her time to glare at Cassian before heading to her chair.

Chapter Four

As everyone took a seat, Cassian realized that there were none left, so he remained standing.

He didn't mind, he wasn't really an invited guest and there was no way he was about to ask for one.

"Devin said that you came to help us with something. What exactly?" Deianira started, her blunt signing showing all that she felt on the inside.

So Devin hadn't filled them in on everything.

Cassian signed as he spoke, flicking his gaze to Salem. "He told me about the Primas. About Emori."

Deianira's cold eyes turned to Devin.

Cassian wasn't exactly happy about the situation that Devin had dragged him into, but he didn't want him to be reprimanded either.

"I can help," Cassian quickly offered.

"How?" was all she asked.

"You need to know more about them, right?" Cassian said quietly. "I can ask Emori."

Cade sighed. "We've already tried that, Cassian. The room's soundproofed for obvious reasons and she can't use the intercom."
"I know. I mean, I think I might be able to-"
"I'm not opening that door before I know it's safe," Deianira said through gritted teeth. "The only one who has a chance of getting through to her is Salem and I'm not going to wear her out in there."
Annoyance rose in Cassian. "So I've been told, but I can-"
"Even if we could speak to her, I doubt she'd want to give us anything," Cade interjected, tipping his gaze to Deianira.
"Oh, here we go again." She rolled her eyes. "Cade, what did you expect me to do? She's a threat to every single one of us," she stressed before laying a hand on her bump.
"I don't disagree," he said, shooting a cautious look in Devin's direction. "But she's not some monster to be contained. All I'm saying is that locking her up might have done more harm than good."
"Are you sure about that? Why don't you ask Salem if she should be contained?" Deianira said, her hands flying.
Even in his annoyance, Cassian could feel Salem tense.
That was low.
He hadn't been around them for the better part of seven years, but even he wouldn't assume that it was okay to bring up the incident so trivially.
Devin stood abruptly. "That was an accident and you know it! She saved our lives that day. Also, if I remember correctly, it was you who Salem was protecting when that happened."
"This isn't the time to dredge up the past," Cade said, raising his voice. "Fighting each other isn't going to get us any closer to working out what the hell we're dealing with."

Cassian huffed, aggravated. "Which is why I'm here. Emori-"

Deianira raised her gaze to Cassian. "If Devin brought you here to ask me to let her go, the answer's still no-"

"Oh my Gods! Let the man speak!"

Everyone silenced at Lia's exclamation.

She sighed and looked over to Cassian.

He gave her a grateful nod before meeting his brother's confused eyes.

"I know you've tried to-"

Shhhh.

Cassian shivered and looked over his shoulder as the quiet noise faded.

What the hell was that?

"Tried to...?" Cade tilted his head, bringing him back on track.

He shook his head, brushing his ear. "Sorry," he muttered. "I know you've been trying to communicate with her," Cassian muttered. "I was saying that I want to try."

Deianira's tone was much less hostile when she started again. "It wouldn't work. The box is soundproofed. I'm not willing to risk opening it for answers she might not even have."

Cassian ran a hand over his head and took a few steps away from the table.

He needed to come clean.

He was trying to tell them something.

Salem could tell by the way he spoke under his breath and rubbed his sweaty palms on his pants.

Whatever it was obviously had him ruffled, so she ran his last few words through her head, trying to piece together what might have been bothering him.

He said that he could help. That he could talk to Emori, even though she couldn't be released.

Salem wasn't getting it. What could he possibly offer them that hadn't been done already? She sat up straighter as an idea struck her.

She knew that it was rude, but her curiosity got the better of her. She just wanted to take a peek. Whatever he was hiding was bugging her almost as much as it was him and she needed to know.

Salem narrowed her eyes at Cassian as he faced the group.

She slowly advanced.

His guard was down. That was good.

He was focused on the conversation at hand.

Salem waited just outside, she waited until he was speaking, until he was distracted, to gently press forward.

And she was in.

I need to tell them-

I shouldn't have come here-

I should've stayed-

What the hell was that?

Cassian turned to look behind him before softly scratching his ear.

Salem stilled.

But then he shook his head and carried on with his sentence.

She let out a discreet breath.

There was no way he could've felt her anyway. She wasn't doing anything, just observing. So Salem dug a little deeper.

This is pointless.

Why did I let Devin-

What is *that?*

Salem's breath caught in her throat as Cassian's head slowly turned in her direction.

It was a coincidence. It had to have been a coincidence. He was just looking at her in passing. It was physiologically impossible that he could-

GET! OUT!

The voice echoed so loudly in Salem's head that she jumped, throwing her chair away from the table, stumbling several steps back.

Everybody in the room startled as Deianira stood out of her chair.

'Salem! Are you okay?!'

She took many ragged breaths, her eyes still pinned on Cassian. She couldn't escape his stare.

'Salem?'

She must've been in shock, because when she responded, she didn't think to keep her mouth shut.

"He's psionic..." she rasped, her gaze trapped by his murderous glare.

Chapter Five

Cassian stood, stark still, staring at Salem.

She tried to get in my head.

He was shocked.

Not that she could, but that she tried.

Cassian had never felt anything like that before. It was encroaching, invasive.

There were some parts of his mind that even he didn't want to explore. Having someone that close was something he never wanted to feel again.

"He's psionic..."

That drew him from his thoughts.

It was the first time she'd spoken since he'd been in the room.

Earlier, Cassian wasn't sure if it was just due to his presence, but he was confused as to why she wasn't speaking. He knew that she could, but she chose to sign everything.

That wasn't the case years ago though. Salem had a beautiful voice and she definitely knew how to use it, so he struggled to understand what had changed.

"Is that true?"

Cassian turned to his brother.

He only offered a nod.

Cade just stared at him for a while. "Why didn't you say anything?" he asked quietly.

Cassian just opened and closed his mouth. He had an answer. He just didn't want to say it.

At his silence, Cade turned to Devin. "Did you know?"

Devin sighed. "Only for a couple days, but yes."

"You told him before you told me?" Cade looked at Cassian like he'd stabbed him.

"No, I didn't tell anyone," he said before he could stop himself. He didn't want to hurt his brother.

Lia brought her head up from her hands. "He didn't have to. It was obvious."

Cade's gaze darkened as he turned to Lia. "You knew?"

She didn't shrink away. "Yes, I knew. And before you ask me why I didn't say anything, he asked me not to."

"So what?!" Cade yelled, startling Deianira. He quickly put a hand on her shoulder, muttering a quick apology, which she rolled her eyes at. "Cassian, that is not something you should have to navigate on your own."

Cassian didn't like the way that the whole room stared at him. "Why not? You did."

"I had no choice!" Cade bellowed.

"But Lia still knew and I didn't!" Cassian yelled back, signing defensively.

As if he had forgotten. Cade started signing while he spoke too. "You know that that is not the same thing. The circumstances were very different."

"They still are."

"No." He slashed a hand through the air. "They're not. I would've helped you."

"That's precisely why I didn't tell you!" Cassian barked. "I don't want your help! Or your pity! Or for you to save me!" Cassian cursed under his breath before lowering his volume. "Seven years and I'm still a kid to you."

"Well stop acting like one and change my mind," Cade hissed.

Cassian immediately took two steps toward his brother, only to be met by Deianira's firm palm against his chest.

"Hey!" He kept his eyes on Cade, both their chests heaving, as he tilted his head down toward her. "You need to pipe the fuck down! Now!" He finally met her eyes and she narrowed them, daring him to test her.

He reluctantly took a step back.

Deianira took a deep breath and whirled on Cade next. "And you!"

"What did I do?" he returned.

She gestured behind her. "Does he look like a child to you?"

Cade didn't respond, but some of the fire left his eyes.

"Cade, I love how much you want to take care of people, I do, but he's a grown man. Stupid as it may have been," she turned to glare at Cassian, "he disappeared for six years and came back to help *us*. Right now, we need him, not the other way around."

Cassian let out a sigh of relief.

It took a while, but Cade eventually nodded and retook his seat.

Deianira sent Salem a questioning nod, and at her responding one, she took her seat before Cade's hand came to rest on her bump once again.

Once everyone was settled, the room silenced as they all looked to Cassian.

They were ready.

Chapter Six

Cassian rubbed his hands together as he stood outside of the assessment room.

He wasn't surprised to find that Emori had been held there instead of in the cells on the sub-level. They were designed for the gifted, not primas. Alternatively, the assessment studio had much stronger dampeners.

Deianira and Cade had already left for the viewing room, leaving Devin, Lia, and Salem waiting outside with him.

"It's okay if it doesn't work," Lia muttered beside him.

Cassian appreciated her effort to comfort him, but he knew that he didn't have a choice in the matter. He couldn't walk out empty-handed after all the trouble he'd caused.

"Cass?"

Cassian sighed out of both annoyance and nostalgia at the nickname. "Yeah?"

Devin's eyes flicked to Salem and Lia before he spoke quietly. "Can you tell her that I'm here? That I'm trying to get her out?"

"Of course," Cassian replied.

He could tell that it was killing Devin to not be able to see her.
He discreetly threw his gaze to Salem. She hadn't even looked at him since her announcement in the council's study.
She still wouldn't.
Cassian shook his head. He was here for a reason, he had a job to do.
'I'm ready,' he signed.
Salem kept her eyes averted as she stepped up to the door and swiped her bracelet.
So she *was* looking at him.
Cassian entered the room and the door slid shut behind him.
He felt a slight tug in his chest at the sight of Emori, curled up into a ball in the corner of the studio.
He understood Deianira's decision, but the room was plain white, no furniture save for the glass box itself.
It was the kind of place that could make a person go mad.
He knew the box was soundproofed and that Emori might not have been aware of his presence yet, so he took the opportunity to study her for a second.
She was obviously scared. Head in her arms, back hunched.
He could see something else though. Feel something else. She was...lonely.
That was to be expected considering that she'd been in there for days, and Cassian used that piece of knowledge to adjust his approach.
It was slightly cruel, but he needed to get her attention.
She missed Devin, he'd give her Devin.
Sort of.

Cassian took a deep breath and sorted through every word, every inflection of voice, and every mannerism he'd seen from Devin. Then he channeled it.

Emori?

Cassian flinched at the speed with which she whipped her head up and crawled to the front of the box.

The second she caught sight of him, the hope drained from her face as it contorted in pain and longing.

She sat back on her haunches, her lips parted, and her chest heaved before the box and the floor started shaking violently.

Cassian had to back up and grab the wall to steady himself.

"What's going on?" Deianira barked through the intercom.

Emori wouldn't stop.

"Cassian, you need to calm her down!"

He kept his hold on the wall and tried to reach her again, as himself this time.

Emori!

One of the light panels went out.

Emori! It's me, Cassian!

"Cassian, get out of there!"

"No! Give me a second!" he yelled.

Emori, I'm sorry I did that! I just want to speak to you!

Emori only paused to take a breath before the screaming started again.

"Cassian, fall back!" Cade was shouting now.

He needed to try something else.

As an idea popped into his head, he realized that it might only make matters worse, but it was something.

Emori! I'm not trying to trick you! Listen!

Cass?

Emori's eyes met Cassian's as she quieted at Devin's voice.

Can you tell her that I'm out here?

She got to her feet and stumbled to the edge of the box, hands against the glass.

That I'm trying to get her out?

She put her forehead against the glass and closed her eyes.

Thank the Gods, Cassian thought.

He tried again.

Emori...

Cassian waited and waited to see if he had gotten through. It felt like hours were passing in that tension-filled moment.

Yes? her small voice whispered.

He was in.

Do you want to hear me or Devin? he asked.

After what he just pulled, she deserved the choice.

Devin, she told him.

Cassian took a deep breath and channeled him again.

I wanted to ask you some questions. Is that okay?

Her entire face relaxed at Devin's voice she nodded.

"What's happening?"

"Is she talking?"

Cassian stepped over to the intercom and flipped the switch. He needed to focus.

Returning to the glass, he took a seat on the floor and crossed his legs.

He waited. He wanted her to go first.

She looked down at him against the glass. *Are Kenny and Ty okay?*

They are. Devin's taking good care of them.

Emori nodded, reassuring herself. He needed to ask now, while she was still relatively calm.

Can you tell me a little bit about Pola?

He watched her visibly tense.

It's okay. Take your time.

Emori fiddled with her hands for a while, her eyes darting around the box. After settling, she sat back down and crossed her legs opposite Cassian, mirroring him.

She's Queen of Patriam.

Cassian already knew this, but he didn't interrupt her.

Emori's hand came to touch her throat. *She's the one who did this.*

It was old and healed, but he could almost feel her pain. Not just from the wound itself, but its everlasting effect on her life.

Do you know what her gift is?

Emori shook her head.

At first, he thought she meant no, but her next words sent a cold shiver up his spine.

It's not a gift. What you have is a gift. A gene given to you by your parents, your ancestors. What she has is not. She isn't an angel of death. She is death.

Cassian swallowed.

He'd seen Deianira in action a few times. On one of those occasions, she was weak and half-dead, but she still managed to rip a man's spine out, right before him.

And the primas were much more powerful.

Eliminating this threat was beginning to seem more and more impossible.

Cassian debated whether he should tell her the next part. It might scare her, but he decided that honesty would be the best approach.

Part of a body was found some miles away from here.

Her eyes widened.

We think it was an azrael. A Prima azrael. Do you know what they might want? What would they be doing so close?

Emori's knee bounced as she started to scan all the corners of the box.

I need to go...

What?

She looked back through the glass. *Tell Devin to get the girls out of school.*

Emori, what are you talking about?

She'll kill me.

His heart rate started to pick up. *Is that why she's coming?*

Emori stood up so Cassian did too. *No, but if she's coming here, she'll do it anyway.*

But why come here in the first place?

She finally stopped her pacing. *She knows your people are here.*

What do you mean?

She's always known.

Cassian sighed and scrubbed a hand over his face.

Emori, I don't understand.

When Emori bared her teeth, he stepped back and realized that he'd stop channeling Devin.

He took a deep breath and turned it back on.

Please, explain.

She pulled back and ran a hand through her hair.

When the members of the resistance left Patriam, she knew that they came to Terra. She didn't follow because she didn't need to. They never escaped, Pola just allowed them to think that they did.

She started to chew her thumb.

Humans have been endangered in Patriam from before I was born. If it's gotten worse since I…left, that's what she'll want.

Humans?

Yes.

Cassian had gotten a brief explanation, but Emori's tone made him feel like there was something more at hand.

For what?

Her eyebrows furrowed. She looked at Cassian like the answer was obvious.

To eat.

His blood ran cold.

They eat humans?

They don't have to. Some choose not to. But it makes u-…them stronger.

Cassian turned away from the box, his hands fidgeting.

The images that were conjured up in his mind were far from tasteful, but he had to consider it.

The primas sounded terrifying. They were stronger, faster, more powerful.

It was almost unthinkable, but what if it was their only choice?

What if we made a deal with them?

Emori's eyes snapped in Cassian's direction.

She shook her head. *You don't understand.*

You don't think they would agree?

I know they would agree.

Then what was the problem?

So, then there's a way out of this. A way where we don't all *end up dead,* he emphasized grimly.

No. You do not understand.

What don't I understand?

Emori's head tilted at Cassian.

You are forgetting that, gifted or not, you are more human than you are prima.

He blanched. There was no way she meant…

They don't care that Devin can conjure fire or that your brother can read people's emotions. You are not above the humans. Food is food. If she's coming here, you're already dead.

Chapter Seven

"So we're fucked," Devin said, nodding his head sarcastically.

"Basically," Eulalia agreed.

"Good to know that *my wife* has been rocking back and forth in a fucking box for the past three days, just for us to be wiped out anyway."

"Devin," Cade sighed.

"Don't Devin me!" He banged his fist against the table, his cold humor gone. "I told you that she would cooperate. That she wasn't a threat. But you didn't listen and now we're all gonna die anyway."

Cade didn't respond, but his wife did. "I did what was best for my people, Jacobs. If she wasn't your wife, you would've done the exact same thing, and if you can honestly tell me you wouldn't, maybe you shouldn't be Head Enforcer."

If looks could kill, Deianira would've been ten feet under.

"As your Head Enforcer," he gritted out. "You should've trusted me. I would never do anything to put Terra in danger."

"And I believe you. I just needed to be sure."

"Well, are you sure now?!"

“Yes,” she said calmly. “I am.”

They sat staring at each other in silence before Cade broke the tension.

“What are we going to do?”

Salem had been watching them go back and forth for over an hour.

There was so much new information. Information that they wouldn’t have been able to get without Cassian. What she couldn’t do in seventy-two hours, he’d done in thirty minutes.

The thought filled Salem with a feeling she hadn’t felt before. She couldn’t even think of a name for it.

Cassian didn’t seem to notice though. He just sat, staring at the table while the others discussed what he had just given them.

“What if it’s a false alarm? I haven’t found anything else by the shore and I’ve been scouting there for months. What if it actually just washed up?” Eulalia offered.

“Unlikely,” Devin huffed. “We wouldn’t have seen that if they didn’t want us to.”

Cade sighed. “By the way Emori described them, they’re advanced. Maybe not technologically, but they’re not completely primitive. They might listen to reason.”

“What reason?” Devin asked. “We have nothing to offer them.” He shrugged. “I mean, unless you wanted to volunteer yourself as an appetizer.”

Deianira gritted her teeth and shook her head.

“What, no takers?”

“This isn’t funny, Devin,” Eulalia chided.

He let out a cold laugh. “Oh, I think it’s hilarious. We-”

Deianira groaned and raised a hand to her stomach.

Salem was out of her seat in seconds, but not before Cade. She had barely left her chair by the time Cade was on his knees, next to Deianira.

"What's wrong?" he breathed.

Deianira couldn't have rolled her eyes back any further. "Dramatic much?"

"Deianira," he said in a serious tone, tilting his head.

"I'm fine, I swear. Just a hard kick."

Cade didn't look convinced.

He turned to the group. "We'll finish this conversion tomorrow."

Chapter Eight

Cassian lay on his bed, staring at the ceiling. The same bed that he'd slept in six years ago.

He was still slightly shaken by what he'd learned today. He didn't presume that their predicament would have an easy fix, but he never expected what he'd heard.

It changed things.

For one, there was no way he could go back home and leave his brother to deal with this alone.

That was an issue.

He hated this place. Not the palace itself, but what it signified. What it reminded him of.

He needed a distraction.

Pulling back the covers, he hopped out of bed.

Echo stood as she watched him march to the door.

He paused and walked back to the bed before rubbing her under the chin.

"Be right back, sweet girl."

Cassian wasn't surprised to find the training room empty at this time. It was why he went down there. Living around people again was a bit of a shock to his system and some alone time seemed like the perfect remedy.

Strangely, it was exactly how he remembered it, yet so different.

He had to admit, Cade did a good job with the upgrades. The dummies were traded in for holograms, the walls were covered in weapons.

Top to bottom, they were equipped with daggers, swords, and so much more.

This was exactly what Cassian needed.

He went straight for an axe.

It was a bit heavier than he expected. He tossed it from hand to hand, attempting to adjust to the weight.

"TerraPod," he said aloud. At the pulse of the light panels, he continued. "Ambush mode. Advanced."

The lights went low and Cassian took his place in the middle of the room.

A large blue silhouette of a man came at him out of nowhere.

Cassian quickly ducked and spun out of the way of the attacker. Just as he dodged the assault, a red figure ran past him in his periphery.

Advanced was the right word.

He swung the axe at the stomach of the first figure and watched it fade before spinning to keep his eye on the second.

It was gone.

He didn't have time to look further as a green figure fell from the ceiling.

If he didn't drop and roll, it would have landed right on top of him. As his axe fell through his fingers, Cassian jumped back to his feet. At his flying spin kick, the green figure faded into the darkness.

Orange.

An orange figure came in, sliding across the floor. Cassian jumped into the air as it passed under him. He dove for his axe before it could get up and swung down onto its head.

He almost made it.

Orange rolled out of his path just as the axe hit the mat. He pulled at the axe wedged in the mat and stumbled back as he freed it. He hadn't even got to turn around before Orange passed through him.

Cassian looked down as lights on the knuckles of his right glove went out.

Fuck.

He tossed the axe into his left hand as Orange ran at him again. It wasn't his dominant hand, but that didn't stop him from running at Orange to meet him in the middle of the room before dropping onto his knees, swinging the axe. As Orange's legs faded away, Cassian brought his left hand up and pulled the axe down into the middle of its back.

Three down.

Before he could even finish that thought, a red arrow flew past his head.

These things have weapons too?

Cassian spun his head in the direction from which the arrow came.

There.

The red silhouette was flying.

Cassian ducked, dove, and rolled to avoid the holographic arrows. As it circled the room, he followed it with his eyes waiting for the right moment.

Hold...

Hold...

Now!

Cassian pulled back and swung the axe, releasing the handle. It spun midair for a few seconds before embedding itself in the wall by the archway.

Red faded away.

"Success," the room echoed.

As soon as the lights turned back on, Cassian jumped as he spotted Deianira standing at the entrance, less than a foot away from the axe.

"Shit!" Cassian blanched. "I didn't see you," he said, panicked.

Deianira snorted. "If I thought it was going to hit me, I wouldn't be standing here." She laid her palm on the handle of the axe and gave it a swift pull. "I'm impressed," she said, examining it in her hand.

Cassian's nerves shot up. He knew Deianira wasn't his biggest fan, but he began to wonder if she would actually try to hurt him.

At the look on his face, Deianira narrowed her eyes and tilted her head. "Oh, get over yourself," she scoffed as she tossed it on the floor.

He released a breath as she walked over to the bench and stepped out of her slippers.

"Do you want the room?" he asked. He had hoped to use it for a couple more hours, but it was her palace.

"Yep," she answered as she started to roll up the legs of her pajama bottoms.

He nodded and started toward the door.

"Where are you going?" A scary smile crawled onto her face.

"You said you wanted the room."

She nodded, a grin starting to form. "I do. We're training."

Cassian thought that she might have been joking at first, but her raised brows and pulled-back shoulders had his hairs rising.

"Are you serious?"

"Why wouldn't I be?" she asked, advancing on him slowly.

"Well, because..." Cassian trailed off before he gestured to her stomach.

She raised a brow. "You won't fight me because I'm pregnant?"

Cassian cocked his head at her. She was being serious.

"You can't actually expect me to-"

A kick to the ribs cut him off. He hadn't even seen her lift her foot.

"How about now?"

"Deianira..." he gasped, winded, holding his stomach.

"I haven't sparred for months," Deianira laughed, jumping up and down.

Seeing her fist coming this time, he managed to dodge it and grab her arm.

Deianira used his hold on her arm to pull him forward and send a knee to his gut.

Cassian doubled over and fell to his knees.

"Ah, this feels so good!" she cheered.

"Deianira. Stop," Cassian breathed as he got back onto his feet.

"Cassian. No." she giggled as she circled him.

She didn't give him a moment to hear the end of her sentence before she jumped and locked her arms around Cassian's neck. He had no idea how she managed to build the momentum, but by the time he had registered the contact, she had swung around onto his back and had him in a headlock.

He slapped her arm in surrender, but she tightened her hold.

She groaned. "Cassian, will you just fight me, for goodness sake!"

Her arm gripped his throat tighter and tighter as black spots started to fill his vision. In a move purely out of self-preservation, Cassian reached back and grabbed her shirt before forcefully dropping to one knee as he quickly bent forward.

Smack!

He went ashen as her body collided with the mat in front of him, her hair in her face.

"Cassian!" she gasped.

"Oh my Gods!" He dashed to her side and hovered over her.

A muffled giggle told him that that was a mistake.

Deianira gripped both sides of his head and brought it down on her knee.

His head flew back with a gut-churning crunch.

Cassian saw stars as he landed flat on his back, his whole face throbbing.

Deianira came into view, hair framing her face, a mischievous smile across her lips.

"Are you okay?" she asked sweetly.

He would've scrunched his face at her if he could. He was too busy trying not to move so she wouldn't see it as a sign that he wanted to continue.

Deianira sat down on the mat next to him and sighed.

They stayed like that for a few moments, Deianira trying to catch her breath, Cassian trying to remember how to breathe.

"You really hurt him, you know?"

Cassian's eyes flew to her at the change in direction.

He knew exactly what she meant though.

"That wasn't my intention." His voice was strained, nasally.

"*I* know that. But, you know Cade. He thinks that he's responsible for keeping everybody safe, especially you. He blames himself when things go wrong. That's just how he is." She started to fiddle with the ends of her hair. "He might not understand why you left, but I do."

Cassian was surprised at how much relief that gave him. For someone who he hadn't spent much time around, he valued her opinion more than he thought he would.

She met his eyes. "You know, as much as I love him, it took me a long time to fully forgive him for what he did to Jude."

That shocked him.

"My own uncle killed my family, double-crossed me, had my husband tortured, then tried to kill me too. And I still miss him sometimes."

Cassian averted his eyes. He didn't like this new direction as much.

"Cade hasn't told me everything about what it was like growing up with Drake, but he was your father at the end of the day. If it was hard for me to forgive Cade, then I know it must be hard for you to forgive yourself. Even after everything he did to you guys." Deianira uncrossed her legs and rubbed her stomach. "It made me feel pathetic, crying over someone who didn't give a shit about me. Someone who used me and took advantage of my love."

When Cassian thought of Deianira, pathetic was the last word that came to mind.

"A word of advice. All of this," she waved her hand around Cassian's torso, "Doesn't make you strong. Doesn't make you feel better or get back at him in some way." She tapped a finger on his temple. "This does. That's how you get stronger. How you build yourself back up."

Cassian wanted to say that he didn't understand, but he did.

He'd spent years trying to make himself less vulnerable, trying to fix what his father had broken. It was easier to act like the problem was external. But he hadn't achieved much. Everything he worked on was surface level and he neglected what really needed healing.

As Deianira slapped a hand on his chest, he groaned.

"Sorry about your nose. I'll call Mikhael," she said as she squatted to stand.

Cassian tried to sit up but paused as the dizziness fell over him. "No, it's late. I'm good."

Chapter Nine

"What's going on?" Finch asked, his hands on his belt authoritatively.

"They've done it again. It was Mila this time," the old farmer cried as he walked with them.

Salem huffed but kept quiet.

"The cow?" Finch smirked condescendingly.

"Yes," the farmer carried on, unaware of Finch's amusement. "She's very old and she'll get cold if she's not back by tonight."

Salem had to speedwalk to keep ahead of them and read their lips.

"You don't have anything better to do than call the guard every time some kids play a prank?" Finch tilted his head.

'Kids' was incorrect.

Salem had been on call for incidents like this at least twice this week already. These were gifted people trying to intimidate an old man into leaving the city.

Some humans did stay behind when The Dome was taken down, but most migrated. Objectively speaking, it was the better option. Better conditions, healthier land, more opportunities.

There was plenty of room for the humans who chose to move onto Old Dome territory too. It made Salem think about how empty The Dome was before. How much they had for such a small amount of people.

While issues often came along with change, this one had re-sparked a long-standing rivalry between humans and the gifted. Earl was a repeat victim of this rivalry.

Some young adults had been stealing his livestock and vandalizing his small farm for months.

"I don't mind them having some fun, but this isn't the first time," the farmer tried to reason.

"Well, Mr. Carr, I think you need to learn how to take a joke," Finch said dismissively.

The farmer stopped and turned to him. "I'm not looking to get them in trouble. I just want her back."

"You want her back?"

"Yes," he breathed with relief.

Finch smiled. "Let's go then."

As they arrived at the house of one of the culprits, Salem chewed on her lip. She already knew how this interaction would go.

The door opened revealing a bright-faced young man.

"What's the problem, officer?" He smiled at Finch as he leaned against the door frame.

Finch's grin matched his. "Mr. Carr says that his cow went missing last night. Would you happen to know anything about that?"

The man tilted his head in thought.

"Sorry, officer. No clue."

"That's a shame. Thank you for your time."

As the door closed, Finch shrugged and swung his eyes to the farmer.

"You didn't even look!" Earl accused.

"Don't have a warrant," he said as he crossed his arms.

"Then get one!"

Finch took a step forward, his hand moving to the side of his belt.

"Are we gonna have a problem here?"

Salem frowned as Mr. Carr seethed.

"No, officer."

"Then, you have a great day." Finch nodded and turned on his heel.

Salem started after him to keep up.

"I don't know why Her Majesty let people like them back in. Just a nuisance."

Salem didn't respond or acknowledge that he'd spoken.

Finch flicked his eyes to her. "I'm sorry you had to see that."

See what?

"I don't like to get aggressive around a lady."

Did I miss something? Salem thought.

"Those humans just bring out the beast in me," he said, shaking his head regretfully.

Salem thought that she must have read his lips wrong. The only thing noteworthy about that confrontation was how uncomfortable it made her. It was a blatant abuse of power.

Not knowing what else to do, she nodded.

"Hey, can I walk you to your room?"

Salem shook her head.

"Are you sure? It's pretty late and you shouldn't be alone...considering your situation."

Salem narrowed her eyes, wondering what situation he was referring to. She was more than capable of finding her room on her own.

She nodded, sure.

He looked reluctant, but he eventually nodded and took off in the opposite direction, waving her an exaggerated goodbye.

She took the long way back to the palace. She liked the feel of the cold evening air on her face. She liked the feel of anything really.

It was said that when you lost one sense, the others were heightened, and while that may have been true for most people, Salem felt the opposite.

She'd never really felt the things that others did. Not in the same way at least. She didn't often feel joy or despair, she was always just there.

While she didn't regret her decision to fulfill her duty rather than protect herself seven years ago, she couldn't help but think that losing her hearing only set her apart even more.

Now, she was disconnected physically too.

She swiped her bracelet across the sensor before stepping into her room, one foot in front of the other. She didn't turn around to turn the lights on, but reached behind her and flipped the switch three times. Then, she removed her shoes, gently nudging them to the left side of the door.

Salem went about her nightly routine. She tidied her bedroom from top to bottom, there wasn't much to clean, but she fixed what she could. She then changed her clothes and smoothed out the bed before taking a seat right in the middle.

As she stretched a hand to the side to pick up her book, a shadow appeared under the door.

Someone was outside.

She waited a moment to see if they'd pass, but the shadow remained. They didn't press the light alert, just stood there.

She debated in her mind whether it was worth getting out of bed and doing her routine all over again when the shadow moved. It didn't leave, just moved.

Salem sighed as she slid off the bed, both feet at a time, and approached the door.

Opening it, she looked from side to side.

No one was there.

A nudge at her leg startled her and she looked down.

Salem almost jumped out of her skin.

It was a cat.

In the palace.

She carefully leaned over it and checked up and down the hall again, just in case someone was close.

All clear.

Keeping her voice low, she leaned forward from a distance. "What do you want?"

The cat tilted its head at her.

"Go away," Salem whispered. She didn't have time for this.

In response, the cat slid past her and into her room.

"No!" Salem hissed. "No, cat!"

The cat just hopped onto her bed before rolling around playfully.

Salem's heart sped up.

There's a cat on my bed.

Fur on my bed.

"Off," she said, voice louder as she approached. "Get off!"

It didn't listen.

"Do you want food? Are you hungry?"

The cat quickly sat up.

"Yes?" Salem asked. "Would you like to eat?"

It opened its mouth, inclining its head at her.

I'll take that as a yes.

"Come here," she called awkwardly.

The cat sprang off the bed and over to her, making her flinch.

That's all it took?

Despite its attempts to get close, Salem kept her distance from the cat the whole way to the kitchen. She had no idea why it was in the palace or who it belonged to but she would at least feed it.

Opening the fridge, she looked for something it might like.

There were dozens of containers and concealed food already prepared for the next day. Spotting a leg of ham, she pulled it out and peeled at the wrap.

The cat started to get excited, and while she couldn't hear it, she was sure that it was making noise.

"Be quiet."

It got closer.

Salem stepped back quickly. "No! Shhhh!"

In an attempt to silence it, she rushed to the counter and cut a small piece off the ham before throwing it at the cat. It hit it square in the face, but it didn't seem to mind.

It jumped at the ham, chomping it down.

Salem cut off another piece and did it again.

As she held up the third piece, the cat turned to face away from her, its attention caught by something else.

"Cat," she called.

It still didn't turn.

She jumped as the door to the kitchen swung open.

And in came Cassian. Shirtless.

Salem had what she could only describe as a brain malfunction.

Abs.

Chest.

Abs.

No shirt.

Abs.

She was so caught up in watching the way that his body flexed as he awkwardly shifted from side to side, she almost didn't notice his face.

'*Your nose is broken,*' she signed automatically.

Cassian absently nodded, staring at her, strictly keeping his eyes on her face.

She wondered why he was looking at her like that before she looked down and realized that she was only in a night dress.

She left her bedroom barefoot, and in a night dress. She had never done something like that before. She hadn't even noticed.

Usually, she'd be halfway to a meltdown, but Cassian's attire settled her somewhat.

Both of them weren't fully clothed. It canceled out.

When she looked up and realized that he was still staring, she got uncomfortable.

Clapping her hands, she repeated herself.

'*Your nose is broken.*'

Cassian shook his head before signing back.

'*Yeah... Deianira.*"

Salem frowned. '*She broke your nose?*"

He only nodded.

'*What did you do?*'

At that, he cocked his head back. *'Absolutely nothing. She just attacked me in the training room.'*

That wasn't necessarily out of character for Deianira so Salem awkwardly inclined her head.

He shook his head and gestured to his face.

'Is it that bad?'

Salem let her eyes assess his face once again. The bridge was swollen and beginning to turn a nasty shade of purple. Also, the tip of his nose was at a slight angle.

'Yes,' she responded instantly. *'You look terrible.'*

Cassian watched her for a second, then his mouth burst open as he bent forward, an amused smile on his parted lips.

Salem lowered her brows.

He was laughing. At her.

'You do,' she stressed. Did he think she was joking? *'I know what a broken nose looks like.'*

'I don't doubt that.' He was still laughing. *'You're just very honest.'*

Salem tilted her head. *'Did you want me to lie?'*

He shook his head, smile still in place. *'Never.'*

As his laugh tapered off and his face slowly straightened, Salem recognized the look in his eye. It was the same look he gave her yesterday when...

'I apologize.'

His brows dipped. *'For what?'*

'Invading your privacy. I should not have tried to get in your head.'

Cassian's eyes flicked to the floor as he bent to pick up the cat.

'It's fine.'

'Okay,' Salem responded, even though his body language said that it wasn't.

Cassian glanced at her, then turned away, only to do it again. He did it a few more times before he finally asked, *'Why don't you talk anymore?'*

Salem tensed.

He shook his head. *'Sorry, I didn't mean to ask so bluntly.'* He winced. *'It's just that you spoke in the council's study and I heard you talking to Echo...so I know you can.'*

He'd heard her. Salem wanted to shrink into the floor.

'Because I don't want to,' she signed more defensively than she intended

'Why?'

Why did he want to know?

Salem straightened her night dress.

'I don't do things that I'm not sure of. I don't know how I sound, so I avoid speaking.'

Cassian stared at her.

He did that a lot. Like he was trying to figure her out.

'Okay,' he eventually said.

His eyes went to the cat as he scratched under her chin. *'I hope she didn't give you too much trouble. I thought I closed my door.'*

Salem frowned. *'Why would a cat give me trouble?'*

He angled his face away as his lips curved. *'I meant, I hope she didn't bother you. It's late.'*

Oh. 'It did bother me. I was about to read a book and it wouldn't leave me alone. I hoped that feeding it-'

'She,' Cassian interrupted.

'She what?'

'She's a she. Not an it. Her name is Echo.'

Echo. The cat had a name.

Cassian shook his head, lips tugging up. *'I'll take her to bed so that* she *doesn't bother you anymore.'*

Salem nodded. *'Thank you.'*

Chapter Ten

Cassian couldn't help the way his eyes kept flicking to Salem.

When he went looking for Echo last night, he hadn't expected to find her with Salem. She'd never been around anyone but him so it was surprising that she was so comfortable around her. Also, he certainly hadn't expected to find Salem standing in the kitchen, wearing next to nothing.

That same image flashed in his mind as he discreetly watched her, flicking his eyes to her next to him every few seconds.

"They already know where we're. It can't hurt to try and talk to them first, see if we can come up with an alternative," Lia started.

"But they don't know that we know about them yet. This could be our only advantage," Devin argued.

"He's right," said Deianira. "I think we should handle this as we do all other threats."

Cade shook his head. "This isn't a threat though. They *are* coming. There are no two ways about that. We should at least try to work something out before inciting a slaughter."

They all had good points.

The truth was, they had no idea what they were dealing with, and approaching the matter peacefully could give them away, but there was also no doubt that a war would result in countless losses.

"How would we even go about setting up a meeting?" Deianira asked, eyes on Devin.

"Why're you looking at me?"

"Because you know the most about them."

He huffed. "These aren't the talk first kind of people. Also, you don't just call Pola."

Cade interjected. "If they really are everything Emori said that they are, then why would they let us know that they're close? Why not just attack?"

"Exactly," Lia agreed. "Maybe, they want to talk first."

"They have no reason to do that." Devin shook his head. "They have everything they could possibly need to end us. Talking first would be doing us a favor."

Cassian glanced at Salem again.

He watched the way her head tilted in consideration. The way her sharp, almond eyes squinted in thought.

He could tell that she had so much to say, but she didn't offer anything.

Before he could stop himself, he tapped the table between them, drawing her eyes up to his and silencing the room.

'What do you think?'

Salem logged all of their arguments in her head.

She didn't know much about the primas, so any move they made would be a risk, but the two potential responses didn't have an equal chance of success.

A hand tapping the table beside her drew her attention to Cassian.

'*What do you think?*' he signed.

Salem froze as her eyes flitted around to the others' faces.

His lips hadn't moved. He was asking her.

It wasn't like no one had spoken to her directly in a meeting before, but it was usually to calculate something or to give an order.

Cassian was asking for her opinion.

It took her a while to catch up but when she did, she blinked back into focus and told them what she truly thought.

'*Taking into account all that we've learned about them, I think that we should try to communicate first. As Devin said yesterday, we saw that head because they wanted us to. Whether it was to instill fear or to send us a message, they reached out. From a tactical standpoint, it is most logical to show that we have received that message, be it to surrender or to respond. I doubt that they would take kindly to our lack of acknowledgment.*'

The room stood still.

They didn't look contemplative though. They looked surprised.

Deianira blinked, nodding.

"I didn't think about it that way." She turned to Devin. "If we were to send a message back, how would we go about it?"

"I can ask Emori," he sighed. He still didn't look on board.

"Okay. It's settled then?" she asked, looking out to the table.

Devin reluctantly nodded and so did everyone else.

When Salem flicked her gaze to the side, she noticed Cassian staring at her again. He'd been doing that the whole meeting but this time, his lips were tipped up at the sides.

Her brows scrunched.

Why was he smiling at her?

And why did it make her want to?

As everybody began to filter out of the room, Cassian finally took his eyes off Salem and waited behind.

"Cade," he called, before lowering his voice. "Can I talk to you for a second?"

Cade looked back at Deianira as she stood by the door. She gave him a small nod and he turned back to Cassian.

Cassian couldn't help but notice her smirk as she sauntered out of the room.

"Sure," Cade mumbled.

He took a deep breath as the door closed.

He just needed to get it out.

"I don't want you to think that you were the reason I left."

Cade barely let him finish his sentence. "Why did you?"

He sighed. "As much as you tried, you couldn't understand what it was like being here, living here, walking past that closet *every day*. One minute, I was in the western sector, and the next I was... I was killing my own father," he whispered. "I'm not saying that he didn't deserve it and I'd do it again for you but-"

"For me?"

Cassian paused. "...Yeah."

Cade shook his head. "Cassian, I didn't ask you to do that."

"I know..." He looked down. "You don't need to ask me to protect you..." he said, quoting him.

Cade blew out a breath as Cassian looked back up.

"Listen," Cassian started again. "My life changed so quickly. And, when it was all done, everyone pretended like it never happened, but I could tell what they were thinking. I could see the pity and the distrust on their faces."

"Of course, we trust you."

"Maybe now, but be honest, you didn't back then. Nobody brought it up around me, I was kept out of the loop. Everybody tip-toed around me, and I'm not blaming you," Cassian quickly added. "But I just needed to get out. And I didn't do it because of you. I did it for me." He took a breath to prepare himself for the last part. "I'm sorry for hurting you in the process, but I'm not sorry for leaving."

Cassian didn't breathe as he waited for a response.

"I would've preferred for you to be here, where I could've helped you. And I don't get it, but I can't change the past." Cade waited for a while before continuing. "Just speak to me next time. Please."

Cassian nodded, blinking quickly. "Of course."

Cade went in and threw his arms around Cassian, patting his back. Cassian returned the hug. He wasn't hesitant or reluctant.

As Cade pulled back, he said, "One more thing."

Cassian inclined his head as his eyes darkened. “Lay a finger on my wife again, and a broken nose will be the very least of your problems.”

With that, he turned to leave the room.

Cassian called after him. “She was the one who attacked me!”

Chapter Eleven

After another patrol shift, Salem emptied her belt into her locker.

First, ammunition, then her flashlight, then the gun, keys, and finally,-

A hand tapped on the locker next to hers, interrupting her task.

"Hey, Salem?"

Salem let out a breath of annoyance as she placed her taser in the locker and closed it, turning to Finch.

She nodded.

"Do you want to grab something to eat?"

Salem shook her head as she swiped her bracelet over the lock.

"Are you sure? The T-Bar's still open."

Salem nodded again.

She was a little hungry but she didn't want to eat bar food. In fact, she didn't eat anything that she hadn't cooked herself.

"I could walk you back to the palace then?"

Salem picked up her wrist and typed out a quick message on her bracelet.

Finch huffed as he bent to read the message.

QIN: I'm not returning to the palace right now. I need to pick up some groceries.

He looked up and smiled.

"Well, I can't let you carry all that by yourself?"

Salem frowned. Why not?

Finch rolled his eyes at her expression.

"Nevermind. I'm going to help you carry your things back to your place."

Salem thought about it.

It wasn't like she needed the help, but she wouldn't stop him if he wanted to carry her things.

At her nod, he beamed.

She soon regretted it though. He wouldn't stop talking as they walked around Grace's tuck shop. Salem tried to keep her eyes on him as he spoke, but soon, she abandoned the task and focused on her shopping.

Finch leaned down to catch her eyes as she placed a loaf of bread and a pack of six eggs in his arms.

"Are you listening?"

Salem sighed, slightly frustrated. She thought that his presence would make the run quicker, but he was only slowing her down.

"As I was saying, the promotion was basically mine. I was supposed to get it when Hewn retired, but Alden practically handed the job to Jacobs. Friends in high places, right?"

Salem wasn't sure what he was talking about but nodded anyway as they stepped up to the counter.

'Good evening, Salem,' Grace signed before she rang her up. Grace didn't even scan the items. It was the same total every week.

She smiled politely as she pushed the reader forward. *'Friend of yours?'*

Salem shook her head as she swiped her bracelet over the reader.

Grace snorted, causing Finch to frown as they placed the shopping into two paper bags.

She was practically shaking with annoyance as she watched Finch place the groceries into the bags.

He was doing it all wrong.

Eggs at the bottom, milk on top of the bread. She should've just refused his help.

As they exited the shop, Finch shuffled the bags over into one hand and tapped her shoulder.

She turned to him, taking note of his tightened features.

"What were you guys talking about back there?"

Salem sighed and lifted her bracelet.

QIN: *She asked if you were my friend. I said no.*

Finch's frown deepened as he read before he paused. Suddenly, his smile was back in full force, but he still laid a hand on Salem's upper arm before she could turn back around.

"Just for future reference, I'd prefer if you didn't do all that in front of me," he said, waving his hand about. "I just have no idea what you're saying."

Salem was confused by his reaction, but in truth, Finch was a confusing person. So, she just turned and continued the journey to the palace, shaking it off. She just wanted to get home as soon as possible so that she could rearrange her shopping and put it away.

As they drew closer to her room, she noticed something sitting at her doorstep.

It was back.

Salem anxiously sidestepped around the cat and leaned over it to swipe her bracelet across the pad.

A finger snapped in front of her face.

She reluctantly faced Finch.

"Who's this?" he asked with a smile.

Salem typed as quickly as she could.

QIN: *It's a cat. Her name is Echo.*

"I didn't know you had a cat."

Salem sighed and wrote another message.

QIN: *It's not mine. It belongs to Cassian.*

She took her hand back and corrected herself.

QIN: *She belongs to Cassian.*

Finch's face soured. "I don't think cats are allowed in the palace."

Salem shrugged. She doubted that Cade or Deianira would have an issue with it.

She pushed the door open a creak, so as not to let the cat in, before she reached out her arms for the bags.

"No, don't be silly. I'll help you put them away."

Salem instantly shook her head.

She'd seen how he packed the bags and she'd go hungry before she'd let him anywhere near her fridge.

"Really. It's no prob-"

Finch's lips stopped moving as his eyes caught something over her shoulder. Salem turned around to see what had interrupted him.

Cassian.

And he was wearing a shirt this time.

Thank goodness.

'Can you take your cat, please?'

Cassian's eyes narrowed a fraction he nodded. *'Yeah. Sorry about her again.'*

Salem turned back to Finch. She put her arms out again.

"I'll help you take them in," he said, eyes still on Cassian. "I've got time."

Salem typed another message as she shook her head.

> ***QIN:*** *I can put them away.*

"It's been a long day. Let me help you ou-"

Salem flinched as Cassian appeared at her side.

"She said she's good."

She tilted her head at him. His words were directed to Finch, but he was still signing.

He glared up at Cassian. "Yeah, well, I'm making sure. I don't know how I feel about her being alone with so many strangers in the palace."

Cassian took a step forward and Finch stepped back. Raising a brow at him, Cassian took the bags out of his arms causing Salem to cringe.

He smiled sarcastically, signing with one hand. “Thank you for your service. You’ve been relieved.”

Finch’s gaze left Cassian and found her.

“Are you sure you’re okay?” he asked, facing away from Cassian.

He spoke as if Cassian couldn’t hear him and as if she could.

Salem nodded.

By the dark expression that quickly flashed across Finch’s face, that wasn’t the answer that he wanted.

Finch flicked his eyes to Cassian before nodding at her.

“Okay, I’ll see you tomorrow.”

Before Salem could even think to object, Finch leaned in and wrapped his arms around her, one around her waist, the other over her shoulder.

Salem went still.

He’s touching me.

As if to test if she could get any stiffer, Finch’s lips brushed against her cheek.

That was enough.

Salem stepped back abruptly.

He didn’t seem to notice her panic as he cut Cassian a look and turned to walk away.

The second his back turned, Salem grabbed the bags out of Cassian’s arms before pushing against the door with her back.

She needed to get in.

Now.

As soon as it opened, Echo took off into her room.

Salem's eyes widened as she looked up at Cassian helplessly.

'Breathe,' he told her, his eyes panicky.

It was only then that she realized that her chest was heaving.

Salem paused and took nine deep breaths before she looked back up at Cassian.

His head was tilted thoughtfully, but he shook off whatever he was thinking to step closer to her.

Salem instantly stepped back, almost tripping. She really didn't want another hug.

'Echo,' he signed before playing his hands out.

Of course. He needed to get his cat.

Salem awkwardly held up a hand and turned before her foot stepped over the threshold.

One foot in front of the other, lights three times, shoes.

Only after she'd completed the last step did she walk over to her mini-kitchen and place the shopping on the counter.

As she turned toward the door, Salem nodded to Cassian.

'Take off your shoes, please.'

Cassian's brows lowered as he carefully stepped into the room and removed his shoes, nudging them right next to Salem's.

Cassian stood in his socks.

He didn't want to move. He could see Echo sitting next to Salem's bed, but he was afraid to ruffle Salem any more than she already was.

He'd almost lost it when he saw Finch embrace her. She was obviously uncomfortable and the son of a bitch was just trying to make a point and upset her in the process.

Her back was turned, so he advanced.

"Echo," he called quietly.

Echo leaped onto the bed.

He cringed. "Get down!"

She rolled onto her back, looking at him upside down.

He wasn't sure what had gotten into her over the past few days but she was constantly whining to leave the room and Salem's was the first place she went. He had to run out and grab her on countless occasions but he was just thankful that Salem wasn't in all of those times.

His attention was drawn back to Salem as she started to move around the small kitchen. She went about putting away her groceries, completely ignoring his presence.

"Echo!" he called again.

Hiss!

Cassian narrowed his eyes.

"I'm not playing. Come here."

The girl started purring.

He groaned and took a few careful steps toward the bed. He glanced at the kitchen.

Salem was still facing away from him.

A few more steps.

Still good.

He advanced the last few and reached out to grab Echo just as she jumped out of his path.

Slapping a hand on the bed, he seethed, "Echo, I swear to the Gods!"

Echo jumped around on the bed, evading his grabs.

Cassian seriously doubted that Salem would like Echo trampling all over her perfectly made bed and his patience was wearing thin.

He flicked his eyes to Salem's back as he slowly kneeled on the bed.

He waited for Echo to slow down, and in a flash, he pounced on her.

Echo hissed and wriggled around in his grip.

This was a game that they always played, but Cassian didn't have games on his mind right now. He just wanted to get her before Salem-

Two soft claps had them both freezing.

Salem stood facing them, her eyes narrowed.

'What are you doing?'

Cassian quickly released Echo and hopped off the bed like a scolded child.

'I was trying to get her off the bed,' he signed sheepishly.

Salem wordlessly turned around and started going through the bags.

Cassian thought that he'd been dismissed until she turned back around with a few pieces of cubed meat on a sheet of tissue.

'Come here,' she signed.

He went to tell her that Echo wouldn't understand before he realized that she was talking to him.

He walked to her cautiously and raised his eyebrows when she held it out.

'Give it to her,' she instructed him, pointing at Echo.

Cassian almost laughed at the way that Salem was eyeing Echo like she might eat her instead.

He picked up a piece.

"Coco."

That was all it took for Echo to jump off the bed and gallop toward him. Salem flinched at her speed and quickly made her way behind Cassian, gripping his arm to keep him between them.

Cassian tried to ignore the way his chest jolted at her touch. At her warm hands on his bicep. He shivered and tossed a piece to Echo, trying to focus.

He slowly turned to Salem as she dropped his arm and stepped back.

'She's friendly, I promise. She just gets excited sometimes.'

As Echo approached again, he gave her another piece to distract her.

'Do you want to pet her?'

She was shaking her head before he'd finished his sentence.

Cassian tried to contain his smile. *'Okay.'*

He watched the way she bounced from foot to foot, eyeing her bags on the counter, and instantly felt bad. She had things to do and he was disturbing her.

'I'll leave you to it. Sorry about the trouble.'

Chapter Twelve

Salem stared out of the window as her mind raced.

She was glad that she wasn't on patrol today, she really didn't want to see Finch after what happened last time.

He'd been acting so weird recently. Talking to her non-stop, asking to walk her home, and that hug.

She shivered at the memory.

The touching.

She just couldn't stand it.

Her low tolerance didn't span across all aspects of contact though.

Before Cade, she was the Queen's most trusted protector.

As a fighter, it wasn't something she could avoid. Honestly, fighting was one of the only times that she truly didn't mind. It didn't feel as invasive, it was choreographed, the movements and touches were calculated.

But when Finch touched her, it made her want to crawl out of her skin.

Salem was just grateful that Cassian showed up when he did.

Cassian.

It felt like she was seeing him more and more every day. Whether it was in the council's study, out in the city, or when Echo would get out.

The lights flickered on and off.

Salem looked up to see Deianira place the remote back on the table.

'Am I boring you?' she signed, amused.

'Yes,' Salem responded. *'I should still listen though. I apologize.'*

Deianira shrugged. *'Sorry, I'm rambling. It's just been bugging me and I don't want to leave it too late.'*

'What has?' Salem asked, tuning back in.

'I still don't have a name.' Deianira sighed as she handed a folder to her. She quickly expanded at Salem's expression. *'For the baby.'*

Oh. 'Does Cade have any ideas?' she asked, trying to engage as she opened the folder.

'I think he does, but he wants me to pick.'

Deianira looked at her thoughtfully. *'You know, you could make a few suggestions. You are going to be the godmother, after all.'*

Salem's brows creased. *'That doesn't make any sense.'*

'What do you mean?' she asked absently.

She sat up in her chair. *'Naming me as the godmother means that I will be your child's guardian, should anything happen to you and Cade. I'm your sentinel. If you're dead, I already am.'*

A deep frown marred Deianira's face as she paused. She took a deep breath.

'A long time ago, I told you that I was your Queen before I was your friend.'

Salem remembered it like it was yesterday.

'I was wrong. I knew it was wrong when I said it. That's never been the case, Salem.'

But she wasn't wrong. *'But it's my job.'*

'In name,' she stressed. *'Salem, when have I ever sent you into danger before I went myself, if I could help it?'*

Salem thought about it.

She hadn't, ever.

'I'm sorry if I don't say this enough Salem, but you're my best friend. Above all. That's why I want you to be the godmother.'

Salem couldn't quite understand what she was feeling, but what she did know was that her chest felt a lot lighter.

'Okay, I'll take your baby.'

Deianira doubled over with laughter as Salem watched her, confused.

Wasn't that what she wanted?

"Can you move over? That shit stinks," Devin complained.

Lia snapped back. "How do you think I feel? I'm the one carrying it."

"Couldn't you have gotten a fresh one?" Cassian asked her, wrinkling his nose.

"And kill an innocent pig for this freakshow? I think not. Besides, all they had was this and a cow's heart. Trust me, this was the better option."

Devin paused with a hand on the tree trunk next to him. "Didn't you used to be a literal hunter?"

Lia narrowed her eyes at him. "Yes, I was. But I didn't just kill animals for fun. I cured the meat, fleshed the hide, and carved down the bones for weapons."

"Whatever," Devin huffed. "You still stink."

"Why don't you carry it, Jacobs?" she hissed as she shoved the bag toward him. "Be useful for once?"

Devin almost tripped as he speedily stepped back. "Get that shit away from me!"

She laughed gleefully. "Bitch."

While they argued, Cassian took the opportunity to appreciate the gradually warming spring air. It had been over a week since he'd left the city and a day trip was just what he needed.

He wasn't even required on this trip.

Lia was Head Scout and Devin was Head Enforcer. They could have completed the task on their own, but he chose to join them.

It was good to get Echo out of the palace too. She was getting out every night now and he knew that it was about time that she got some fresh air.

"Okay," Lia called as they broke the tree line out of the forest. "Over there. That's where I found it." She pointed to the water line across the rocky beach.

They all stopped to look at where she gestured. Even Echo paused at Cassian's feet.

"Who wants to do the honors?" she asked openly.

No one responded.

"I've been carrying this thing for hours, come on."

"I'll go," Cassian offered, reluctantly taking the tote off her shoulder.

"Thank you, *Cassian*," she said, eyeing Devin.

He wasn't bothered in the slightest.

"Coco, with me."

Cassian held the bag out in front of him as he carefully stepped from rock to rock, descending onto the beach. Echo, on the other hand, was having the time of her life, leaping across the rocks.

He finally reached the small strip of sandy stones and opened the tote. Despite the events of the past week, Emori had been surprisingly helpful in advising them. She thought it was a bad idea, so did Devin, but helped anyway.

Evidently, she was aware of the threat they were facing.

"Offerings and sacrifices are very important in my culture. The head was a message. If you wish to respond, you must give them something of equal value."

"We need to sacrifice a human?"

"No. Humans are like animals to them. You would only need to offer something proportional to that."

"Okay, and how do we tell them we want to talk?"

"When do you want to meet with them?"

"A week? That should give us enough time to prepare."

"Mark the seven cuts into the offering. They'll be there in seven days."

Cassian grimaced as he pulled the marked pig's head out of the bag. He picked up a few small stones and placed them around it to keep it in place before shuffling back and surveying his work.

It looked good enough.

He wiped his hands on his cargos and stood.

In the corner of his eye, he caught a little tail wag further down the beach.

"Echo! Not too far!"

She scurried further away, too focused on whatever was between the highly stacked rocks.

"Echo!"

Cassian jogged over to her and picked her up.

"Sorry. Hometime."

Echo wriggled and whined before slipping out of his hold and running straight back to the rocks.

She scratched at them, over and over again.

"What is it, Coco?" he asked as he followed after her.

As her paw slapped against the surface again, a lone rock fell out of place.

Cassian squinted his eyes as he leaned closer.

There was nothing behind it.

His brows lowered.

The rocks were built too high to be held up by one layer.

He bent down and joined Echo in pushing aside the rocks, but the hole only got bigger.

"Echo, stay," Cassian commanded as he peered through the small opening.

He could just about fit his head through.

Thin rays of sunlight streamed through the tiny gaps in the wall of rocks, but he couldn't see much in his position. He cringed and groaned when the sharp stones scraped him as he tried to rotate his body through the gap.

As he managed to flip on his back and look up, his eyes widened.

It wasn't just a hole.

It was a tunnel.

A tunnel leading right in the direction they came from.

Terra.

Cassian ignored the pain in his shoulders and backed up as quickly as he could, worming his way out of the hole. The second he was out, he ran to where Devin and Lia could see him.

He waved his arms. "Guys! You need to see this!"

Credit to them, they were running onto the beach before he'd finished speaking.

He led them to the opening.

"It's a tunnel," he said urgently. "It's pretty dark so I can't see how far it goes, but it's facing Terra. I would take a look if I could fit through."

Devin stepped back and waved a hand. "Welp. Ladies first."

"Me? You're the one with fire fingers. I won't even be able to see in there."

He gasped. "Fire fingers? How-"

"Can one of you just go?!" Cassian yelled. He seemed to be the only one taking this seriously.

Lia kicked away as many rocks as she could to widen the gap before getting on her knees to crawl through.

"What do you see?" Devin asked as soon as her head disappeared.

"Your mom!" came Lia's echoed voice.

She wriggled and shifted before she made it through.

"I can't see anything!"

Cassian walked a couple of feet away and picked up a few small branches before finding one that wasn't damp. He wordlessly handed it to Devin, who quickly opened his palm and used the roaring flame to light the end.

He carefully passed the log through the gap. "Watch your feet, Li!"

"Thanks."

He waited anxiously.

"Guys..."

"What?" He quickly leaned down to see if he could find anything.

"Someone's been here. Recently."

That's enough.

"Lia, come out!"

She didn't argue at all. "Gladly."

After they'd both helped her back through the gap, Cassian finally allowed himself to breathe.

"What was it?" Devin asked.

"There were footprints," Lia explained grimly, looking back at the gap. "There were only two sets, but they were deep, like multiple people had stepped in the same spot."

"How do you know it was recent?"

"I've scouted down here before. You see the water line?" They both turned to where she pointed. "When the tide rises, it moves all the way up here and it would've filtered through the rocks and into the tunnel. The sand was damp."

A pit formed in Cassian's stomach. "How often does the tide come in?" he asked quietly.

Lia's face told him that he wouldn't like the answer, but her response was worse than he expected.

"Twice a day. Any more than twelve hours and they would've been washed away." She flicked her eyes to Devin. "And there were no footprints coming back."

Oh Gods...

"Emori..." Devin breathed as he looked in the direction of Terra. "The girls..."

Everyone was in Terra. They would have no idea anything was even coming. That's if they weren't already there.

Cassian needed to act quickly.

Think, think, think.

Devin's voice cut through his thoughts. "We need to go back!"

"No!" Cassian protested. "We won't make it there in time."

Lia's head spun to him. "What? We need to warn them!"

"I'm going ba-"

"Just let me think!" Cassian snapped.

Think, think, think.

His eyes caught the half-burnt, abandoned log near the opening.

That's it.

"Devin."

Devin didn't respond but met his gaze.

"Light it up."

"What?" he finally asked.

"Burn it, all the way through. Then collapse it."

Lia stepped up. "Cassian, we have no idea how far it goes. He might not be able to-"

Devin was off before another word could be said. He ripped off his thick vest and removed his jacket before stepping up to the opening. He took a deep breath before he drew his hands back and pushed them out. The wall blew apart at the gust of wind he threw, leaving a ten-foot hole where the small gap used to be.

It was open, exposed.

With the new light, Cassian could take in the depth of the tunnel.

It was terrifying.

Devin rubbed his hands together and wrung out his wrists. As he pulled his arms back, a strained grunt tore from his throat as he pushed forward, two steady streams of fire pouring from his hands, lighting the tunnel further.

Cassian just had to watch for a second.

He knew that Devin was powerful, but the display was nothing short of spectacular.

The fire stretched as far as he could see, but Devin held firm, even as the cuffs of his shirt started to burn away.

Lia shook her head. "Devin, that's enough!"

Cassian put a hand out as she tried to approach. "He needs to do this."

She slapped his arm away. "Cass, he'll kill himself."

He set his eyes on Devin again.

Even from a distance, he could see his scrunched face, the sweat dripping down the sides of his forehead.

"Dev-" Before he could finish, the fire began to wither and Devin lowered his arms, his breaths labored.

He didn't stop there though.

He stretched his palms out, both of them facing the ground, and closed his eyes, his stance haggard.

The ground began to shake under Cassian's feet as Lia quickly bent and picked up Echo. He watched as dirt started to fall from the top of the tunnel, and before long, rocks were falling, and they fell faster until the hole gave way and caved in on itself.

As soon as the last rock stilled, Devin fell to his knees.

In seconds, Cassian was running to him, telling Lia to stay put.

"Devin!" he called as he dropped beside him.

Beads of sweat fell from the ends of his locs as he struggled to keep his head up.

"I did it..." he rasped with a goofy smile.

Cassian's shoulders fell with relief. "Yes, you did."

"I d-..." Devin swallowed, gasping for a few seconds. "I did..."

His body slumped to the ground, his head colliding with a blunt stone.
"Shit!" Cassian pulled him up. "Devin!" he slapped his face gently. "Dev, wake up!"
His head lolled over Cassian's forearm.
Shit, shit, shit...
"Lia!" he bellowed over his shoulder. "Lia! Get the rover!"
Cassian grunted as he turned Devin over and lifted him onto his shoulders.
"Oh my Gods!" Lia's face drained.
"Run!" he roared as he started toward the forest. "Get the rover! I'll meet you at the tree line!"
Lia broke into a sprint while he ran as fast as he could, Devin bouncing in his grip.
Cassian could barely breathe, and it wasn't just because of Devin's weight on his shoulders.
He'd told him to do it. He asked him to collapse the tunnel, knowing that he might not have had the power to do so. He prevented Lia from stopping him, even when he could see the toll it was taking on him.
Devin couldn't die.
Not like this.
Not because of me.
He used that thought to spur him on, to push himself even as his muscles threatened to give way under the pressure.
It had taken them over two hours to walk to the beach from where they had parked the rover so Cassian was thankful to whatever entity of strength that possessed him because he made it back in forty minutes.

"Come on!" Lia called from the rover as she drifted right into their path.

She grabbed onto the external bar and propelled herself out of the large window to open the door for Cassian.

Time ticking, he laid Devin across the seats and called to Lia.

"I'll drive! I can't fit back there with him!"

Lia didn't even respond, just hopped into the back and kneeled on the floor between the front and back seats.

Cassian jumped into the driver's seat and stepped on the gas before the door even shut beside him, wincing as Echo jolted in the passenger seat.

"Hold him down!" That was the only warning Cassian gave Lia before he spun the vehicle around and set off for Terra.

He tried to stay calm, so as not to land them in an even worse predicament, but there was nothing he could do to steady the frenzied beating in his chest.

As they neared the city, he didn't take his foot off the accelerator, only steered.

"He's not breathing!" Lia shrieked.

No, no, no, no, no...

Cassian scanned his eyes over the interior of the truck before turning back to the road. Just his luck that they took a rover without a radio.

He knew that it probably wasn't the safest thing to do while driving at such a high speed, but he didn't know what else to do.

Cassian focused, even closed his eyes for a few seconds.

The link was already established. He just needed to find it, tug on it.

The cool draft across the back of her neck alerted Salem to Cade's presence.

'She's asleep,' she told him as he stepped through the door.

Cade nodded and went to close it, wincing as it hit the frame too hard.

He dropped his bag by the door and approached the bed where Deianira lay with a soft smile.

'How long has she been out?' he asked, eyes on Deianira.

Salem waited for him to look up before responding. *'Three hours and forty-seven minutes.'*

He chuckled as he leaned down and kissed her forehead before moving further down to kiss her bump. *'Sorry, I'm late. I had to stand in for Devin.'*

'It's okay. She didn't give me any trouble,' Salem responded, recalling her conversation with Cassian.

He snorted.

She tilted her head. *'What's-'*

Salem.

She flinched.

The second she thought about him, she was hearing his voice. She shook her head before gathering her papers.

'I'll leave you two alone now. Goodbye.'

She closed her binder, then stood.

Salem!

Again?

She spun to look over her shoulder.

Only Cade and Deianira were there. But she knew that already.

Whatever it was wasn't coming from inside the room, it was too far. Loud, yet far.

In the last seven years, Salem only had the voices in her head to remind her of what people sounded like, and while it was startling, hearing a voice that she didn't have to conjure up was strangely comforting, so she wasn't surprised that his voice was replaying in her mind when she thought of him.

Cade waved to get her attention. *'Is everything okay?'*

'Yes.'

Salem stepped to the side and pushed her chair back under the desk.

SALEM!

She jolted and dropped her binder at the roar. Salem spun in a circle, plagued by confusion.

What in Terra was that?

Looking up, she found Deianira sitting up and Cade approaching her.

'Hey, are you feeling alright?'

'Salem, are you okay?'

She couldn't answer their questions. She was too busy searching for the source of the voice.

Salem, can you hear me?!

That was a question.

This wasn't just a voice in her head.

Cassian was speaking *to* her...and she could *hear* him.

Sal-

Cassian? she asked hopefully.

Salem, thank the Gods!

Deianira and Cade were both standing now, watching her carefully.

Salem, I need you to get Mikhael and meet us outside! It's Devin.

What's Devin?

He's hurt. Real bad, he's not breathing.

Deianira cautiously rested a hand on Salem's shoulders.

'Salem, what's going on?' Cade asked beside her.

'Devin's not breathing,' she told him before returning to the link.

Where are you?

Northwestern border. Just outside the city.

Salem ignored Cade and Deianira's frantic gestures and left the room.

In her periphery, she could see that they were following, but that didn't stop her from picking up into a run in the direction of the infirmary.

As soon as she arrived, she swiped her pass and stepped into the room.

Mikhael wasn't there, but Octavia was.

She jumped at Salem's abrupt entry.

'Where is Mikhael?'

Octavia blinked at her cluelessly.

She didn't understand.

Salem had just been about to open her mouth when Cade rushed into the room.

'Salem, what the hell is-'

She pushed his hands down.

'Ask her where Mikhael is?'

Cade watched her suspiciously but still asked.

"Where's Mikhael?"

Salem spun to catch Octavia's response.

She placed a hand on her hip and narrowed her eyes at Cade. "Why do you want to know?"

Salem swung her gaze back to Cade, her eyes darting between them.

"Octavia, this is serious."

She rolled her eyes. "He has a shift in the clinic."

Salem didn't watch the end of the conversation, she just took off for the clinic.

She ignored the way her stomach turned too.

The clinic was the last place she wanted to be anywhere near, but this wasn't about her.

Don't come to the palace. Head for the clinic.

Okay. We're five minutes out.

Cade caught up and was running beside her as they made it to the clinic entrance.

She needed to catch him up if she was going to communicate the situation to Mikhael.

She stopped outside and turned to Cade, signing as fast as he could comprehend.

'Cassian called me through a psionic link. I'm unsure of the circumstances, but something happened resulting in Devin getting injured. He's on his way over here now, so I need you to help me get Mikhael ready for them.'

Cade's eyes darted from her left hand to her right, and once she'd finally finished, it only took him a second to nod and head into the clinic.

Salem followed behind him, then paused at the door, her feet not allowing her to go any further.

She wasn't sure what he was saying as he marched in, drew curtains, and banged on desks, but before long, Mikhael's head peaked out from behind a door in the back. Cade yelled something and motioned for him to follow before three other doctors came rushing toward Salem with a gurney.

She hopped out of the way and followed them away from the clinic as a rover drifted to a halt right outside, almost taking out a passerby.

Cassian practically threw himself out of the driver's seat and met Salem's eyes for a split second.

He yanked the door open at the same time that Eulalia hopped out.

Two of the doctors, with the help of Cassian and Eulalia, reached in and pulled Devin onto the gurney.

Salem turned to follow the doctors as they wheeled him in, like everyone else, but a hand gripped her forearm, spinning her. All of a sudden, Cassian was in her face, hands holding both sides of her head.

He was so close.

His words were written so clearly in his deep blue eyes, so plainly that he didn't even need to say them, but he still did.

"Thank you..." he breathed.

Salem was still. Not from fear or discomfort.

She was entranced.

By everything about him.

The way his pupils dilated as his gaze dipped to her mouth, the way his chest heaved, the way his lips parted. His eyes were so big, so blue. The look in them almost made Salem think that he was about to...

Then in the next second, he was gone.

Cassian stepped back, head down.

'I'm sorry. I shouldn't have done that.'

You shouldn't have stopped... she wanted to say.

Chapter Thirteen

Cassian's head rested in his hands.

He didn't want to look up. He knew exactly what he'd find if he did. Devin lying still on the bed hooked up to a heart monitor, a tube down his throat.

The doctor clasped his hands together before addressing the room.

"My name is Hiram and I'm taking over for Mikhael on this case," he said quietly, flicking cautious eyes to Deianira. "As far as damage goes, he's torn his right brachialis and left deltoid. There was also a minor brain hemorrhage but we were able to reverse most of this in one healing session. While the majority of the physical damage is repaired, his body is fatigued. He's not strong enough to breathe on his own for the time being so we've induced a coma to aid his recuperation." Hiram picked up his clipboard before turning back to the group once more. "As some of you may know, Mr. Jacobs underwent the restoration process some years ago and his abilities have been... somewhat enhanced. The amount of power he has isn't designed to fit in his body. Any body for that matter. You'll need to

watch him closely, because if he tries to exert that much energy again...he will die."

The door swung open, drawing Cassian from his flashback. Emori skittishly entered the room in front of Cade. She ran to Devin's bedside and put a hand to his face.
Cassian couldn't take much more of this.
"Cass?"
He blinked his eyes quickly as he looked up at his brother.
"Let's give them a minute, yeah?"
He didn't trust his voice not to break, so he only nodded and got up.
Cade led him past the waiting area and into an unoccupied room where Cassian found everyone waiting.
Everyone but Salem.
He kept his eyes on the floor as he shuffled into the room and put his back to the wall.
Cade closed the door.
Deianira's voice was scarily calm as she filled the silence. "Does somebody want to explain to me how I sent two members of my High Council to make a simple drop, and only one came back breathing?"
Sometimes, being around Deianira in an informal setting made him forget this side of her.
The Queen in her.
Lia started. "It was an accide-"
"It was my fault," Cassian interjected.
"How is that?" Deianira asked, eyes boring into his.
Averting his eyes, he told the truth. "We left the message, but then we found something. There was a tunnel, facing Terra."

"Where?" Deianira asked bluntly.

"On the beach." Cassian looked to Lia for the next part. She could explain it better than him.

"There was a gap between a few rocks and I went in to look. Since I've been scouting there, the tide rises every twelve hours, give or take, and the tunnel was close enough that the water would've reached it. The sand was damp too, and there were footprints. Two sets. People were in there today."

That seemed to break through Deianira's ice. "So they're coming?" she asked quietly, sitting straighter.

"No." Lia shook her head.

When Deianira narrowed her eyes, Cassian took over. "We knew that they must have been in there recently, but we didn't know if they were already on their way, or how far they'd gotten. Either way, the tunnel would've been a problem for us at some point. So, I...I told Devin to burn it...and cave it in. I just didn't want them to get here before we could warn everyone."

Deianira stayed silent for a while, nodding slowly.

She looked up at Cassian. "Devin is Head Enforcer. He doesn't take orders from you, so whether it was too much for him to handle or not was within his discretion."

So she wasn't mad?

The next look she gave him had him questioning that. "And if you wanted me to put you to work, you could've just asked."

She slid off the bed and made for the door.

Chapter Fourteen

Never again.

Those were the only words echoing in Cassian's head as he swept up another broken glass. He was starting to understand why Lia laughed at him when he offered to take the job.

"Alright! Naptime!"

"No!" the two little demons yelled at the same time.

"Guys, please. We played hide and seek, and tag, and I don't think Echo wants another makeover," he groaned, gesturing to Echo, who was half-hidden under the bed.

Kendria looked him up and down contemplatively. "Make fire."

Tyla nodded along. "Yeah, make fire."

Cassian was just drained. "I can't make fire."

"But daddy makes fire," Kenny argued.

He felt a small stab of guilt at the mention of Devin. The reason he was watching the girls was so that Emori could stay with him at the clinic.

"Okay, if I make fire, will you guys take a nap?"

Kenny beckoned Ty closer before they started whispering to each other. After much discussion, Kenny finally turned back to Cassian.

"Make fire and let me do makeup and naptime."

"On me?" he asked.

She nodded with a wide smile.

Cassian was well aware of the fact that he was negotiating with two five-year-olds, but he needed the break, so he conceded.

"Deal," he said as he ran over to his dresser, rummaging through it before he found what he was looking for.

He went back to the girls and sat crossed-legged in the little circle that they had created.

Cassian flicked the lighter on for about three seconds before snapping it shut.

"There's your fire. Makeup time."

Kenny's face scrunched. "That's not how daddy does it."

"I can't do it how daddy does it," he mocked back, imitating her.

Kenny's face burned red but Ty went very quiet, very still.

They were identical but it didn't take Cassian more than a day to learn to tell them apart.

They were literally their parents.

Kendria was bold, outspoken, and scarily intelligent. She was a handful to deal with alone, but it was Tyla that he truly feared.

It was clear that she had a mind of her own, but she still followed Kenny, allowed her to lead.

She was quiet, like her mother, however, Cassian just knew that there was a storm brewing. He could see it in the way that she tilted her little freckled head at him. She looked unstable, like she was always planning his murder.

Maybe, she did have a little bit of Devin in her.

Kenny went on. "You have to make it with your hands," she told him, holding up her fingers.

Cassian shook his head and placed the lighter behind his hand. Concealing it in his palm, he flicked it on with the other hand. "Woooow..." he said enthusiastically.

Neither of them even cracked a smile.

"I saw you put it behind your hand," Kenny said, bored.

Cassian tossed the lighter on the floor and stood, holding his hands out. "Okay! Naptime. I mean it."

Kenny crossed her arms while Ty stood and reached for Cassian's hand.

"Thank you, *Tyla*," he emphasized, glaring at Kendria.

She only stuck her tongue out at him.

Ty tugged on his hand. "Hug."

Kenny nodded. "Yeah. Daddy gives us hugs before naptime."

Anything to get them asleep quicker.

Cassian picked her up and hugged her as her little arms came around his neck. He hoped that her obedience would prompt Kenny to do the same, but she remained seated with a mischievous smile on her face.

He should've known that something was up when she looked up at him like that because it was the last thing he saw before a pair of teeth sank into his shoulder.

"Fuck!" he howled, instantly pulling her away.

Kenny's jaw dropped. "You said a bad word!"

"Because your sister bit fucking me!" he growled, holding Ty at arm's length.

Enough was enough.

Cassian shifted her under his arm and grabbed the back of Kenny's dress, holding her like a duffle bag.

The girls squealed with laughter as he marched them across the room and launched them onto the bed. Ty still had her shoes on, but he didn't even care. He just pulled the covers from under them and used them to trap them in, tucking the corners as tightly as he could. They were still laughing.

Knock, knock.

"Stay!" Cassian instructed them as he went to open the door.

Lia was standing at the threshold with a wide smile on her face.

"How's your day going, Cass?"

He said nothing as his eyes narrowed.

"Someone's pissy. Did Ty give you a hug?"

The glare that Cassian threw her way should have had her quieting, but Lia burst out laughing.

Out of annoyance, he went to close the door, only stopping when Lia held a hand out.

She steadied herself on the door frame.

"I'll take them," she said, her laughter sobering. "Go get something to eat. You look like you could use it."

He couldn't pass up the offer. "Thank you," he said earnestly.

"Girls!" he yelled. "Get out!"

Chapter Fifteen

Snap.

Salem turned to look at the owner of the hand that had just snapped in her face.

"Hi," Finch greeted her.

She raised a hand and turned back to the groups.

With Devin still in his coma, the members of the High Council had been taking turns covering his shifts with the program.

Today, it was Salem's turn. With Finch.

Snap.

Salem took a deep breath. She really didn't like that.

"Hey, were you okay the other night when Little Alden interrupted us?"

Salem squinted her eyes at the word 'little', but nodded.

"Good. I didn't want to have to pull him aside."

Salem's head tilted.

For what? she thought as she moved down the arena to keep in line with the groups as they traveled down the course.

"So, are you busy tomorrow night?"

Salem thought about it. She had to meet with Deianira in the morning, but after that, she was free.
She shook her head.
"Great." Finch smiled. "The T-Bar is doing a little prima celebration tonight."
Her eyes widened momentarily.
"I know it's usually in winter but the guard can get a little pissy about it. It's great though. Food, drinks, music, all that good stuff. I can pick you up."
Oh. As in Prima Day.
She let out a breath, then she frowned. She quickly typed out a message.

***QIN:** Celebration?*

"Yeah, for the few of us left that still believe in putting the gifted first. You know, with The Dome gone and all?"
Salem thought about it. Prima Day hadn't been celebrated in six years due to its history and the meaning it held for the humans who lived on Old Dome territory. She wasn't sure that she wanted to attend an event that celebrated the holiday.

***QIN:** I would prefer not to.*

Finch's smile slipped before he pulled it back. "If I didn't know any better, I'd think that you didn't want to spend time with me, Salem."
I don't, Salem thought, but she didn't say it.

It was one of those things that Deianira warned her might hurt someone's feelings. She went with a different reason, a true one, but not the main reason.

QIN: *I don't eat bar food and I can't exactly listen to music.*

Finch shook his head. "What? Don't worry about all that. Trust me, you'll love it."

She was sure she wouldn't.

QIN: *No, thank you.*

"We'll do dinner then. You pick the spot."

Salem moved up the field again.

It was hard to walk and type.

QIN: *I cook for myself.*

"Perfect." Finch beamed. "Your place then."

Salem didn't remember suggesting that he come over, but it seemed like a better alternative to the T-Bar.

Why he couldn't eat on his own, she had no idea, but if that's what he really wanted then fine.

Salem had a lot of quirks and preferences of her own so she wouldn't judge Finch for his.

She nodded.

Cassian pulled up on the bar above his door frame one last time before dropping.

With the arena and training gym being used by the program, he had to find an alternative. It wasn't so bad. In his room, he could turn off all the lights and draw the curtains.

It almost felt like home.

Almost.

He'd also managed to get his hands on a real pair of sound-canceling headphones, thanks to Cade.

Since Cassian arrived back at the palace, he and Cade had spent more time together than they had their whole lives. They met up to just hang out, even when there was nothing to do. He was surprised at how much he liked spending time with his brother.

Like today when Cade asked him for help to plan a surprise baby shower for Deianira. He had an exact plan and just needed Cassian and Lia to help execute it. During their planning, he asked why he hadn't asked for Salem's help too, seeing as she had known Deianira the longest, but Cade informed him that Salem couldn't keep secrets, she didn't lie.

It was a genuine question, but in truth, he just wanted to see her. They hadn't spoken since the day that Devin washed rushed into the clinic. He thought back to that tension-filled afternoon. It was tense for a lot of reasons, some of which had nothing to do with Devin.

When he called on Salem through the mind link, he wasn't sure if it would work. She'd been in his head before, but he'd never been in hers. Apparently, that was all it took for him to reach her.

When she responded, the relief that he felt was indescribable. Then he arrived and she was outside of the clinic with Cade and Mikhael. Everything around her was moving so fast, but there she stood, motionless, like an angel in the chaos.

He had no doubt that Devin would've died if she hadn't responded so quickly. There were only seven minutes between the time that he called her and when they arrived, so she must've been sprinting to make it from the palace to the city clinic in time to help him.

When he got out of the rover and grabbed her, so much adrenaline was pumping through his veins that his vision was blurring. He was seconds away from kissing her when he remembered how she responded to Finch's touch that night outside her room.

He'd be damned if he ever made her feel uncomfortable, so he got a hold of himself and backed up.

That didn't stop him from thinking about her constantly though.

As Cassian went to fill Echo's bowl, an idea struck him.

"Coco," he called.

She looked at him but didn't move.

"Echo, come here."

She lazily padded over to him.

"You want to see Salem?"

Energy instantly entered her body as jumped up and weaved through his legs, giving him a high-pitched *meow*.

He opened the door and stood back.

"Go find Salem!" he whisper-shouted.

She was out of the room before he had finished his sentence.

As Cassian closed the door and waited, he smiled to himself.

The lights pulsed.

Salem stepped away from the stove and creaked open the window before walking to the door.

She pulled it open and paused.

He was wearing a suit.

And holding flowers.

"Salem, hi," Finch greeted, his smile spanning from ear to ear. "These are for you," he said as he handed her the roses.

Huh.

Salem nodded her thanks to him.

She didn't necessarily dislike flowers. They looked nice, but it was often the smell that put her off. And she didn't like the red so much either.

She stepped to the side to let him in and instantly cringed as he waltzed right in, shoes on her floor. Salem speed-walked to the counter to put the roses down before rushing up to him, typing as she moved.

> ***QIN:*** *Please, take your shoes off.*

Finch looked down and tilted his head at her. "Uh, sure."

He toed off his loafers and kicked them to the side of the door.

The wrong side.

Salem huffed before looking up to find Finch's mouth moving.

"... are you wearing?"

She let her eyes fall over her body.

> ***QIN:*** *They're compression clothes.*

Finch's eyes narrowed, but he shrugged as he removed his jacket and placed it on the back of Salem's chair.

"Wow, you've really got everything in here."

Salem took the opportunity to distract herself, taking a look around her room.

It was true. Over the many years she'd spent in the palace, she'd worked on all of the adaptations herself. The kitchen took longer than she had intended, but with minimal help, she was able to have her room fitted with everything she could need in a whole house. It was almost the size of a small house too.

A nod was her only response as she took a deep breath and hoped she wouldn't regret this.

But half an hour in his company proved that she'd never regretted anything so much.

She didn't often have strong feelings toward people, but she really wanted Finch out of her room.

He'd complained about the blandness of the meal that she'd cooked, he chewed with his mouth open, and he wouldn't. Stop. Talking.

Salem shoveled her food into her mouth as fast as she could before standing and taking her plate to the sink.

She returned to take his plate.

"Oh, I wasn't done with th-"

She pretended not to see his words as she picked up his plate and walked it over to the counter.
She scraped the food from his plate before putting on a pair of gloves and proceeding to wash them. As she tossed the gloves in the trash, Salem turned to come face to face with Finch.
She blenched.
"Thank you for tonight," he said.
She nodded as she sidestepped him to remove the glasses off the table.
He followed and beckoned her again with a tap on the shoulder.
"I had a good time."
She nodded again.
He didn't ask her a question, it was just a statement, so Salem turned back to the kitchen, both glasses in her hands. She pretended that he wasn't behind her as she pulled on another pair of gloves.
Salem didn't like waste. He was distracting her.
She huffed as she threw away the second pair of gloves after placing the glasses on the dry rack.
She knew he was right behind her when she turned around so she thought that she might not be so startled this time. That would've been the case had his hands not found her waist and his lips, hers.
She didn't freeze though, she switched.

After waiting a good five minutes, Cassian set off to follow Echo.

He wasn't in a great mood after the events of the past few days, but he knew that one sour face or blunt comment from Salem would change that.

It didn't take him long to reach her room, they were on the same floor, but when he arrived, Echo was sitting on the doorstep.

Usually, Salem would've opened the door by now.

Cassian sighed.

She wasn't in.

Echo scratched and sniffed under the door.

"Me too, Coco," he said quietly. He called her over. "Come on,"

Just as he turned around, a high-pitched wail sounded from inside the room.

He was at the door again before the sound had even ceased.

"Salem!" Cassian called as he banged on the door, hitting the light alert a few times. "Salem!"

He tried the handle.

Locked.

Cassian knew that it wasn't going to work, but he swiped his bracelet over the panel anyway.

Denied.

Salem! he yelled through the link.

No answer.

Echo was already scurrying out of his way as he backed up a step and threw his body into the door.

The doors in the palace were engaged with electromagnetic locks so Cassian knew that it wouldn't be easy to force his way in. That didn't stop him from trying again though. And again, and again.

It took seven tries before the door gave way and flew off the hinges.

The scene that unraveled before him was not at all what he was expecting.

Deputy Finch lay on the ground, stomach first, his arm twisted up behind his back.

And Salem?

She was the one pressing a knee into his back, holding his arm, drawing animalistic cries from him.

He didn't stand to make any more observations though.

Wordlessly, Cassian marched up to them and pulled Finch out of Salem's grasp by his collar. She stepped back as Finch fought Cassian's grip.

He shot her a dark look. *'What did he do?'*

Her eyes flicked to Finch. *'He tried to kiss me.'*

Whatever Finch saw on Cassian's face had him stuttering. "S-she's lying! The fucking psycho attacked me out of nowhere!"

Cassian didn't need to look over at Salem to know that it wasn't true.

Deianira? Sure.

Salem? Never.

Cassian tightened his grip on him before pulling his arms back and throwing him as far as he could.

As Finch's body collided with the far wall and fell to the ground, Cassian strode over to him once again and picked him up by his lapels with a humorless laugh. "It's like you want me to throw you back to her," he growled.

Finch's head lolled before he groggily looked between the two of them.

"You can have her," he said through gritted teeth.

Cassian released him suddenly, letting him fall to the ground. He angrily picked himself back up and made for the door.

"Hey, Finch?" Cassian called after him.

He reluctantly turned. "Wha-"

The fist that connected with his jaw cut off the rest of his question.

Cassian's words were much calmer than the rest he'd spoken tonight. "Look at her again and I'll dig your fucking eyes out."

He gasped, choking as he dragged himself onto his feet, stumbling toward the door.

When he'd managed to stumble out of the room Cassian finally took his eyes off him, turning to Salem and the wrecked room.

She stared at him silently for a moment. *'You broke my door.'*

Cassian blinked at her and tilted his head.

Is she serious?

Chapter Sixteen

Cassian stayed behind to help Salem clean her room, and to say she was pleased was an understatement.

He did everything exactly how she asked. Even when he didn't look too sure, he watched her to see what she was doing and replicated it almost perfectly. He packed the dishes away, arranging them in the cupboard in size order. He tucked in the chairs, leaving a small gap between the frame and the table.

She couldn't have asked for more.

As a result, the job was done in under thirty minutes.

Cleaning finished, she started toward the door.

Salem.

A shiver went up her spine at the closeness of his voice.

It would take a while to get used to that.

She turned to him.

'*Where are you going?*' he asked, standing awkwardly in the middle of the room.

'*The workshop,*' she responded plainly.

'*Why?*'

Salem flicked her eyes to the doorway.

'You broke my door. I need to get a new one and fix it.'

Cassian frowned.

'You want to go out, get a new door, carry it up here, and put it in by yourself, at this time?'

She was frowning now.

'Why wouldn't I?'

He stared at her blankly before blinking.

'No, I'll do it,' he said. *'Sorry about that. I thought you were in trouble.'*

Huh?

'Why would you think that?'

'I heard a cry outside the door.'

'Why were you outside the door?'

Salem instantly noticed Cassian's flushed cheeks as he took a while to respond.

'Echo got out again,' he replied, inclining his head to where she slept under the table.

'Okay,' Salem responded. That happened all the time. *'While we're in the workshop, you can find a new lock for your door.'*

He absently nodded then took a step forward as she went to turn around.

'It's 11:30.'

It wasn't a question, but she found herself inclined to respond to him.

'It is.'

He shook his head.

'No, it's late and I'm the one who broke it. You can sleep in my room tonight.'

Salem refused vehemently. *'I need to sleep on my bed.'*

He shrugged. *'Take mine. I'll sleep on the couch.'*

'No, my *bed,'* she stressed before settling. *'But thank you for the offer.'*

Cassian ran a hand over his buzzed hair and sighed.

'Salem, I can't let you sleep in a room with no door.'

'You don't have to. I'm going to fix it.'

Isn't he listening?

'I'm *going to fix it. First thing tomorrow. For now, I'll put a board up. But you need a room. I have one.'*

How did her predicament affect him?

She glanced at her bed.

When Cassian caught her eyes, he narrowed his.

The next thing she knew, he was stepping away and stalking toward the bed.

Salem almost screamed as she watched him stretch out his long arms and gather up the bed sheets before grabbing two pillows.

She had just made that.

'What are you doing?!' she signed manically.

Cassian shifted the covers under one arm.

'Would it make you feel better if you slept on your own sheets?'

Oh.

Her breath hitched as she stared at him, frozen.

He was trying to accommodate her.

At her silence, he cringed and went on. *'I can come back for the mattress.'*

She was still in shock but she knew that it was only reasonable to meet him halfway.

'No, the sheets are fine.'

Cassian couldn't help his grin as he trailed behind Salem to his room.

She stuck as close to the wall as possible, keeping away from Echo, and occasionally flinched or jumped when she would get too close. Echo might have been excitable, but she'd never scratched or bitten him in the four years he'd had her.

Salem obviously wasn't taking any chances.

As their short journey drew to an end, Lia appeared from down the hall and drew to a stop. She tilted her head at Cassian with an amused smile.

"Do I even want to know?" she asked, eyeing the light blue cotton bed sheets gathered in his arms.

The grin dropped off his face. "No."

"Oh, I think I do." She nodded, her smile growing as she turned to Salem. *'What's going on?'*

Salem flicked her eyes back to Cassian and held her book at her side. *'Cassian broke my door and insisted that I sleep in his room.'*

He could've sworn he saw the slightest blush on Salem's face as she explained.

Lia didn't even hold back her laughter. He could still hear her as she left and turned at the end of the hall.

Salem reached his door and stepped aside for Cassian to awkwardly swipe his bracelet with the sheets in his arms.

The second the door opened, nerves racked him.

He hadn't planned for company, and while his room was relatively clean, he knew that Salem had a particular way of doing things.

He cringed as he watched her remove her shoes, nudge them to the left and stand to the side. Cassian entered as quickly as he could and dropped the sheets onto the couch before moving to the bed to remove his.

Looking over his shoulder as he stripped the bed, he noticed that Salem was still standing by the door.

He paused his task. *'Do you want to sit? I can run to the kitchen and grab you a drink if you want?'*

'No, thank you.'

He anxiously returned to the bed. He'd seen how she made hers and copied it to the best of his ability.

'Is this okay?' he asked, turning to her.

Her eyes glided over the bed, assessing it. After a minute, she swung her gaze back to him.

'Yes.'

A huge weight lifted off of his shoulders.

'I'm gonna go take a shower and let you change.'

He didn't wait for a response as he stalked into his en-suite.

Cassian stayed in the shower for way longer than necessary.

He was nervous.

Inviting her to stay with him had been an impulsive decision, but once he'd made it, he was glad that he did. While he didn't regret offering, he had no idea what he would do when he re-entered the bedroom. Honestly, he hoped that Salem might be asleep when he got out.

Cassian wrapped the towel around his waist and took a deep breath as he walked back into the room.

Salem wasn't asleep.

She was sitting on the bed, legs crossed, reading a book.

As he stepped into the bedroom, her eyes shot to his before lowering.

The deep breath that Cassian took flew out of the window as he stilled.

Her gaze was plain, examining, critical.

As if realizing that she'd been staring, Salem flinched and cast her eyes back down to the book, even turning a page.

He wasn't sure what to say, so he didn't say anything. He just ambled over to his dresser and pulled on a pair of long black sleep pants before removing the towel. As he turned back around, Salem's eyes flicked to her book.

She was watching me.

It would've been a lie if he said he didn't like that.

Tamping down his smirk, he walked back over to the small couch in front of the screen and threw himself down with an *oomph.*

Despite his current company and nerve-filled thoughts, he found himself struggling to keep his eyes open as his back hit the couch.

"You think you can just get rid of me?"

Cassian stood, gun held up, in the entrance of the supply closet as Drake went on.

"I made you, I raised you. I'm not going anywhere."

The anger coursing through Cassian's veins almost had him dropping the gun and killing his father with his bare hands. He didn't even speak, he feared that his words wouldn't hold as much venom as he intended.

"Pull the trigger," Drake snarled.

He squeezed the trigger...but nothing happened. He tried again, even holding it down, but it didn't go off.

"Just as I thought," Drake laughed. "Weak."

"I'm not weak..." Cassian whispered, shaking with rage.

"Are you sure about that?"

In the next second, Drake had Salem held against him, his own gun to her head.

"No! Don't!" Cassian bellowed.

"If you're so strong, try that trigger again."

They were standing too close. He couldn't risk hitting her.

"Come on, son! Show the girl how strong you are!"

His hands weren't steady enough.

"It's okay, Cassian."

He met Salem's eyes as she whispered to him.

"I can't do it..." he told her, voice cracking.

"It's okay," she said quietly.

He shook his head. He couldn't do it.

"Once weak, always weak," his father smirked. "Just remember, you could've avoided this. This is your fault."

"It's okay..."

BANG!

"SALEM!"

"It's okay," a small raspy voice whispered into his ear.

Cassian jolted into a sitting position and threw his gaze around the pitch-black room.

Even when he squinted his eyes, there was nothing to be seen.

But there was no mistaking the little stuttered breaths he could hear to his right.

Salem? he sent down the link.

It took a while to get a response. He almost thought that he'd imagined the voice until it finally came through.

Yes?

He shivered. *That was you?*

He couldn't see her face, but he knew that she was there as he bowed his head, allowing her small breaths to fan over his cheek.

It had been her voice. She'd comforted him, anchored him.

Yes. You had a night terror.

Cassian grimaced. He really didn't like the thought of her hearing th-

How did you know?

He could hear her move an inch. *You were shaking.*

That only made him feel worse. Not just for waking her up, but that she was there to witness it.

I'm sorry for waking you, he said quietly.

It's okay. Deianira used to have them too. It's no problem. There was a long pause. *I'm going back to bed now.*

As he heard shuffling, Cassian blindly reached out, gently grasping her hand as she went to stand. She didn't shrink away from his touch, so he held on.

You have a beautiful voice...

He didn't know what made him say it, but it didn't make it any less true.

She didn't respond. She didn't leave either.

Cassian gently tugged on her hand, drawing her closer.

Can I hear it again?

Silence.

Nothing.

As she slipped her hand from his, Cassian closed his eyes.

He'd pushed her too far. The touching, the talking, the-

"I don't know what you want me to say..."

His head snapped in her direction at the sound.

While clear, her voice was quieter than it used to be. It was slightly brittle from lack of use. Raspy from sleep. There wasn't much intonation or change in tone.

The only thing he could liken it to was a gust of wind.

And it was the most peaceful thing he'd ever heard.

"Cassian?"

Heat rose to his cheeks. He'd heard her say his name through the mind link, but nothing compared to the real thing.

Carefully, slowly, he reached for her again. This time, he felt her arm. He traced her with his hand. He made sure his touch wasn't too rough or too light, it was somewhere in the middle. Upper arm, shoulder, collarbone, neck, chin. Goosebumps rose under his fingertips as he passed over her skin. She shivered when he reached her cheek, but he knew that it wasn't from fear.

Did I say something wro-

Can I kiss you?

Cassian didn't so much as breathe as he waited for her response. He knew that he was pushing his luck, but he couldn't help himself.

Yes...

He didn't make her repeat herself.

Cassian splayed his fingers across her cheek, spanning to the back of her head. He didn't pull her in, he bent forward and slowly pressed his lips to hers. There was no rush, no urgency, he wanted her to set the tone. And she did.

Salem placed a hand on his chest and leaned closer to him. He followed her movement and slowly fell back as she pushed forward.

She could take whatever she wanted.

Since she'd been able to speak, Salem was prepared for a life of service.

While she knew who her parents were, they weren't the ones who raised her. She was schooled, trained, and had lived in the palace all her life. That's how she met Deianira.

There were many others in her class, but Salem stood out. While that had never been a good thing in her experience, it was what got her the position as Deianira's sentinel.

Though combative skills and intelligence were very important, the choice was ultimately hers. And she chose Salem.

No one had ever chosen her. Not even her parents.

Out of fear that she would change her mind, Salem devoted herself to being the perfect sentinel. She was obedient, loyal, and as organized as she could be. Even though Deianira treated her like a friend, Salem knew that quitting wasn't an option.

Her life wasn't hers.

There wasn't much she did just for herself, wasn't much she *could* do just for herself.

But then Cassian asked that question.

Can I kiss you?

Salem wasn't blind. She knew that Cassian was attractive.

A lot of people were. Even Finch, though she wasn't in a hurry to kiss him.

But Cassian was more than that.

She got this tingly feeling in her stomach when he was around, he was observant, he never assumed. It was almost as if he wanted to please her.

The thought was outlandish to her.

She couldn't quite understand why he wanted to kiss her, but she knew that she wanted to kiss him.

Yes...

Cassian didn't hurry. He was slow, he was tender.

That feeling in her stomach multiplied when his lips touched her. She didn't know what the sensation was but she wanted more of it. A lot more.

Tonight, she was taking, and Cassian was willing to give.

Salem put a hand to his chest and leaned into him.

It was firm, smooth.

Everything she'd expected after seeing him that night in the kitchen.

He slowly laid back down, following her silent direction fluidly.

As she hovered above him, lips on his, she flinched when she felt his free hand crawl up her hip and gently shift her. Taking a breath between kisses, Salem gave up control for only a second for him to pull her body up onto his. She straddled him, her chest to his as his tongue pried at her lips.

Instinctively, she parted them, giving way for him to explore.

Then she stilled for a moment.

She wasn't too sure about the feeling. That changed though when Cassian pushed up and brushed his tongue against hers.

She liked that.

A lot.

The hand on her back lowered.

Is this okay? he sent.

Yes, she responded enthusiastically.

Cassian gripped her bottom and gently squeezed as he ground her forward a fraction. As her sweet spot skimmed along his length, she couldn't help her shiver or stop the moan that tumbled into his mouth. She slid her tongue against his as he aided her by moving her hips back and forth.

Salem beamed with pride as a muffled groan fell from Cassian's lips.

He was enjoying it as much as she was.

As they built a steady rhythm, her pleasure only increased. She ground harder on every pass.

It was never enough.

Cassian's hand on her cheeks spanned to her hair as his lower hand shifted her to the side half an inch.

There.

That spot right there.

She wasn't even sure if she thought it or sent it, but it was perfect.

He matched her on every stroke, pulling her tighter against him, gripping her bottom more roughly, angling her face toward his.

His lips moved against hers, saying something as his chest shook.

She couldn't focus on it though. She was too busy climbing higher and higher up her mountain to pleasure. Cassian took his hand off her face and slid his palm down her body, grabbing her hips with both hands, forcing her down against his length.

In seconds, her climax came cascading down over her.

"Cassian..."

Salem had no idea what she sounded like or how loud she was, but whatever came out of her mouth set him off as she rode out her high.

He clung to her as his lips parted from hers and he buried his face in her neck, grinding more frantically.

His chest shook against hers as he shuddered, grunting into her neck.

Then finally, their pace slowed.

For a moment, they just stayed there, breathing against each other.

Her intrusive thoughts interrupted her declining waves of pleasure.

She just kissed Cassian. More than kissed him.

What was she supposed to do now?

Wait for him to say something? Say something herself?

Cassian gently tapped her thigh, pulling her attention back to him.

Give me a second.

She went to ask him what for when he quickly added, *I need to go.*

She stiffened at his request.

He wanted to go.

She didn't assume that they'd spend the rest of the night in that position, but her chest still tightened.

Numbly, she extricated herself from his grip as he stood and his heavy footfalls gently shook the floor.

As soon as the bathroom light turned on, Salem speed-walked back to the bed. Her hands were shaky, her movements uncoordinated, as she climbed onto the bed and pulled the sheets over her body.

She'd felt many things tonight that she hadn't before, but this was a wild contrast from how she was feeling a few seconds ago.

Moments later, the room brightened as the door reopened. Salem discreetly watched as Cassian squinted over at the couch. She couldn't see his features very clearly because of the backlight, but she saw him look to the bed.

He tilted his head when his gaze caught her. He knew that she was awake, so Salem didn't break eye contact.

They watched each other for a while before Cassian shrugged and turned the light off.

Salem rolled over and swallowed, trying to ignore the ache in her chest.

It was suffocating.

She let out a small gasp as the bed dipped. Something patted the bed before a hand lightly tapped her leg. Her first instinct was to move it away, but she held out as the hand slowly traveled to her waist.

Her breaths light, she closed her eyes as the hand firmed its touch before rolling her over into a hard chest.

Just like that, the sinking feeling dissipated a fraction every time his chest rose against her face. It lessened even more when both of his arms moved to hold her, banding tightly around her like a cocoon.

It didn't take long for Salem to relax. In fact, she'd never felt more relaxed. She just let herself be and counted as his heart thumped against her cheek.

His heart beat sixty times a minute.

It was perfect.

Chapter Seventeen

Cassian had never slept so soundly. Not in the western sector, not in the palace, not even in his little home just outside of Terra.

Never.

When he woke, he didn't dare move. He'd never move again before he'd disturb Salem's sleep. Not when her soft snores were filling his room like a quiet melody.

He had things to do, starting with fixing her door, but they could wait. Everything could wait.

He never expected last night to go how it did. He didn't invite her to his room with the intention of being with her like that, but he regretted nothing about it.

Salem shifted in her sleep.

Cassian watched with nerves crawling up his throat as she lifted her head from his chest and looked up into his eyes. He saw the moment that it all came back to her.

The first thought that came to mind was-

Does she regret it?

Good morning, she sent.

She didn't look…upset. She didn't look like anything really, just Salem.

Morning, he replied cautiously.

As she took a breath, a buzz from her bracelet had her halting.

Cassian averted his eyes as she read.

Salem froze in his arms, drawing his eyes back to her wide ones.

I need to go.

That was all she said as she rolled out of his arms and jerkily climbed off the bed.

As she got to her feet, she looked back to the bed and her panic only seemed to increase.

'Don't worry about it. I'll bring them by later,' Cassian offered automatically.

She looked hesitant, but eventually replied, *'Thank you.'* and set off into the bathroom.

As soon as the door closed, Cassian rolled onto his back and picked up a pillow. He held it to his face and let out a long, undignified groan.

Salem was never late. To anything.

One might have blamed her current predicament on the absence of an alarm clock, but that wasn't a legitimate excuse in her case. She woke up at the same time every morning, alarm or no alarm. She showered at the same time, dressed at the same time, ate at the same time.

So why am I about to walk into Deianira's study over an hour late?

She was spiraling.

What would Deianira say about her tardiness?

What would Deianira think about what happened between her and Cassian?

What if she already knew?

Though it was never clearly stated, Salem knew that her oath to the crown barred certain lifestyles. Her purpose was her duty. She wasn't supposed to have sleepovers, or kiss guys, or...

Especially not her Queen's brother-in-law.

Salem tried to casually speed-walk to Deianira's office, pushing down her roaring anxiety.

She had only knocked once when the door swung open, a shadow receding as Deianira came into view behind her desk.

She quickly got to her feet and beckoned Salem into the room before closing the door.

'Are you okay?!' she signed frantically.

Salem's brows furrowed as she took a step back, overwhelmed.

'Yes,' she responded warily.

'What happened?!'

She mentally sputtered. She couldn't lie to-

'I was worried about you!'

Salem paused her panic.

Worried?

'Why?'

'You didn't show up this morning and you didn't reply to any of my messages! I sent Cade to your room and he told me that your door was busted in! He's still out looking for you.'

Deianira lifted her wrist. "Found her," she watched her say into her bracelet.

Salem was both shocked and relieved.

Deianira wasn't mad.

She was worried.

About her.

'I apologize. I overslept.'

Deianira's brows creased. *'You overslept?'*

Technically, it wasn't a lie.

'Yes.'

She didn't look convinced. *'Salem, is everything okay?'* she asked, looking into her eyes intently.

Salem's hands were shaking at her sides. She had no idea what reaction her next words would be met with, so she rushed it out as fast as she could.

'I did oversleep, but not in my bedroom. I slept in Cassian's room last night because he broke my door in because he thought I was in trouble, but it was just Finch, and then he insisted that I stay with him and then he accidentally woke me up early this morning and asked to kiss me and I said yes so we did and then we-'

Deianira slowly grasped Salem's hands and lowered them, her mouth open.

This was it.

One hundred and seventeen years of service down the drain.

'You kissed Cassian?'

'He kissed me,' Salem responded as if that might help her case. *'Then I kissed him back.'*

Deianira's face was frozen for a second before an abrupt laugh burst from her.

'I did not see that coming.'

Salem didn't say anything.

She waved at her and snorted. *'Why do you look like somebody sat in your chair?'*

'You're not terminating my service?'

The humor drained from Deianira's face. *'What? No! Why would you think that?'*

'Because I told you that I kissed Cassian,' Salem said, stating the obvious. She still wasn't convinced that she wouldn't be reprimanded.

'You think I'd have you discharged for your poor choice in men?'

At Salem's confused expression, Deianira shook her head. *'I'm kidding. But I'll always think that you can do better.'* She smiled. *'On a serious note though, I'm happy for you. If you like him, kiss him a thousand times. Just not anywhere near me.'*

So, she was okay with it?

'Salem, wipe that look off your face. I really am happy for you. It's your life.'

Salem was taken aback by those words.

They were given so flippantly, as if she'd said them a hundred times, but Salem had never heard them before.

It's your life.

Chapter Eighteen

Cassian stood up from where he'd been crouched and tested the door, swinging it from side to side.

"What are you doing?"

He jumped as he turned to face Cade.

"Just fixing the door," Cassian replied as casually as he could.

Cade put a hand to the door, surveying Cassian's work. "Yeah, it was busted this morning. Do you know what happened?"

Cassian didn't know how to respond. He didn't have an issue with his brother knowing what happened last night, but Salem might.

"No clue."

Cade shrugged. "Well, thanks for getting on it. I was about to run to the workshop to-"

He paused.

Cassian held his breath when he saw Cade's nose twitch as he eyed his brother with a lot more suspicion than he had a second ago.

Meow...

Cassian thanked whatever was above for the interruption.

“Coco! Off!” he instructed as he spotted her making herself comfortable on Salem's bed again.
She promptly hopped off the bed, galloping up to him.
Cade bent down to stroke Echo playfully.
“Don’t encourage her,” Cassian told him.
“How can I not?” Cade laughed as he ruffled her fur.
Bzz. Bzz.
Cassian’s eyes dropped down to his wrist.

SAMBOR: *Devin’s up.*

He abruptly turned to Cade. “He’s awake.”

Lia was leaving the room as Cassian and Cade entered.
“I’m just gonna grab a drink. Be back in a sec,” she smirked as she passed by them.
What’s she so happy about?
Cassian erased the thought as quickly as it popped into his head. Of course, she’d be happy, Devin was okay.
As he stepped into the room, all the guilt that he felt on the day of the accident came rushing back. Sure, Devin was awake, alive, but his pale skin and straight face said anything but.
“Hi,” Cade said cautiously.
“Hey.”

Cassian's chest clenched.

He did this. If he'd just-

"Cass?" Devin rasped.

Cassian swung his gaze to him.

Devin lifted a hand, beckoning him forward, so he gloomily stalked over to his bedside.

He gestured for him to lean in closer.

Cassian obeyed.

"You gotta get me out of here, man."

What?

His breath caught as his eyes snapped back up.

"Why?" he choked out.

"If I have to watch Lia flirt with the nurse for one more minute, I'll kill myself," he breathed. "For real this time."

It took Cassian a few seconds to let his words sink in. Then he let out a ragged laugh.

This is Devin.

"Good to know you haven't lost your sense of humor, Dev," Cassian guffawed.

His face scrunched up. "I wasn't joking. They were practically eye-fucking each other, right over me. It was sickening."

Cade joined in with the laughter as Lia sauntered back into the room with Deianira and Salem.

Cassian's back went straight.

He didn't know where to look. Every time he tried to find a corner to look at, his eyes somehow made their way back to hers. Because she was looking at him too.

Salem didn't seem to be bothered by the others in the room though, or the unclear note that they were left on this morning.

She just stared right back.

"Ahem."

Cassian quickly looked to Devin, who eyed him with suspicion.

The room was silent.

Everyone was looking between Cassian and Salem.

"Anyway," Devin said as he turned to the group. "What'd I miss?"

Lia took the question. "After you imploded the tunnel, you passed out and we had to rush you back here." A smirk danced across her lips. "Doc says your power can't fit in your weak little body."

Devin sighed and turned to the room, facing away from Lia. "Can someone *with two brain cells to rub together* explain what happened? In fact," he said, raising his brows as he turned to Salem. *'Want to fill me in?'*

She looked from his hands to his lips and back to his hands before responding.

'She's not entirely incorrect. Your power is enhanced beyond what a gifted person should be able to hold. While gifts can sustain and exert such power, your body can't. You almost tore yourself apart.' Salem nodded as she stepped back, leaving Devin open-mouthed in disbelief.

He sputtered. "So, what I'm hearing is, I have all this power and I can't use it?"

"Yep," Deianira answered, gently patting his foot at the end of the bed. "I've already decided to instate Cassian as interim Head Enforcer." At Devin's protesting whine, Deianira held a hand up, silencing him. "Shush. You need to rest. Don't worry, your job will be waiting for you when you can pee on your own again."

While Devin frowned at the last part, Cassian paid particular attention to the first. Deianira didn't tell him that he'd be taking over for Devin.

"Are you sure?" he asked, flicking his eyes to Salem, trying to work out how she felt about the arrangement. It would mean that they'd be working together.

As usual, there was nothing to decipher.

"Yes. You were my first choice actually."

That surprised him. Cassian didn't think that Deianira disliked him per se, but he wouldn't have guessed that she'd be in a rush to give him such a position.

"I'm not trained," he told her. She needed to be fully informed.

"Yes, you are. Just not by me."

If that's what she really wanted, then he'd take the job. Getting to spend more time with Salem was not a problem at all.

He nodded. "Okay, I'll do it."

Deianira shook her head with narrow eyes and looked up at Cade. "He thinks he had a choice."

Chapter Nineteen

Deianira stepped out of the closet, putting an earring in.

'Okay, let's go.'

Salem quickly stood from her seat at Deianira's desk, closing the report folder. She didn't remember anything being marked on her schedule.

She even checked her bracelet to make sure.

Nothing.

She'd been really distracted recently.

'Where?' she asked nervously.

'My baby shower,' Deianira signed as she gently lowered herself onto the bed to put on her heels.

'I thought you weren't having a baby shower.'

'I wasn't. Cade just told me to meet him in the ballroom. He thinks he's smart.' Though she looked like she was trying to hide it, Salem saw the small smile on the edge of Deianira's lips. *'Oh, well. It's already planned and I'm not about to pass up good food.'*

She looked so beautiful.

She wore a stunning black wrap dress that complimented her perfectly. In color, in style.

Deianira noticed the look in Salem's eye. *'Do you want to borrow a dress?'*

'No,' Salem responded instantly. She hated dresses. They were too loose. She could just about stand her night dresses and she only wore them because sleeping in pants was true agony.

'Makeup?'

'No.' She'd tried it before but didn't like the way it felt on her skin.

'Shoes?'

'No.' While Deianira looked amazing in hers, Salem doubted that heels would pair well with her thick tank top and practical cargos. And then there was the issue of walking in them.

Deianira sighed. *'At least let me do something with your hair.'*

Salem cringed.

'I promise, your head won't depressurize if you take down that bun.'

She thought about it. She wasn't very explorative when it came to her appearance.

Not because she didn't want to be, she just never had a reason to.

Maybe, she could try something new.

'Okay.'

Salem didn't like the new hairstyle.

At all.

Her chestnut brown waves bounced just above her shoulders as the ends tickled against her skin. It made her want to shave her whole head.

Deianira loved it though. Salem saw how much pride Deianira took in her work, so she didn't even complain as they walked up to the entrance of the ballroom.

Salem jolted as they stepped through the archway. She knew that there was going to be a party, but she didn't expect nearly a hundred people to jump out at the same time.

Deianira wore a shocked expression on her face as Cade approached her with wide arms, a wide smile on his lips.

"Oh my Gods! You shouldn't have!" Deianira exclaimed.

Cade went right up to her and kissed her as the guests clapped. As he pulled back and looked her up and down, the smile dropped off his face. He reached out and gently grasped her chin, pulling her face closer to examine.

He narrowed his eyes. "You knew."

Deianira didn't lose her smile. "I did, but it was cute that you thought you could put something like this together without me finding out," she said, patting his cheek in a condescending manner.

Cade shook his head and kissed her lips again.

Salem looked away and ambled over to the nearest table. She found herself automatically scanning the room for a specific person.

Tap.

She turned abruptly. And there he was.

Just when she'd been looking for him.

Cassian paused, mouth open, as if he hadn't expected her even though he'd tapped her.

'Hello.'

He blinked. *'You-, you look beautiful.'*

She raised her brows as heat rose to her neck.

'Your hair, I like it.'

'I don't,' was the first thing that came to mind.

'Why?' He frowned.

She answered honestly. *'It's touching my shoulders.'*

Cassian tilted his head at her for a moment. Then confusing her, he reached down and gently picked up her wrist.

Salem lowered her brows as he slid her two hair ties off her arm. He didn't ask her to turn, just stepped around her.

She turned with him, wondering why he was moving behind her, but he huffed out a laugh and grasped her shoulders, pivoting her back around.

Just as she tugged on the link to ask what he was doing, she felt her hair sweep back over her shoulders.

She let out a satisfied sigh at the instant relief.

After a few cautious tugs and pulls, Cassian turned her back around.

'Better?'

Salem reached her hand back and felt her hair.

It was up. He'd tied it up in a ponytail.

Something in her tightened at the gesture.

Then she felt further and frowned.

Not only was the ponytail loose, but there were bumps and flyaways all over her head.

As she looked back to Cassian, he winced.

'I tried my best,' he signed with a shy smile.

She dug her fingers into the band and pulled it out. *'You're best isn't very good.'*

Salem ignored his parted lips and bewildered expression as she reached up and started tying her hair back herself.

By the time she'd pulled it tight, he was still staring at her.

'What?' she asked.

He shook his head, blinking, before looking between her eyes. *'Are you okay?'*

'Yes.'

Why did he always ask that?

He subtly turned his back to the room. *'I mean, after what happened.'* He paused. *'In my room. We haven't had a chance to talk about it yet.'*

Salem's cheeks burned at the memory.

'Yes. Deianira is fine with it,' she replied in case that was one of his main concerns too.

His eyes widened. *'Deianira knows?'*

'Yes, she does.'

Was she not supposed to tell her?

Salem thought that she saw Cassian mutter something about Deianira cutting his balls off when Devin interrupted them.

He limped toward them, a crutch in his left hand.

Cassian quickly helped him into a seat.

"Shouldn't you be in a wheelchair?" Cassian asked, concerned.

Devin fumed, shaking him off. "No. Doc said I'm good with crutches." His hands were moving with such aggression that Salem almost didn't understand him.

Cassian looked down, then back up. "So, where's the other one?"

"Ask Lia," Devin hissed. "She's the one that's been hiding them every chance she gets."

Cassian stared at him for a second before he burst out laughing.

His whole face lit up.

Before she could stop it, Salem found herself smiling.

It wasn't even what Devin said that set her off. It was Cassian finding the humor in all of it.

"I'm glad you find that so funny, Salem." Devin glared. "Go on, mock the cripple."

Before she could apologize, everybody turned to the center of the room. Salem turned too.

Lia stood in the middle of the ballroom, a bright smile on her face.

"It's game time!"

Chapter Twenty

Cassian was confused. Not upset, just confused.

And it had everything to do with a certain someone.

Every time he spoke to her or even looked at her, he found himself choking or tongue-tied, but she seemed to be handling their tension with ease. Nothing about her behavior suggested that she was even slightly ruffled.

It made him wonder if she was a good actor or if she just didn't care. Considering what Cade had told him about her not being able to lie, he was highly doubtful about the former, which was an even bigger ego hit.

Instead of sulking about it though, he took it as a challenge.

Today, he would find out what made her sweat, what made her squirm. He wanted to wipe the bored look off her face.

That started with picking partners.

Lia turned to the room. "Jacobs, I'm assuming you're with Emori?"

He tilted his head at her. "Who else?"

She threw him a mock glare, turning around to write their names. "Cade?"

He turned in his seat to incline his head with a smirk. "My beautiful baby m-"

Cade choked as Deianira's flat palm collided with his chest. "Call me your baby mama one more time, and I'll find this baby a new daddy."

Even as he patted his chest, trying to breathe, he was still laughing along with a few guests.

Cassian turned in his seat, facing Salem, away from the board.

She frowned as he met her eyes, tilting her head.

He offered her a bright smile, confusing her even further.

"And Ca-"

"Salem," he said, smirking at her. "Me and Salem."

Lia nodded slowly and turned to write their names on the board, but he was still watching Salem as she looked from left to right, as if he might have made a mistake.

But she didn't just seem surprised that he'd picked her. She looked surprised that she was involved in the game altogether.

That had him frowning.

Why wouldn't she-

"Oh. Fuck. No-" Devin was silenced by Emori's elbow to his ribs. He looked back at the girls playing a few feet away.

"Sorry, baby," he said to her before turning to Cassian again. "I object to this pairing. They can speak to each other in their minds. You're just asking them to cheat." He ended it with a swift hand through the air.

Cassian smirked. He hadn't even thought of that.

Lia shrugged, still writing their names. "It won't matter for the first game anyway."

Emori and Devin.

Deianira and Cade.

Cassian and Salem.

"Okay!" Lia clapped. "This is a game I created myself, so listen carefully!"

She went on to explain the rules of a game she called 'Daddy Deianira'.

It was basically a scavenger hunt around the city with different tasks that Deianira did every day. When a task was completed, you were given, or had to find, a small silver crown and the first pair to get back to the ballroom with three crowns won.

Lia clapped again once they'd all lined up a few feet from the grand entrance. "Any questions?"

It seemed simple enough.

There was also the fact that he had Salem on his team. She was with Deianira every day. If anyone would give him an advantage, besides Deianira herself, it'd be her.

When Devin raised his hand, he thought that he might bring that up.

"Why isn't the game just called Deianira? Where did the 'Daddy' come from?"

Deianira snorted as Lia cut him a dry look. "Because I like it. Any more stupid questions?"

Everyone shook their heads.

"Good. On your way out, grab a diaper bag and it'll have your clues in there. There are four tasks in each bag, but remember, you only need three to win." She paused. "Are we ready?!"

"Yeah!" Devin shouted over the silence.

Lia shook her head. "Three! Two! One!..." She paused again, smiling at the impatient faces.

Cassian felt Salem ready herself at his side.

I'll grab the bag, he told her. *You run.*

"DADDY DEIANIRA!"

Salem was halfway out of the door before he'd even let his foot hit the marble.

Cassian sprinted after her, not even looking down as he bent and swiped a diaper bag off the floor. His eyes left her for a split second to make sure he wouldn't fall down the steps, and when he looked back up, she was gone.

Salem?

Meet me at Emori's.

As in Dev-

Her bakery, not her room.

Salem yanked on the handle of the bakery door as she arrived.

Locked.

She ran back a few steps and peered through the window, only to be met with Devin's grinning face.

She jumped back.

'Too slow,' he signed.

That wasn't right.

Salem knew that she was the first person out of the door. On a normal day, Deianira would've beaten her, she was the fastest, but Salem saw her lagging behind. She saw Devin behind her too.

Then it clicked.

He jumped.

Salem wasn't sure if it was against the rules or not, but it certainly didn't seem fair.

She went back to the door and pulled the handle again. He followed her on the other side of the glass and held up a keycard, smirking.

'Open the door.'

He shook his head. *'No.'*

Pretend to faint.

Salem whipped her head around.

He was here. Somewhere.

Fall down and pretend you're having a heart attack or something.

What?

The ground looked dirty.

Salem, just fall down.

Why?

His laugh rumbled down the link. *You'll see.*

All objections fled at his joy-filled voice. She chewed on her lip as she scanned the ground again.

Okay.

Salem looked back at Devin and started breathing lighter. Dyspnea.

Then, she started rubbing her chest. Angina.

Lastly, she started to roll her eyes back, blinking rapidly. Dizziness.

She didn't need to display all the symptoms. A heart attack often only presented through one or two, so the third wasn't really necessary.

She wavered on her feet before gracefully slipping to the ground. She even shook on the sidewalk a little.

Peering through squinted lids, she flinched as Devin disappeared from behind the glass and reappeared in front of her.

"Salem, are you-" he started to say before he was mowed down.

She rolled as fast as she could to avoid the collision as he hit the ground.

As she stood, her eyes widened.

It was Cassian.

He laughed like a crazed person as he tackled Devin to the ground. After a few seconds of wrestling, Cassian stuck his hand back toward Salem.

He was holding the keycard.

Go! he laughed. *I'll hold him.*

She snatched the keycard from his grip and swiped it across the panel before barrelling into the bakery.

She knew what she was looking for. Heading straight for the counter, she hopped over it and squatted down to pull back the door of the glass cabinet.

There was only one cinnamon bun. That wasn't a coincidence.

She quickly grabbed a serviette and picked it up.

There was nothing under it. Maybe it was-

Salem, hurry!

She jumped and before she could take a second to think about the mess, she ripped it apart. Sure enough, a small crown, just bigger than a ring, sat in the center.

There was no stopping the way her lips tipped as she dug it out.

She did it.

Salem placed the bun back on the shelf and ran out of the bakery to find Cassian still tussling with Devin. She couldn't see very well because of how fast they were moving, but she caught the words, 'cheater' and 'dick' from Devin.

Cassian.

He turned his head to her.

She held up the crown.

Cassian's smile only grew as he shoved Devin away from him and jumped to his feet.

He grabbed her hand and they both took off.

Chapter Twenty-One

Once they'd made it to the city center, Cassian slowed down to take a breath, prompting Salem to do the same.

That was the most fun he'd had in years.

But even in his joy, his awe didn't escape him. He'd expected that having Salem on his team would put them ahead, but she was in and out of the bakery in under a minute. That was leaving out the part where she hadn't even read any of the clues.

That reminded him.

He finally took the diaper bag off his shoulder and opened it. There were five baby bottles in it and he made quick work of popping the lids off and reading the clues on the pieces of paper inside.

1. *Winter wonders*
2. *1300*
3. *Oh baby*
4. *Sweet Tooth*

That was it.

Sweet tooth.

The bakery.

He turned to her, his smile bright. *'How did you know?'*

Salem wasn't nearly as tired as him.

'How did I know what?'

'To go to the bakery.'

She nodded, understanding. *'There are a few things Deianira does every day without fail. Getting a cinnamon bun from Emori's is one of them. Even with the other tasks, there were bound to be repeats across the clues with the other teams. The probability of us having that clue was too high to pass up or waste time reading them.'*

Cassian's face was blank, but his mind was buzzing.

She'd done all that in the seconds between Lia announcing the rules and sending them off.

'How the hell do you just do that?'

'Do what?' she frowned.

Cassian sputtered. He didn't even know where he was going with that.

'Just be so smart all the time.'

She shook her head. *'I know her schedule.'*

'But I bet it would've taken her longer to put that together.'

'Maybe. But that's only because of the pregnancy-'

Cassian laughed as he cut her off. *'Salem. You got it because you're smart. Not because she has baby-brain.'*

As she lifted her hand to protest, he grasped both of them.

Take the compliment, he sent.

I don't-

Salem.

She scrunched her brows.

Repeat after me. I am smart.

Cassian-

He shook his head. *Nope.*

Salem huffed.

I am smart, she sent, bored.

He beamed, releasing her hands. *Hell yeah, you are.*

Hard as she tried to narrow her eyes, there was no missing the way her whole face softened.

'Do you know what they're gonna name the baby?'

Salem thought back. *'She said she doesn't know yet. They don't know the sex either so I don't understand the clue.'*

Cassian nodded absently before his brows raised.

He snorted. *'They didn't make the game. Lia did.'*

Salem still wasn't following.

'It's Eulalia. It's a trick question. She's saying that they should name the baby after her.'

'Do you think the crown is in her room?'

He nodded. '*Yeah, and what about this one?*' Cassian asked, pointing to the second clue.

1300

Salem closed her eyes.

1300

Thirteen hundred.

One thousand, three hundred.

No.

Not a number.

13:00

A time.

She blinked and lifted her eyes to Cassian again.

'The nail salon.'

He tilted his head. *'How did you get that from thirteen hundred?'*

'It's one o'clock on a twenty-four-hour clock. She gets a manicure on Thursdays at one o'clock every two weeks.'

He raised his brows. *'Is it close?'*

'Yes, but the lake is closer.'

'Lake?' he frowned.

'Winter wonders. She goes skating every year when the lake in the woodlands freezes over.'

He nodded with a smile. *'Palace, then the lake. Lead the way.'*

Considering how quickly they'd gotten the first two crowns, Cassian assumed that they were ahead, so they took a light jog through the woodlands.

The first was all Salem, but he was quite proud of himself for figuring Lia's clue out. He found the second crown inside a folded blanket on her mantle. It even had her name stitched into it. It couldn't have been more obvious.

As they jogged between the trees, he followed behind Salem, taking in every detail. It was only a game but he'd never seen her so invested in something before. Her eyes lit up with every clue she worked out, every angle she thought over.

She was actually enjoying herself.

And then that 'almost' smile. It was barely anything but he was surprised that it peeked out over the smallest amount of praise.

Salem slowed to a stop. She pointed into the distance and he followed her eyes.

The lake.

'*Where would she hide a crown here?*' he asked.

She looked like she was thinking about it before she started toward the lake, getting closer. Again, Cassian followed.

Do you think-

His mental message stopped abruptly as Salem reached for the hem of her tank top and pulled it over her head.

He quickly turned his back to her.

Uh... He scratched his head. *Salem?*

Yes?

Why are you taking your clothes off?

A graceful *plop* answered his question before she did.

I'm looking for the crown.

Cassian turned back toward the lake, and just as he expected, she was gone.

I could've gone, he huffed, his arms out even though she couldn't see him.

I like to swim.

That was fair, but he would've preferred to go. He felt like he wasn't pulling his weight.

He leaned over the edge, watching her blurry figure move quickly beneath the surface.

Can you even see down there?

Yes. It's quite bright actually.

Cassian nodded, lazily swinging his foot over the dirt.

I think I see it.

He leaned forward eagerly. *Are you sure?*

I've got it.

Letting out a loud, *whoop*, Cassian cemented his decision to stick with Salem for the rest of the party games.

I'm coming up, she told him.

"Can you walk any slower?"

Cassian ducked and rolled behind a trunk at the voice.

Salem, stay down.

Why?

Incoming.

"It's not like you're the one lugging an extra twenty-five pounds."

"You literally have a super baby in you. That's like...double the energy."

"At least you have proper shoes on. I wouldn't have worn heels if I knew you'd have me trekking through the woods," the first voice hissed.

They were getting closer.

Cassian stayed low as he army-crawled to the edge of the lake, and then as quietly as he could, he took a deep breath and rolled into it.

He almost let out all of his air as he opened his eyes to see Salem, right in front of him.

She tilted her head questioningly.

He let out a few bubbles as he pointed upwards.

Deianira and Cade.

Salem ran both hands over her face, moving her hair out of the way.

Wait.

Where is it? he asked.

As she parted her lips, Cassian thought she was about to smile, but then he noticed it. She held the small crown clenched between her teeth.

"Don't...stupid. It's not...of a deal."

At the muffled voice, Cassian wrapped his arms around Salem and moved closer to the edge of the lake to make it harder for them to be spotted.

She shivered against him.

Are you okay?

A look passed between her eyes. *Yes.*

Do you need air?

Not ye-

SPLASH!

Both of them startled as a body landed in the lake.

Go, go, go! Cassian yelled.

They broke the surface and scrambled onto the dirt.

Right up to Deianira.

"Told you I saw bubbles," she giggled.

Cassian flicked his gaze over his shoulder, and there Cade was, treading water, a grin on his face.

"Where is it?" he called with a smile.

Cassian shrugged. "Didn't find it," he lied.

"He's lying," Cade drawled as he climbed out.

Forgot about that.

They were so close, they had all three crowns. All that was left to do was get back to the ballroom.

Deianira turned to Salem with a sweet smile. *'You wouldn't try to make me lose at my own baby shower, would you?'*

Salem blinked. *'I would. I want to win.'*

Damn.

There was nothing Cassian could do to hold back his snort.

'So that's how it is?' She faced them both, signing and speaking. "Who has it?"

They both stayed silent and Cassian couldn't help but grin at the annoyed pair.

But suddenly, Cade didn't look so annoyed.

"Cassian?" he smirked.

"Cade?" Cassian returned in the same tone.

His brother advanced a slow step.

"Were brothers, right?"

Cassian's eyelids grew heavy. "Yes..."

"And brothers help each other out...right?"

Of course. I'd do anything for-

Cassian shook his head.

Where the hell did that come from?

Trying to pry open his eyes, he caught Deianira's proud expression.

Cade stepped even closer. "You see, my wife *really* wants to win this thing...and because I love her, I want her to win too."

Cassian blinked groggily.

What is happening?

"And because you love me, you want me to help her win."

"I want you to help her win."

No! No, you don't!

"No, I don't!" he shouted.

Cade narrowed his eyes. "Yes...you do," he said in a low voice.

"Yes, I do."

Cade smiled. "So tell me who has the crown."

Cassian, don't-

"Salem has it."

And just like that, the haze ceased.

Cassian shivered. "What the fu-"

"Get her!" Cade bellowed.

It was only then that Cassian realized Salem had taken off, Deianira on her tail.

Good girl.

Then he turned to his brother. "Did you just fucking compel me?"

Cade shook his head with a smile and clapped Cassian on the shoulder. "Nothing personal."

As Cassian went to make a comeback, his eyes fell to the bag sitting next to the tree.

The diaper bag.

The diaper bag he'd put the crowns in.

Salem was running like the fate of Terra depended on it.

Thorns and low branches scratched her bare legs as she dashed through the woods, but she never slowed. Even in her mad dash, she could feel the dirt pounding beneath her feet. And it wasn't just hers.

She didn't need to turn to know who was behind her. Her footfalls were way too light to be Cade, even with the extra eighteen–not twenty-five pounds–pounds on her.

Salem knew that she would've been caught already had it not been for the pregnancy, she'd never met anyone as quick as Deianira. The advantage didn't dim her roaring adrenaline though. Everyone had their own gifts, their own advantages. She could use this one.

It took her too long to notice that the footsteps behind her had halted. Salem was too cautious to waste a second to look behind her.

That was a mistake.

If she had looked back, she would've seen that Deianira hadn't stopped. She'd taken flight.

Advantages.

As if it was even possible, Salem quickened her pace as she breached the tree line.

The palace was only a quarter mile from the woodlands and it was even harder to evade Deianira in the open. She would swoop down low, try to land ahead of her, but each time, Salem made it away.

Her saving grace was the knowledge that Deianira was only trying to stop her, not to make it to the ballroom first.

Salem was a short distance from the steps when she saw something on the other side of the training fields.

No, someone.

Or someones?

Emori and Devin were side by side, sprinting toward the steps at full speed. Salem knew that she couldn't move any faster, but she didn't need to.

Her bare feet slapped against the stone steps seconds before Devin's. She sprung up the last few and dashed through the entrance.

Eulalia stood up from her seat when she saw them coming.

Pumping her left arm, Salem lifted her right and fished the other two crowns out of her bra.

The second Cade had started speaking to Cassian, she slipped her hand into the bag and took them. She knew she'd have to finish the job.

Devin was almost on her as she made it to Eulalia and slapped the crowns onto the podium. Then she quickly parted her lips, grabbed the last from her mouth, and threw it down next to the other two.

As she closed her eyes and took a breath, a hand grabbed her arm and lifted it into the air.

She quickly turned her wide eyes to Eulalia to catch her say, "...winners are Salem and Cassian!"

Movement burst around the room.

People were laughing, cheering, and clapping.

For her.

She turned to the other contestants. Even though Deianira was the one trying to stop her, she looked happy. She looked...proud.

And as much as Devin tried to tamp down his smile, there was no hiding his grin as he nodded at her, panting.

Seconds later, Cassian barrelled into the ballroom, bag in hand.

Then he paused and looked around.

His eyes met Salem's.

You took the crowns?

She nodded.

He huffed out a disbelieving laugh as he stalked toward her.

Salem was overwhelmed.

The joy, the praise, it almost knocked the breath out of her.

Actually, it did.

Salem bumped her chest with her fist as her lungs tightened.

Salem?

She coughed and looked up to see Cassian's blurry figure dancing before her.

Cassian?

Salem, are you-

She thought that it was her vision failing her as the room began to darken, but a look toward the entrance let her know that she wasn't seeing things. The doors began to close, shutters began to descend on the windows.

And the air.

It grew foggy.

Cassian?

It was getting harder and harder to see. Harder and harder to breathe.

The lights in the ballroom didn't do much to help the blur, but she could make out the figures darting around the room, panicked.

Her head grew lighter with each shallow breath she took.

Focus! she told herself.

Salem wheezed as she ambled over to the game table and grabbed a baby blanket. Grabbing a glass of water, she doused the material in it before wringing it out to the best of her ability and holding it to her face.

Cassian! she yelled as she allowed herself to take a full breath.

Salem, where are you?!

She didn't know. The fog was too thick.

Somebody smacked into her, almost sending her to the ground. Righting herself, she tried to move through the crowd, one hand holding up the makeshift mask.

Even though the features were hard to make out, Salem knew exactly who it was when she saw a body lying across the arms of a large figure a few feet from her.

The bump gave it away.

Her heart sank.

Deianira.

Her Queen.

Cassian was the first person she called out to, not the woman she was bound to by duty. Not the woman she'd sworn...

Her eyes grew unbearably heavy.

Just as she went to call out to Cassian again, he appeared only steps away from her.

Salem!

He reached out to grab her.

But it was too late.

She was already sinking to the floor.

Chapter Twenty-Two

Salem's pulse pounded in her skull as she woke. She had to fight down her rising nausea as she sat up slowly.

Her bed was harder than usual.

Maybe I slept in Cassian's bed again.

No, Salem didn't remember spending the night in his room. In fact, she didn't remember going to bed at all.

Reaching up to touch her face, she removed a damp piece of cloth.

Huh?

It was only when Salem started to blink that she took note of the scene around her.

Bodies.

They were everywhere.

Looking up at the high windows, she instantly recognized the stained glass.

The ballroom.

The baby shower.

The challenge.

Cassian.

Deianira.

Salem did her best to stand on her shaky legs as her gaze circled the room.

She was the only one awake.

The cloth.

She must not have inhaled as much of the gas as everyone else. But after thinking about it more, she realized that she couldn't have held the cloth to her face as she passed out. Someone else had.

As she turned to the entrance, she caught sight of Cade.

He was asleep.

Deianira was still cradled in his arms, unconscious too.

She staggered over and dropped beside them. She tugged and tapped at Cade until his eyes flickered beneath his lids.

He blinked up at Salem, confusion written in his gaze.

She couldn't see very well so she assumed that he couldn't either.

Cade. Let me in, she sent.

It was easier to communicate with a psionic than someone that wasn't. With a psionic, there was an open link that could be used at any time once established, like leaving messages on each other's doorsteps. However, when someone wasn't psionic, the only way for her to send or receive a message would be to enter.

Salem could've forced her way in if she wanted to, but it was only right for Cade to make that decision. It would be giving her access to his whole mind and she wanted him to trust her not to abuse that power.

Cade.

What's going on?

Salem sighed with relief.

I'm not completely sure. I need you to help wake everyone up.

Cade looked down at his chest, only then noticing Deianira, and paled.

After a few shakes, Deianira was looking up at her with the same confused look in her eye, but Salem left him to it.

She went around waking everyone. Some took longer than others, but eventually, they snapped out of it.

Salem wasn't satisfied though. There was someone she still hadn't found yet.

She'd just woken the twenty-seventh guest, but still no Cassian.

How far did he go? she thought.

He was right there when she went down.

Cade came up to her as she stood from one of the last guests.

Start sending people to the side exit. Deianira's got the guest list and she's taking a headcount.

Okay. Have you seen Cassian?

His eyes widened. *He wasn't with you?*

Salem tried to steady her breath as her heart started to beat quicker.

No.

I'll look.

Her knee bounced as she sat in her cot. She couldn't settle.

Cade had to force her to get checked out while he got himself looked over with Deianira but she wanted to be anywhere else.

Salem had been living in silence for years, but sitting in the stillness of the clinic was what did it apparently.

She yanked the IV out of her arm and left to seek out Cade and Deianira. Sticking to the walls, she discreetly looked left and right, keeping all angles in sight while keeping out of it. Salem didn't have to look far, they were in the next room.

Mikhael stepped out as she entered.

He paused when he saw her, about to say something, but Salem turned away from him and set her eyes on Cade before he could.

'Did you find him?'

Cade sat up and shook his head grimly.

As her eyes caught on Deianira, a pit formed in Salem's stomach. Deianira was the one she was supposed to be protecting.

'Is the baby okay?'

She nodded stiffly.

Cade drew her eyes back to him with a short wave.

Her anxiety only rose as he took a while to get his words together.

'There are only three people missing out of the one hundred and two.' His eyes were regretful. *'Cassian, Devin, and Lia.'*

Deianira finished for him. *'It wasn't an attack. It was an abduction.'*

Chapter Twenty-Three

Cassian could barely hear anything over the thumping in his head.

"Ah..." he groaned as he tried to put a hand to his temple.

But he couldn't.

He pulled at his hand again.

It was stuck.

They both were.

Tied.

"He's awake," he heard to his left.

He swung his head in the direction of the sound.

"It's just me."

Lia.

"What happened?" he rasped.

"Well, we're not in the palace," she drawled

His vision began to clear.

He could see the bright sky, blurry trees, and Lia on his left, tied to another tree stump. To his surprise though, he found Devin to his right, in the same position, looking at him.

"Devin?" he asked.

"Yup," he said, bored.

"Where are we?"

"Stop talking."

Cassian flinched at the deep, unfamiliar voice.

He didn't have to wait long for the owner to come into view.

He strode leisurely into the triangle formed by the three of them.

Cassian looked from his bare feet to his ungodly stature to his clear eyes.

His eyes had no color.

His hair had even less.

His white wisps swayed as he stepped out in front of them. What really caught Cassian's eye though was his hands. He only had six fingers.

In total.

While he was stunned by the sight of him, the others didn't seem phased.

How long was I out?

Lia huffed and leaned her head against the tree. "What do you want?" she whined as if she'd asked a hundred times.

Devin slid his eyes to her blankly. "Isn't it obvious? Look around. He's probably mad about the tunnel."

Primas.

She glared at Devin and hissed, "I'm not blind. I made the connection an hour ago, but on the off chance that it might not have had anything to do with the tunnel, I didn't want to give us away!"

He scoffed. "What are the chances that the three of us get taken days after what happened for a completely unrelated reason?"

She smiled bitterly. "I guess we'll never know now thanks to you."

He smiled sarcastically. "Your wel-"

"STOP! TALKING!"

All three of them flinched at the pure base that resided in his voice.

Lia and Devin only then seemed to realize the gravity of their situation.

The man took a deep breath.

"I am Podak. This is my brother, Potek," he said, gesturing to his side.

Cassian's trepidation battled with confusion.

There was no one there.

The others' faces seemed to portray exactly what he was feeling on the inside.

After a good ten seconds, Devin could barely contain his grin.

"Uh, Podak?" he snorted. "Is Potek...with us right now?"

Midway through Lia's muffled giggle, a figure appeared out of thin air next to Podak.

"Shit!" Devin cursed, but Cassian was speechless.

He had many similarities to Podak, but he was bigger, if that was even possible.

Cassian had been subconsciously expecting the primas to look a little more like Emori, maybe taller, but he never imagined them to be giants, even bigger than him.

The longer he looked, the more differences he was able to find between them. Potek's white hair fell to his shoulders while Podak's came to his ears.

And Potek's face. It was covered in long deep cuts from his brows to his lips.

"What the fuck do you guys eat?" Devin asked, grimacing.

"Potek," Podak called. "Silence him."

Like a dog given a command, Potek kneeled in front of Devin and swiped a thumb down his throat. Devin tried to back up, but he could only go so far tied to the tree.

When Potek drew back, Cassian tried to look closer to see what he had done, but there was nothing, he didn't notice any difference.

Until Devin tried to speak.

His mouth opened, but no sound came out. His chest began rising and falling quicker as he tried to get words out, but nothing left his lips.

Cassian whipped his head to Potek as he stood, fear entering his body.

"What did you do?" Lia demanded.

"He talks too much," Podak responded.

Devin halted his panic to narrow his eyes at Podak.

Cassian knew why they were here, but he didn't know what they wanted.

That was a start.

"What do you want from us?"

Podak turned to him, his face dark. "Nothing."

"Then why are we here, asshole?" Lia fumed.

He only spared her a glance before continuing.

"Some weeks ago, my wife asked me to do something for her." He paused, staring off into the distance. "Of course, I accepted. I would do anything for her. All she asked was that I find her a way into this little place called Terra." He started strolling as he went on. "Immediately, I set out to complete the task. I was almost finished with it too. Then three little half-breeds destroyed it," he said, glaring at Devin. "My wife doesn't know about that yet, but when she finds out, she'll need something to bear the brunt of her anger. Who better than the culprits themselves?"

There were a few seconds of silence.

"Your wife sounds a little nutty," Lia concluded.

Cassian had never seen someone move so fast.

One second, Podak was in front of Devin, and in the next, he had a hand around Lia's throat.

"No!" Cassian bellowed as Lia gasped and Devin let out a muffled growl.

"You speak against Pola, you never speak again..."

Cassian didn't know why he noticed it, but he watched Potek's eye twitch at his brother's words before they dawned on him too.

"Wait...Your wife Is Pola?"

Podak turned his empty eyes to Cassian. "So you've heard of her?"

That seemed to please Podak enough for him to release Lia. "Potek, unmute the yapper."

Potek only looked at Devin, and just like that, he gasped, relieved. "Gods..."

"Yes, I have," Cassian responded, trying to keep him in a good mood. "We wanted to meet with her."

Podak smiled. "Oh, we received your message. But I don't think *she* would receive your invitation so well after you killed the twenty-two of her men in that tunnel."

So there were people in the tunnel.

Maybe Cassian should've felt guilty, but he was relieved. If he hadn't asked Devin to collapse it, Terra would've been attacked, ambushed.

"Wait, wait, wait."

Cassian sighed as Devin opened his mouth again, his lips tipping up.

"So, your name is Podak, you're Potek, and your wife is Pola? Did y'all plan that or was it a coincidence or fate or some shit?"

"When each of us joined with her, we changed our names. It is a great honor," Podak responded, not picking up on his humor.

"Hold up. You're both married to her?" Devin asked, his face scrunched.

Podak didn't seem to understand his confusion. "Joined. Yes."

Devin looked like he was about to say something else before he shook his head. "None of my business."

Podak's gaze flitted over them. "You made a big mistake. Pola does not like to be disappointed," he said, absently stroking his thumbs over the stubs on his hands.

Pola did that to him?

Cassian looked back to Potek's face. That must have been as well.

Devin broke the silence, yet again. "Don't choke me out or anything, but I don't think your girl likes you very much."

Chapter Twenty-Four

"I want the surveillance checked, I want to know how they got in, I want to know how they got out, and I want to know what the hell the scouts were doing when intruders breached the border and took three members of my family!"

Salem had followed Deianira as she went through the systems for hours. The footage came up empty, the scouts were knocked out. There was no trace of them.

They were almost certain that it was the primas, but with Salem's knowledge of their society and low technological advancement, she concluded that they wouldn't have been able to clear the security footage, let alone loop it.

None of it made any sense.

It had almost been a full day.

Countless times, she'd tried to reach Cassian, but he wasn't responding. Either he was too far away, or whatever was in that fog was still in his system, blocking his power, or he was...

She didn't know what else to do.

Old Dome territory was huge, but Terra was even bigger. They wouldn't even know where to start.

The lights pulsed thrice.

Salem checked the time.

Who would be at her door in the middle of the night?

No one just showed up uninvited.

Well, expect a certain furry guest. But she couldn't have initiated the light alert.

She stalked over to the door, her hand hovering over the knife strapped to her thigh. Laying one hand on it, she opened the door a crack

Oh.

Emori.

With Kendria and Tyla.

Salem pulled the door open.

She hadn't spoken with Emori since that last day in the assessment room, and while she was acting under orders, she couldn't help the small feeling of regret that tugged at her as she stared at Emori.

What did she want?

Emori moved Kendria's hand to her right and tapped the side of her head.

Salem didn't understand.

She pointed at her and then tapped her head again, more urgently.

It clicked.

Her mind.

She was letting her in.

Emori?

I'm trying to track him, but I need help.

Devin.

Salem stepped aside as she ushered the girls into the room. She forced herself to look away as their shoes plodded across the floor. All Emori had to do was point at the couch as she walked to the dining table, and the girls, holding each other's hands, ran over before sitting.

Salem still stood at the door.

Emori turned to her with a desperate look on her face.

Come here! she urged her.

Salem closed the door and went to her side.

I've already tried, but my search is too wide. I can see that he's not in Terra, but that's it.

What do you need my help with? Salem asked.

I only have Devin's belongings, but I need more to narrow it down. I need an anchor. Do you have anything of Lia's or Cassian's?

Salem thought about it before an idea hit her.

Would his cat work?

Emori nodded emphatically.

Salem didn't wait another second to pull up her sleeve and write a quick message to Cade.

To his credit, he was at her door in less than five minutes.

"What's going on?" he asked as he shuffled into the room holding Echo.

'Emori is going to track them.'

Cade swung his head to Emori. "You can do that?"

She inclined her head stiffly.

"Why didn't you tell us earlier?"

As Emori's eyes narrowed, Cade sent his to the ground.

He shook his head regretfully. "What do you need?"

She turned to Salem.

Bring the cat.

'Bring the cat,' Salem reiterated.

He quickly brought Echo forward, Salem cringing as he picked her up and dropped her on the table.

"Sit."

Echo obeyed, eyeing his hands excitedly.

Salem watched Emori snap her fingers twice.

The girls' heads popped up from the couch. She pointed to one of them, then pointed to the table. Immediately, Kendria hopped up and skipped over to her mom, smiling as Emori stroked her head and lifted her to sit next to Echo before dropping a kiss on her forehead.

Salem and Cade stepped back as she placed a hand on the fur of Echo's neck and the other on Kendria's cheek. She closed her eyes.

She didn't mutter any words or mumble like Devin did. She just breathed in and focused.

South, she sent.

The southern sector?

Outside of Terra.

Emori's brows furrowed.

I need more.

She needed a link to Eulalia.

'More,' Salem told Cade.

His eyes darted all around the room before he started patting his chest. Reaching under his shirt, he removed a chain with a ring looped on it. He carefully dropped it on the table and stepped back again.

"I've had it for a long time, but she gave it to me."

Emori grabbed it before he could finish his sentence and palmed the ring, placing her hand back on Echo's fur.

Her eyebrows shot up.

I can see them. There are two men with them, but I can't see their faces.

What do you see around them? Salem inquired.

Forest. Miles of it- Wait. One of them is turning-

Salem inched around the table to look at Emori, to see why she'd cut herself off, but Emori pulled her hands back.

"What happened?"

She backed away from the table.

"Emori. Where are they?"

At her silence, Cade turned to Salem.

'She saw them. In the forest, some miles from the Southern Sector.'

'Then why are we still here?'

Salem was asking herself the same question, but something about Emori's body language told her not to act yet.

Emori, can you show us where they are?

He can't see me, she sent quietly, eyes flicking between the girls.

Who?

Devin?

I can't let him see me. One of you has to do it.

Do what? Salem asked.

Cutting off her momentary panic, she whipped her head to Salem, grabbing a hold of her arm.

I can send you there.

She didn't even need to think about it.

Do it. Send me.

“How long is this gonna take?” Devin whined.

Cassian wanted to throttle him. Even Lia, who had a high tolerance for Devin, was at her wit's end.

Podak glared at him. “Pola works on her own time. You would do well not to rush her.”

“Yeah, well,” Devin shrugged. “At this point, it’s starting to look like you made her up.”

“Devinnn...” Lia groaned.

“I mean, I don’t blame you. I can’t imagine the prima dating pool having a large sector for six-fingered behemoths.”

“Potek.”

Cassian could hear the impact of Potek’s meaty fist against Devin’s face.

“Son of a bitch!” Devin choked.

Sighing, Cassian leaned his head back against the tree, thankful for the momentary silence.

There was nothing left to do.

A while ago, he’d discovered that he couldn’t use his abilities. It wasn’t that he’d called and Salem didn’t answer, the messages just weren’t being sent. He kept hitting a wall, over and over again. Figuring that it had something to do with whatever they were drugged with, he stopped trying.

He also wasn’t sure exactly how much time had passed, but he could see that it was well into the night. That had him thinking about her again. If she was here, she would be able to tell him the time down to the second.

Despite the circumstances, Cassian found his lips tugging up as he smiled into the night.

She's so smart.

A sparking sound, had his eyes opening.

Right behind Podak and Potek, Cassian caught sight of a small spark of light. It disappeared into the air before it lit up again.

What was that?

Cassian vaguely heard Devin clearing his throat on his right, but he was too busy trying to see if that light would return.

Devin cleared his throat again as the light flared.

This time, it stretched before it disappeared again. He squinted his eyes in the dark, straining them to see where it had gone.

Abruptly, Devin started coughing obnoxiously loud. He sounded like he was hacking up his lungs.

He spun his head in Devin's direction and was met with an authoritative glare.

What's his problem?

Devin looked Cassian in the eye, then slowly cast his to the ground.

Cassian frowned.

Banging his head against the tree stump and sighing, Devin repeated the action.

The movement was so exaggerated.

Warily, Cassian looked to the ground to see what he was motioning to when he saw Devin's hands moving covertly.

He's signing.

Cassian quickly focused.

'Distract them, you idiot!' he signed curtly.

Cassian met his eyes with confusion before looking down again.

'The light, it's a portal. Emori's coming for us.'

Oh.

He discreetly nodded.

As his gaze flicked to Lia to relay the plan, she was watching him with an exasperated expression. Apparently, he was the only one who hadn't gotten the message.

Lia started for him. "Uh, hey, polar bear?"

Podak turned to Lia. "Podak," he corrected.

"Po-what?" she asked, tilting her head.

"Podak," he repeated, frustrated.

"Boback, right." Lia nodded earnestly. "I need to use the ladies' room."

Podak turned to his brother with a bewildered expression.

No, they needed to look forward.

He flicked his eyes behind them to find the light growing again. If he could see it, they would too if they turned around.

They just needed to stall.

"She means the toilet," Cassian blurted. "To, you know...relieve herself."

"Go ahead. No one's stopping you," Podak told her.

Devin feigned irritation. "Are you serious? Come on, she's a lady."

"Yeah, you can't expect me to go here. It's unsanitary," she spat out, wrinkling her nose.

Podak snarled at Devin. "I do not care what she is. She can go where she is or she can hold it."

Lia started blinking speedily, looking up into Podak's eyes before she hiccuped.

A real tear fell from her eye as she scrunched up her face. "Please... It's been hours."

"Hours!" Devin chimed in.

"I was just at a baby shower and I didn't even do anything and then you kidnapped me-"

"Despicable." He shook his head.

"-and now you're gonna make me pee on myself and I have a skin thing-"

Devin grimaced. "Real nasty thing."

Podak's face soured as his knee bounced.

"-and you're being so mean to me for no reason and-"

Podak slashed a hand through the air. "Potek! Don't let her out of your sight."

Potek got up and kneeled beside Lia as he began untying the ropes.

They actually bought that.

Lia coughed, evidently struggling to hold back her laugh.

The second she was free, Cassian jolted as a figure leaped out from the spot where the light had been. They rolled as they hit the ground before springing to their feet, simultaneously drawing two guns.

She came.

But it wasn't Emori.

It was Salem.

Cassian saw the next few moments in slow motion.

The first bullet went through Podak's knee. The second was aimed at Potek but missed. He was too quick.

By the time Cassian had turned to him, he had an arm around Lia, holding her to his chest.

Salem only waited another second before narrowing her right eye and pulling the trigger again. Potek released Lia as the bullet tore through his shoulder.

Lia, being closer to Devin, ran straight for him, untying his restraints.

"Potek! Kill them!" Podak roared as he clutched his knee and lept for Cassian. Mid-jump, he crumpled to the ground as three more shots went off. Salem, still pointing a gun at Potek, fired as many shots as she could into Podak before tossing the gun at Cassian.

How am I supposed to-

The knife that was sent into the tree stump a second later, half an inch from his hands, answered his question. Cassian quickly reached for it as the ropes fell from his wrists. He looked down again.

She wasn't giving him the knife, she was freeing him.

He didn't have time to be awed because Podak was on his feet again. He was obviously in pain but that didn't stop him from throwing himself at Cassian.

Cassian rolled just before he made impact and cursed his dead legs as he stumbled when trying to get to his feet.

From the corner of his eye, he caught a glimpse of Potek charging toward Salem from behind. She was too busy trying to get to Lia and Devin. She didn't know he was behind her.

Cassian knew that he wouldn't be able to get through, but he still called out.

SALEM!

Salem must have been more aware of Potek's presence than he thought because she dove for the ground just as he reached her and rolled onto her back right before he landed on top of her. Cassian couldn't peel his eyes away as she pulled her legs apart, brought them up, and locked them around his neck. Salem twisted with her legs around his throat until she was on her knees and he was beneath her. His arms locked around her thighs at the same time that she threw the first blow to his head.

A hand locked around Cassian's ankle, bringing him right back to the ground. He blindly threw his arm out and grasped the knife from the tree stump, bringing it to Podak's neck.

But Podak didn't throw a punch, he didn't kick, didn't fight. His hand came up and gripped the side of Cassian's head.

He stilled.

Cassian wasn't sure what Salem was wearing but he wasn't complaining the slightest bit.

As hard as he tried to keep his eyes averted, there was no way he could stop himself from stealing a look. Those long tanned legs, that neckline dipping just an inch lower than he allowed himself to look-

'Yes. You look terrible.'

Finally snapping out of it, he tried his best to hold back his laugh.

'You do,' *she signed more urgently, making him laugh even harder.* 'I know what a broken nose looks like.'

Snorting, Cassian steadied himself. 'I don't doubt that. You're just very honest.'

'Did you want me to lie?'

'Never.'

Cassian held onto Salem's thigh as his tongue delved into her mouth, pushing up against her more urgently.

Is this okay? *he sent.*

Yes, *she responded.*

"Hey, Finch?"

"Wha-"

Before he could finish his outraged exclamation, Cassian sent his fist flying into his jaw.

"Look at her again, and I'll dig your fucking eyes out."

Cassian gasped as he came to, gritting his teeth at the high-pitched buzzing in his head.

Podak wore a cruel smile as he stood up and stepped away from him, but not before whispering something to Cassian, his lips almost touching the shell of his ear.

"I'll remember her..."

Cassian's heart was moving a mile a minute, his head still spacey, but he didn't let any of that stop him from getting to his feet and bolting over to the others.

By the time he made it over, Potek was on the ground, face down. Podak, however, stood in front of the same tree, giving Cassian that same eerie look.

To describe it as unnerving was an understatement.

He wasn't doing anything. He was just standing there.

Devin limped over to Cassian and Salem, an arm around Lia's shoulders.

Cassian watched as Salem closed her eyes and scrunched her brows.

The next thing Cassian knew, he was tumbling onto the ground.

No, not the ground. The floor.

The floor of Salem's bedroom.

What?

He peered up as he shakily stood from the ground.

Lia ran straight into Cade's arms. Devin fell to his knees, holding the girls while Emori held onto him from behind.

Then Cassian's eyes flicked to her.

The only person he was actually interested in seeing, blunt as that may be.

She was the one standing behind them, her gaze steadily on him. She seemed so unsure of herself, so different from how she looked a second ago. She shifted from foot to foot, absently rubbing her arm.

After everything she'd just done, she was standing alone.

Cassian didn't think, he just acted.

He got up and started marching in her direction, side-stepping and skirting around the others. He absently noticed the way her eyes widened as he approached, the speed at which she stood straighter, readying herself for his words.

She didn't need to though. Cassian didn't have any.

As soon as he was within reach, he picked her up by her kevlar vest and crushed her lips to his.

There was only a moment of stillness before Salem's hands grasped his face and she kissed him back with just as much ferocity. He shivered as her blunt fingernails caressed his scalp.

It wasn't like the last time, there was nothing sweet or innocent about it. It was raw and passionate. He just wanted to make her feel a fraction of what she made him feel.

He gave her everything he could. And she took it every time.

Cassian didn't realize that he hadn't stopped walking until Salem's back hit the wall, but he still didn't slow down. He pressed his body against hers, lapping up her sharp breaths and soft moans.

Her legs gripped his waist, trapping him as if she thought he might leave.
Like that was going to happen.
Almost to reassure her, he grabbed her bottom lip between his teeth and tugged. Sa-
"Uh...do you mind?"
He froze at Devin's voice.
Oh yeah.
They weren't alone.
"Cass, there are children in the room," he chided.
Cassian sighed and finally removed his lips from Salem's as he slowly lowered her to the ground.
Rolling his eyes, he slowly turned back to the room. "If you want to get technical, this is Salem's room. You don't have to be here," he drawled.
Cade stood still, open-mouthed.
Lia didn't look surprised at all. In fact, she wore a knowing smile.
And Devin? His face was a mask of pure horror.
Cade sputtered, staring between Cassian and Salem.
"I'm going to bed," he settled on.
Cassian nodded to his brother as he walked past them, stopping to look between them again, and left. Lia followed after him, but not before patting Cassian on the shoulder.
Devin was the last to recover.
He curled his lip at Cassian, wrinkling his nose. "Girls, let's go someplace where people have manners."
As they neared the door, Cassian heard Kenny's hushed voice.
"Daddy, what was Uncle Cass doing to Salem?"

"He was trying to eat her face." At the girls' simultaneous gasp, he nodded. "Mhm. I know. Nasty, right?"

Chapter Twenty-Five

As the door closed behind them, Salem looked back up at Cassian.

He was wearing the same clothes from the baby shower, he had a little dirt on his face, a few spots of blood too.

Those were all things that should've had Salem running in the opposite direction or kicking him out of her room.

But all she wanted to do was kiss him again.

Cassian finally moved.

'Do you have any idea how amazing you are?'

She wasn't sure how to answer the question.

Wasn't quite sure what he was referring to.

Oh. The rescue.

'I've been training for a long time. It's not amazing, it's muscle memory-'

'Salem, I'm not talking about your skills, I'm talking about you,' he signed, shaking his head. *'That's the second time you've saved one of our lives in the past* week.*'*

This was true. But why did he seem so surprised by the fact?

'I'm a sentinel. It's my duty.'

'No, Salem. Duty or not, that was still you.'

'I know.'

Of course, it was her. He wasn't making any sense.

'You don't.' He huffed. *'What you did back there didn't come from years of training or because it was just your job. Someone else could've been in the exact same position as you and they wouldn't have been able to do that. It was you, Sae. You.'*

She narrowed her eyes. *'My name is Salem.'*

He watched her face for a moment before he snorted.

'That was your takeaway?'

When she went to respond, he shook his head.

'It's okay.' He gestured to the side of her face. *'Come on. Let me have a look at that.'*

Salem was surprised that she felt no inclination to object.

'Okay.'

She usually handled her injuries on her own, depending on their severity, but for some reason, she didn't want him to leave just yet.

After kicking a sleepy Echo off the table, Cassian gripped Salem at her waist and picked her up. At first, she startled, but she settled as he placed her on the end.

She stared at his back, confused, as he went to retrieve the med-kit from the kitchen.

She could've gotten up there by herself.

Cassian was soon coming back to her side.

'This might hurt a little bit,' he told her as he poured a few drops of the disinfectant on the cotton pad.

Salem nodded, neglecting to tell him that he didn't need to use disinfectant on her. Thanks to her immune system, she'd never had an infection before and neither had most of the gifted population, but she knew that Cassian wasn't raised gifted. He obviously wasn't aware that water would've done the job. That didn't mean that she was going to stop him as he shuffled forward to stand between her legs though.

At once, that same fluttery feeling she'd felt when he kissed her came rushing back. It didn't even leave as the sting just below her hairline flared. In fact, it multiplied when she looked up at Cassian and watched his brows drawn with concentration as he cleaned her wound.

She didn't think that her heart could beat any faster until he angled her head up and gently blew on the cut. She closed her eyes and let the soft breeze fan over her face before she felt a band-aid being stuck in place.

Salem cautiously opened her eyes expecting to see Cassian stepping away, but he was in the same place. Actually, he was standing even closer, right between her thighs, staring deep into her eyes.

Her mind scattered.

'You didn't ask,' was the only thing that came to Salem's head.

His brows lowered. *'Didn't ask what?'*

'To kiss me.'

He'd asked that night in his room, but not today.

A different look crossed his eyes as he looked down. This one seemed much less intimate.

'I'm sorry,' he responded.

What did he have to be sorry for?

Salem would've asked, but she was too excited to ask her own question.

'Can I kiss you without asking?'

His eyes flew to hers, seconds ticking between them before he finally responded.

'Salem, there isn't anything you could ask me that I'd say no to.'

She let out a breath.

Good.

She liked that.

Her eyes darted around the room before locking onto Cassian again.

In the blink of an eye, Salem grabbed the front of his shirt and tugged him down. She straightened her back, leaning up as high as she could reach to drop a chaste kiss on his lips.

As she drew back, the smile on his lips threatened to split his face.

Salem slid off the table, coming face to face with his chest but she skirted around him, walking to her closet, releasing the straps of her vest. She tip-toed to slide it on top of the shelf, then turned to find Cassian in the exact same place she left him, still smiling.

'What?'

He shook his head, revealing a faint blush to his cheeks, and looked away. *'Nothing.'*

Cassian started moving around the room, tucking the chairs that were scattered around the room back under the table before heading to the utility room.

When he reappeared with the broom, Salem realized that he was cleaning.

She couldn't help the way her heart sped up at the sight. He wasn't even near her, but she warmed all over for him.

Chapter Twenty-Six

Deianira placed her palms on the table.

"So what's stopping one of them from tracking you guys and opening a portal, just like Emori did?"

The question was directed at Devin.

"Honestly, nothing. I don't know how we managed to get away in the first place."

That had Cassian pausing, thinking.

He was so distracted by their escape, by Salem, that he forgot the way that the last few moments had gone.

The way that Podak behaved.

"I think they let us go," he said under his breath, in deep thought.

Lia shook her head. "No, you saw the fight they put up."

As he tried to remember, his mind traveled to last night.

Salem on the table, him cleaning up her cuts, that kiss.

Cassian shook his head to focus. "I know that. But at the last second, I think Podak let me go. He just backed up."

The more he thought about it, the more sure he was. "He let me leave."

Just as he'd said the words, Cassian winced.

There was a short...buzzing sound.

The others didn't seem to notice.

"What do you mean he 'let you leave'?" Cade leaned in.

"I mean exactly that." Cassian closed his eyes, trying hard to recall. It was as if the memory was fading. "Right before, he said something, did something."

"Cassian, did what?" Deianira asked, growing impatient.

"It's all foggy but he did something to my head. He said..."

The buzzing increased, grew higher in pitch.

"I'll remember her..."

Cassian shook his head and steadied his breathing, looking up at the concerned faces around the table.

"'I'll remember her.' That's what he said."

Deianira frowned, watching him carefully. "What does that even mean?"

"I don't know."

"Are you sure he didn't say, 'I'll remember you'?" Cade offered.

Lia nodded. "Yeah, that would make more sense."

Those words were one of the only things that Cassian could remember clearly.

"No, those were his exact words. 'I'll remember her.' He was in my head, said it like he knew something that I didn't," he said grimly.

He could tell that they wanted to believe him, but they didn't look as sure as him.

"What did he do?"

He turned his gaze to Devin. He'd been watching Cassian this whole time, but only chose to speak now.

"I don't remember."

Devin looked at him in an almost clinical way. "You said, you think he got in your head. What did he do right before he said that to you? Think."

Cassian tried his best, but he could only remember one thing. "He touched my head, it wasn't rough, but it felt like I couldn't breathe."

Devin cursed under his breath.

Deianira quickly asked, "What is it?"

"Seer," he said.

Lia's gaze snapped to him. "Devin, not everyone in the room is a mind reader. You're gonna need to elaborate."

He sighed. "He was reading you. Not in a psionic way or like an empath. He was reading your past and or future."

Cassian blanched.

"They can see into the future on command?" Lia asked anxiously.

Devin dropped his eyes to the table.

"How the hell do you beat someone who knows exactly what you're about to do?" she snapped.

"It doesn't work that way," he huffed. "Gifted seers see random events involuntarily. Primas seers? They don't see events, they see individual pasts and futures. They have to touch you to read you, but if they do, they can find exactly what they're looking for."

"Well, what was he looking for in Cassian's head?" she asked. "There were three of us there. Why not me or you?"

"I'm not sure. It could've just been a coincidence. But if he let you go," Devin turned his eyes to Cassian. "Then he found it."

Cade looked at him too. "Do you have any idea what he might have seen? He said 'her', not 'you'. That has to mean something."
Cassian's gaze fell on Salem's empty seat across the table.
It probably did mean something.
That's exactly what he was afraid of.

As her words were displayed on the screen, Salem kept her head down, typing.

> ***QIN:*** *There are three sections in this paper. You are allotted forty-five minutes to complete each one, but if you wish to use more or less time on a section, you are allowed to do so. The total time for this paper is two hours and fifteen minutes. The time is 11:30, you may begin.*

Salem waited for the inmates to flip the first page before exiting the cafeteria and making her way to the viewing room.
Deputy Finch was supposed to be assisting her with the examination, but when she arrived at the cafeteria this morning, he wasn't there. She wasn't really hoping to see him anyway, so she went along with the day as usual, beginning the examination herself.
Upon arriving at the viewing room, she swiped her bracelet across the keypad and entered.
The room was supposed to be empty.

It wasn't.

Finch was sitting on one of the chairs facing the screens that displayed the live footage of the cafeteria. That wouldn't have been unusual if Octavia wasn't sitting on his lap, her legs on either side of the chair, her mouth on his.

It took a moment for them to separate.

Finch's gaze spun to Salem with a look of shock.

"Salem," he said, with wide eyes. "I didn't know you were going to be here."

She narrowed her eyes. They were both on the schedule to supervise the exam. He should've known.

Maybe he forgot, she concluded. Not everyone had a good memory.

Octavia got off his lap with a sultry smile on her face.

"I'm so sorry," she said, looking between the two of them. "I should probably go."

Salem stepped to the side for Octavia to exit.

As soon as the door slid shut behind her, she pulled up the other chair and sat in front of the monitor. Finch fixed his clothes before pulling his chair to the right, next to Salem.

At his tap against the desk, Salem looked at him.

"I didn't mean for you to see that."

Salem could've sworn she saw his lips tug up the smallest bit as he spoke. That also made her notice the rest of his face.

He didn't necessarily look unusual as she glazed her eyes over him, but Salem looked further, she always did. Not only was his jaw faintly swollen, but it was pointing at the slightest angle from the rest of his face.

The altercation had taken place days ago so unless he wasn't keeping up with his healing sessions, some serious damage must have been done.

She waved a hand.

What he did was his business. Granted, he shouldn't have been doing it during work, but ultimately, it had nothing to do with her.

"I would understand if you were upset."

Why would that make me upset?

She shook her head.

Finch sighed and looked back to the monitor.

She was just about to turn too when he swiveled his chair back to her.

"I'm sorry for getting handsy the other night."

Salem nodded.

She didn't expect him to apologize. He certainly didn't seem very remorseful after the incident, but she appreciated his apology. Especially considering the fact that he didn't necessarily walk away scot-free.

"I know how you get about stuff like that. Next time, I'll take it slow."

Next time?

She didn't want to keep talking to Finch, she would've preferred to focus on her work, but she felt that she needed to make things clear. Sighing, she unlocked her bracelet.

***QIN:** I think it would be best if you didn't kiss me at all.*

Finch looked from Salem to the hologram, then back again.

"Is that a joke?"

Joke?

She shook her head.

"You tell me we're more than friends, then invite me to your place and get all jumpy when I kiss you?"

Salem was all too happy to correct him.

> ***QIN:*** *You misunderstood. I didn't tell you that we were more than friends, I said that we weren't friends. And I did not invite you to my room, you did.*

If Salem thought that Finch couldn't get any redder, she was wrong.

"So that's how you're gonna play this?" he asked, nodding.

Play what? she thought.

"You're gonna pretend that it was all in my head?" He laughed even though he didn't look like he found anything funny. She had no idea what to say, and when she didn't respond, he stood, shoving his chair back. "Fuck this. We're done, Salem."

She blinked.

Done with what?

She didn't have time to ask because Finch was already making his way out of the room.

She stared at the door for a while, utterly bewildered.

Considering the way he left, she assumed that he wasn't coming back and moved her focus to the monitor.

Easy as it may have been, this was the least favorite of Salem's tasks. She just had to watch the screen for the whole exam. If she wanted to, she could've brought up a book or some paperwork to do in the meantime, but she knew herself. If she got engrossed in a new task, the other would be abandoned.

Where are you?

Salem jumped at his voice.

I'm in the viewing room above the cafeteria. Why do you ask?

On my way.

She frowned. He ignored her question.

It didn't take five minutes for the lights to pulse.

She spun her chair toward the door.

Use your bracelet.

Oh yeah.

The door slid open revealing Cassian with a shy smile on his face.

'I forgot about my new title.'

As he stepped into the room, Salem noticed a small plastic box in his hand. He dropped it on the table and sank into Finch's abandoned chair as the door slid closed.

'Why are you here?'

Cassian snorted. *'I missed you too.'* He scooted closer to the desk and opened the box. *'You weren't in the study this morning, so I checked the schedule and it said you were overseeing the exam, but you weren't in the cafeteria either.'*

That didn't answer her question.

Salem went to ask again, but he opened the box and pulled out a bandaid.

Grabbing the armrests of her chair, he pulled her to him so that her knees were between his before gently grasping her chin and tilting her head up.

Salem didn't ask what he was doing. She liked the way that it felt when he touched her, so she let it happen.

Cassian slowly pulled the bandaid off of her head and balled it up before scooting over to the trash can and tossing it in. Wheeling back, he picked up the new one and opened it before carefully placing it on her forehead.

He only rolled back to pull something else out of the box.

A sandwich.

Cassian held it out. *'Lunch.'*

'You brought me food,' she stated, frowning.

He flicked his gaze over her face, smiling a fraction. *'I did.'*

'Why?'

He shrugged. *'My schedule's pretty much open today. You're in here for another hour. Figured you'd be hungry.'*

Salem's brows scrunched. *'I can get myself food.'*

He raised his brows as he sat back and tilted his head. *'Never said you couldn't.'*

'Then why did you bring me this?'

'Because I wanted to.'

'You wanted to feed me?'

His eyes dipped as his lips curved. *'I did. Is that a problem?'*

'No, but why are you looking at me like that?'

Come here and I'll show you... his voice rumbled down the link.

Salem shivered, her eyes widening seconds later as she processed his words.

Deciding to ignore his proposition, Salem subtly pulled at the neck of her tank, hot all of a sudden.

She looked down at the sandwich.

To be honest, she was hungry. But...

'I don't eat food from the cafeteria.'

Cassian narrowed his eyes before nodding.

'That's good because I didn't get this from the cafeteria.'

She only ate what she cooked, that way she'd know exactly what she was putting in her body. But she didn't exactly want to refuse his gesture either.

'What's in it?'

He leaned his head, looking at the sandwich from different angles as he listed off the ingredients. *'Ham, tomatoes, lettuce, red onions, and mayonnaise.'*

Just hearing them made her feel nauseous, but then she looked up at Cassian's face.

He looked so hopeful, and the gesture was kind.

She could at least try it.

'Thank you,' she said before she picked it up.

Salem pulled it out of the bag and gave it a little sniff to test the waters.

It didn't smell...bad.

She averted her eyes from Cassian as she took a bite. Looking back up, she chewed a few times.

'Good?' he asked.

She chewed some more.

Salem wanted nothing more than to be able to say yes, but she couldn't.

It was horrible.

She shook her head grimly and waited for him to get angry, to call her ungrateful.

He didn't.

Cassian quickly wheeled over to the trash can and brought it to her, his shoulders shaking. When Salem spit it out and met his eyes, she realized that he was laughing. He put the trash can down, still grinning as he passed her a water bottle.

'I didn't like it. It had too much,' Salem told him before she took a swig.

'I could tell,' he replied with an amused smile before opening up his sandwich and picking things out of it. When he was done, there was only ham and bread.

'Don't worry, I didn't put any mayonnaise in mine,' he said as he handed it to her.

Salem looked at him, tense. *'What will you eat?'*

'Yours.'

She thought about it, then nodded.

As she tried the second sandwich, she wrinkled her nose as she waited for her tastebuds to reject it, but they never did.

Much better, she thought.

Even though they ate in silence, Salem quite liked his presence. It wasn't overbearing or irritating, he didn't distract her from the monitor either. He was just with her.

She was noticing a pattern. As opposed to most others, when Cassian was around, she felt at ease. She wasn't constantly wondering if she'd say the wrong thing or do something to offend him.

He just made everything so...easy.

He made her want to be around him a lot more.

This is bad.

Chapter Twenty-Seven

Standing outside Deianira's study, Cassian tried to get a hold of himself.

She hadn't told him anything about why she wanted to see him, so naturally, he'd been dreading it since he received the message during his lunch with Salem.

Spending some time with her had calmed his nerves, but standing outside the door had his pulse rocketing again.

A voice in the back of his mind told him that the call had something to do with Salem and their...situation, but he wasn't going to voice his suspicions unprompted.

"Hey."

He flinched at the voice to his side. He'd been so lost in his thoughts that he hadn't even noticed Lia approaching.

Cassian straightened up. "Hey," he said, giving her a short wave, expecting her to walk past, but she stationed herself right beside him.

"You were summoned too?" she asked lightly.

He frowned.

So maybe it wasn't about Salem?
"Uh, yeah."
Before she could respond, the door swung open, Deianira sitting behind her desk.
"Well don't look so scared," she smirked.
That didn't help ease his nerves at all, but he walked in anyway, Lia overtaking him to grab the seat in front of the desk.
As he closed the door, Deianira shed the smile off her face, looking between the two of them. It might not have had anything to do with Salem but Cassian was sure that this wouldn't be good.
"I need to ask something of the two of you. As you're not under my command, Cassian, you are well within your rights to decline." She swung her gaze to Lia. "You, on the other hand, are. So this is an order."
While Cassian became uneasy, Lia didn't appear perturbed.
"As you both know, we have very little information regarding our current situation. That needs to change. Thanks to what we do have, provided by Emori, we know that there is an upcoming...event. A traditional prima event that I want you two to attend."
What?
"I'm sorry," Lia frowned. "You want us to go to Patriam? The place where people would sooner eat me than shake my hand?"
Deianira nodded. "I know it's a lot to ask. But I can't think of anyone else that I trust enough to do this," she briefly flicked her eyes to Cassian, "and that I know can get it done."
He could already feel himself declining her request.
"Wait," Lia held a hand up. "Podak and his brother have already seen us. How can we get around if they know what we look like?"

"According to Emori, while it's a popular event, it isn't a sanctioned one. It's unlikely that either of them would be in attendance, especially without Pola."

He could sense Deianira's eyes on him, waiting for his answer, but he was still reluctant.

Lia was just full of questions. "Okay, but how are we going to fit in?" It seemed that she'd already decided that Cassian would be joining her. "Have you seen them?"

Deianira had all her answers prepared. "The only noticeable differences are their size and eye color." She pulled a box from below her desk. Opening it, she presented two pairs of colored contact lenses. "I had Devin design these. They work as normal contacts would, except they have a microscopic camera embedded in the lens."

Cassian shook his head. "Wait, Devin knows about this?"

Deianira nodded.

The fucker.

Devin knew Cassian would have declined right off the bat, but seeing the preparation that had already gone into it had him somewhere in the middle.

"Regarding their size," Deianira swept a hand in front of the pair. "That's why I picked you two."

Both of them looked down at themselves, then looked at each other.

It all made sense now.

Lia was the tallest woman at Deianira's disposal and Cassian was a whole other matter.

He wasn't sure if it was a side effect of presenting late or that paired with the training he put himself through, but something changed during those years away. While he hadn't paid much attention to it at the time, his transformation became glaringly obvious when he came back to the palace. Evidently, Deianira had noticed it too, if she wanted to use his size to their advantage.

Even though Cassian was almost a head taller than his brother now, Cade was still a big guy and surely Deianira trusted Cade more than him.

It was like the question was written across his forehead because Deianira shook her head at him before he even mustered the confidence to ask.

"I can't," she said quietly. "I hate that I have to ask this of you, but I can't send him." Her thumb absently stroked her stomach cradled in her palms.

Cassian understood. He didn't want to, but he did.

What's one more road trip?

Chapter Twenty-Eight

"And I thought you looked good with blue eyes..."

Cassian squinted his eyes against the sting to glare at Devin.

"Who knew you'd look so pretty in purple?"

"Shut up," he muttered, too tired for Devin's tomfoolery.

He sat back in his chair. "Seriously, I could kiss you right now."

Emori threw a look his way and cleared her throat.

"I *won't* because I have a beautiful wife, who I am wholly in love with," he said loudly. "But for real though, it's confusing."

Cassian gaped at him.

He shrugged. "What?"

Lia snorted. "And how do I look?"

Devin didn't even glance at her. "Like a troll."

Her neon green eyes narrowed. "At least I'm not an actual troll. Remind me again why you weren't picked for this op?"

He spun her way. "Oh, please. I'm literally taller than you."

"By like three inches. Look around, Dev. Not much of an achievement."

"Well, I'm so sorry I wasn't born with a long ass neck like you," he spat back. "Fucking giraffe," he said under his breath.

Lia gasped at the same time that Cade's hand made contact with the back of Devin's head.

"*Owww!*"

"Thank you," Cassian sighed.

"Okay," Cade stood, placing his tablet down. "This isn't going to be a regular sort of party. It's the only event of the year where all five affinities meet, so you don't have to worry about them knowing you're not one of them."

They both nodded.

That was good.

"There's something else." He quieted for a moment. "They're going to be... hunting."

"Humans, I'm assuming?" Lia asked conversationally.

Cassian threw a look her way as Cade continued.

"Yes. Which makes your job of blending in that much more important."

She nodded. "Because if they catch us, we could be thrown in with the prey."

"Yes, again," he sighed. "What you're going to see won't be pleasant, or even humane, but you can't intervene. You can't even appear disturbed by their practices. No matter what, you keep your head straight."

The room was cold, all the humor from earlier gone.

"And what happens if they do find us out?"

Cade looked to Cassian. "We're hoping that they don't. But if they do, we'll track you and have Emori bring you right back."

Emori nodded from her seat.

Cassian took it all in.

While he was gifted now, he was *normal*, whatever that meant, for most of his life. He knew what he was, but he still thought of himself as more human than anything. And now he'd have to watch the people he identified with be hunted and slaughtered, all while showing no emotion.

This assignment was starting to become a lot more than what Deianira described it as.

"Okay." Lia stood from her seat. "I'm ready."

Devin spoke as he and Emori moved to the open space in the middle of the operations room. "We only know that the event is held in the forest, but not exactly where. It could be a long walk from where you're dropped."

Cassian nodded, reminding himself why he was doing this.

"We'll see what you see and hear what you hear, but we can't talk to you. We're not sure how powerful they are and I don't want to risk them hearing us over the line."

Emori was occupied with getting the portal open, but noting the way that she flicked her eyes to Devin, Cassian assumed that that was almost certain.

"You ready?" Lia peeked up at Cassian.

The portal opened before he could respond.

He watched it for a moment, taking a discreet breath.

"Okay, get gone," Devin quipped, gesturing to the flickering gap.

Cassian stood to the side for Lia to go first. She rolled her eyes and strutted through, closely followed by him.

Once his feet hit the dirt, he looked back through the portal.

Devin waved before it abruptly receded and disappeared.

Almost in the same second that he turned to begin walking, a distant burst of laughter had his feet stopping.

Lia froze as well.

It was quiet for a moment before another laugh sounded.

He snapped his head in the direction of the sound, and when he focused enough, he could hear voices. Multiple voices.

"What is it?" Lia whispered.

"You don't hear that?"

She shook her head.

"Follow me,"

There was no point in trying to be quiet seeing as they were there to meet the primas. It wasn't long before they did too.

As they neared, light danced between the trees.

It was a fire, a large campfire standing in a cleared-out piece of forest.

And primas.

Dozens, by his count, laughed and danced around the open fire.

Cassian now fully understood why he and Lia had been chosen for this assignment.

They were huge, some not as big as Pola's husbands, but huge nonetheless. Even a large number of the women were his size or taller.

Lia nudged him. "Come on, party time."

Apparently, he was the only one feeling anxious about this.

Side by side, they stepped out from the trees.

Cassian let out a relieved breath when no one seemed to appear suspicious or stared for too long.

He subtly leaned down. "So what's the plan?" he whispered.

Lia stared straight ahead. "What Cade said. Fit in."

"I know, but how do you want to play it? I could ask some questions and you can-"

A slender, purple-haired woman stepped into Lia's path, forcing his words to trail off. He noticed Lia's hand go to the back of her belt and quickly put his hand over hers.

The woman noticed his movement and frowned.

He frowned right back.

He'd just saved her life, or more realistically, saved her face from a slash across her cheek.

Her gaze went back to Lia and she plastered on a smirk.

"How much?" was all she said, her voice deep and accented.

Now Lia was frowning too.

She cleared her throat. "How much for what?"

Cassian had to press his lips together to keep from laughing at her attempt to make her voice sound more guttural.

The woman's head tilted at Lia. "For your husband," she replied, narrowing her eyes as if it were obvious.

His eyes widened. "Oh, we-"

At the same time that Lia's elbow connected with his gut, he noticed everyone else around the fire. Every man that wasn't sitting on the ground was walking behind a woman, some being dragged, some holding onto their shoulders.

"Does he always speak out of turn?" the woman asked Lia.

She recovered quicker than he did. "Yeah, so rude," she laughed awkwardly. "Trust me, you don't want this one."

Cassian didn't dare glare at Lia and kept his lips shut.

"It's no problem. I'll fix him for you."

Lia's smile was almost earnest. "Thank you so much for the offer, but I think I'll keep him close for tonight."

"Oh." The woman nodded, finally understanding. "Then we swap."

She gestured over to a tree where a large, red-eyed man stood, leaning against it, watching her closely. "He's very good," she assured Lia. "You take him, I take the little one."

Cassian stiffened.

Lia sputtered, eyeing the man that looked almost double her size. "Oh, I'm sure he is. But I like my... husband. I think I'll keep him."

They both waited for her response, tense.

The woman looked between Lia and Cassian before smirking at him and shrugging.

"Next year."

And with that, she stalked off, her husband following after her.

Cassian had to bend down and blow out a breath but his attempt at calmness was swiftly interrupted by a muffled giggle. He looked up at Lia before she erupted into true laughter.

"You think that was funny?" he asked, glaring.

She was grabbing her stomach. "Oh gods, that was so worth the trip."

"That was terrifying, she looked at me like I was a piece of meat," he hissed.

Lia's laughter sobered a fraction. "Oh, you poor thing. I can't imagine what that's like."

Cassian toned down his glare. "Well, you don't have to act like me being fucking sold is hilarious," he said in a raised voice, throwing his arms out.

He winced as heads popped up all around them. The women scowled, the men looked up in wonder.

But they weren't all watching him. Most were watching Lia, waiting for her reaction.

She looked around and let out a poorly stifled snort.

Smacking his arm, she barked, “Bad, Cass!”

‘Are you hungry?’

Salem knew what that meant.

Deianira was hungry but didn’t want to eat alone. She knew what she’d want as well.

Salem didn’t really understand why she wouldn’t just ask directly, but she didn’t mind buying something from Grace’s to appease her enough to get her own food. They had just finished a workout so it was actually preferable for Deianira to get something to eat.

Salem returned a question rather than answering hers. *‘Do you want to go to the tuck shop?’*

Her lips tipped up as she shrugged. *‘I could eat.’* Then she looked away for a moment. *‘We can stop by the clinic after.’*

Her signing was smaller somehow, more understated.

Salem spun to her. *‘Why?’*

Was something wrong?

‘No, nothing’s wrong,’ she assured Salem. *‘I meant for you, not me.’*

‘For me?’ Salem looked down at herself.

Deianira averted her eyes again as she reeled in the battle rope. She walked it over to the shelf before facing Salem.

‘For the...shot.’

The shot. Right.

What shot?

Salem had learned about vaccinations in her studies, but they weren't widely practiced among the gifted. They simply didn't need them.

'I don't understand.'

Deianira brought her hands to her cheeks and looked up to the ceiling.

"Gods, why me?" Salem caught her saying.

Deianira met her eyes again and took a breath.

'Birth control,' she rushed.

The birth control shot.

Not a vaccination. But still, why would Deianira think she'd need-

Cassian.

Salem shot her eyes back to Deianira. *'I'm-'*

She closed her eyes. *'No, no, no! I don't want to know. I'm just saying that we can go today.'*

When she reopened her eyes, Salem started again. She needed to tell her.

'I'm not having sex with Cassian.'

Deianira nodded awkwardly. *'That may be the case now, but I just want you to be prepared.'*

Prepared.

Wait.

'Did he mention it to you?'

Deianira grimaced. *'Gods, no! This is coming from me!'*

Oh. Okay. 'Do you think we should have s-'

Deianira waved her arms about the place. *'Salem, Salem, Salem, please do not make this harder for me. Do you want it or not?'* she asked desperately.

Salem paused and thought to herself.

She didn't need to have experience in that department, any at all, to know how these situations progressed.

The question was, did she want it to?

Despite already knowing the answer, she still weighed her options.

It would've been a lie to say that she hadn't thought about it, but initially, she had objections, reasons not to go there with him.

The main one was her duty, but seeing Deianira's standing on this had that flying out the window.

It's your life.

She'd never forgotten those words. She never forgot anything, but those words had been at the forefront of her mind for the past week.

It was *her* life.

Salem looked back to Deianira. *'I want to get the shot.'*

Cassian kicked at the dirt as he rested his head back on the tree stump and plotted Lia's murder.

Maybe he'd push her off a cliff.

No, too impersonal.

Strangling was personal.

Yeah, he'd strangle her.

He tried to focus everything he was thinking into a searing hot glare as he watched her over the fire, having the time of her life.

It wasn't as if Cassian was in a rush to party with these people, but that didn't exactly mean that he wanted to be left with a group of men like a child being dropped off at daycare. She even patted his cheek before sauntering away to speak with the other women.

"You're hers?"

Startled, he turned to the man that walked up to his side. Ignoring Cassian's face, he sighed as he took a seat on the ground next to him.

He asked a question.

"Yeah...hers," he stuttered.

The large, dark-haired man nodded. "That explains a lot."

"I'm sorry?"

The man laughed, patting Cassian on the shoulder.

He smirked. "Why you're looking at her with murderous intent, but it isn't truly in your heart."

Cassian stilled. He was-

"Empath," he finished.

Huh?

Cassian would've guessed psionic. His reading was too specific.

Just how powerful were these people?

He extended a hand. "I'm Sven."

Cassian forced himself to get it together and grasped his hand. "C-...Connor."

Stupid.

It was only in the last second that he thought to not give his name, but he doubted he got away with that.

"You're lying." Sven smiled. "But it's okay. Nice to meet you, Connor."

"You too," Cassian lied again.

Sven snorted.

If the empaths were like this, he needed to stay far away from the psionics.

Sven stiffened and turned away from the fire. "It is time."

For what? Cassian almost asked.

He nodded like he knew what Sven was talking about and stood, dusting off his pants.

Sven quickly stood and grabbed Cassian's arm, forcing him back down.

"What-"

"Wait for your woman!" Sven hissed quietly.

Shit.

He didn't look as angry as his words came across, more concerned.

"Oh yeah," he said, nodding. He really needed to keep his head on straight if they were going to make it out.

Noticing something, Cassian looked up at Sven, who was yet to take his seat again.

"What about your woman?" he asked.

At that, Sven's smile came back.

"I don't have one."

Chapter Twenty-Nine

'That wasn't so bad,' Deianira signed before reaching to untie the last restraint.

Once she had, Salem sat up on the bed and rolled her shoulders back, not giving her an answer.

It was bad. It was horrible.

That's why Salem requested that she be restrained after she sent the third needle into the wall, smashing it to pieces.

It wasn't the pain that was the issue. Pain was nothing new to Salem. It was the sensation that had her yanking the first needle out of her arm and kicking the doctor away on her second attempt.

Just the thought had her tensing again, but Salem pushed them out of mind. It was done.

She slipped off the bed and was about to head to the door when she noticed that Deianira hadn't moved.

She just stood, watching her.

'Are you okay?' Salem asked.

She looked like she was about to nod then she shook her head.

'What's wrong?' Salem was already on her way back to her.

'No...it's just.' She looked away for a second as Salem paused. *'I trust you, okay?'*

'I know.'

'And I want you to be happy.'

'Okay. Thank you.'

Why was she telling her this?

Deianira huffed and met Salem's eyes, her face darkening. *'If he hurts you, if he upsets you, if he even looks at you the wrong way, I want you to tell me.'*

'Who?'

Deianira huffed. *'Cassian.'*

Oh.

But, why?

Salem shook her head. Her job wasn't to question Deianira.

'I will.'

She took a step forward. *'I mean it, Salem. 'Cause I'll chop his balls off.'*

Salem's eyes widened.

Deianira may have developed a sense of humor in the past few years, but she didn't look like she was joking.

In truth, Salem didn't think that Cassian would or could do any of that to her, so Deianira's threat had a low likelihood of becoming reality.

Still, she reassured her. *'I'll tell you.'*

She let out a breath and subtly wiped the corner of her eye.

Salem didn't miss it though.

Just as she went to ask what had caused her upset, Deianira interrupted her.

'Good. I'm still watching him though,' she signed, pulling on a smile. *'You can tell him that when he gets back.'*

That had Salem's question dying on her tongue and a new one springing up.

'I can tell him that when he gets back from where?'

Deianira tilted her head. *'He's on a research op with Lia.'*

He didn't mention anything about that. In fact, he said that his day was practically open and a research operation wasn't often a small task.

That brought another thought. A research operation on what-

Deianira laid a hand on her shoulder. *'Woah. You okay in there?'*

Salem blinked back into focus. *'Yes. I just didn't know that he had an assignment tonight.'*

'You didn't get the message?' She frowned as she lifted her wrist. *'I must have forgotten to patch you in. Sorry, baby brain.'*

Salem's bracelet buzzed and she lifted it to read.

She went to lower her wrist after skimming over the memo when she caught a word.

A name more accurately.

Her heart sank as she lifted her gaze to Deianira again.

'They should be back in a few hours. Do you want to watch the feed with-'

She cut herself off when she saw Salem's face. *'Is everything-'*

'He's in Patriam?' she interrupted.

Salem didn't have it in her to recoil at her own rudeness. She'd never interrupted her before.

Deianira slowly nodded. *'Yeah...they're gathering intel.'*

She didn't care what he was doing. She needed to understand something because she was almost sure her mind was failing her. *'You sent him...to Patriam?'*

The same Patriam that was filled with man-eating monsters that they barely escaped the last time.

Deianira straightened, her face hardening. *'I did. Is that a prob-'*

'Yes. That is a problem.'

She looked shocked at her bluntness, but Salem wasn't paying her any mind.

'Salem what's wrong with you? You've been on ops far more dangerous.'

'Yes. Me. Not him,' she signed curtly.

Deianira's brows lowered. *'Well, I think he can handle himself. Why don't you? Is there something I should know?'*

No, that wasn't it.

But there were plenty of people at Deianira's disposal.

Her hands shook. *'Why him?'*

Deianira took a step back. *'Wow. If I knew I'd be interrogated today, I wouldn't have bothered with this little detour.'*

She was avoiding the question.

'Why not send me?' Salem was always the first person she called for assignments like these.

'Because it wouldn't have worked, Salem.'

She wasn't lying, but that did nothing to ease Salem's racing heart.

Stumbling toward the door, she threw a look over her shoulder that she could only assume was a glare. *'I need to go.'*

Cassian followed behind Lia as they trailed through the woods, primas at their sides, in front of them, and behind.

Lia blindly reached an arm behind, her fingers attempting to intertwine with his.

"Fuck off!" he quietly hissed, smacking the offending hand. She tried to stifle her responding snort, but Cassian still heard it.

As the line slowed, he thought that they might be stopping, but a look ahead had him breathing lighter.

Weapons.

They were handing out weapons along the line.

Why would they even need them?

Cassian kept his stride even, trying not to shrink away as they moved closer to the weapons station.

As Lia passed, she looked down into the wooden barrel, her body language betraying nothing. Then she reached in, her eyes cast down, and pulled out a machete.

What the-

He sped up to reach her when a hand pushed at his shoulder. He turned, and there stood Sven.

He narrowed his eyes. "You left this."

Cassian went to ask what he meant when he felt the cool metal against his arm.

An axe.

He'd passed the station without picking up a weapon.

"Thank you," he said as evenly as he could, plucking it out of his grip.

Sven nodded, watching him closely, but Cassian pretended not to notice as he moved to Lia's side.

"What are you doing?" he whispered.

Lia kept her face forward. "Fitting in. What are you doing?"

He almost stopped walking. "Li-"

Whatever Cassian was going to tell her evaporated as he looked out at the clearing that they approached.

There were houses.

Huts more like, but they were homes.

He wasn't exactly sure what he was expecting, but for some reason, he imagined the humans in Patriam to be more…uncivilized, to live like animals, especially considering that they were hunted like animals.

But this was a small village.

Curtains were drawn, doors were closed, animals were locked away in their pens.

They had no idea what was coming to them.

Chapter Thirty

Chaos.

Absolute chaos.

He couldn't even remember how it all started.

One second, they were watching from the trees, the next, men were dying, women were being dragged into the night, and children were screaming.

And Lia.

The moment the clearing burst out in disarray, she disappeared.

They didn't have comms. There was no way to talk to her, to find her.

A hard hit from the left knocked him out of his own head.

The woman who'd bumped into him lay on the ground, staring up at him with wide eyes.

She screamed, her hands coming up to guard her face.

Cassian leaned down. "I'm not-"

"Please! I have children, please!"

He took a quick look around to make sure no one was too close. "I'm not gonna hurt-"

A piercing sensation split across his cheek.

Cassian winced and looked down to find a knife in her hand.

He touched his face, drawing back his hand to find blood on it, then looked back at her. Her eyes had doubled in size now.

He huffed. He couldn't do this here.

Reaching out, he grabbed her. She kicked and punched to no avail, but he still held her against him, her back to his chest, as he marched to a small gap between two huts.

He set her on her feet and spun her. "Where are your children?"

She froze at his question as her eyes went to his hands.

Cassian looked down and instantly dropped the axe.

"I'm not going to hurt you," he gritted out. "Where are your children?'"

She still remained silent.

Cassian looked in all directions as he ran a hand over his head. "Listen, if you don't tell me, someone else is going to find them and kill them anyway," he emphasized. "Is that a risk you're willing to take?"

This isn't working.

He locked eyes with her and just as he went to hone in, she lifted a hand and pointed to another hut, smaller than the others, across the clearing.

He drew his thoughts back and took a breath.

His words were firm. "Stay here."

As he stepped back into the clearing, he looked from left to right. It didn't seem possible that things could've gotten worse, but they did.

A man swayed several feet in the air, his arms and legs held tightly together by...nothing.

He was just floating in the air, his body stiff.

His mouth hung open, but not a sound escaped.

Cassian didn't have to look far to see who was holding him.

A young girl, sixteen at most, stood on the ground, her face a mask of pure bliss as she waved her hands around in an almost rhythmic motion.

Setting his eyes back down, Cassian tried not to be sick as he made his way to the hut.

There was so much death.

Most of them weren't even being eaten, just killed.

As quick as he could, he flattened his back against the wall on the side of the door. Sparing the clearing one last glance, he shoved the door open and hurried into the dark room.

And in an instant, there was a blade to his throat.

"Leave. Or die."

The voice was deep, familiar.

Cassian raised his hands even though they wouldn't see. "I'm not here to hurt anyone."

"Cass?"

Huh?

"Lia?"

"Oh thank the Gods. He's with me."

Cassian squinted as a bright light flashed directly in his eye. Lia turned her bracelet skyward.

Then Cassian finally recognized the person to his right, the one who'd put a knife to his throat.

"Sven?"

"Connor," he smirked.

A whimper drew his gaze to the corner of the room.

Children.

At least a dozen of them.

They couldn't have all belonged to the woman he'd just met outside. They were too close in age and she didn't look old enough.

He turned back to Lia. "What's going on?"

She walked over to the children and picked up one of the toddlers. The child clung to her. "We're taking them."

Cassian swung his questioning eyes to Sven who still stood behind the door.

"It's okay," Lia assured him. "He's on our side."

Since when?

"Cassian, snap out of it and help me with the small ones."

He looked back at the group. "How the hell are we supposed to get them all out of here?"

"Sven," was all she said.

Sven gave her a nod and made for the door.

"Lia, what the hell is happening right now?" Cassian hissed as the door closed.

She propped the toddler up on her hip and reached for another. "Do I look like I have time to exp-"

BOOM!

"Shit. That's our cue." She turned to the kids. "You," she said pointing to an older girl in the back.

The dark-haired, blue-eyed girl stepped forward warily. As she stepped into the light, Cassian realized that she was older than she appeared at first. She was just so thin.

"I need you at the front. Can you carry one of them?"

She didn't speak, but she nodded.

As Lia started to get them into order, Cassian shook off his shock and joined in.

There were sixteen in total. He carried two on his back and one in each of his arms. Lia took two while the older girl took one and the rest seemed able enough to walk on their own.

As he started to open the door, Lia stopped him.

"No," she said. "Back door."

He followed her to a small arch with a dirty sheet draped across it. Taking the lead, Lia looked left and right before sneaking out of the back and picking up into a quick jog into the surrounding trees. Cassian stayed at the back as they hurried along in a single-file line out of the clearing. Then, he remembered.

"Wait," he whisper-shouted.

"Cass, we don't have-"

He bent to let the kids down. "Go ahead, I'll catch up."

She looked at him for a while before she practically growled, "Hurry!"

Free of the extra weight and the need to be discreet, Cassian sprinted back into the clearing. He spun in all directions looking for that small gap. The madness was yet to die down and every direction looked exactly the same.

Blood.

Bodies.

Trees.

There.

He was off before he could second-guess himself. He even shoved a few people out of his way to reach it. Prima or human, he didn't know.

He had one thing on his mind.

Just before he made it to the gap, he stopped.

Not because someone had intercepted him, but because he'd found her.

Well, part of her.

Seeing as he'd witnessed the unthinkable tonight, he wasn't prepared for the grim wave of horror that hit him as he stared into her dead eyes. That was practically all that was left of her.

Why didn't I take her with me?

He could've carried her, could've snuck through the clearing in the midst of the commotion.

But he didn't.

And she was gone.

Her kids would never-

Her kids.

Cassian shut his eyes and took a breath before turning back the way he came.

They were still alive. They needed help now, not her.

It was said that time sped up in adrenaline-fueled situations, but it was the opposite for Cassian. It didn't actually take long to find the others, but the minute walk through the clearing felt like hours.

"Cassian."

He finally looked up and met Lia's stare.

She didn't ask what he went back for, but his eyes evidently told her everything she needed to know.

Giving him a once-over, she threw him an almost comforting nod and tapped her ear.

"Dev, we need an evac."

Chapter Thirty-One

Tying up his boot, Cassian pulled the laces as tight as he could.

Even with the screaming in the background, he was careful in his quiet steps out of his bedroom. He checked both sides before making his way across the landing and slowly beginning to descend the stairs.

As a blood-curdling scream tore through the air, he released a shuddery breath, quickly wiping the tear that fell from the corner of his eye.

Just one step at a time.

He paused as his small boot touched the floorboards, releasing an eerie creak.

When nothing happened, he continued to the door as he rehearsed his lines in his head, over and over.

My name is Cassian Alden, *he repeated as he mouthed the words in the dark.*

I'm nine years old and I live at the Western Council Lodge.

My-

"Where do you think you're going?"

Cassian's gut sank as the voice sounded from behind him.

The lights flickered on and Drake Alden came into view.

"I asked you a question."

His mouth opened and closed silently, his words stolen by his fear.

"Take your hand off the door, Cassian."

Everything in him told him to obey, but his fingers wouldn't move.

Finally finding his voice, Cassian shakily whispered, "She needs help."

Drake closed his eyes and shook his head. "Come here."

A sob broke free as he stood in his place, unmoving.

"Cassian, come here," he said more firmly.

"No..."

Cassian's eyes widened at his own words, he hadn't meant to say it out loud, and the second it left his mouth, he wanted to rewind time.

When Drake's eyes snapped open, he knew that he wouldn't be leaving the house tonight. Maybe not for a long time.

Charging like a bull, he advanced on Cassian and grabbed him by the lapels of his thin coat. In seconds, he was being marched back up the stairs.

But for the first time in his life, Cassian fought back. He kicked, he screamed, he punched, but Drake barely faltered as he ascended the steps.

"Dad, please!"

Drake remained silent as he dragged him back into his bedroom.

"Please, let me g-"

The air rushed out of him as he landed back on his bed.

Drake didn't wait a second to pin his arms down, his face a show of pure fury, his gaze so cruel that Cassian had to look away.

He screamed out. "Please-"

His father cut him off with a hard shake. "When you find a butterfly stuck in a cocoon, do you help it?!"

Cassian squirmed, his throat growing raw from his cries. "Dad! Please!"

Drake shook him again. "DO YOU HELP IT?!"

"NO!" Cassian screamed back, his fear blending with anger and frustration.

"Exactly!" he exclaimed, his eyes growing wide.

"She's gonna die!" Cassian hiccuped.

"The weak, DIE! That's the world we live in!"

"NO!" he screamed out again, fighting as hard as he could.

"Say it!"

Cassian could barely breathe, his cries trying to claw their way out of his throat at the same time.

"SAY IT!"

Chest heaving, he shrieked at the top of his lungs, "THE WEAK DIE!"

Drake finally released him, giving him a shove, as he backed away from the bed.

"The sooner you accept that, the better..."

Cassian didn't leave that position for nearly two days.

Not when Drake left the room, not when the screams from the other room silenced, not when Cade came and sat next to him on the second day, telling him that it was all okay.

Nothing was okay.

Maybe if he'd been quieter he could've made it out, made it far enough to find someone and tell them the words he'd been repeating to himself since the screams began.

My name is Cassian Alden.

I'm nine years old and I live at the Western Council Lodge.

My mom's having a baby and she needs help.

"Cassian, I need your help."

He jolted and threw his gaze to Lia as she stared at him, her arms outstretched.

"Cassian?"

"What?"

"You can let go."

He was about to ask what she was referring to when something moved in his arms.

A boy. His age was hard to tell, but he looked like one of the youngest.

His little arms clung to Cassian's neck as he slept.

Lia lowered her voice. "We need to get them to the clinic. Can you help me out here? I'm in enough trouble with Deianira for the rescue mission."

It only took one look around to realize that the room was waiting for him.

Cade stood at the entrance, a few of the older kids with him, Devin and Emori were surrounded by the younger ones. And Deianira stood behind Lia, watching him.

He tried to steady his heart as he snapped out of his haze, carefully handing the child over to her.

Before he could open his mouth to say something, he didn't even know what, Deianira stepped closer.

"It's okay," she said quietly. "We'll debrief tomorrow."

Good.

He needed a second to breathe, a moment to-

"Cassian?"

What now?

Deianira snuck a look over her shoulder as the council and their new guests left before leaning in close to Cassian.

"I think..."

He didn't want to rush her, but he also wanted to get out of the room as quickly as possible.

"I think I might have upset Salem."

His eyes flew to hers. "What do you mean upset?" he asked the second the last word left her mouth.

Deianira took a step back, her eyes flicking around the now-empty room. "I think she's...mad at me."

Salem? Mad?

Cassian took a breath, but the calm he was hoping for didn't come.

"What did you do?"

Deianira narrowed her eyes and cocked her head back. "Nothing actually. She found out about this research op and went all...I don't know. I've never seen her like that before."

This wasn't making sense.

In truth, Cassian hadn't been around Salem for a long while, but she *was not* the type to get upset for no reason, or at all.

Deianira sighed, irritated. "I'm just asking you to make sure she's okay."

He watched her suspiciously, still not entirely convinced, then nodded.

Chapter Thirty-Two

Obsessions.

Salem knew them all too well. After all, she'd dealt with them her whole life. Even as a child, she would fixate on anything and everything that she took interest in. They were volatile, lasting for any amount of time, be it a whole day or five years.

She had virtually no control over it.

For someone who prided themself on how much control they had over their life, or any given situation, one would think that this would be an issue.

However, it never was.

Salem's job was her obsession.

Training, weapons, safety.

Her fixation on these things may not have always been healthy from time to time, but they always made her better at her job, better at being a sentinel.

Nothing got by her, no problem was left unchecked.

Salem's duty didn't allow for her to obsess over much else, so throwing herself into her work was all she could do.

That had changed though.

She couldn't exactly figure out when or how, but there was a new obsession on the horizon.

Again, this wouldn't have been a problem if she didn't have to see him every day, didn't have to work with him, didn't live with him.

She knew she couldn't stop it once it had started, but she doubted that reinforcement would help her case.

The lights strobed, sending her thoughts away.

Salem tilted the jar of sugar upright and stopped her pacing.

She really didn't want to speak to Deianira right now.

That was also something that hadn't happened before.

The lights pulsed again.

Salem squared her shoulders and placed the jar on the table before making her way toward the door. Her duty came before her feelings.

Pulling the door open, she didn't find Deianira, but instead, the face of her growing obsession.

Then she promptly slammed it shut.

Well, tried to.

Cassian stuck his foot in the gap.

Salem, what the hell are you doing?

She pushed back against it.

Closing the door.

Why?

So you can't get in.

Why are you-... Salem, open the door, he sighed.

I- I don't want to.

That was almost a lie.

She knew that it would only take a look at his face to ease her nerves, to settle her. But that would only reinforce her behavior, reward her. She couldn't afford for this to get any-

Wait.

That was it.

Conditioning.

If she could provoke him with a negative stimulus, he'd give her a negative reaction and then she could just learn to associate that with him. The same way she didn't like spending time with Finch because of his behavior.

She needed to make him angry.

Why no-

Before he could finish sending the thought, Salem pulled the door back and slammed it onto his foot as hard as she could.

FUCK!

Salem opened the door all the way and stood at the threshold, waiting for his reaction. She really hoped it would work.

Cassian hopped on one leg, his face flaming as he looked at her with wide eyes.

What the fuck was that for?!

She didn't respond, just waited for him to lash out. Waited for something hateful to ignite in herself toward him.

Salem! he called again.

She remained silent.

Cassian tilted his head with narrowed eyes before shaking it and limping past her.

No.

That was not supposed to happen.

He was meant to yell at her, or storm off, or both.

He dropped down onto her bed, then lifted his left foot onto the sheets, untying his laces.

Salem cringed and shut the door before marching up to him.

Your shoe is on my bed.

Cassian's gaze spun to her, his lips parted in pure disbelief.

And you broke my fucking foot! I think we're even!

Salem almost scowled, unimpressed by his tone.

I only did it to make you angry, she retorted.

Why the hell are you trying to make me angry?

So you'd go away.

His glare softened. *You want me to leave?*

She tried to say it. She really did. But he was already inside and leaving was the last thing she wanted him to do.

No.

He released a short breath and watched, he looked half relieved, half on edge.

Salem slowly walked toward the bed.

I apologize for breaking your foot, she sent. He looked like he was in a lot of pain, it wasn't helping her rising guilt.

Cassian looked down as if he'd forgotten it was hurt in the first place. Sliding his foot off the bed, he laid back and stared up at the ceiling.

Salem wasn't sure what to do until he wordlessly stretched a hand out in her direction.

Keeping her eyes down, she reached out and grasped his hand. Cassian gently tugged her down next to him, pulling her tight against the side of his chest.

You're fucking crazy, you know that? he said softly.

Salem rolled over on his arm and met his eyes, frowning.

I'm not crazy.

He tilted his head at her. *Really?*

Yes, she shot back.

He nodded. *Okay. Then would you like to explain what the hell just happened?*

Salem looked away for a moment. Then she narrowed her almond eyes at him.

No.

He snorted and pulled her closer.

As her gaze returned to the ceiling, he turned his head to her, watching her profile.

What happened between you and Deianira today?

Cassian flinched at the speed with which she stood up.

Woah, you okay? he asked, sitting up. He went to follow her, but the burning sensation in his foot told him to sit back down.

Salem didn't answer, just marched to her closet and grabbed a broom.

What are you-

Cassian's words were cut off as he finally allowed his gaze to circle the room properly.

She was grabbing the broom to clean, which was a very normal thing for Salem to do.

What had him stopping though was the state of the room she was cleaning.

It was a mess.

An actual mess.

And not just in Salem terms.

The dining chairs were all in different corners of the room. The sink was full to the brim with dishes and cups, they looked clean from where he was sitting, but it was full nonetheless. Her clothes were draped just about anywhere that there was space. It looked like they'd just been tossed up in the air and left where they landed.

And then there was the mess that made the least sense.

Sugar or salt, he couldn't tell, covered about seventy percent of the floor. And it wasn't even scattered, it looked like it had been poured in a long trail, swirling around the whole room.

Cassian blinked his wide eyes as Salem started with the broom in the far corner of the room.

Salem?

Yes? she responded without looking his way.

What happened in here? he asked calmly. He wasn't sure what to expect, wasn't sure if he might set her off.

I made a mess.

She made a mess?

You mean, you did all this?

Yes.

He swallowed. *Can I ask why?*

She paused, turning to face him. Cassian braced himself.

I was trying to distract myself. It didn't work.

Okay?

How do you know?

She looked pretty distracted to him.

Because you're here.

He paused, utterly confused.

Too much was going on and not enough was making sense.

Salem, why are you mad at Deianira?

Her eyes shot to his, making him want to recoil.

I'm not mad. I don't get mad.

Based on the way her eyes bored into his alone, he seriously doubted that. That was ignoring the way her hands tightened on the broom too.

Okay, he said evenly. *Are you happy with her?*

No, she responded before he could finish.

Why?

Salem took a breath, frowning.

It's done now. It doesn't matter anymore, she huffed.

He narrowed his eyes. *Then why are you still m- not happy with her?*

For the first time tonight, Salem didn't look like she was trying to order her words or phrase them in the right way.

She just blinked at him, as if she was just as confused as he was.

I don't know.

Chapter Thirty-Three

"Check again," Deianira told Cade.

"If she saw something, she would've told us by now," he replied.

She turned to Devin. "Are you sure Emori got the message right? It's the seventh day."

He looked out to the sea. "Trust me, they'll be here. After what went down with Po-squared, I'm sure she's dying to meet us."

Cassian stared down at his new cast, trying to block out the others. He agreed with Devin. He did think that they'd come, he just wasn't sure if he wanted them to.

After thinking over Podak's words, he was left with a bad feeling. That feeling only multiplied as he stood next to Salem on the beach. He didn't want them anywhere near her.

Cade lifted his arm and tapped his bracelet twice. "Lia, can you get a higher vantage point? We don't see anything and they should be here by now."

"I would, but there's a bird's nest on the branch above and I don't want to knock it off. I can try to jump it?"

"Please don't. I don't need you getting hurt."

"I can hear the hatchlings," she whined. *"I really don't want to-"*

Devin scoffed and grabbed Cade's wrist. "Lia, I swear to the Gods, if you don't start climbing, I'll come up there and fry whatever's in that basket."

"Funny. I don't remember asking for your opinion."

"You do realize that there is a *literal* man-eating lunatic on her way here right now. I can assure you, she wouldn't give a fuck about knocking *your* ass out of that tree."

"Gods, fine! If one of these hatchlings die, it's on you."

Devin's face was blank. "I'm throwing up with guilt."

"Wait, guys? I see something."

"Where?" Deianira demanded, coming up beside Devin.

"Oh my Gods..." she whispered. "They're-" Krr.

Cade snatched his arm back. "Lia, I lost you. Can you repeat that?"

Cassian stepped closer, yearning to hear her response.

But there wasn't one.

"Lia?" Cade called again. "Lia, can you hear me?"

Thump.

They all spun at the sound from behind, Salem following seconds after.

Lia rolled across the rocky sand, coming to a halt as she hit a large stone.

Where did she even come from?

Lia was at least half a mile out when they split up.

They all sprinted for her, Devin, in the lead, Cassian doing his best to keep up on his bad leg.

"Lia!" Devin yelled, shaking her as Cade held her up.

Cassian watched in horror over their shoulders as her head lolled over Cade's arm, blood dripping from her nose.

"I don't like being rushed."

Once again, the group spun in the direction of the sound.

The voice rather.

The deep silky voice.

Straight away, he recognized Podak and Potek. They were the ones standing on either side of her.

The woman in the middle, however?

Cassian had never seen her before. In fact, he'd never seen anyone quite like her.

Pola.

She didn't look real.

Aside from her bright big yellow eyes, it wasn't so much her features that struck Cassian. It was the air around her. It was like she was glowing.

Knowing that she was an azrael, Cassian expected something dark, something akin to Deianira.

She was nothing of the kind.

Her skin held the same tone as honey and it glistened like it too.

And the jewelry.

Like molten gold, it hung from her ears, wrists, and bare ankles. Even her barely-there wrap dress had golden rings along the hem and across the split at her stomach.

While her hair was as black as Deianira's, it flowed over her shoulders in thick braided ropes, a curl poking out here and there.

"I like being scouted even less. But I'm sure you've noticed that by now," she smirked, her eyes flicking to Lia, who was still out in Cade's arms.

Devin seemed to be the only one who wasn't still in shock.

"What the hell did you do?" he demanded as he stood.

Pola only smiled at his tone. "I don't think you're in any position to be questioning me considering you killed twenty-two of my men. I should kill you where you stand."

Devin didn't respond, but Cassian could tell that he wanted to. He was holding back. His actions could heavily influence the course of their future.

"Settle. I only had Potek toss her around a little. She'll live." She sighed. "It's unfortunate that I can't say the same for my men. What are we going to do about that?"

It was Deianira who advanced slowly, her long black mesh dress swishing in the rising water.

"You are going to do nothing about it. You sent us a message, we sent one back. The attack you coordinated was unprovoked."

Cassian was once again impressed at Deianira's ability to be so calm yet so threatening.

Pola narrowed her eyes at Deianira before her lips tipped into a smile. "I like you. And you make a good point."

Lia began to wake, her wide eyes darting across their faces, as Cade turned to Pola.

"What do you want?" His voice never wavered.

Pola's voice was sweet as sugar. "I think you know what I want."

Devin responded to her this time. "No. You could've taken what you 'wanted', but you didn't. You decided to contact us, then you tried to get into Terra underground. There's something else. What is it?"

Her almost imperceptible scowl told Cassian that Devin was right.

He was also aware of the fact that neither Podak nor Potek had spoken a word since the beginning of this exchange. It was a huge contrast for Podak in particular. The last time he saw him, he had an authoritative nature about him. Now? He stood behind Pola, head down. Cassian also couldn't help but notice his hands too. One had three fingers, the other had two.

As if sensing his gaze, Podak's eyes shot up to Cassian. He had to steel his spine in order not to shiver. Podak's gaze slowly passed over him, then shifted to his right before a sickening smile took over his face.

Cassian looked over his shoulder to see what caused that reaction when his heart dropped.

Salem.

He was looking at Salem.

Cassian almost snarled, his eyes warning Podak away, but his smile only grew.

Pola's watchful stare momentarily darted to Cassian at his shift in stance, then swept back to Devin.

She plastered a grin on her face. "You are one smart cookie. I don't know who I want more. You or the grumpy blond?"

Devin held both hands up. "Not for sale, and let me tell you right now, you are not pretty enough to play that dumb. Answer the question." His tone may have seemed light, but Cassian could almost smell what was bubbling just beneath the surface.

That got a reaction out of Podak. He snarled as he stepped forward, but promptly halted when Pola lifted a hand.

She pulled a fake frown. "No need to be mean. I was getting to it."

Pola turned her eyes to Deianira. "The azraels."

She lifted her chin as she corrected her. "Azrael."

Pola's shoulders shook with amusement. "So quick to assume. I don't want you," she laughed.

Cassian was truly confused.

"I want *the azraels.*"

Devin huffed. "Saying the name shit twice doesn't make it make any more sense."

Pola flicked her gaze to him, her face much less pleasant. Narrowing her golden eyes, she pointed a hand at him, then flicked it out toward the water.

Cassian could only watch as a large shadow appeared out of thin air, enveloped Devin, and dragged him out into the sea.

Before Cassian, or any of the others, had even processed what they'd seen, Salem dashed past him. She was sprinting in a matter of seconds before she reached the water line and dove right in.

"I don't think so," Pola muttered under her breath before another shadow dove into the sea.

He wasn't sure what that meant, but he was already moving toward the water.

The next thing he saw was Salem being pulled from the sea and thrust onto the beach. He dragged himself those last few paces to get to her.

Salem!

Dropping beside her, he ignored the twinge in his ankle as he rolled her onto her side.

Cassian patted her back firmly, trying to keep her still as she flailed to sit up.

Finally, she gagged, coughing up the water.

Let it out, he encouraged her as he released a sigh of relief.

He let her sit up as she wheezed, clinging to his shoulders as he rubbed her head.

With a splash, Devin resurfaced, drawing Cassian's attention back toward the scene. He heaved in a breath as he started to pump his arms, only to be yanked back down.

"Stop! Let him up!" Cade bellowed.

"No," she said evenly before turning to Deianira again. "I want the azraels."

There were ripples and bubbles on the surface, but no more splashing, and he knew that Devin could swim.

She was holding him down.

"You will get nothing until you bring him back!" Deianira was starting to lose her icy exterior.

Pola shrugged. "Then we'll wait until he dies and I'll move on to the next."

Deianira didn't look like she wanted to back down.

"What azraels?!" Cade asked, shaking with anger.

Pola gave him a bright grin. "Yes! That's the real question, isn't it?"

Cassian's eyes darted between Salem, the sea, and Pola. "Stop stalling!"

She threw him a wink. "You know, I've been waiting and watching Terra grow for many, *many* years." She started strolling around in the sand. "While you have done very well, if I say so myself, there was something that your people did that saddened me greatly." She feigned anguish. "Those poor azrael children. Wasted because no one could control them, control their power." She paused her short walk. "Well power isn't meant to be controlled, it's meant to be set free. That's what I've come to do."

Cassian was shaking with fury.

She was drawing this out on purpose.

Devin had been under for too long.

"Do what?!" Lia growled as she stood on shaky legs.

Pola looked like she was struggling to contain her elation at everyone's newfound urgency. "I've come to set them free," she said with both arms held out.

"He will die," Deianira whispered, her voice laced with something that sounded a lot like fear.

"And how unfortunate that would be."

Enough was enough.

Cassian moved in front of Salem and set his focus on Potek.

Even though he caught him off guard, his walls were high, strong.

But Cassian pushed, shoved.

He was practically throwing himself at Potek's door until his eyes finally flashed to Cassian's, his face contorted in horror.

He was in, and Potek knew it.

He poked.

Potek fell to his knees with a cry of agony.

Everyone's attention swung his way as Cassian prodded.

Potek's roar was animalistic.

He needed to make a point. One more time, he sent a pulse.

Potek was writhing on the floor, clutching his head.

Cassian made sure his voice was even, venomous.

"Let him up, or I will turn his head inside out."

He didn't once take his focus off of Potek as he waited for a response.

He didn't get one though, he didn't need it.

The splash and thump he heard to his right let him know that he'd accomplished what he set out to.

"You've made your point." Something else had entered Pola's voice. It wasn't so sweet anymore.

Cassian stepped out of Potek's mind, politely closing the door behind him, leaving him in a shaking heap.
He turned his cold gaze to Pola to find her watching him with a lot more caution than before. She didn't look scared though, she looked surprised. Impressed even.
"Speak, and speak plainly," Deianira gritted out as Cade rushed for Devin.

Pola kept her gaze on Cassian for a moment longer before looking back to Deianira.
"The power to give and take life," she said thoughtfully. "You can take a life with a simple thought, you can bring a person back from the dead. Do you really think that kind of power dies with the body?"
Deianira kept her face illusively straight. Salem knew that face though. She would've left already if she wasn't interested in what Pola had to say, but she wasn't going to entertain her theatrics either.
"I want them. All of them."
"Why?" Deianira asked.
"That's my business."
"Not good enough."
"If it's a problem, I can get them myself."
Salem was having a hard time keeping up. She understood why the others didn't sign. The less that Pola knew, the better. While she was

aware that her difference wasn't a weakness, she knew that it could be taken advantage of, given the right circumstances.

Deianira tilted her head. "No, you can't. You don't know where they're buried. That's why you dug the tunnel, why you wanted to negotiate. If you could've, you would've."

Pola shrugged. "I have time. I have power."

Salem wasn't even looking at Potek, but somehow she spotted the way his eyes flicked to Pola before going back to the ground.

She was lying.

But, about what?

She did have power. That much was obvious if Salem's scraped side and Devin's drenched clothes were anything to go off of.

Time.

She needed the power and she didn't have time.

Why?

"That's not all."

Cade stepped beside Deianira. "What?"

Pola beamed. "I must say, I do love how much better you guys are getting at listening the first time."

"What. Do. You want?" Cade was in no mood to play around.

"One hundred," she said with finality.

One hundred what?

"One hundred what?" Cassian echoed, impatient.

"I honestly don't have a preference," she said, raising a shoulder. "But I want one hundred. Each year. Including the bitesize ones you took from me a few nights ago."

She knows.

She set her sights on Cassian. "Don't ever think that you can pull one over on me."

"No," Deianira said immediately.
"It's win-win. Your entire kind doesn't get wiped out and we get an unlimited source to feed on."
Salem's stomach twisted.
"No."
"Think about this, Your Majesty. The population of Terra is two hundred and nine thousand, four hundred and sixteen. I'm sure you can spare a few."
She was right. Salem didn't have to do the calculations to know that not only did she have the correct figure, but that if she took one hundred people a year, with the current rate of growth of the population in Terra, their numbers would be practically unaffected. And they could probably avoid Pola ever touching their bloodlines.
Logically, it was a no-brainer.
Morally...
"I said no."
Pola pouted. "You're not being very fair. I came here to negotiate, to compromise. I even let you pick. You really ought to open your mind. After all, it's not like I asked for *your* child."
At Deianira's sharp intake of breath, Pola smirked.
She quickly recovered, but Salem noticed the way her hands yearned to touch her belly. "The answer. Is no."
Pola watched Deianira for a moment. While she tried to keep her face straight, Salem could easily pick up on the signs of her irritation at being denied. Fidgety hands, pinched brows.
"I'll give you time to reconsider." She nodded. "It's been lovely meeting you all." She turned her gaze on Cassian. "Especially you."
Salem didn't like that.
She didn't like that at all.

She wasn't sure exactly what the feeling was, but she hated it. So much so that she took a step forward and a step to the left, blocking him from her view.

Well, as much as she could with him being over a foot and a half taller than her. She didn't let that deter her though as she cut Pola a deadly look, one as cold as she could muster. A warning of sorts.

The feeling lessened when she felt Cassian's hand slowly curl around her waist. In fact, while that feeling decreased, another increased.

His hold wasn't just protective, it was possessive.

Pola let her eyes pass over him once more, her lip curling a fraction before she turned to Deianira.

"We'll speak again, soon," she drawled.

With that, she walked backward and grabbed a hold of Potek's hand. Podak came up on her other side before a spark of light zapped across the beach.

Then, they were gone.

Chapter Thirty-Four

Cassian stood in front of the bathroom mirror as he held up the clippers.

Everyone went their separate ways after they arrived at the palace. What they had been given was a lot to take in and no one wanted to spend the night in the council's study going over it again.

He dragged the clipper back over his head.

Azraels, he thought.

Handing them over would be at no loss to Terra, but it could create a bigger problem for them in the future. Pola was terrifying as it was. He wasn't sure if he wanted to see her with the power of hundreds of azraels too.

And then there was the message from Podak. Cassian didn't want to say anything in the study, but he knew exactly who 'her' was. And if he had any doubt in his mind before, it was erased when he saw the way that Podak looked at Salem.

He'd seen the flashbacks.

Salem in the kitchen, Salem in his room, him threatening Finch.

In the back of his mind, he knew it would be used against him. How and when was the real mystery.

He turned off the clippers and ran a hand over his head, brushing away the stray hairs.

There was a lot to work out, but for now, he needed rest.

"Do you take this man to be your lawfully wedded husband, to have and to hold from this day forward, for better, for worse, for richer, for poorer, in sickness and in health, to love and to cherish, until parted by death?"

Salem's eyes twinkled as she looked up at him.

"I do."

He couldn't contain the smile that came over his face.

This was it.

She was really about to be his.

"Cassian. Do you take this woman to be your lawfully wedded wife, to have and to hold from this day forward, for better, for worse, for richer, for poorer, in sickness and in health, to love and to cherish, until parted by death?"

He squeezed her hand as he spoke his words to her. "I do."

"By the power invested in me by the Gods-"

"Stop!"

Cassian's head spun to the end of the aisle.

Drake's smile was nothing short of cruel as he swung the gun from left to right, pulling gasps from the guests.

"Did you really think that you could just kill me and move on? Just pretend that it didn't happen?"

Cassian's chest heaved. He wasn't just scared, he was angry.

Taking a step down the aisle, he seethed. "Why can't you just leave me alone?!"

Drake tilted his head. "And miss all this? Never. I already missed out on being a grandfather."

His heart clenched.

"You took that from me, Cassian." The smile slid off his face. "Now, I'm going to take something from you."

BANG!

Cassian turned slowly, grimly, to find Salem flat on the floor, an oozing hole through her head.

He dropped to his knees and cradled her still body. "SALEM!"

Chancing a look over his shoulder, he saw that Drake was nowhere to be found.

"SALEM!" he bellowed again, gently shaking her.

Nothing.

"Salem, please!"

He could distantly hear a muffled sound behind him, but he kept his focus on his woman in his arms.

"Come back..." he breathed. "Please, Salem, come back." He stroked her hair out of her face. "Don't leave me..."

KNOCK! KNOCK! KNOCK!

"Cassian!"

He threw himself upright at the loud noise.

"Cassian! Open the door!"

He knew that voice. In his state, he couldn't properly work out where from, but he knew that voice.

KNOCK! KNOCK! KNOCK!

The door.

He didn't know how long he'd been asleep, but sprung out of bed and darted to the door, pulling it open with an apology locked and loaded.

"I'm so sorry, I was asl-"

Huh?

Salem stood at the door in only a sleep shirt, her brows stiff, breathing heavily as if she'd been running.

She was the one shouting?

"Salem?" he muttered in surprise.

'You called me,' she signed as her chest rose and fell.

Cassian shook his head, reeling. *'No, I just woke up.'*

Salem huffed and tapped her temple. *'You* called *me,'* she signed again, emphatically.

The mind link.

He stiffened. *'I-I didn't mean to.'*

Salem's shoulders dropped an inch. She nodded and stepped back.

'Do you want to stay?' he blurted before she could leave. Again, he hadn't planned to ask her, but he couldn't think of anything that would make him feel better than her sleeping in his bed next to him.

Salem froze at his question.

Her eyes darted around what was visible in his room, around the hall, and up and down his body. But as usual, her face betrayed nothing as she continued her hurried assessment.

That's why Cassian was so surprised that he managed to catch her fist before it connected with his face.

He gaped at her, brows drawn, her hand concealed in his.

Again?! Really?!

He thought she was over that, but evidently not.

Salem looked up at her hand, and just when Cassian thought that he might get an apology, he was greeted with a wave of nausea as her knee collided with his balls.

He doubled over, clutching his groin in agony as she pulled her fist back from his grip.

SALEM!

Thankfully, she didn't knee him as hard as she could've. He knew that he might not have been able to come back from that.

Cassian took deep breaths before trying to stand upright again, silently thanking Cade for the healing session he'd forced him to take with Mikhael.

She hadn't moved from her position.

Keeping both hands out defensively, he tugged on the link.

Are you gonna hit me again? he asked slowly.

Salem frowned before schooling her features again. *I don't know.*

He huffed disbelievingly. *What do you mean you 'don't know'?*

She looked away for a moment.

I don't want to but I think I have to.

What-

Cassian scrubbed a hand over his face. *Can you just come inside? Please?*

He could see her eyes darting around again.

He stepped back.

Salem...

She swung her gaze to him.

Salem, think about this-

He didn't know what he was about to say, but he didn't have to think about it because she leaped at him with a fly kick.

Cassian closed his eyes and he grabbed her mid-air, hauling her to his bare chest.

That was it.

Fine! he seethed, dragging her into his room.

You wanna be crazy?!

She kicked and fought against him, but it was too late.

She'd made her choice.

Let's be fucking crazy! he gritted out as he kicked the door shut with a *slam* and marched back into the room, throwing her onto the bed.

The second she hit the sheets, she sprang off, ready to go again.

Cassian didn't give her the chance. He launched himself at her, pinning her to the bed with his whole body, grabbing a hold of each arm.

When she jerked her head away from him, he moved both of her hands into his left and grabbed her chin, pulling her gaze to his.

This is what you wanted, right?!

As she squirmed, Cassian didn't have it in him to hold back his groan.

But there was something in her eyes too, something fiery.

You wanted to make me angry?

Yes, she sent back, a strand of defiance in her voice.

Good. He nodded darkly. *I'm angry.*

Salem wasn't sure how she was expecting Cassian to react, especially considering her new strategy didn't work last time, but she couldn't stop herself from trying one more time.

She'd practically thrown herself out of bed when she heard his voice in her sleep. He sounded so scared, so angry. No amount of self-control could've stopped her from sprinting through the palace like a madwoman to find him. Their rooms weren't that far apart, but she ran like they were miles away.

She called out to him too. Before her feet had even touched the ground, she was pulling on the link, but his mind was too hazy, too unfocused to hear her.

So she called out.

At that moment, she didn't even fear that someone else might hear her. She didn't care either. She just needed to know that he was okay.

Finding out that it was just a nightmare brought her more relief than she wanted it to. There was only one person whose welfare she should have been caring about, but without her permission, that short list had grown.

Despite the progression of this problem, she was still fighting on the inside. She knew there was nothing she could do at this point, but some part of her wanted to believe that she could reverse it or at least lessen it.

Maybe it would've worked if Cassian had responded accordingly to her attack. She would never find out though, because he didn't.

He grabbed her chin, his eyes burning holes through hers.

This is what you wanted, right?!

She couldn't answer.

No, this isn't what she wanted, this wasn't the desired result. But as she raised her hips, pushing up against him, Salem couldn't think of anything she wanted more.

You wanted to make me angry?

Yes.

She still fought against him, relishing in the sensation she was rewarded with every time he pushed back.

Good. I'm angry.

For a moment, Salem considered whether she'd made the right choice, whether she'd said the right thing.

But when he yanked her lips to his with so much force that she winced, she couldn't come to a conclusion. She wasn't sure what she'd gotten herself into.

Whether she could handle it or not though, she didn't care anymore. She just kissed him back with just as much force, doubling it even.

As his chest rumbled, she pushed up again, biting his lip.

Cassian tore his mouth from hers, staring down at her.

She inched back a fraction.

Had she gone too far?

He narrowed his eyes and huffed out a short laugh before pulling her back in.

Salem knew that she could throw him to the far wall if she wanted to, but in the moment, it was a struggle to even pull her legs apart beneath him.

The second he was seated between her thighs, Cassian pushed forward with renewed energy.

She groaned aloud as he ground hard against her.

As if in response, he gave her hip a rough pat.

Up.

Automatically, Salem lifted her hips, trying not to shiver as his guttural voice echoed in her head.

Cassian only lifted himself off her to dig his fingers into the top of her underwear and forcefully tug it down.

Just to be non-compliant, Salem went to sit up, only to be pushed back to the bed by Cassian's large hand against her chest.

Grabbing both her thighs, he almost dragged her halfway down the bed, tugging her closer to him.

Uncertainty entered her as she saw what he was about to do, but he didn't give her a second to think about it. He held her hips in a vice grip as he lowered himself and brought her center to his face.

There was no helping the way her hips jolted when his tongue swiped at her clit. But yet again, Cassian's hands were there to hold her in place as he quickened the assault.

It was almost too much.

Salem lifted a hand to his head, dragging her fingers through his sharp buzz.

A hard lick had her bucking again, but there was no escaping his hold. Not even when he freed a hand to prod one finger at her entrance.

Salem tensed at the intrusion, unsure, but as he curled it upwards and flattened his tongue against her bud, her body melted.

Stay still.

Even as she fought to disobey him, her legs shook as she steadied her hips.

Rewarding her, he wrapped his lips around her clit and sucked.

As if that hadn't already torn a scream from her throat, he flicked his tongue faster before slipping another finger in, thrusting faster.

Salem detonated.

His orders forgotten, she arched up, her legs clamping around his head as she opened her mouth and let out what she was sure was an unrestrained cry.

Cassian continued, drawing every hiss and moan from her.

Just when she thought she couldn't take anymore, she felt his teeth graze against her clit. She screamed, pushing against his head, and only when her legs clamped around him harder did he slow his rhythm.

He rose up, kneeling between her trembling thighs, his eyes hard.

Salem was almost sure of what she'd find if she looked down, but she still did. His thick length bulged from beneath his loose pants. She could almost see it twitch.

She met his eyes again and saw the uncertainty.

The hunger, the wanting.

She was there, open and waiting for him, but he wasn't taking.

Then she realized his hesitation. It was her call.

Salem's breath was light as their eyes held each other's, heated seconds passing between them. Then she said the only thing that she could think of.

I got the birth control shot.

Cassian's brows shot up as understanding visibly passed his eyes, then in the next second, it was gone and replaced by pure, unadulterated lust.

Before she could rethink her words, his rough, authoritative voice sounded down the link.

On your stomach.

Salem didn't have time to ready her shaky legs to move before he grabbed her hips and flipped her onto her front.

For a few seconds, there was nothing.

She couldn't hear him, couldn't see him.

But then she felt his breath on her neck.

That was all she felt before a pair of teeth sank into her nape. She arched against the bed, only to be met with calloused hands on her hips, roughly lifting them skyward.

She hadn't fully seen his length before she turned, but she felt it now. Thick and bare, pressing against her back.

Her body was practically shaking with anticipation as he pushed her shirt up and slid down her body, kissing and biting his way down her back.

Finally, she felt him where she really needed him, the tip nudging at her center. His hands came back to her hips, holding her steady as he pushed forward.

Salem fisted the sheets as she felt him breach her entrance. The initial sting was more than she anticipated, but she held on as he continued to push, never pulling back an inch.

He wasn't fast, but he wasn't slow either.

She gasped as he brushed against a sensitive spot deep inside and released a hand to reach back and hold his thigh.

It was too much.

He halted.

Cassian lowered himself onto his elbows, his forearms caging her in on either side. She groaned as the new position shifted him inside her, his tip caressing that spot again.

His lips brushed her ear.

A little more, he rasped.

Maybe it was the closeness, but his words sounded so much louder like this.

Nervously, she removed her hand from his thigh, focusing on the feeling of his heart pounding against her back.
Cassian placed a sweet kiss on the side of her forehead, and that's where the gentleness ended.
In a flash, his hips were flush against her as he drove in the last few inches.
Cassian! she squealed down the link.
The impact had Salem rocking forward. Not too far forward though, because soon, one of his arms came down under her neck, holding her shoulders as he drew back and thrust back in with just as much force.
Salem's breath caught in her throat as she tried to scream, Cassian pounding against that spot, over and over again, making her want more with every thrust.
His whole chest shook against her when she clenched around him.
Grabbing a hold of her neck, Cassian drew back all the way, until he sat just at her entrance again. Then squeezing her throat a fraction, he rammed his way into her channel to the very base.
Salem let out an open-mouthed cry even though she was sure no sound escaped.
He was relentless, brutal even.
Then suddenly, he was lifting himself off the bed, but not before looping an arm under her and dragging her up with him. He replaced his hand on her neck and held her to his chest as he resumed his punishing thrusts.
She grasped his legs as she jostled in his lap, the new angle only intensifying the building sensation in her core.
She was close. So close...
Not yet, he told her, his voice soft yet firm.

She thought she'd heard wrong as she felt her channel involuntarily pulse.

The heel of his palm quickly found her clit, applying just the right amount of pressure to push her over the edge.

But then his voice was there again.

Hold it.

Her release was so close, she could almost see it as her vision began to blur. But she forced it away with a ragged breath and braced one arm on the headboard and the other around the back of his neck.

His hand rubbed a small circle around her clit.

Salem bit down on her tongue. *I can't!*

If anything, his thrusts grew faster.

Are you gonna stop attacking me every chance you get?

She should've taken the time to consider his question, but in the moment, she would promise anything to get her release.

Yes!

He slammed into her harder.

Are you done pushing me away?

A piece of the wooden headboard crumbled beneath her grip as she tried to fight her release while comprehending his question in her muddled mind.

Yes, I'm done!

Cassian slid his hand further through her folds. Then pinching her clit between two fingers and tightening his hold around her neck, he pulled her earlobe between his teeth.

Then come.

Her eyes rolled back in her head and she dug her fingers into his neck as her release hit her like a freight train.

At first, it was euphoria.

Complete and utter euphoria.

It fell over her in blissful waves, the next one stronger than the last.

Then, it was darkness.

She vaguely remembered being racked with aftershocks as he pulled her close, but it was all so hazy. Then she felt herself being lifted. But it went black after that.

Salem slowly peeled her eyes open.

Looking down, she found herself sitting on the toilet.

Cassian was on his knees, his side facing her as he dipped his finger into the bathtub. When he caught her eyes, his face dropped and he reached a hand to her cheek.

Are you okay?

Truthfully, she was drained. Achy.

But she was okay.

Salem groggily blinked and nodded as he shifted to her side. One arm around her back and the other just under her knees, he lifted her from the lid.

She winced as her legs rubbed together.

Sorry, he said quietly as he lowered her into the tub.

It was a little bit on the hotter side, but when it reached her hips, she was sighing with relief.

He knelt beside the tub before reaching for something behind her.

"What are you doing?" she mumbled when she felt the warm rag against her back.

Cassian's eyes were on hers in a split second.

Why is he looking at me like that? she thought.

Giving you a bath.

Salem frowned as she swayed under his touch.

First, he was feeding her, and now he was bathing her.

Does he think I'm a child?

Cassian's shoulders hitched as brought the cloth down between her breasts.

No, I don't think you're a child.

Salem's eyes widened before narrowing again. "I didn't mean to say that out loud."

His eyes darted between her eyes and lips, his chest visibly trying to steady itself.

He nodded. *I figured.*

Her head lolled as her fatigue threatened to pull her under, but she sucked in a sharp breath, sitting upright once again. She needed to ask.

"Why are you doing this?"

Cassian looked away, shrugging.

Because I like taking care of you.

As his hand neared her face, Salem leaned against his forearm.

"I can take care of myself," she yawned.

Cassian nodded again, seemingly trying to stop looking at her.

You can. But I like doing it too.

He liked it.

Salem thought about that for a moment.

Did she mind him wanting to take care of her? No.

Did she think it was strange considering no one had ever wanted to before him? Yes. Very much so.

Her own parents didn't even want to take care of her, so what did he stand to gain from-

What?

Her eyes flicked back up to Cassian as she squinted them sleepily. "Are you in my head?" she asked slowly with a quirk of her lips.

He briefly looked down. *I didn't mean to. You were thinking really loud. But what did you mean about your parents?*

Salem forced herself to shrug. She wasn't trying to be deceptive, but she knew that it would be best if she downplayed the situation.

"They didn't want me."

Cassian's hands were slightly more tense as he washed down her arms.

So you're...adopted?

Salem shook her head.

As he sputtered, she saved him his breath.

"I wasn't an easy child to deal with. I wasn't bad but got in trouble at school a lot. My mother used to get really stressed because of me. She'd get embarrassed around the other parents." She rolled her head onto his arm as he wiped under her neck. "It was worse on my father because he had a reputation to uphold." Cassian paused as Salem took a breath. "When I turned five, she made me take the entrance exam for the sentinel program. I passed and was originally in the class training to work for Calliope Rikar, Deianira's younger sister, but I excelled, so they moved me up. And with her family's passing, none of the other trainees would've been ready for initiation by her eighteenth birthday." She closed her eyes as she remembered. "So I became Deianira's sentinel by default at fifteen. I've lived in the palace ever since."

Salem blinked out of the memory and looked up.

Then she frowned. Cassian's eyes weren't curious like they were a second ago. They were dimmer, more pensive.

She was surprised that she could pick up on all of that when she could barely keep hers open.

"Did I say something wrong?"

No, he responded almost immediately. Then he took a breath before resuming with her bath. *Are they still alive?*

She absently nodded. "They live near The Haven."

Cassian's head snapped up. *That's like thirty minutes away.*

She nodded again as she swished her hand in the water.

Have you...seen them since?

She tilted her head as she strived to recall. "The last time I saw my mother was the day that Cade was set to be executed. And I last saw my father two weeks ago."

Cassian nodded, his hand still tense. *You visited him?*

"Not necessarily. The only time I did try, he wouldn't speak to me. He told security to escort me out. That was fifty-two years ago and I haven't tried again." She hadn't planned on seeing him that day but she couldn't control everything. "Though this time, I didn't have a choice. Devin needed help."

His eyes squinted with confusion. *What are you talking about?*

Salem sighed. "Do you remember the day that Devin was injured when you, him, and Eulalia were making a drop on-"

Cassian waved a hand. *I remember, but what does that have to do with your father?*

"He was at the clinic. Hiram Qin, he's Devin's doctor."

Chapter Thirty-Five

Waking slowly, Cassian slowly tried to move, his muscles achy, his body fatigued.

It was a while before anything from the night before hit him, but his ruffled sheets and sore back had those images quickly bombarding his mind. That and the imprint of wavy hair on his chest.

The only problem was that the head that was supposed to be there wasn't.

He groggily patted the sheets around him.

No Salem.

Being a light sleeper, he knew that he would've heard something if the door closed.

He sat up and rubbed his eyes, trying to abate the sinking feeling in his chest.

He'd overdone it. He was too rough, too invasive, too-

"Let go."

His eyes swung to the corner of the room.

The stick end of Echo's mouse toy was in her mouth, and the other was in Salem's hand. She tried her best to pull up the ridiculously large sleeves of his bathrobe that he'd put her in last night.

"I can't throw it if you don't let go."

Echo let out a low muffled hiss but Cassian was too awed to pay attention to anything but...

Her voice.

His heart had skyrocketed when she started speaking to him last night. He knew that it was probably temporary, a reward he was only granted because of her loopy state. But that didn't stop him from holding onto every moment, engraving every sound into his memory. He even spoke to her as he wrapped her up in his robe and carried her back to bed, smiling at her nonsensical mumblings.

It was the most talkative he'd seen her and she was half-conscious.

What made it hard to enjoy her warm voice though were the words she'd said.

It wasn't only hearing about it that made him feel like a dick for sulking about his father, it was the fact that he'd never even thought to ask about her past.

Now that he knew though, he wouldn't be forgetting anytime soon.

Salem took a few steps back, her bare feet padding against the floorboards.

"Shhh. Cassian is sleeping."

He couldn't stop the snort that rose out of him.

Not anymore.

Salem's gaze quickly fell on him as she dropped the end of the toy.

I apologize. I told her to be quiet.

So they were back to the mind link.

I was up anyway, he sent, mildly disappointed.

He pulled back the sheets and started toward her.

'She doesn't know how to play fetch,' Salem informed him.

Cassian nodded before taking the toy from Echo. *'That's because she's not a dog. Try this.'*

He held the stick and dangled it over Echo's head. She jumped up, trying to catch the mouse. Cassian smiled and handed it back to Salem.

'See? You just shake it.'

Salem picked it up out of his hand and turned it over, inspecting it. Nodding, she drew her arm back and swung, slapping Echo across the face with the mouse. Echo hissed and ran to the other side of the room.

Woah! Cassian grasped her hand. *You shake it gently.*

Salem winced.

It's okay, he laughed. *I think she'll live.*

Bzz. Bzz. Bzz.

He'd just lifted his wrist when Devin's face was projected from his bracelet.

"What's up?" he asked as Salem's eyes met his over the screen. *'Devin,'* he told her so she wasn't out of the loop.

"Okay, so basically-" He looked back at the screen as Devin cut himself off. *"What the hell happened to you?!"*

Cassian frowned, then looked at himself in the corner of the screen. Bright red scratches ran along the sides of his neck, his chest, and even his arms, a few disappearing as they curled round to his back. And that was excluding the small bruise beside his left eye.

He sputtered, eyes flicking to Salem.

She frowned. *'What's wrong?'*

"Uh...I slept pretty rough." He looked back up. *'One second.'*

Devin's eyes narrowed.

"Cassian?"

"Yes?"

"Is there someone in the room with you?"

He kept his eyes on the screen. "...No?"

Devin blinked, tilting his head. *"Are you lying?"*

"Yes," Cassian sighed.

Devin nodded, his face straight. *"Does this person go by the name Salem?"*

Cassian warily nodded. "Yeah..."

"Can you put her on?"

He narrowed his eyes before turning to Salem. *'Devin wants to talk to you.'*

At her nod, Cassian swiped a hand down his arm and across his bracelet. The screen vanished then reappeared on Salem's wrist a second later.

She waved at the screen.

Cassian frowned as he stood opposite her, arms folded.

He could only see Salem's responses, but he could've sworn he saw her lips tip up.

'No, he's not,' she signed back to Devin.

Who was 'he'?

Salem tilted her head. *'Around six minutes.'*

Six minutes?

What the hell does that mean?

Because if she's talking about last ni-

'Short.'

That's it.

Done with being polite, Cassian shoved himself into the frame next to Salem.

"Oh, hey Cass. Bye," Devin smirked before the screen disappeared.

He turned to Salem. *'What was that about?'* he signed curtly.

'He wanted to know if we were free this morning to take the girls to school. I have a short schedule for the day and so do you. I said we'd be there in six minutes.'

Relief shot through Cassian instantaneously. Then he looked back up.

'Wait, you said yes?'

She nodded. *'Why wouldn't I?'*

No wonder he asked her.

Cassian lifted his head to the ceiling and groaned.

Cassian had to pry Kenny's fingers from his eyes as he walked, almost bumping into someone.

"...and then he pulled my hair and then I told the teacher and then he called me a bad word..."

"Mhm. And what else?" Cassian asked as she started kicking her legs and patting his head.

"Then I told Ty and then she stepped on his hand," Kenny giggled from his shoulders.

Cassian looked down at Tyla. "You stepped on his hand?"

Tyla's little smile told him all that he needed to know.

He shook his head trying to hold back his smile. He shouldn't encourage them.

Just as he went to look away, he absently caught Ty reaching out to hold Salem's hand. This time, he couldn't hide his amusement as he watched Salem slap her hand away.

At least she'd think back to this moment before accepting Devin's requests in the future.

"What's a ass-will?"

Cassian almost choked. "A what?"

"A ass-will."

Salem caught his eyes before looking at Kenny as she repeated it again.

Azrael, she told him.

Oh.

Cassian sighed with relief. "You know Aunt Deianira?"

"Yeah."

"She's an *azrael,*" he emphasized.

Kenny slapped the top of his head.

"Ow!"

"No! Not Aunt Nira. She's not dead," Kenny told him as if he was stupid.

Cassian frowned. "What do you mean?"

Kenny sighed. "The *dead* ass-wills."

His steps faltered momentarily.

A dark feeling nudged him. "Ken, you shouldn't be thinking about dead people. You're too young for all that," he said seriously.

"But she asked me!" she argued.

Cassian immediately halted and lifted her off of his shoulders, turning her to face him. "Who asked you?"

Kenny shrank.

"Ken, you're not in trouble," he said softly. "Who asked you about dead azraels?"

Her bottom lip started to wobble.

Oh no.

Tears sprang in her eyes as she threw her head back. "I didn't do anything! She told me to ask daddy but I don't know!" she cried.

He blanched.

From the corner of his eye, Cassian could see Salem watching the display in horror, and probably not because of Kendria's words.

A small foot kicked his shin with surprising strength.

He almost dropped Kenny but managed to pull her to his chest before looking down.

"You made her cry!" Ty seethed.

"It was an accident!" Cassian argued defensively.

Ty's face got redder and redder.

Cassian looked to Salem helplessly.

She reluctantly grasped Tyla's hand and walked ahead. She looked like she wanted to be sick.

Cassian rubbed Kenny's back as he started walking again.

"I'm sorry I yelled, okay?"

Kenny nodded into his shoulder.

He wanted to ask more, he wanted to push, but he knew he wouldn't get anywhere while she was in this condition.

As they neared the school, Cassian watched Salem practically shove Tyla toward the teacher at the door. He bent and let Kenny down.

"Are you okay?" he said, at eye level with her.

She didn't say anything, but she nodded.

He wiped away a stray tear. "You sure?"

She nodded again.

"So you don't want this piece of candy?" Cassian pulled out the lollipop he'd swiped off Devin's desk earlier. He'd gotten it for himself, but his friendship with Kendria was rocky at best. He needed to up his points.

Her face lit up as she snatched it out of his hands.

Tears gone, just like that.

He smiled back. "I have to go to work now, but mom-"

"Bye, Uncle Cass."

She was skipping toward the school gate without a glance back.

Cassian wanted to laugh at her complete one-eighty, but his mind was stuck on something else. Something far more important.

Pola got to the twins.

Chapter Thirty-Six

Taking a deep breath, Cassian let the damp smell of the night's summer rain fill his nostrils.

Times like this made him think of home the most. It almost never rained in Terra, let alone on Old Dome territory.

It was no surprise that the weather was more favorable in the heart of Terra. The land being spellbound for thousands of years was bound to have side effects.

But it was the rain that he liked the most.

Something that so many people saw as an inconvenience, but couldn't live without.

It gave life to the crops, quenched the thirst of hundreds of thousands, and yet, it was the one thing that people blamed for ruining a summer's day.

Cassian didn't agree.

In his opinion, there was nothing more refreshing, nothing more calming.

And he would take all the calming he could get.

Especially now.

As he heard the automatic doors slide open and he spotted the figure leaving the building, he stepped out from the shadows.
It didn't take more than three long steps to reach him.
"Excuse me?" Cassian called politely.
The man looked up as the clinic doors slid shut.
"Yes?"
"I'm looking for someone," he said contemplatively. "Hiram Qin."
Hiram slipped on a pleasant smile. "Speaking," he quipped.
Cassian nodded with a smirk, already knowing this.
"Perfect," he murmured. "I wanted to ask you about a former patient. She was admitted at your clinic for two weeks seven years ago."
He shook his head kindly. "Sorry, son. I wouldn't be able to disclose patient data unless she gives me her permission."
Cassian waved a hand as he winced at the word 'son', taking a quick look around. "I'm sure you can make an exception."
Hiram tilted his head, his face still relatively warm.
"I really can't," he said, his feet already moving again. "If you come back with her tomorrow, I'm sure you'd be able to find someone to help you. I should get going. The family's waiting," he laughed pleasantly.
Cassian cocked his head back an inch.
Family?
"You have kids?" he asked quietly.
Hiram's face softened. "Well, my boys aren't kids anymore. But they still live at home so what can I say?" he sighed warmly with a chuckle.
Cassian narrowed his eyes, nodding distantly.
"I really should get-"

"You know the patient I'm talking about?"

Hiram shook his head, shrugging his shoulders impatiently.

Cassian gave him a hard look, his act up. "Salem Qin."

Hiram's eyes narrowed with confusion for a few seconds before they widened.

That had Cassian stepping back.

He didn't even remember.

As Hiram started walking backward, Cassian snapped out of it.

He began stalking him.

"You heard that name before?" he asked, approaching slowly. "It should be familiar considering she has your last name."

His lip wobbled as he sputtered. "What do you want?"

Cassian let out a rough laugh. "What do I want?"

He saw the moment Hiram flicked his eyes behind him, the second he decided to run.

Cassian didn't let him.

Catching him in one step, he grabbed him by his coat and spun him around, holding him in place.

"I want to know what type of sick fuck abandons their own child, only to go have more and pretend she doesn't exist," he gritted out. "I want to know why I should let you go home to those kids. I want to know why I shouldn't kill you right here and let them forget about you the same way you forgot about her..."

Hiram trembled in his grip. "Please...I did everything I could."

Cassian shook him. "What did you do? Please enlighten me."

"I had her tested for everything," he breathed. "For years it was endless appointments, scans, different types of therapy and nothing worked! She screamed when you touched her, threw a fit if she didn't get her way, cried herself to sleep every night-"

His words cut off as Cassian threw him to the ground, sending his glasses flying into the dark.

He stalked over to where he'd fallen and picked him back up. "You know what you just described to me?" he asked darkly. "A kid! A little kid that you chose to have and treat like a burden!"

"No!" Hiram shook his head vehemently. "There was something wrong with her. I've had two boys and they were nothing like that."

Cassian's blood boiled at the reference to his other kids. "And it never occurred to you that she was just different?! You're a fucking doctor! You deal with different cases every day and treat them accordingly. Are you telling me that you couldn't work out what to do because her case wasn't visible?"

Hiram's eyes were on everything but Cassian as his chest heaved.

"Let me go..." he whispered.

Cassian scoffed. "No, I don't think I'm gonna do that," he breathed, shaking his head.

"This is assault."

Cocking his head back, Cassian released him.

Just as Hiram stumbled to his feet, he spun his jaw with a right hook.

Hiram crumbled to the ground, gasping.

"That was assault," Cassian corrected.

"I'll have you arrested..." he wheezed, trying to get to his feet again.

Grabbing a fistful of his hair, Cassian pulled his head back.

"Go ahead," he said with a smirk. "Matter of fact, why don't you put in a formal complaint with the Head Enforcer? I'm right here."

As his eyes widened, Cassian pulled his head back further and forcefully sent it into the ground.

"Ahh..." Hiram cried, gurgling on the blood coming from his mouth.

Cassian pulled his head back again. “Here’s what you’re gonna do when you wake up,” he said quietly. “You’re gonna write her a letter. You’re gonna tell her that it wasn’t her fault. You’re gonna tell her that you’re a dickless bastard that has no business having kids. And you’re gonna ask her, and when I say ask her, I mean beg her for the opportunity to see her, to even be in her presence, so that you can get it out of her head that there’s something wrong with her. You will write those words, and sign them. From you and your shitty wife. Do you understand?”

When he only groaned, Cassian tightened his grip on his scalp, causing him to cry out.

“I SAID DO YOU UNDERSTAND?!”

“Yes!” he cried.

Cassian nodded, breathing heavily. “Good. That’s good.”

Hiram started grumbling, saying something.

He leaned closer.

“Who are you?” he rasped.

For the first time tonight, a genuine smile touched his lips.

“Your son-in-law...” Cassian responded pleasantly before raising his right fist and clocking him, knocking him clean out.

Chapter Thirty-Seven

"We can raise troops. We might not be as powerful, but we outnumber them by thousands."

That wouldn't work and Cassian was sure that his brother knew it too. All their ideas at this point had been wishful thinking.

"Cade, it's still not enough," Lia drawled.

Everyone was tired. They'd been at this for hours and still hadn't been able to come up with a solution.

She shook her head, exasperated. "You saw what she did to Devin." She gestured to his seat. "What Podak did to Cassian, what Potek did to me. It will never be enough."

"You're bringing up an awful lot of problems and no solutions," Deianira said into the silent room. "Do you have any suggestions?"

Lia flicked her eyes to Deianira before looking down at the table. "I don't need one. We already have a solution."

Cassian spun his head in her direction.

She's not seriously saying...

Lia turned to Cassian with dark eyes. "Don't look at me like that. You're all thinking about it."

"Lia." Cade gave her a narrowed expression, disappointed at her suggestion.

"Speak for yourself." Deianira glared. "Those are *my* people that you are talking about handing over like it's a simple trade."

Lia pinned Deianira with a look that Cassian had never seen before. "Since when?"

Everyone waited for Deianira's reaction, but she only tilted her head. "If you have something to say, Eulalia, I suggest you make it quick."

Lia met her eyes, looking uncertain about her next words for the first time.

"I think that it's a little late to be inclusive." She shrugged.

"And that's meant to mean?"

"You really want me to spell it out?" Lia shook her head and huffed. "Fine. You're like a hundred and forty fucking years old, what's six years? You sat idly by while 'your people' starved and worked themselves into the ground to put a roof over their heads." She rolled her eyes and sat back. "But now they're 'your people'. We," she emphasized by pointing a finger around the room, "are 'your people'."

Deianira's face fell for a nanosecond. Cassian had never seen her do that before.

"Lia." Cade had a new depth to his tone. "Out. Now."

"Seriously, Cade?" she questioned, offended. "Am I lying? We were both out there, and while you might have had a comfy lodge, not all of us did. You saw what I had to do. I've jumped from bad situation to worse my whole life and now it's on the line to prolong the lives of a few people that won't even be around in a hundred years."

Cassian was shocked at her words but there was one in particular that Cade seemed to hang onto.

"Comfy?" he echoed, taken aback.

Lia sighed, running a hand over her curls. "I'm just saying, we should at least consider it."

Cassian was genuinely curious as he asked his question. "We should consider sacrificing innocent people and an infinite amount of power to an unstable dictator to save our own skin?"

As Lia's head whipped in his direction, he knew that it was his turn.

"Humans are the 'innocent people'?" she laughed humorlessly. "I forgot, we weren't exactly on the same side of things back then."

Cassian stilled at the waters that she was entering.

"While you were playing daddy's little soldier, I was literally picking through scraps in the forest to survive. If I wasn't being attacked for being gifted, it was for my skin or who the hell I chose to sleep with. Those 'innocent people' made my life a living hell."

He took a deep breath, trying to let the words roll off his back. "That was wrong, and that shouldn't have happened to you, but who are we to play God and say that their lives are worth less all of a sudden? You were in Patriam, with me. Is that what you want to happen here?"

Lia huffed, shaking her head. "If I remember correctly, I was the one who saved those kids. But that was it. They were kids. Given the right circumstances, they would've turned out just like any other human in the western sector."

What?

"Lia, I'm not disregarding what you went through, but we have ALL suffered. You, of all people, know that."

Cassian caught his brother's subtle nod from his side.

"You suffered?!" she almost screeched. "You suffered at the hands of the big, bad humans?" She squinted her eyes in disbelief. "You can sit up there and judge me for wanting to survive, but don't ever forget that you're one of them, *Alden*."

He froze.

One of them.

Alden.

He knew that she hadn't necessarily lied, but he couldn't understand why she would bring that up, now of all times.

They'd been friends for years.

They'd grown.

He'd grown, changed.

Along with the hurt, he felt a mountain of guilt. To be honest, that was the only thing keeping him in check. His guilt.

But apparently, that guilt didn't apply to someone else in the room, because before Cassian could even open his mouth to make a rebuttal, Salem was getting out of her seat.

Salem was unsettled.

At first, she wasn't exactly sure why, but she knew that it had nothing to do with the frustrating amount of time they'd been discussing the matter. Or the fact that they were still yet to make any advancement.

This feeling came about right when Eulalia started her verbal attack on Cassian.

Not only was it unnecessary, but it wasn't factual.

Maybe it was true of the Cassian she'd met seven years ago, but not the one sitting on her left with his eyes in his lap.

She was upsetting him.

At first, Salem found herself wanting to correct her, to tell her all the reasons why she was wrong, but all of a sudden, she wasn't in the mood for words. Not when Eulalia's words were hurting Cassian like they were physical hits.

She'd always taken pride in her ability to handle matters pragmatically, and maybe she could've if Eulalia hadn't said that last word.

Alden.

But unfortunately for her, she did.

Before Salem could silence the impulse, she was out of her seat and sliding across the table.

Salem! she heard through the link as she wrapped her hands around Eulalia's throat.

Seconds later, she felt the vibrations of the chairs being pushed away from the tables and hands wrapping around her waist, tugging her back. But Salem had a strong grip so the pull had them both being dragged back over the table.

Eulalia's eyes widened in fury as she gripped Salem's hands, bashing them as she gasped for breath.

Salem! Cassian bellowed.

Yes? she responded as she tightened her grip.

Let her go!

Salem huffed as she released her.

Eulalia fell to the table, her chest heaving, and reached into her back pocket.

Salem never got to see what she went to pull out because she was being pulled against a hard chest and hauled backward. As she was backed up out of the room, she finally noticed Deianira's wide eyes and Cade's bewildered face, but the door closed in front of her before she could see more.

She was set roughly on her feet and spun around.

Salem frowned as Cassian stepped back and put his hands on his head.

He nodded and shook his head multiple times, then took a few short steps away before coming back and taking a deep breath.

Salem? he called, his voice shaky yet deceptively calm.

Salem perked up. She wasn't sure what he was doing before but she was glad that he was finally speaking to her.

Yes?

He put his palms together and pressed them against his lips, his knee bouncing.

Why did you just try to attack Lia?

Salem shook her head.

I didn't try to attack her. I did attack her, but you got in the-

Okay. Cassian lifted his head to the ceiling, scrubbing both hands back over his face.

But why?

She answered honestly. *I didn't like the things she was saying.*

He bent down so they were at level, squinting his eyes, speaking slowly.

Doesn't mean you strangle-

Cassian paused and tilted his head. *Salem, she was talking about me, not you.*

I know.

He stood back up, his gaze still pensive. *You did that because she was lashing out at me?*

Salem nodded. No matter how much work he put into that frown, she couldn't miss the way his lips curved.

I thought you didn't get mad.

She gave him a bored look. *I'm not mad. I'm unsettled.*

Cassian sighed, looking her in the eye.

You can't just fight everyone that says something you don't like, Salem.

She straightened her back. *But you broke Finch's jaw because he called me a psycho.*

He narrowed his eyes.

That was...different. He came at you first.

She shook her head, remembering it perfectly. *No, he didn't. He just tried to kiss me.*

He sputtered. *Same thing.*

Salem frowned. *You kiss me all the time. Does that mean I should let him?*

Cassian took a step forward, his eyes fixed to hers as they darkened.

Try it if you want him to go missing next...

Despite the fact that he was quite literally trying to scold her, Salem allowed herself a small smile. She didn't know why, but she really liked the thought of Cassian not wanting her to be with anyone else. She didn't want him to be with another woman either.

He shook his head again. *What was the plan anyway? Were you gonna kill her or just strangle her?*

Salem shrugged. *I don't know. I didn't think that far.*

Cassian narrowed his eyes before swinging his head to the door at whatever he'd heard. He turned back to her.

Are you settled enough to apologize?

But, I'm not sorry.

Salem...

Yes?

He sighed. *Can you at least say the word? Because I'm pretty sure Lia's throwing a fit right now.*

She considered it. *That would be lying.*

You don't have to mean it-

Cassian looked at something over her shoulder and turned to find Devin, strolling toward them.

"Hey, sorry I had physio..." He trailed off as he looked between them, settling his eyes on Salem. "What's with the crazy hair-" Devin's eyes widened as he recoiled, looking at Cassian. "You really couldn't wait to get back to your room?"

She wasn't sure what he was talking about, but Cassian's brows rose.

"No!" he hissed. He flicked a hand to Salem. "Crazy face here tried to kill Lia."

Devin's jaw dropped.

"What?"

Salem frowned at Cassian as she turned to Devin to correct him. *'I didn't try to kill her. She was saying horrible things to Cassian and I just wanted her to stop talking.'*

Devin lifted his gaze from her hands to her face.

Then he burst out laughing. "Damn!"

Holding his chest, he lifted a hand in her direction.

Before she could high-five him, Cassian slapped his hand down.

"Don't indulge her!" he chided.

Cassian held onto Salem's hand as the three of them ambled back into the room.

Lia was on her feet and marching toward them as the door opened, but Cassian quickly took a step in front of Salem.

"Hey!" he called, blocking her.

Lia pulled her arm out of Cade's grip. "Don't 'hey' me!" she hissed violently. "Your dog is the one who-"

He fixed her with a dark look as he squeezed Salem's hand. "Watch your mouth..."

Lia spun around to Cade, and when he didn't say anything, she huffed out a laugh. "You can't be fucking serious." She looked at Devin for support, then turned to Deianira. "So this is what we do now? Attack each other and it's all good?"

"No, we don't," Cassian answered, stepping to the side.

Salem? he prompted, watching her as she stepped forward.

She flicked her eyes to him then back to Lia.

'I feel that it is my responsibility to remind you that the only reason that Cassian returned was to help us. Regardless of the lifestyle he upheld before coming to the palace, we wouldn't know a thing about the primas if he didn't come back. If you *didn't send Devin to beg him to. You wouldn't have asked for his help if you thought he was the same person that he was those years ago, so saying that he's 'one of them' is for nothing except to hurt his feelings. While he has given us everything that we have, you have done little except suggest that we make a deal with a sociopath. Accepting her terms would not only be unethical, but it would be shortsighted. With*

the hostility between humans and the gifted already present on Old Dome territory, we would be asking for civil war. And they outnumber us.'

Cassian put a hand to his head, wishing he had hair that he could rip out.

Salem, he said roughly as he gave the back of her knee a soft kick.

'And I apologize.'

For a while, no one said anything. Then, Lia was storming toward the exit, knocking Devin's shoulder.

He shook his head seriously. "I swear, I leave you kids for two seconds and one of you almost catches a murder charge."

He dropped his bag on the table as Cade blew out a breath.

"She wants to take the deal."

Devin nodded slowly as he stared off into space.

Cassian turned his gaze to him. "Please, don't tell me you-"

"Shut up. Of course, I'm not agreeing. I was thinking."

Deianira took a deep breath. "Care to share?"

Devin shrugged. "I don't know. I was just wondering what she actually gets from this. I mean, I get the one hundred thing, but it's the azraels I'm hung up on."

"She wants their power," Cade pointed out. "You heard her."

"I know that," he said, narrowing his eyes at Cade. "But why now? She said she's been watching us for ages." He averted his eyes before looking at them again. "There hasn't even been an azrael born in a good hundred years, so why did she choose now?"

"Obviously, to cause problems, up the pressure," Deianira sighed. "She wants me to sacrifice my people, dig up dead children, and now Eulalia looks like she wants to fight me for the throne."

Technically, that could've been it, considering they knew so little about Pola, but Devin was right. There must have been a trigger.

Cassian?

He looked down at Salem to find her eyes narrowed.

How often do the combat trials take place?

Blinking back into focus, he thought about it.

Every ten years. Why?

She ignored the last part. *When is the next one?*

Cassian hadn't answered yet, he was still forming the words as he caught onto her line of thought.

He huffed. *You fucking genius. Start of next-*

Devin's arms waving between them disrupted the conversation.

'Hey, time and place. Y'all can talk dirty to each other later.'

Cassian rolled her eyes while Salem frowned.

'That is not what we were doing.'

'Then, do tell.'

When she looked up at him, he nodded. He knew how antsy she was about things being sure, being definite, and this was only a theory. But it was all they had and he practically beamed with pride as she went for it.

'I think she needs the azraels now because of the combat trials. The next one is in less than a month and now she comes here asking for power. In my experience, things like this are rarely coincidental. For some reason, she thinks that she might not win. She needs more.'

Chapter Thirty-Eight

It had been days, but Cassian was still reeling from the meeting in the study.

It was just so unexpected.

A lot of the time, Salem could go a whole meeting without uttering a word. Someone would usually have to speak to her first, but not that day.

Sure, it was nice to think that she would want to defend him, but he never expected her to choke someone out over a few comments.

Despite his rage bubbling at what Lia had said in the first place, Cassian wasn't angry when he'd dragged her out of the room.

He was more surprised, but he shouldn't have been.

As opposed to the wallflower she'd been since his arrival, the past few weeks had shown him that he could never know what to expect with her.

His shock aside, he liked this new Salem. She was more blunt, demanding, uninhibited.

He'd take her over the timid Salem he'd seen in the study that one morning any day.

Turning the corner, he pushed those thoughts out of his mind.

While he could've thought about her all day, he had something important to do. Something he'd been dreading for the past few days.

Knock, knock.

Cassian put his hands in his pockets and waited.

The door opened.

He looked into the room, confused.

No one was there.

"Hi."

He didn't even need to look down to know it was Tyla.

Cassian frowned and bent down, picking her up. "Should you be opening the door by yourself?" he asked, stepping into the living room and closing it behind him.

"No," she grinned as she held onto his shoulder.

"Tyla Wesley Jacobs!"

As Ty jumped and hid her face in his neck, he walked straight into the weight room to see Devin marching toward him.

He ignored Cassian's presence and pulled Ty up out of his arms, placing her on his hip. "How many times have I told you not to open the door?"

"Lots and lots."

He walked her to the end of the hall. "Yeah, so why don't you listen?" he asked, disappearing into a room on the left.

Another little voice sounded from behind the door. "But, daddy, you open a door all the time."

Devin reappeared, empty-handed, and slowly closed the door as he argued back. "Yeah, well, one, I'm a grown-up, and two, nobody asked you, Ken."

He closed the door before either of them could respond and walked right past Cassian.

"What's up?" he asked, speeding back into the weight room.

Cassian threw a look over his shoulder before following. "Uh, I just wanted to talk to you about something. Where's Emori?"

"Work." He jumped up and grabbed the bar on the stand.

Cassian sighed.

They should both be here for this.

"Dev, can you listen for a sec?"

Devin pulled up. "I'm listening," he said as he pushed up above from the bar and extended his arms.

He shook his head and started anyway. "When I took the girls to school the other day, Kenny said something." He rubbed a hand over his head. "She was talking about dead azraels."

Devin's head whipped to face Cassian. "What do you mean 'talking about 'em'?"

Just say it.

"She said that someone told her to ask you where they were." He took a breath. "Said it was a 'she'."

Devin paused his pull-up midair.

Cassian could quite literally see his pupils constrict before he dropped from the bar and slowly advanced on him.

His face remained straight. "Are you trying to tell me that the same woman who slit my wife's throat, who tossed her out like she was trash, managed to get to my child?"

Cassian cast his eyes down, struggling to find the words. "I'm just telling you what she told me. Something felt off and-"

He vanished.

Cassian blinked, turning to look behind him, when he heard a door open down the hall.

"Devin! No!" he yelled, running to the girls' room.

When he was a foot away, Devin whirled on him. "What?!"

Cassian ran past him and closed the door, hauling Devin back into the hall.

"You need to calm down!" he whisper-shouted.

Devin yanked his arm out of Cassian's grip before gritting his teeth. "No! What I need to do is find out what the hell is going on?"

He shook his head. "You'll scare her."

Devin took a step forward, coming chest-to-chest with him. "If she was close enough to talk to her, what else do you think she did, huh? Ty's in there too."

Cassian had to pause.

That hadn't occurred to him.

He'd seen what Jude did to his brother years ago, what he did to Deianira.

The primas were far more powerful too. Pola could've done anything.

He shook the thought away. "We'll talk to her, and Ty. But as you said, we don't know what she could've done. You need to approach this very carefully."

Devin took several breaths before reluctantly nodding.

Yet again, Salem was in a mood.

Not because of any specific cause.

It was because of who she was with.

For some reason, since the night of the research operation, she hadn't been able to make her peace with Deianira.

A lot of the time, when something bothered her, it would eventually wane, very quickly too. But these negative feelings didn't seem to want to leave.

Cade walked past the bedroom and did a double-take, backtracking and entering.

"Nope," he said immediately.

Deianira rolled her eyes, dropping the plank of wood with a huff.

"D, I said I'd do it," he told her.

"Well, you were taking too long."

"An hour is too long?"

Salem picked up the plank and took it over to the half-constructed crib. She turned around, giving them privacy as she slotted the piece of wood into the frame.

She'd been helping out a lot in the nursery. She hadn't necessarily enjoyed it, but helping Deianira came before her emotions, work-related or not.

A hand tapped her shoulder.

'You don't have to do all this, you know,' Deianira told her.

When Salem shrugged, she looked back at Cade

He held his hands up, walking backward. *'I'm going to grab something for dinner. Do you guys want anything?'*

Deianira's face flipped. *'Two boxes of sweet potato fries from Grace's. Tell her it's for me, she knows how I like them. And some of those cinnamon buns from Emori's. But I don't want them if she isn't in. I don't like her assistant. And we're out of orange juice.'*

Cade nodded. *'I can get that from the kitchen.'*

Deianira shook her head vehemently. *'No, that carton stuff makes me want to be sick. I mean the fresh juice from that cutie at the market.'*

He tilted his head. *'Cutie? Should I be worried?'*

She nodded *'You should. He makes me feel seven again.'*

Cade snorted, pushing her arm playfully. *'Got it. Salem?'*

'Nothing for me, thank you.'

He nodded. *'Back in a second.'*

As soon as the door closed, Deianira went to pick up the mobile. She gently spun it as it dangled below her fingers, watching it closely. When Salem started watching too, Deianira dropped it inside the half-made crib and faced her.

'What's wrong?'

Salem met her eyes. *'Nothing's wrong.'*

It was true, nothing was wrong with her.

Deianira rolled her eyes. *'Fine. Why are you mad at me?'*

'I'm not-'

'Salem, why are you being off? What did I do?"

She stepped back from the crib, ready.

'You sent Cassian on a dangerous assignment. The risks outweighed the rewards and he could've been seriously hurt or killed.'

Deianira took a breath and nodded before shaking her head. *'Salem, I'm sorry that you didn't like that and that you were worried for him, but I didn't force him to go. I asked and he accepted.'*

'But you still requested it.'

'Yeah, Salem, I did,' she signed, shrugging. *'But what other choice did I have? Almost everything we do these days is dangerous, but I have to take those risks so I can make it a little safer for us.'*

Salem tilted her head. *'But you're not the one taking the risk. You're not even risking the people you care about.'*

Deianira cocked her head back. *'What the hell is that supposed to mean?'*

'It means that I ran through all your possible reasons for sending the two of them and there was more than one common denominator. Granted, they were more suited considering the size component, but Cassian disappeared for seven years and I've been beside you for long enough to know that you don't trust that easily, let alone allow others to regain your trust. As for Eulalia, while she is well trained, she is the least powerful of the members in the High Council and also the individual you've made the least amount of effort to form a relationship with since she was appointed as Head Scout. These limitations should have made them the biggest liabilities, yet they were your first suggestions for such a dangerous operation. It seems that you chose them based on expendability rather than suitability.'

Deianira's lip shook as she narrowed her eyes at Salem. *'Are you kidding me?! You think that I would risk their lives so carelessly because we're not best friends?!'*

Salem didn't respond. Deinaira already knew what she thought.

'That is absolutely ridiculous!' she signed curtly, tears welling in her eyes. *'Of course, I didn't want to send Cade! He's my husband, I'm carrying his child! But don't you dare think for one minute that I wanted to send either of them into the hellhole!'* She gritted her teeth as she took a step forward. Salem didn't step back. *'If I could've gone myself, I would've! And you can read me if you think I'm lying...'*

Salem didn't read her, she didn't need to. She went to tell her that when Deianira continued, not finished yet.

'I'm not a number, Salem..." She sighed. *'You are the most intelligent person I've ever met, but not everything can be quantified. Those readings may match up, but I'm a person, with thoughts, and feelings. Things aren't always true just because the math adds up. There are extraneous variables, uncontrollable factors.'*

Salem looked to the ground as a strange feeling settled in her.

She wasn't used to being wrong.

Deianira's hand brushed her arm. *'It's-'*

'I apologize,' Salem interrupted.

She shook her head, rolling her eyes. *'It's okay.'* She wiped her face with the back of her hand. *'If I asked you a year ago for the probability of you dragging Lia over a table because she upset Cassian, what would you have said?'*

She didn't need to think about it. *'Zero.'*

Deianira snorted. *'But you went full sentinel on her for that exact reason. See? Variables.'*

Salem frowned as the words registered in her mind. *'I attacked Eulalia.'*

'You did.' Deianira nodded.

'I need to apologize.'

She tilted her head. *'You already did.'*

'Yes, but I didn't mean it that-'

The door opening cut her words off.

Shuffling into the room behind Devin, the first thing Cassian noticed was the dark colors. He definitely hadn't been in a little girl's bedroom before, but he was expecting a lot more pink and a lot less...black.

While both sides of the room had their fair share of black and gray, Kenny's side had a pop of green. After thinking about it, it kind of made sense. It suited them.

"Kenny, can I talk to you about something?" Devin started as he took a seat on the corner of the bed. Cassian stayed standing.

While Kendria looked at him in her periphery, Tyla continued drawing on the wall as if no one had spoken.

Kenny closed her coloring book, swiveling to sit up. She eyed Cassian as she crossed her legs.

"Okay, but I'm very busy."

"Thank you for making time for us," Devin said, bored. He took a deep breath, facing her. "Have you seen any strangers recently?"

Her gaze flicked back to Cassian for a moment. "I see strangers all the time."

Cassian narrowed his eyes and she glared right back.

Apparently, that piece of candy hadn't bought him that many points.

Devin sighed. "Have you *spoken* to any strangers recently?"

She looked at Cassian again. "Mhm, when Salem and-"

"Not, Cassian!" Devin said, raising his voice. He put his head in his hands, blowing out a breath.

Cassian took a step closer. "Dev, I can show her."

"Show her what?" he responded, looking back.

He tilted his head to Kenny, not wanting to say the name. "I can *show* her."

He watched Cassian for a minute, then nodded, but not before standing up, getting really close to him.

Devin tilted his head down when he spoke to Cassian. "If you make one mistake, one wrong move, and mess up something in my baby's head, there won't be anywhere in Terra or Patriam you can run."

After punctuating his threat with a hard look, Devin sat back down.

Cassian was hesitant to try this all of a sudden.

"Kenny?" he called.

Kendria slowly lifted her eyes to Cassian's.

"I'm gonna try to show you something, okay?" he said, squatting down in front of the bed.

"Show me what?" she asked, gaining enthusiasm.

"A picture. But first, it's going to feel like..." He thought about how to phrase it. "It's gonna feel like I'm knocking on a door in your head. I need you to open it."

She briefly looked to Devin. "Daddy said I shouldn't open the door."

"But-"

"You can open this one," Devin interrupted.

Cassian honed in on Kendria. Her mind wasn't weak, but it wouldn't have been hard to get in at all. He just didn't want to hurt or scare her.

"Do you feel that?" Cassian asked carefully.

Kenny brought her hands to her head. "I don't like it."

Devin immediately stood, but Cassian put a hand up. "Wait," he whispered. "Ken, I'm gonna knock so you know where I am, okay?"

He didn't wait for a response for fear that Devin might change his mind. He just tapped lightly on the surface.

Kendria's head spun in his direction, her bottom lip pouting.

Shit.

Just when he was sure that Devin would kill him, the door opened.

Cassian almost fell to the floor with relief.

"I'm in," he said to Devin. "Kenny, I'm gonna show you a picture of a lady. Can you tell me if you've seen her before?"

He recovered multiple images of Pola from their talk on the beach, every angle that he could find.

Kendria's eyes were closed.

"Ken?" Devin prompted.

"She's very pretty."

He sighed. "Okay, baby, but have you seen her before." He quickly amended. "Before today."

She tapped her chin for a while before shaking her head.

Cassian drew back.

"Are you sure?" Devin asked.

She nodded, chewing on the end of her finger.

That didn't mean much. She could've been compelled to forget.

Devin's look at Cassian said that he'd concluded the exact same thing.

Chapter Thirty-Nine

For the past three hours, Cassian had been sitting on the couch, watching Devin seeth. He understood his pain, there was no way not to.

Pola had gotten to his daughter.

He didn't know when or how, and as a result, he couldn't stop it from happening again.

Cassian had to talk him down multiple times as he panicked. Devin suggested pulling them out of school at one point. He knew how social the girls were, especially Kendria, but their safety came first.

Cassian just wanted him to calm down before he made any decisions.

"We can't take the deal," Devin murmured, pacing.

"We were never going to," Cassian sighed.

"I know, but even if it's our last option, we can't do it," he stressed. "If we cave, she'll only come back for more and we'll have nothing to defend ourselves with. She's already gotten inside. Imagine what she'll be able to do with that kind of power."

Cassian blew out a breath as he caught onto Devin's line of thought.

"She needs to die," Devin said to himself, nodding.

He didn't disagree. "How? Even if we had the power, it's not us against her, it's us against them."

Devin turned away, his face dark. "What if it was one on one?"

He frowned. "Even if we managed to catch her off guard, which is highly unlikely, Podak and Potek are practically extensions of her. How would that work?"

He met his eyes. "The combat trials."

Cassian stared at him blankly. "What about them?"

Devin let out a deep, shuddery breath. "I'm of prima blood, and I'm over the age of sixteen..."

Wait.

For a few seconds, Cassian just stared at him. Then, he exploded.

"Are you out of your goddamn mind?!" Flicking his eyes to the girls' room, he lowered his voice. "Devin, you couldn't walk two weeks ago. What makes you think you can just waltz into a prima battle and make it out alive?"

When Devin didn't respond, his blood ran cold.

He wasn't planning to.

"Devin," he breathed. "You're mad, you're scared, and understandably so, but you need to take a fucking breath." His own heart was pounding.

"Cass, if we don't do anything, we'll die anyway." His eyes were glossy. "There's no point in surviving this if I can't protect them," he whispered.

Cassian shook his head. "We'll find something else, there's always a way."

"Not this time." He looked away before turning to Cassian again. "Look, I don't think she'll attack if we don't give her the azraels." He was speaking so fast. "I know where they are and she won't find them without us. This could work-"

Cassian balled his hands into fists. "Yes, it could work, but you'll just be dead!" he bellowed.

"You're gonna die?"

They went deathly still as the little voice echoed in the room.

At her sniffle, Devin slowly pivoted to face the archway where Tyla stood, eyes shiny. He choked out a breath as he went to her, picking her up and holding her to him.

Cassian glared at him over her shoulder.

Anything that Devin said to comfort her would be a lie.

Tyla pulled back. "You don't have to die."

"Ty..." he breathed as rocked her from side to side. "I know-"

"You just have to tell her where they are."

The glare slid off Cassian's face at the same time that Devin stopped swaying.

Cassian stared dead into his eyes.

Careful... he told him silently.

Devin began swaying again. "What do you mean, Ty? Who told you to say that?" he whispered.

"You just need to tell her where they are and you and mommy don't have to die."

Cassian could see Devin's shoulders tense. "Where were you when she told you this?"

"In my room," she responded.

Cassian sucked in a breath.

She was in the palace. In their home.

Tyla had always been intelligent, perceptive even. She read Devin instantly. "Are you gonna make her in trouble?"

Devin's eyes cast to the ground before he lied. "No, of course not. I just want to know how she got in. Where was I when she was here?"

"I can't remember," she answered cautiously.

"That's okay," he said evenly before setting her on the couch and squatting in front of her. He picked up her wrist and gestured to her little bracelet. "Ty, if you see her again, I want you to call me. Immediately."

She looked up with a frown. "Why?"

Devin's mouth opened and closed a few times.

He didn't want to scare her.

"I just want to talk to her."

She looked even more confused. "You can talk to her now."

Cassian spun his head to the door, then around the room as Devin did the same thing.

No one was there.

Devin's voice was a mere whisper when he asked, "Can you see her?"

Ty slapped a hand over her mouth and giggled. "No, daddy." She grabbed Devin's wrist. "I'll call her."

Both of them went to object, but Ty had already tapped on his bracelet and the quiet trill began to fill the room.

Standing behind Devin, Cassian couldn't see his initial reaction. He saw the way that he stilled though, the way that his whole back stiffened.

Devin turned to him slowly and held up his wrist.

Cassian's gaze briefly snagged on his bracelet before he did a double take.

He blinked and read the name again, at least ten times.

It had to be a mistake.

Devin didn't seem to be able to speak, so he did.

"Tyla?" he asked grimly.

"Yeah?"

She had to have pressed the wrong name. "Who told you to ask your dad where the azraels were?"

She huffed, seemingly frustrated by their need for clarity.

Tyla pointed at the bracelet as the person on the other end of the line picked up.

She looked up at him, a bright, oblivious smile on her face.

"What do you want, Dev? I'm busy."

"Aunt Li."

"Hello? Devin?"

Chapter Forty

Salem wasn't sure if Eulalia had knocked, but by the look on Deianira's face, the visit was unwanted.

"What do you want?"

Eulalia flicked her eyes to Salem briefly.

"I just wanted to-"

She winced as she lifted her wrist.

"What do you want, Dev? I'm busy," Salem watched her say.

She wasn't sure what Devin said on the other end, but Eualia brought her arm closer to her ear.

"Hello? Devin?"

After a beat, she shook her head and cut off the call.

"Sorry," she said. "Probably an accid-"

The ground beneath Salem's feet jolted.

Eulalia and Deianira both turned to the wall. Salem did too.

Another quake.

This time, the vibrations were stronger, closer.

Salem grabbed Deianira's arm and threw herself in front of her as Devin appeared out of thin air.

His gaze flitted across the whole room before landing on Eulalia.
In the blink of an eye, she was pinned against the wall, Devin growling in her face.
"WHAT DID YOU DO?!"

Devin disappeared. Again.
"Daddy?"
That was the only thing that pulled Cassian out of his shock.
It was Lia.
He shook his head and grabbed Tyla's hand, hastily walking her back to the bedroom. "Ty, I need you to stay in your room. I'll call your mom and tell her to come home but don't answer the door. To anyone."
Despite her panic, she knew that what he was saying was important. Cassian's pride warred with his trepidation as she nodded, pulling the door closed.
As soon as he left Devin's, sending off a quick message to Emori, a loud crash had him halting.
He was going after her. Now.
There had to be some sort of explanation but Cassian knew that Devin wouldn't be so eager to hear it in his state.
He bolted in the direction of the noise.
CRASH!
He took a left at the end of the corridor, pumping his arms faster.

"WHAT DID YOU DO?!"

Cade's room.

Cassian didn't slow as he dashed to his brother's room and pushed past the ajar door.

Lia was against the wall and Devin had an arm at her neck.

"Devin!" Deianira yelled.

Cassian caught Salem's gaze as she stood in front of Deianira.

Her eyes held so many questions, but he shook his head, turning his attention back to Devin.

"Dev, let her explain!"

There had to be an explanation. There just had to.

He turned to Cassian with orange eyes. Glowing orange eyes.

"EXPLAIN WHAT?!"

"Devin, what the hell?!" Deianira clutched her stomach and took a step back.

"Devin!" Lia choked. "Stop!" she gasped.

The door hit Cassian's back as Cade rushed into the room, two paper bags in his hands. "What the fuck is going on?!"

Devin's fiery gaze turned to Cade. "She's working for Pola!"

Suddenly, all the noise ceased.

No one said a word. Except for Lia.

"No, I'm not!" she yelled, clawing at Devin's arm.

Evidently, he wasn't convinced. "Then, why were you asking about where the azraels are?! Telling *my daughters* that they'd lose their parents if they didn't tell *you* where they were?!"

She quieted but continued to pull at his arm.

"Lia?" Cade dropped the bags and took a slow step toward them. "Is that true?"

Her eyes welled as she stared into Devin's.

"Tell them!"

"I'm not working for Pola!" she gritted out.

Devin practically roared. "STOP! LYING!"

"I'm not lying!" she yelled right back.

Deianira shoved Salem's arm out of the way. "Somebody better explain what the fuck is going on! Right now!"

When no one moved, she growled, "JACOBS!"

It looked like it physically pained Devin to release her.

"Lia," Deianira said coldly. "Tell me that he's lying."

Lia looked at everyone in the room before she let out a shaky breath. "I swear to the Gods, I'm not working for her," she whispered, throat bobbing, eyes darting everywhere.

Devin's chest heaved. "You already fucking said that, but I'm not hearing any other explanations..."

Cassian wasn't sure what to believe. "Lia," he said, his hands shaking.

Her eyes brimmed as she looked at Devin pleadingly. "I had to."

He took a step in her direction again. "You what?"

She backed up into the wall. "I'm sorry, but I had to."

Cassian's heart unclenched a fraction as he spoke up again. "She compelled you?"

Lia's eyes didn't stray from Devin as she shook her head grimly.

Devin advanced again, but Lia held a hand in front of her face as she screamed, "He showed me!"

That was the only thing that had Devin pausing. His curiosity.

"Who showed you?" he asked darkly.

"Podak."

"Lia, you will start from the *very* beginning," Deianira told her calmly.

Well, it would've sounded calm if he didn't know Deianira.

This was practically a warning.

Lia shook her head and looked up to the ceiling. "I was just trying to save you. All of you." Her shoulders sagged. "He showed me the future. When he dragged me out of that tree and Potek portalled me to the beach, he showed me what would happen if we didn't take the deal."

"Why didn't you just tell us?" Cade asked. "We would've found a way, there's always a way."

"You don't get it! There was no other way!" Lia fumed, tears streaming down her face. "He didn't just let me see it, he *showed* me. I lived it!"

Cassian was struggling to understand.

"When I wound up on that beach, two weeks had passed. I was actually in the future!" she stressed. "We left the meeting and came back to Terra, thinking everything was fine. Then she came back and gave us one more chance." She let out a pained sob. "We didn't take the deal and they *slaughtered* us! I watched all of you die! Horribly! I was so scared to see all of you because as far as I knew, you were all dead. Not one of us made it." She flicked her gaze between Cade and Deianira. "Not even your son."

Cassian looked back at them just in time to see their eyes widen.

It's a boy.

"I couldn't let that happen. I've had visions for most of my life, but this was nothing like it. When I died, I was still there, in my head. Alone. I can't do that again," she hiccuped.

It felt like an eternity had passed before someone spoke again.

"In the future...did I enter the combat trials?" Devin asked.

Not this again.

"Devin," Cassian said firmly.

"Do I enter the trials?!"

Lia wiped her eyes on the back of her sleeve. "The what?"

Devin nodded, satisfied with her confusion.

Cade's voice was thick as he asked, "What is he talking about?"

Cassian shook his head. This was madness. "He wants to enter the prima combat trials. To kill Pola."

"Two from each affinity. I'm coming."

Cassian spun back to Cade. "What?!"

He's seriously indulging him?

"You can't," Devin gritted out, eyes on Lia. "If more than one of us enters, one of us would have to kill the other. If we didn't, they'd kill us both."

"You can't be serious!" Lia exclaimed.

Devin whirled on her in seconds. "I don't want to hear a word out of your goddamn mouth!"

She silenced as she stepped back.

Cassian tried to reason. "Devin, you'll kill yourself."

He threw his arm out to Lia, a cruel smile on his face. "Well, as you've heard, I'm gonna die anyway."

Cassian shook his head.

This time, it was Deianira's voice that filled the silence.

"He's right."

Cassian almost choked.

Had they all gone mad?

Sure, Devin was a bit of a loose cannon, but Deianira? He wasn't sure how many more surprises he could take tonight.

"We need to do something they won't see coming. The trials are the only way," she said distantly, almost detached. "But Devin's not going."

"Deianira-"

She cut him off, turning to Salem. *'I want you to work out which one of us has the highest probability of success. Take everything into account. Ability, power, intelligence,'* her eyes flitted back to Devin momentarily. *'Durability.'*

For a while, Salem stared blankly at Deianira.

She looked lost. But Cassian knew that she wasn't.

She was calculating.

Then something happened.

Something small.

He wasn't sure what made him notice it, but as Salem lifted her hands to respond, her left eye twitched slightly. It was an almost imperceptible tell, but when her eyes snapped to his for a fraction of a second, he was almost certain that something was off.

Every eye in the room was on her.

She'd seen the question. She knew the answer before Deianira had even dropped her hands.

In skill alone, Deianira and Salem came out on top, but if she quantified it and compared it to power, Devin, Cade, and Cassian surpassed them by far.

It was common knowledge.

They were all affected by the restoration.

Between the guys, Devin was out due to durability, so it was between the brothers.

The problem was that she didn't like the answer.

She couldn't even begin to explain the dark feeling that swam below as the name repeated in her head.

Cassian. Cassian. Cassian.

She didn't want it to be him. But it was.

Cade might have trained for longer, but Cassian was more skilled, no questions. Physically and perhaps mentally. And if that wasn't enough, Cassian's power was better suited to the task. Cade was strong, but you could only get so far as an empath on a battlefield.

She knew that everyone was waiting on her, but she just couldn't push the name past her lips.

Not him... she thought as her eyes passed over him.

Salem had always believed in numbers, but at this point, she'd lost faith in them.

I'm not a number, Salem...

Not everything can be quantified...

There are extraneous variables, uncontrollable factors...

He might have had the highest chance of success, but those were just probabilities. He could still lose. He could still die...

Salem couldn't let that happen.

So she did something.

Something she'd never done.

Something that was so against her core programming, it nearly hurt.

She lied.

'Me.'

It wasn't the first thing that sprung to her mind because it was the only thing she could allow herself to say. Any other name out of her mouth would've been a betrayal.

She'd be sending them to their death.

Deianira frowned, obviously suspicious. *'Are you sure?'*

No.

Salem couldn't stop her eyes from finding him.

At first, she assumed that she'd thought the word, but when she caught his eyes across the room, she knew that it wasn't her that said it.

'Salem?'

'Yes, I'm sure,' she quickly responded to Deianira.

Deianira nodded stiffly, then flinched as she spun to look over her shoulder.

No.

He wasn't even sure if he meant it as an exclamation or an instruction, but he knew that there was no way in hell she was going.

'Yes, I'm sure,' he watched her sign to Deianira.

The words were leaving his lips before she'd turned back around.

"I said no!"

Deianira jumped and clutched her stomach. "No, what?" she retorted.

For the first time since he'd learned to sign, he didn't. Even though Salem was right behind Deianira, trying to understand the interruption, he spoke.

Right now, it wasn't an open discussion.

"She's not going."

Deianira narrowed her eyes. "Says who?"

He pushed past Cade. "Says me and anyone in this room with a fucking brain cell," he gritted out.

Suddenly, Cade was in front of him again, right in his face. "Watch yourself..."

Cassian wasn't backing down. Not on this.

"If you think I'm letting her step foot in that forest, you've got another thing-"

Cade was pushed out of the way as Salem stepped up to Cassian, brows stiff, fists balled.

And there it was.

That was the look he remembered.

She was looking down at him. No amount of fear or anger he was feeling could make him miss it, could stop pride from soaring in his heart.

Stop it, she hissed.

He took a look around as the others watched them intently.

Cassian took a step forward, shielding her from view.

No, he sent right back.

Why?

Are you serious, right now? he asked, squinting. *Why won't I let you run into a battle with monsters ten times more powerful than all of us?*

She did it again.

That thing with her eye.

If anyone can do it, it's me.

Cassian narrowed his eyes, taking a step closer. Salem tilted her head up, her chin almost touching his chest.

What are you doing, Salem?

Her chest brushed against his stomach as she fixed him with a look that said she was done with the conversation. *Saving everybody.*

He wasn't though. *What happened to 'there's always a way', huh?!*

There is always a way. This is it.

"A way that doesn't get you killed!" he snapped aloud.

"That's. Enough."

Deianira stood beside Cassian, her eyes beckoning his.

His never left Salem's though.

She spoke anyway. "Jacobs, take a walk. Cade, call a guard for Eulalia. She's under house arrest until further notice. And Cassian?" She leaned close, lowering her voice. "One more word, one more sliver of resistance out of you, and you'll find yourself on the sub-level."

Slowly, feet shuffled as Devin left the room and Cade went for his tablet.

Cassian had heard Deianira's warning, but he didn't leave the room without sending Salem one last message.

Try to leave the city before the trials. I dare you...

Chapter Forty-One

Salem wasn't one to not follow orders. She had always done as she was told.

It was restrictions that she had trouble with at times.

Try to leave the city before the trials. I dare you...

This particular order was an issue for two reasons though.

One, she didn't take orders from Cassian.

Deianira was her superior.

Technically, as her second in command, Salem outranked Cassian.

And two, she wasn't planning on leaving Old Dome territory *before* the trials anyway.

It was like telling someone not to think about something that they weren't thinking about in the first place.

Him telling her not to leave sparked something in her. Now all she could think about was leaving, testing him.

It was almost inevitable.

Salem could've blamed it on her compulsive thoughts, but in truth, she wanted to push him. There wasn't even a true reason for it. She just needed to prove that she didn't have to listen to him.

She knew that he was being serious when he spoke those words too, she could feel it. However, if she was going to go against him, she'd have to be discreet. There was no point in trying to make a point if she was going to get caught before she'd even attempted it.

So she did one of the things she did best.

She planned.

With Deianira forcing her to take leave for training, she didn't have much else to do.

Salem already knew his schedule like the back of her hand, she only had to see it once.

In the days since the outburst in the study, he'd been on patrol twice, running drills with the trainees three times, and today, he was on program duty at the gun range. That's why Salem had been sticking to the training room. She didn't want to run into him, but she knew that he knew she was up there.

How could he not when he'd been spying on her?

Salem looked over at the spy in question.

'You okay?' he asked.

She nodded, her eyes flicking to the mats. *'After this round, I'm going to go for a run.'*

Devin's shoulders dropped before he shook it off and threw her a smile.

'I'll come with you.'

Salem had to force a frown to stop her lips from tugging up. He'd insisted on joining in on her training sessions for days now, and no matter how hard she worked him, he stayed for more.

Devin had trained with her before the incident, so his overall presence wasn't out of the ordinary. What gave him away was the way he looked down at his bracelet every five minutes.

Cassian must have been peppering him with questions.

There wasn't much he could do with Deianira breathing down his neck, but Salem wanted to see just how far that grace stretched.

An experiment of sorts.

Once again, Devin lifted his wrist and typed out a message as they started their walk out of the palace and into the training fields.

Salem gave her head a subtle shake.

So obvious.

'How many laps were you thinking?' he asked, eyeing the perimeter of the field.

She held two fingers up.

"Oh," he said.

He let out a breath, evidently relieved to only do a short run.

Salem let his relief sink in before she gave him the rest. *'Around the city.'*

Devin's smile dropped. *'As in...Old Dome territory?'*

'Yes,' she signed brightly.

His eyes flicked away briefly. *'Why don't we do a few more laps around here?'*

She shook her head. *'No. The city.'*

He fidgeted with his hands as they made it to the end of the field, just by the entrance of the woodlands.

Devin nodded. *'Okay. Just give me a minute.'*

Just as she'd expected, he turned away from her and lifted his wrist.

She was done playing games now.

Salem approached from behind and tapped him on the shoulder. Devin jolted and turned to face her.

Before he could say anything, she asked him a question that made him still.

'Why did he send you?'

Devin sputtered. *'What? What are you even talking-'*

At her bored look, he winced. *'Okay, fine. I'm sorry, but I owed him big time. I didn't even want to-'*

Salem reached out and pushed his hands down, shaking her head.

'No. Why did he send you?*'* she emphasized.

He frowned. *'What do you mean?'*

'He claims that he doesn't want me to leave the city, but he sends someone that I can so easily incapacitate.'

Devin cocked his head back. "Excuse me-"

She took a step forward.

Devin...

His eyes widened as he stilled.

Give me your bracelet...

Without hesitation, he unfastened his bracelet, slid it off his wrist, and placed it in her open palm.

Thank you. She leaned in close and tip-toed to reach his ear.

"Sleep..." she whispered.

Salem didn't try to break his fall as he dropped to the ground, he deserved it for siding with Cassian.

She took a step back and a quick look around to make sure they were still alone. When she saw no one but a few servants some distance away, she bent down and grabbed Devin's index finger, tapping it on the bracelet.

It unlocked.

She knew what she'd find, but she still read through the messages.

CASSIAN: *Where is she now?*

JACOBS: *Here's an idea. Why don't I just tell you when something changes instead of you blowing me the fuck up?*

CASSIAN: *Okay, but what is she doing?*

JACOBS: *Hmm. That's a toughie. What do people usually do in a training room, Cass?*

CASSIAN: *...*

JACOBS: *Wait...something's happening.*

CASSIAN: *What?!*

JACOBS: *...she's drinking water.*

CASSIAN: *I fucking hate you.*

JACOBS: *Kisses.*

JACOBS: *Wait, she wants to go for a run.*

CASSIAN: *No.*

JACOBS: *I already said I'd go with her.*

CASSIAN: *Why?!*

JACOBS: *I don't know! You didn't say she couldn't run!*

CASSIAN: *Whatever, just stay on the fields.*

JACOBS: *I tried. She said no.*

CASSIAN: *What do you mean 'she said no'?*

CASSIAN: *Devin.*

CASSIAN: *Hello!*

CASSIAN: *Is she okay?!*

Salem narrowed her eyes. Initially, she was going to leave Devin there and go on her run, but now?

She rolled Devin's body over, so that he lay facing up, and pushed his arm away from his face. Standing back, she pointed his bracelet at him and snapped a quick picture.

Loading it in the box, she typed a message of her own.

JACOBS: **image**

JACOBS: *She's fine. But she doesn't appreciate being spied on.*

Before he could reply, Salem tossed the bracelet onto the ground beside Devin and started a leisurely walk into the woodlands.
She didn't need to run, he'd find her either way.

Servants and workers darted out of his way as Cassian tore up the distance between the gun range and the arena. He was already on his way into the palace when Devin stopped responding to his messages, but that image had him doubling his pace as he ran through the palace and out to the training fields.
She was doing this on purpose, she had no reason to even leave the palace today. For some reason, that annoyed Cassian even more.
She was pushing his buttons.
He instantly recognized the body lying on the grass a few feet from the entrance of the woodlands.
As his feet thudded against the earth, Cassian saw him stir but didn't stop as he flew past Devin and into the woodlands. That was the only way out, she had to have gone that way.
As the air grew darker, shaded under the tall trees, he slowed his pace.
He wasn't chasing her, he was tracking her.

Footprints, snapped twigs, bent branches.

After a few minutes, Cassian stopped.

It wasn't that he'd gone the wrong way, he knew she was close.

That was the problem.

It was too easy.

She was way too smart and way too small to make leave the wrecked trail that-

Cassian almost fell to the ground.

Partly out of fright, but mostly because of the weight that landed on his shoulders.

An arm locked around his neck as legs wrapped around his waist from behind.

Long, toned, tanned legs.

He grabbed the arm around his neck just as it tightened.

What are you playing at?!

She squeezed harder. *You sent Devin to spy on me.*

Cassian reached both arms back, one grabbing her shirt, the other grabbing a fistful of her hair. As he tugged and leaned forward, keeping a hand under her to cushion her fall, Salem went flying over his shoulder.

Gently lowering her, he hovered over her face.

I did. Next time, I'll send someone better.

Salem swiveled her legs in a circle and jumped onto her knees, coming face to face with him.

There won't be a next time.

Before she could fully stand, Cassian was there, pulling her close by her nape.

Yes, there will. He tightened his grip when she tried to shake her head. *There will be a next time for as long as you keep up whatever the fuck you think is.*

She narrowed her sharp eyes at him as he forced her to look at his.

You can't stop me, she sent cautiously.

Cassian raised a brow at her. She didn't even sound like she believed the words she sent. It seemed more like a dare than anything else.

You sure?

Eyes dipping to his lips and back up, Salem nodded.

Cassian only bent his knees to grab a hold of hers and sprung back up, tossing her over his shoulder.

Put me down, she said calmly.

No.

Holding her legs together, he turned around and began his march back out of the woodlands. By the time he reached the tree line, Devin was sitting up, arms back, legs spread, looking from left to right.

He quickly got to his feet as Cassian approached.

"One job, Dev..."

He held his hands up as he fell into step beside Cassian. "Hey, she snuck me. I was caught off-guard."

No, I didn't. I compelled him.

Cassian's snort was cut off as he realized something.

She heard what Devin said.

She was listening in.

Reaching up, he gave her a swift smack on the behind.

Get out of my head.

Put me down.

No.

Then no.

Cassian shook his head.

When did she get such an attitude?

When you started behaving more like an ape than a man, she drawled.

He almost tripped as he processed what she had insinuated.

He didn't even know how to respond.

Walking back through the gardens, he hadn't even set foot on the first step up to the palace when a shrill voice filled the air.

"Cassian!"

He turned to his left to see Deianira and Cade approaching. She released Cade's hand as she quickened her pace toward him.

"Put my sentinel down!"

He sighed. "I'm sorry, but I can't do that."

Just as Deianira cocked her head back, Cade put a hand on her shoulder and looked at Cassian, exasperated.

"Why are you carrying Salem like a bag of rice?" Cade sighed, frowning.

Cassian briefly looked at Deianira. "Because she doesn't listen."

Cade tilted his head to the sky, closing his eyes before looking back at him pleadingly.

"Can you please put her down?" he asked softly.

He panned his eyes over his shoulder.

Are you gonna run away if I put you down?

There was a beat of silence.

Probably.

Cassian rolled his eyes.

Can you please not?

More silence.

Fine.

Chapter Forty-Two

"Wake up..." the voice whispered in his ear.

Cassian blindly reached out and grabbed the figure, throwing them onto the couch as he blinked rapidly.

"Cassian!" a deeper voice scolded at the same time that a high-pitched squeal filled the air.

He immediately released the small body as his eyes adjusted to the light.

Kendria looked up at him, her face lit up in glee.

"Can you not maim my child please?!"

Cassian sighed, running his hands over his face as he got up off the couch.

He leaned from side to side, pulling out the knots in his back.

His bed was way more comfortable than Devin's couch, but he couldn't sleep there. Everything smelled like her and it wasn't doing wonders for his desire to stay mad at her.

"Sorry," he murmured. "Reflex."

As Devin snapped his fingers in front of him, Tyla grabbed the comb off the kitchen counter, passing it back to him. He swiveled her chair an inch and pulled half of her hair up, combing out the ends.
"Well, can you reflex your ass over here and make yourself useful. I'm already late and I haven't even started on Ken."
Cassian looked down at Kendria, frowning at the curly mess on her head as she smiled up at him.
He looked back to Devin.
"What makes you think I know how to do hair?"
Devin threw him a bored look. "It's two pom-poms, Cass."
He glanced down at her again.
That scary smile was still in place.
"I don't know... She's looking at me funny."
Devin sighed. "You're fine, trust me. She hasn't bitten anyone in like two weeks."
He narrowed his eyes. "Wow. A whole two weeks sober? Well, I'm sold."
"Cass-"
"Fine," he huffed. "Come on," he told Kenny as he picked her up by her leg and walked her to the open kitchen upside down.
Devin brought his shoulder up to his ear as she giggled and screamed before Cassian dropped her onto the chair beside Ty.
"You're gonna need to walk me through this," he sighed, stretching.
By the time he'd wrapped the hair bobble around the last time, Cassian was thanking his past self for making the decision to shave his head.
Not only did it take way too long to comb her hair out, no matter how much water he spritzed or hair butter he rubbed in, but he

couldn't move a finger without her crying or complaining that something was too tight.

And the best part?

Devin didn't lift a finger to help him. He even snorted a few times.

Maybe Salem was right when she told him that he was no good when it came to hair.

Oh.

That reminded him.

Walking around the counter, Cassian washed his hands then opened up the fridge, pulling out a small chunk of ham wrapped in foil.

"No, no. Go ahead and raid my fridge. I don't mind," Devin quipped from the counter, fixing Kenny's hair.

Cassian threw him a sarcastic smile as he opened the bread bin.

He got to work, although it wasn't much work at all, then loaded the sandwich into a small lunch box.

Just as he went to find a lid, he frowned.

She'd be hungry again in an hour.

His eyes caught the fruit bowl.

Snagging an apple and an orange, he popped them into the box next to the sealed sandwich.

Better.

He turned to the cupboard when he noticed two pots on the stove.

Curiosity getting the better of him, he lifted the lids. He practically groaned as the aroma hit his nose.

A lot could've been said about Devin, but no one could say he couldn't cook.

He turned around, lids in hand. "Dev, can I get some of this pasta?"

Devin stared at him blankly. "The fruit theft wasn't enough?"

When he tilted his head, Devin waved a hand.

Cassian closed the pot with the pasta sauce and grabbed a small container, filling it with plain pasta. He popped on the lid and then set it into the lunch box, sealing it.
Devin narrowed his eyes as he turned. "What's even the point-"
"Can you drop this at the arena before lunch?" Cassian asked, holding out the box.
He wrapped the bobble around Kendria's pigtail once more.
"Why?"
"For crazy face," he said quietly, turning back to the counter to clean up.
When he was met with silence, he looked back again.
Both Devin and Kenny were looking at him with blank faces.
"What?"
Devin nodded. "Let's do this then." He picked her up and set her on the floor, waving her away. Placing both palms on the counter, he tilted his head at Cassian.
"Why can't you go?"
Cassian looked over at him, his eyes bored. "Because she doesn't want to see me," he mumbled.
Devin raised his brows, then huffed. "So stupidity runs in the family?"
"Bad word!" Kenny and Ty yelled in unison.
"Hushup," Devin shot back before they turned back to their breakfasts on the couch.
Cassian pinned him with a look. "What's that supposed to mean?"
He snorted as he reached for the lunchbox, shoving it into his work bag. "It means you're both stupid."
When Cassian didn't respond, he sighed.

“First it’s Cade thinking that Deianira hated his guts when the woman was practically drooling over him. And that's when she thought he was a criminal. And now you, pretending that you don’t know Salem’s in love with you.”

Cassian’s heart jolted as he took a step back. “Don’t say that.”

Devin turned to him. “Say what? That’s Salem’s in love with you,” he said with a smirk.

“Yes, that!” he hissed.

“Why not?” he questioned.

“Because it’s not fu-” He swung his eyes to the couch. “Not *fudging* true.”

Devin watched him for a while before shrugging with a smile. “Okay.”

“She’s not,” Cassian insisted.

He nodded. “Okay.”

“Stop it.”

“I’m agreeing with you,” Devin laughed.

Cassian lowered his voice as he gritted his teeth. “No, you’re not. You’re messing with my head.”

His smile only grew as he shrugged again and stalked out of the kitchen.

“Gremlins! Get your shoes on and roll out!”

Cassian followed him, dissatisfied.

“She broke my foot, kicked me in the balls, and literally ran away from me in the space of like two weeks!”

Devin turned back to him as he picked up the girls’ book bags by the door. “Exactly.”

“What?”

He wasn’t making any sense.

"Look. Have you ever seen Salem stress over someone she doesn't care about?"

He thought about it. "Well, no but-"

"And if she really didn't want you around, would she have pushed you away and then baited you into chasing her?"

"I don't know, but that doesn't mean-"

His voice dropped as he looked at Cassian more intently. "Cass. She jumped through a portal into the unknown for you, she went all cage fighter on Lia, of all people, for you, and she's about to fight in a death match, for you." He sighed. "Salem... she doesn't express herself the same way as everyone else, but it doesn't mean that she doesn't feel the same things. She might think that she's stuck beside Deianira all these years out of blind loyalty or because of some oath she swore, but she cares about her. Really cares. For the Gods' sake, she went deaf for her. She knew the consequences and chose to protect Deianira that day. It's the same thing she's doing with you right now. No amount of training can make you disregard self-preservation like that."

Cassian was trying his best to listen to all that Devin was saying, but he couldn't help himself from hanging onto the first few words he'd said.

"What do you mean she's about to fight in a death match for me?"

Devin blinked, then leaned back his head back, eyes to the ceiling. "Gods, you really are stupid." He huffed then looked back at Cassian with a smirk. "Don't tell 'crazy face' I said that. I'm not tryna get mollywhopped next."

Cassian brought his hands to his head, the words moving around too fast for him to process. "Dev, I'm gonna need you to spell it out for me," he said quietly, shakily.

Devin shifted the bags into one hand and groaned, pinning him with a hard look. "Salem's not going to the trials. She never was. I knew it, Deianira knew it, I'm pretty sure the only people who didn't were you and Salem."

"Knew what?!" Cassian exclaimed.

What is he talking about?

"That she's not supposed to go!" Devin yelled back. "Someone has to go, but it's not supposed to be her! Put it together! You know it's not Deianira, so who else would she have done that for?!"

When Cassian's face fell, Devin nodded, satisfied.

"I'm already late soo good day to you. Lock up when you decide to get the fudge off my couch."

Cassian was hearing him, but he wasn't listening to him. He couldn't focus on anything, but the two words that played back and forth in his head.

She lied.

Chapter Forty-Three

Salem gasped for air as she resurfaced.

Looking down at the shimmering lights on the floor of the pool, she considered taking another lap, but she was tired in every sense of the word.

It had been almost a week since she'd seen anyone on the Council.

Well, that excluded Devin.

He'd turned up to her training sessions every day with food and talked to her for a few minutes.

She wasn't stupid, she knew who the meals came from, she just didn't understand why he wouldn't bring them himself, why he didn't want to see her.

Her time away had been...miserable.

Salem liked her own space, liked being alone, loved training, but it wasn't the same anymore.

It felt wrong.

It didn't help knowing that in just over a week, she'd be fighting for her life in a battle against the most powerful beings in Patriam.

She'd only learned about their existence weeks ago, only met one of her opponents days ago.

Time wasn't on her side.

Salem let the air fill her lungs again before descending for the thirty-second time.

In the water, she got to pretend that she wasn't a week away from certain death. Because that's what the trials would mean for her.

Death.

She knew it, she had a feeling that everyone in Deianira's room that day knew it.

But it was their only chance.

Salem broke the surface and accidentally swallowed a mouthful of water.

Someone was standing at the edge of the pool.

Not just someone.

Him.

She coughed, patting her chest.

It was inevitable that they would see each other at some point, and even though a part of her wanted to, she couldn't help but feel overwhelmed. He was the whole reason she was doing this. Facing him would mean admitting some things to herself.

Things she wasn't ready to admit.

She caught her breath and stared right back.

Salem didn't speak. She knew that he had something to say so she let him.

You lied.

The breath she took threatened to choke her again.

In Deianira's room. You lied.

Salem couldn't bring herself to do it again, so she didn't respond.

At her silence, Cassian shook his head disbelievingly.

She struggled to read him. His chest was heaving, like he was mad. But his eyes were curious, questioning. She didn't dare enter his mind either, she didn't know if she was ready for what she might find.

Cassian's gaze passed over her one more time before he lifted a foot to his hand and tugged off his boot.

What is he doing?

Then the next boot was off.

Then his socks, then his shirt.

Salem's breathing picked up as he reached for his pants.

No slower than he'd pulled them off did he drop onto the edge of the pool and lower himself in.

Against her better judgment, she didn't move, didn't back away.

He turned to her, a hand on the edge.

I know you did. I might not have figured out why you were acting so weird if Devin didn't say something, but it makes sense now. You lied.

What did he want?

Admit it.

Salem finally listened to herself and began to tread water, away from him.

She should've known he'd follow.

Salem.

She just kept backing up.

Stopping would mean caving, would mean admitting it.

She wasn't ready.

She didn't realize how long they'd kept this up for until her back hit the wall at the other end of the pool.

Cassian took the opportunity to cage her in, arms on either side of her.

Salem... he mouthed while speaking through the link.

Her eyes widened.

It was like he was actually talking to her. Like she could hear him.

Please.

His tone wasn't as firm, it was more desperate. As if he needed her to say it.

But she still couldn't do it.

He got closer, and closer. Until his mouth was within a hair's breadth of hers.

Before he could say another word, she silenced him with her lips.

This wasn't giving in. This was fine.

As she predicted, Cassian couldn't resist.

His hand was on her nape in a second, taking control. He was rough, demanding.

Salem loved it.

Before she could stop herself, her legs were around his waist. Cassian pushed her up against the edge, one hand steadying them. The second he parted his lips from hers, she could feel the words on the tip of his tongue.

Salem went for his neck. Just like he did to her that night in his room.

His answering groan and responding grind told her that it worked.

Regardless of her motives, she relished in the sensation.

Cassian drew back and took her lips again, more aggressively this time. He rocked against her core, drawing a moan from her.

It was like he couldn't get enough.

Salem couldn't either.

The pool was freezing at this time of night, but they were both panting.

Sa-

Cutting him off, she ran a hand down his abs, only pausing at the top of his underwear.

Yes.

Salem didn't hesitate this time. Her hand slipped into his boxers before she brushed her fingertips against his length. The muffled groan against her lips only motivated her to grasp it.

The sheer feel of it left her wanting.

She wanted more, and not just as a distraction.

Cassian seemed to know exactly what was on her mind because the hand on her neck moved down to cup her mound. It wasn't long before he was pushing aside her swimsuit to tease a finger around her opening.

Salem parted her lips to ask for more, to beg, but he didn't make her wait.

She didn't tense as he pushed one finger into her opening. She'd been expecting it, though that didn't stop the open-mouthed groan that left her.

They were barely even kissing anymore. Just breathing into each other as they brought the other to the edge.

Cassian reached out again. *Salem, please-*

Salem tugged at his boxers, pulling them as far down as her arms would allow as she brought her center closer.

He practically shuddered.

She held his head in her hands, bringing their lips together once again.

Cassian used the arm on the edge to shift them into shallower water.

With a hand on his length and the others holding her up, he aligned their centers, pulling his head back.

Salem almost sprung out of his arms with anticipation as she felt the tip at her entrance.

She waited for the intrusion, was yearning for it.

But it didn't come.

She hesitantly peeled her eyes open.

Cassian was watching her intently.

Hard as she tried, she couldn't read him for the life of her.

Salem.

The base was back in his voice.

Tonight, Salem wanted to lose herself, not pour her heart out.

Cassian, can you-

Tell me.

It was on the tip of her tongue, but she just couldn't.

His brows scrunched as he brought his face closer.

He looked like he was breaking.

That wasn't what she wanted. Not at all.

Cassian closed his eyes and rested his head in the crook of her neck.

Salem couldn't stop her hand from coming up to his head, running her fingers through his scalp affectionately.

Every move he made rubbed against her core, she was close to begging.

I'm not asking you to tell me why you did it. I just want you to admit it.

He didn't understand. It was the reason that mattered most.

You can tell me that you didn't lie and I'll leave. I swear, I will. But I just need an answer.

So did she.

Salem ran everything back. The words, the kisses, the looks, the touches.

She wasn't stupid enough to try and convince herself that she didn't care for him. She knew that she did.

Just, how much?

Salem rubbed her thumb against his ear before lifting his head with a hand under his chin. The words felt like gravel in her throat but Cassian had done it time and time again. He'd exposed himself, made himself vulnerable.

It wasn't balanced, it wasn't fair.

Cassian didn't meet her eyes at first. It may have been out of sadness or fear, but Salem didn't give herself a second to ponder over it.

She took a shaky breath.

"I didn't want you to go..."

Cassian's eyes snapped open and flew to hers.

It was what he'd been waiting for, begging for. Now that he had it, it seemed like he didn't know what to do with himself.

To his credit though, recovered fairly quickly.

Salem flinched at the speed with which he covered her mouth with his. She had even less time to brace herself for the forceful intrusion from below.

She tore her lips away with a gasp.

It was everything.

They couldn't have been any closer.

Cassian ran his lips across her throat as she squirmed, trying to accommodate him. As her little breaths turned to moans, he drew back slightly before giving her a shallow thrust. Followed by another.

Salem didn't hold off as she threw her head back and allowed the small cries to flow freely from her lips.

Apparently, the water wasn't allowing him to do what he really wanted because he held onto her thighs, still inside, as he walked them to the steps.

He'd only walked up three of them when he kneeled on the stair, her body wrapped around his.

The first full upthrust had Salem wincing.

This was harder, deeper.

He must have heard because, if it was even possible, he brought their bodies closer, dragging his pelvis across her clit with each stroke.

Salem wrapped her arm around his neck, letting that ball of pleasure in her core grow tighter and tighter.

She was doing it.

She was letting go.

Not only was it not as hard as she thought it would be, but it was easy.

It was liberating.

"I didn't want you to go..." she rasped again.

Her voice only spurred him on as Cassian's thrusts quickened.

I know...

"I wanted to keep you safe..." she moaned.

Cassian breathed into her neck.

I know... he murmured as he drove into her, hitting that spot deep inside her core.

Salem squealed as she almost jolted out of his grip.

But he was relentless.

Cassian's grip on her thighs grew harsher, almost painful. All she could do was hold onto him as he took her to a new world.

One hand took hold of the hair at the base of her scalp, tugging her head back, allowing him to continue his assault on her neck as he hit harder.

The sensation was almost too much.

I don't want you to go either, he told her.

Salem didn't know that it was possible for him to go any deeper, but he did.

I want to keep you safe too.

She wasn't even moaning anymore, just grunting and squirming in his hold.

She was almost there.

Cassian drew back for another harsh thrust as he uttered his next words.

So, I'm going.

Before she could protest, he began hammering into her violently and she shattered.

She screamed as her nails dragged across his wide back, as her walls clamped down around his length, as he groaned into her neck.

He just kept going, drawing every cry from her.

"Cassian..." she tried to say, but he was lost in his mind.

Again and again and again, he slammed into her.

She dug her nails into his shoulder. "Cassian...I-"

His chest vibrated against hers as he wrapped an arm around her waist, pulling her tighter against him as his teeth skimmed her neck.

She was so sensitive.

"Please..." she begged. She didn't even know what for.

Just when she reached her breaking point, his movements became twitchy and he shuddered as warmth flooded her channel.

Cassian kept her in his arms the whole time, his thrusts slow, shallow, as he pumped her with everything he had.

By the time she'd caught her breath, her throat was raw, legs were shaking.

He finally stilled and drew his head back.

For the last time, he moved his lips while sending his words down the link. But what Salem heard made her wish he'd never spoken.

I'll tell Deianira in the morning. I'm going.

Chapter Forty-Four

She's not going.

Cassian should have been over the moon. He should have been ecstatic, rejoicing.

But he wasn't.

Instead, he was scared. More scared than he'd ever been.

Not because he'd be fighting for his life in just over a week. That thought hadn't quite registered in his mind yet.

The reason for his fear was that Salem hadn't spoken to him since last night.

Not one word.

Not when he told her what he was going to do, not when he wrapped her in a towel and carried her to his room, not even when he laid her down on his chest, the chest that her head still rested on this morning.

Salem hadn't spoken, sent him a message, or even signed.

In recent weeks, he'd seen a new side to her. A side he liked a lot. She'd been vocal, vibrant, argumentative even.

But now?

Nothing.

The thing was, Cassian wasn't regretful over the reason for her silence. There was no way he could let her enter the trials, especially knowing that she was only doing it to protect him.

He knew that he was doing the right thing. He just wished that Salem could see it that way too.

To be honest, maybe she did understand. She was the smartest woman he'd ever met. Cassian would just never know what she was thinking because she wouldn't talk to him.

Salem hadn't even blocked him out completely. She still allowed his presence, responded to his touch, she even kissed him before she allowed sleep to take her.

He wasn't sure if that was better or worse. It certainly felt like the most painful thing he'd ever endured.

As she turned in his arms, he wondered if she might end his suffering today, put his mind at ease a little.

She didn't.

Salem rolled over and looked at him with dead eyes.

Her gaze was brutal.

Considering that it was one of the only ways she would interact with him, he didn't know if he wanted her to stop or never take her eyes off him again.

He tried to call to her.

Salem.

She finally blinked and slowly extricated herself from his hold.

It felt like a knife to the heart.

All he could do was sit back and watch her stalk over to her pile of clothes and pick them up before heading to the bathroom. On her way, she even leaned down to give Echo a small head rub.

As soon as the door closed, Cassian let his head fall back to the pillows.

I'm doing the right thing.

He repeated those words over and over in his head obsessively.

He was doing the right thing.

But at what cost?

As the water rained down on her, Salem stared at the tiles.

She'd never felt so dead.

That might have been surprising to some considering how people saw her, but it had never felt as true as it did right now.

She was positively numb.

The second those words were sent down the link last night, it was like a flip had been switched.

For the first time in her life, she had a problem and couldn't do anything to fix it. She was truly helpless.

Her previous joy at finally giving in had evaporated.

Letting go was supposed to free her, but it felt like a trap. She was stuck and had no idea what to do.

Salem didn't expect Cassian to take her place, but she should've. If she had foreseen it, she would've sent him away at the pool, she would've lied a thousand more lies.

But she couldn't take it back now.

So, despite her numbness, all that was left was...anger.

The anger she felt was at herself for her shortsightedness, but she redirected it.

Punishing Cassian was punishing herself.

She knew that she could never shut him out completely, she just couldn't deny herself his affection, his touch. But she wouldn't give him any more than that and make him think that she was okay with his decision.

As she changed, quickly and uncomfortably, into her clothes from last night, Salem realized that she had nothing to do today.

She had time off work, but she wasn't training for the trials anymore.

Her schedule was just...empty.

That had never happened before.

She frowned as a thought occurred to her.

She didn't have any hobbies or pastimes. She'd never had time for one.

Quickly running through possible activities in her head, she gathered her hair up.

At this point, she didn't care what it was, she just needed something to distract her from the never-ending pit in her gut.

She got an idea. It wasn't the most tasteful in her books, but it was something that she'd found herself enjoying recently.

Salem didn't even look in Cassian's direction as she walked out of the bathroom.

He sat up. *Sae, can we talk?*

She walked over to her activity for the day before reaching up onto his shelf on her tiptoes to grab the lead.

Salem.

Everything in hand, she made her way to the door.

Salem, where are you taking my cat?

At the lock panel, she quickly tapped a few buttons, giving herself access to his bedroom. She'd bring Echo back later.

After she swiped her bracelet to confirm, she opened the door.

Cassian must have said something because Echo looked back into the room.

Salem didn't.

As she stepped over the threshold and snapped her fingers, Echo enthusiastically followed her out.

Salem!

Salem was immensely proud of her resolve as she shut the door.

Where to now? she thought.

Chapter Forty-Five

She wasn't sure what she was doing as she stood outside Devin's door, but today, Salem was going to learn about herself. A big component of that was having friends.

She told herself that she would just ask him if he wants to hang out, or eat food, or something of the sort.

Knock, knock.

She didn't have to wait long for the door to open. Except it wasn't Devin. It was one of the twins.

Salem wasn't sure which one exactly, but the open-mouthed smile that split across her lips and the way she jumped up and down at the sight of Echo told her that it was Kendria.

Salem didn't like kids. She didn't even like kids when she was a kid.

They were far worse than adults.

They cried when they were upset instead of trying to work toward a solution, and they threw tantrums when they didn't get their way instead of reasoning or accepting. She knew that she wasn't the poster child for well-behaved children, but she could acknowledge that most of their behavior was completely illogical.

She sighed.

Today, she was doing something different. So she pushed her notions out of mind and looked down at Kendria.

"Hello..." she said very quietly.

"Cat!" was the only thing that she said as she bent down and threw her arms around Echo's neck.

Salem frowned. "Her name is Echo. Not Cat."

Just as she spoke, something startled both Echo and Kendria.

It wasn't long before she found out what it was.

Devin rounded the corner. "Kendria, I swear to the Gods!"

"I forgot." Kendria smiled as he yanked her off the ground.

"Yeah, I'm sure you did," he huffed. "One more time, and I'm taking away your bracelet."

He was turning as she protested when he noticed Salem.

Devin put Kendria down and pointed to a door on the other side of the living room.

'Hey, what does she want?' he asked as Kendria reluctantly made her way to the room.

What did who want? Salem thought.

Devin's eyes finally lowered.

'Why's Echo here?'

'I brought her,' Salem responded confidently.

He seemed confused for a second, but he shook it off.

'Is there a meeting?' He checked his wrist. *'I didn't get an alert.'*

'There isn't a meeting,' she told him.

Now, he just looked bewildered.

'Then...why... Did you need... What's up?'

Salem took a deep breath. *'I've come to hang out.'*

Devin looked at her, then stepped past her to look into the hallway.

Stepping back, he blinked.

'With me?'

'Yes.'

Why was he so surprised?

'Did Cass put you up to this?'

Salem's heart squeezed at his name.

She wanted a distraction, not a reminder. Maybe she should've just gone back to work, or taken Echo for another walk or-

'Hey, hey, I'm sorry. It's okay, you can come in,' Devin said in response to whatever he'd seen on her face.

He signed as he walked and Salem followed, tugging Echo behind her.

'Emori's asleep, but the girls are in their room if you want to hang with them for a minute. I'll have dinner on the table in an hour.'

Salem nodded and parted ways with Devin to enter the girls' room.

She wasn't sure why she was nervous. It wasn't like she hadn't been around them before. This time though, she was alone.

She carefully opened the door.

Kendria looked up from where they'd been putting makeup on something that looked a lot like a men's t-shirt, and Tyla quickly palmed something in her hand.

They watched her like hawks as she awkwardly shifted over to the corner and took a seat on a little green chair. That made her notice the rest of the room.

It was all green, gray, and black.

There. A starter.

"I like your bedroom," Salem stated.

The girls looked at each other, then back at Salem before Tyla spoke up.

"Do you wanna see my pet?"

Salem wasn't expecting the question. She didn't see any pets as she looked around the room, but now she was curious.

"Yes."

Kendria followed behind Tyla as she made her way to her.

Just as she opened her mouth to ask where this pet was, Tyla opened her hands.

Salem couldn't hold back the screech that tore from her throat as a frog jumped into her lap. She leaped out of the chair, uncaring of the twins in front of her, and ran to the bed.

As she turned back to the girls, she found them running around, chasing Echo.

Huh?

Salem cautiously took a few steps toward the chaos when she noticed a little green leg hanging out of Echo's mouth.

Tyla's mouth was wide open, mid-scream, while Kendria started aggressively slapping Salem's leg.

"She got him! Do something!" Kendria wailed.

"Echo!" Salem tried quietly. "Echo, put it down!"

In the next few seconds, Echo made it abundantly clear that she didn't care what Salem had to say.

She watched in frozen horror as Echo tossed her head back, opened her jaws, then snapped them shut.

Then, she started chewing.

Tyla's hands were on her head as she let out a sound that Salem could feel in her sternum. She couldn't focus on it for long though because she was distracted by the burning sensation in her leg.

Kendria's nails dug into her legging painfully.

"Your cat ate our frog!" she cried.

“She’s not my cat!” Salem argued back.

She had just about pried her fingers out of her skin when the door swung open.

Everybody froze.

“What the hell is going on in here?!” Devin exclaimed.

Oh no.

They’re going to tell him and then he’s going to ask me to leave and then I won’t have anything to distract me from-

Her eyes snagged on Tyla’s mouth. “Nothing.”

Salem narrowed her eyes.

Devin didn’t seem at all convinced, but he looked to Salem for confirmation.

‘Is everything okay?’

She stiffly nodded.

Maybe my new hobby should be lying, she thought, scolding herself.

Devin looked over the girls one more time before nodding to Salem and slowly closing the door.

The girls both whirled on Salem.

It was quite intimidating actually.

“Why didn’t you tell him what happened?” Salem asked quietly, leaning down.

Tyla wiped her red eyes, glaring at Salem while Kendria answered.

“O’viously ‘cause we can’t have a frog!” she said, throwing her arms out to the sides.

Oh.

“I apologize.”

They watched her for a long time before looking at each other, silently communicating.

Kendria shrugged sadly as if she was about to deliver the worst news to Salem.

"Now, you have to let us do makeup."

Bzz. Bzz.

> ***JACOBS:*** *What the hell did you do to that girl?*

Cassian frowned as his eyes skimmed over the message.

"TerraPod, pause!"

He stood up, confused, and read it again before responding.

> ***CASSIAN:*** *Devin, what are you talking about?*
> ***JACOBS:*** *What else, dumbass?*
> ***JACOBS:*** *I swear to the Gods, I'mma smack the shit out of you if you did something stupid.*

Salem?

His heart immediately picked up.

> ***CASSIAN:*** *What's wrong? Where is she?*

He wrote as he marched to the corner to pick up his boots.

JACOBS: *...*

JACOBS: *First off, chill. She's not dying. She's just at mine.*

Somehow, that didn't help.

JACOBS: *Care to explain why SALEM QIN would rather hang out with my* children *and* your cat *than spend the day with you?*

Ignoring his question, he wrote one of his own.

CASSIAN: *Why is she at your place?*

He absently noticed the way his chest began to rise and fall faster. He didn't like that one bit.

JACOBS: *That's what I'm asking you! What did you do?*

He'd tried to protect her, that's what he'd done.
But he didn't have it in him to get into it with Devin.

CASSIAN: *I'm on my way.*

JACOBS: *Why?*

That made him pause.
Why?
What was he going to do?
As anxious as her actions made him, Salem was her own person. She'd been her own person a long time before he was even born.

Even if he tried to haul her out of Devin's and force her to talk, he was sure he'd end up in the clinic.

CASSIAN: *Is she okay?*
JACOBS: *I honestly don't know. I mean, she always seems okay, but I mentioned your name earlier and she looked like she was having a stroke.*

His heart tightened painfully.
That was the last thing he wanted.
But he couldn't go to her and try to make it better without disrespecting her boundaries.

CASSIAN: *Can you please ask her to call me?*
JACOBS: *Fine, but don't think I didn't notice that you ignored my question.*

Kendria dragged the brush across Salem's forehead prompting a cringe. It felt so cakey on her skin.
"Why do you talk to my daddy like that?"
"Like what?" Salem responded, bored. She was getting really tired of the questions.
Kendria waved. "With your hands."

Salem wasn't ashamed of it. In her mind, it was a battle scar. Proof that she'd done her job well.

"I'm deaf."

Both girls looked at her, aghast.

She quickly realized their misunderstanding.

"I'm not dead. I'm deaf. It means I can't hear."

They both sagged with relief, but Tyla frowned.

"Then how come you can hear *me*?"

Salem shook her head. "I can't hear you. I look at your lips when you talk and work out what you're saying."

"That's so cool," Kendria said with wide eyes.

Tyla still wasn't having it. "If you can see me talk then why do you talk with your hands?"

She thought of an explanation that they might understand.

"I can read your lips, but if you talk too fast, it's difficult to see what you're saying. Using your hands makes it easier for me to understand."

Tyla looked at her for a good minute before nodding and looking down at her hands. "Can you show me?"

"Me too," Kendria joined.

Salem was slightly taken aback by how easy the conversation felt. They asked way too many questions, but they weren't judgemental. They were just curious.

She spent the next twenty minutes teaching them a few basic signs, the same ones that she'd learned first.

With the knowledge of her own schooling experience, Salem could tell that they were very advanced. They were inquisitive, good listeners, and they never asked a closed question. They always wanted to know more.

Kendria and Tyla reminded her of herself. The Salem that she used to be at least.

The door opened.

Devin popped his head in and did a double-take when he saw Salem. She didn't have to look far to imagine what he was seeing. The little mirror on the desk in front of her gave her a perfect view of the three ponytails her hair was in, the bright green eyeshadow on her lids, and the glitter covering her face.

Salem slowly turned to face him as he put a fist to his mouth, obviously trying to push down his laughter.

"Dinner's ready," he announced and signed, an amused smile still in place.

Kendria practically jumped up to dart out of the room while Tyla looked at her dad.

Something in Salem's chest melted as she brought her two fingers to her chin before balling her hand into a fist and rubbing her chest.

He beamed and grabbed her, throwing her in the air. "That was so good!"

Tyla was in a fit of giggles as he dropped her and sent her to wash her hands.

Once alone, Salem moved to stand but Devin put a hand out.

'Did you teach her that?'

She internally winced. He might not have been okay with that. She should've asked.

'Yes, I apologize.'

He frowned. *'Why? That's amazing.'*

Oh.

'I've been trying to teach Emori, but the girls don't pay me any mind. They listen to you though.'

'They're very intelligent,' she responded. *'Easy to teach.'*

Devin shook his head. *'I know they're smart. But they are not easy to teach. Emori's the only one they take seriously,'* he said, with a smile. *'And you now.'*

Strangely, Devin didn't seem to have a problem with that.

He looked down at the ground before looking back at Salem.

'Are you going to speak to Cass at some point?'

Her back went straight. *'You told him I was here.'*

She didn't want to see him right now.

Devin bowed his head. *'I did, but don't worry, he's not coming.'*

Though that seemed like a relief, Salem felt a small tug of disappointment at the fact.

'He's just worried about you.'

She knew this, but it wasn't enough.

Devin shook his head.

'It's okay. Go wash up, we're about to eat.'

Salem nodded and made her way to the bathroom. She also took the opportunity to wash her face and try to push all thoughts of Cassian out of her mind.

Arriving at the table, Salem remembered that she'd never eaten at Devin's before. She frowned as she stepped up to the table, trying to work out a polite way to let him know that she wouldn't be eating with them when she noticed what was on the plate at the empty seat. There was some plain chicken, potatoes, and a few vegetables, none of them touching each other.

She looked at everybody else's plates.

Not only were their dishes heavily seasoned and drizzled with sauces, but they had different drinks next to their plates, as opposed to the water that sat beside Salem's.

She didn't have to be a genius to work out what had happened.

Cassian.

She hadn't spoken to him in almost a day but he was still looking out for her, taking care of her.

That only made her feel worse.

She kept her head down and finished her food without much interaction with the Jacobs. At times, the girls would look at her, probably wondering what caused her change in behavior, but Salem just wanted to get out. She was tired of being around people.

As soon as Cassian received the message that Salem had left Devin's, he ran out of the room and waited on his doorstep.

He knew it was wishful thinking that Salem might finally cut him a break, but he knew that she had to give him his cat back, so he hoped that he might be able to talk to her.

The footsteps that he heard from down the hall only had his hope growing.

Eventually, Salem came into view, Echo trotting on her leash beside her.

Cassian's heart sped up as she drew closer.

'*Hi*,' he tried.

Salem looked up at him and held out the end of Echo's leash.

As he watched her face closely, he could've sworn he noticed a slight shimmer to her skin. He bent forward a fraction.

Glitter?

What had she been up to?

He took it from her, intentionally brushing his hand against hers. It wasn't much, but it was something.

Before her hands returned to her sides, she hesitated.

This was it.

She was going to speak to him.

He tried to steady his heart as he watched her.

'She ate a frog.'

Cassian blinked.

Echo?

'I thought you should know.'

He went to respond, thankful for the opening, as strange as it was, when something interrupted him.

Bzz. Bzz.

E#612: *Visit Request - Eulalia Sambor*

Lia?

He hadn't seen her since that last day in Deianira's room. Knowing that no one else had visited her yet, he struggled to understand why she'd reach out to him first over Cade.

Looking up again, he only had time to see Salem nod and spin around to leave.

Chapter Forty-Six

Knock, knock.

She could've been angry, apologetic, or lonely. He had no idea what to expect.

He didn't know which one would've been worse too. There was nothing he could do about her situation and while she didn't do anything to him in particular, Devin was one of their best friends. There was no excuse for what she did, good intentions or not.

An enforcer opened the door.

Not just any enforcer.

The deputy.

Finch.

Cassian sighed. This was the last thing he needed.

"Cassian!" came a voice behind the door.

Finch puffed up his chest. "I'm gonna need to check your-"

Cassian stepped around Finch, refusing to make eye contact as Lia came into view by the bed. She stopped as she came within a few feet of him.

Cassian understood her hesitation. He didn't know where they stood either. It wasn't like they got to say their goodbyes.

"Hey," he said quietly.

Lia looked behind him before beckoning him over to the corner of the room, away from unwanted ears.

"She's back."

Cassian didn't need to ask who she was referring to.

"Where?"

"The border."

By the dampness on Lia's forehead, Cassian guessed that she just had a vision.

"I don't know when they'll be here, but you need to go now," she whispered.

Cassian watched her for a second.

If there really was a threat, he couldn't ignore it. But he wasn't sure if he could trust Lia's information. He would never believe that she had malicious intent, but she could still be lying. She pulled what she did last time because she thought that she was saving everyone.

Lia must have seen the conflict on his face.

"I know I haven't given you any reason to trust me, but it's true. She's coming."

Cassian's knee bounced as he argued with himself.

Lia was his closest friend.

"I really hope you're telling the truth," he told her as he walked back toward the door.

“Why would I trust a word that comes out of her mouth?” Devin hissed.

“Because I trust her and I hope you trust me,” Cassian retorted.

Cade tried to reason. “Lie or not, what do we have to lose by being safe.”

“It could be a trap,” Deianira offered.

He disagreed. “She thought she thought she was helping us last time. She wouldn’t lie to trap us now.”

Cassian stepped up. “I don’t know how long we have, but these things don’t usually have a wide timeframe. It’s now or never.”

Deianira sighed. “Devin, call Emori.”

Devin huffed disbelievingly and tilted his head to the ceiling.

Cassian was a lot more nervous than he was letting on.

He wouldn’t be able to forgive himself if he convinced the group to walk straight into a trap. That could have been the reason that Lia requested him and no one else.

Easy to manipulate.

The thought was nothing new to Cassian. He’d been manipulated his whole life. He just hoped and prayed to any higher power that Lia wouldn’t do something like that to him.

As soon as Emori arrived, Cade explained to her what was happening.

She only nodded, seemingly disgruntled at being woken up, and directed everyone into the middle of the room.

Cassian discreetly tried to get as close to Salem as possible as they waited for the portal to open.

Emori stopped.

Pointing to Deianira, she shook her head.

She was refusing?

Deianira looked just as confused until Emori gestured to her stomach.

"I can't go because of the baby?"

Emori nodded.

"Then I'm staying," Cade offered instantly.

Devin looked over his shoulder at Salem, then Cassian.

"Oh, this should be fun," he scoffed.

Cassian rolled his eyes at Devin's observation and turned to look ahead as the sparks began.

As soon as the portal was big enough, Devin jumped through. Cassian stepped to the side allowing Salem to go first. She only spared him a look over the shoulder before she made a cat-like leap through the gap. Cassian followed soon after.

On the other side, he looked left and right, hoping that they weren't too late.

Grass.

That was the only thing he saw.

They could've been late, early, or already sitting in the trap. There was no way to know.

"What are we supposed to do now?" Devin asked, looking around.

He went to open his mouth when Salem drew Devin's gaze, cutting Cassian a look.

'We wait.'

“Well this is just painful,” Devin groaned from where he lay sprawled out on the ground.

Cassian agreed, drawing up a knee where he sat.

The only one still standing was Salem.

She hadn’t left her position since they arrived. She just stood, hands locked behind her back, staring out into the distance.

Though almost all that he’d been feeling recently was worry, some part of him was...annoyed.

He couldn’t understand why it was so easy for her to ignore him when he felt like he was dying inside.

At any given moment, all he wanted to do was reach out to her, talk to her, do anything with her. But Salem didn’t seem to have a care in the world.

The last couple of months had brought something out in him that he’d never truly felt before.

Happiness.

He thought that he was happy in the western sector, when the veil of lies was still over his eyes, when he had people that ‘cared about him’. But that wasn’t happiness. Not real happiness.

Not the feeling that took over him every time he looked at her, or woke up with her in his arms, or was on the receiving end of a blunt comment.

He wasn’t one to assume, but based on what he’d learned about her, about her past, he thought that it might have meant something to her too. It certainly seemed like it a few days ago. But he was starting to wonder if he was wrong.

Her nonchalance was killing him, and while he wished he could direct all of his anger toward her, he knew he couldn't.

Salem snapped her fingers three times.

His gaze immediately went to her.

She held both hands open and facing the ground as she slowly backed up two steps.

Cassian practically sprung up off the ground to flank her.

He didn't have time to ask what was wrong before a large portal opened in the middle of the field, much larger than the one they had taken here.

Devin quickly rose to his feet as Pola, Podak, and Potek gracefully stepped onto the field.

Neither Cassian, Devin, nor Salem did anything as they waited for something to happen.

But nothing did.

The trios just stood, maybe thirty feet apart, facing each other.

If Pola was surprised by their presence, she certainly didn't show it.

Of course, Devin started.

"What the fuck do you want now?" he drawled.

Just like that, Pola's wide smile made an appearance.

"I've missed you, Mr. Jacobs."

"Good for you. Why are you here?"

She tilted her head. "Straight down to business. I like it." Pola took a step forward. Though graceful, every move she made was calculated. It may have looked carefree or effortless, but Cassian couldn't miss the slight stiffness of her shoulders or the way her fingers didn't even twitch at her sides.

She was tense.

"I'm here to see if you've given my offer further consideration."

Devin shrugged. "Then you can go back to whatever rat's nest you crawled out of. The answer's still no."

To her credit, her smile only dimmed the tiniest bit. "You know, Devin, if you keep talking to me like that, I'm going to have to add you to the roster," she quipped as she gestured to Podak and Potek behind her.

He winced. "I would just say I'm a married man, but honestly, I don't know how I feel about sharing a bed with coo-coo, yeti, and no-fingers," he retorted.

Cassian let out an exasperated breath, but at the look of outrage on their faces and Pola's bared teeth, he hastily stepped in front of Devin.

Is he trying to get us killed?

He tried to calm them. "He didn't mean any of that,-"

"-I most certainly did-"

"-we're just not interested."

Pola quickly schooled her features. "That's disappointing," she sighed. "Don't tell Devin but you were kinda my favorite."

Devin snorted behind him. "You can have her."

She ignored him. "Well, I admire your strong will either way. But you know what I have to do now."

Cassian narrowed his eyes. "No... I don't think you'll do anything."

Pola feigned a grin. "What are you talking about, pretty boy?"

He slowly straightened his stance. "I'm talking about how you don't know where the azraels are buried. Killing us will mean you losing that."

She shook her head with a smile. "As I said before, I have the power, and I ha-"

"-and I have the time," Devin mocked. "Yeah, we remember, coocs. It would be a lot scarier if it were true though."

As Pola's expression morphed, Cassian was finally able to understand the link between her and Deianira.

She had darkness, just in a different way.

Devin carried on, obviously not noticing her shift in demeanor. "I actually think that you're on a very tight schedule."

Pola had lost all her sweetness. "Why do you think that?"

To Cassian's utter shock, it was Salem that responded.

"The combat trials," she said plainly, ignoring the way that Devin's head almost did a one-eighty.

To be fair, it was her theory, but Cassian wished she hadn't spoken. The less attention she had on her, the safer she would be. But by the way that Podak's lips tipped up, he knew 'safe' was the last thing that Salem was right now.

Pola's eyes widened before a smile crawled back onto her face. A real one. "She speaks," she beamed before pouting. "But she doesn't hear very much, does she?"

She knows.

It only took Cassian a few seconds to figure out how too.

Podak. That day in the forest.

She knew because of him.

Pola practically giggled. "You didn't really think that you could slip that one past me, did you?"

If anything, Salem stood straighter. "No, I don't hear. But I do listen. If *you* did, you'd know that your deal just became invalid. You need us, not the other way around."

"I'm sorry?" Pola said, narrowing her eyes, her body tensing further. "I need you?"

This was bad.

"Yes," Salem responded. "You need the azraels, we don't need anything from you."

Pola scoffed. "Is that so?" she asked, taking a step forward.

As Salem nodded, taking a step of her own, Cassian reached for her arm, only for his hand to be slapped away.

What are you doing?

Silence.

His heart hammering, he subtly reached for her again and was met with the same refusal.

"You don't need anything from me?" Pola questioned, her lip curling.

"Are you sure *you* can hear *me*?" she asked, tilting her head.

Salem, stop. You're gonna-

Cassian quietly winced as he hit a wall.

Then he shuddered as the link receded.

He stared at the back of her head in shock.

She blocked him.

"I would like to think that not dying would be pretty high on your list of needs."

Her recklessness aside, he needed to get Pola's attention off her.

"But you're not gonna kill us," he blurted, hoping to draw her eyes. "You'd be killing yourself."

Pola only spared him a glance. Her lips quirked as she gestured between Cassian and Salem. "What happened here?"

He took a deep breath, reminding himself that she was just deflecting.

"Last time, there was so much tension, I could practically taste it." She frowned at Salem. "He's not treating you right? I'd be happy to take him off your hands."

Cassian almost popped a blood vessel trying to push down the fresh wave of anger that assaulted him. What had him settling though was the way Salem pulled back her shoulders and inclined her head at Pola, her stare threatening.

He shook his head.

Get attention off Salem.

"You have a new candidate for the trials," he announced.

That pulled Pola out of her act. She tilted her head at him questioningly.

"I'm entering."

Pola's face was blank for a second. Then she burst out laughing. "While I would love to see you all shirtless and bloody, you're not eligible."

Devin responded for him. "Two individuals from each affinity, of prima blood, over the age of sixteen," he recited.

Cassian watched closely as she paused before bringing that smirk back. "From each *affinity*," she emphasized. "What affinity would you be from?"

She's grasping.

"Gifted," Devin declared. "We may be distantly related, but we've been part human for centuries. We're probably not even the same species anymore."

She turned her eyes back to Cassian. "So who'll be joining you? Your-"

"Just me," he said, cutting her off before she could make a comment that could change the course of the night.

She narrowed her eyes. "All that technology and you don't know that one doesn't equal two?"

Before he could even panic, Devin stepped forward. "Really? That card?"

When she only frowned, he continued with a smirk. "All that power and you're worried that a gifted little twig's gonna put you on your ass?"

Cassian looked back at him, both confused and offended.

Devin leaned to the right and addressed Podak and Potek. "You hear that? Your big, bad wife is scared of a little half-breed."

When Pola's eyes briefly flicked behind her, he realized what Devin was doing.

He was baiting her.

Pola's chest heaved. "Do what you like, but I'm getting those azraels."

Devin's smile was nothing short of condescending. "As my brother here said, there's nothing you can do."

Checkmate.

But something happened the very next second.

Cassian had to blink three times to make sure that he was seeing correctly.

Pola's eyes went white. Not the kind of white that Lia's went when she was having a vision. They were giving off light, glowing.

Shit...

Her hair began to rise, her curls separating to frame her head.

"I must admit," she said quietly. "What you tried to do here was very cute."

The sky darkened as shadows started to flow from her body. "It was a well-thought-out plan."

Cassian and Devin began to slowly step back as Pola's feet left the ground. "But you forgot one thing."

She halted, a few feet off the ground. "You don't pick a fight with someone who has nothing to lose."

That was all the warning they got before Pola let out a blood-curdling scream as the shadows extended rapidly toward them.

"RUN!" Cassian bellowed.

The three of them broke into a sprint in the direction of Old Dome territory.

Devin was a few paces ahead of Cassian with Salem in the back. Cassian slowed his pace so that she could pass him, so that he could see her. She'd only just made it beside him when a shadow swept her off her feet.

"NO!"

Cassian barely had to look at Devin for him to turn back and hurl a ball of fire at Pola.

The second the shadow receded, he ran back to where Salem had fallen and hauled her off the ground.

They kept in line with each other as they pumped their arms for dear life.

At the speed with which they were running, they didn't have time to slow down as a portal opened right in front of them.

Before Cassian knew what was happening, he was falling. He felt like he was falling forever until he smacked onto the hard ground.

Right in front of Pola.

Her scream sounded like an eagle's cry as she brought shadows down on him, holding him to the ground.

His focus wasn't even on her as she neared.

Instead, his head was whipping from left to right, looking for the others.

When he opened his mouth to call out, a shadow darted through his parted lips. After the initial shock, he became aware that he couldn't breathe. She was drawing the air from his lungs. He squirmed and writhed to no avail while Pola laughed and cackled over his shaking body.

But one look at her face made him realize something.

In her anger, in her rage, she'd left her mind unguarded.

He could use that.

Cassian didn't just poke, he dug deep.

In his condition, he couldn't focus enough to even read anything in there, he just marched around, pulling on every string he could find, trying to cause as much damage as possible.

Pola was cut off mid-laugh as she cried out, spiraling to the ground.

He used his first full breath to call out "DEVIN!"

Even with Pola down, her manipulation of the sky was still in effect.

It was hard to see, but as Cassian squinted his eyes, he managed to make out Devin and Potek hurling everything and anything at each other, but no Salem.

Salem! Where are you?!

He hit a wall.

He was still blocked.

Just as Pola started to shift on the ground, Cassian caught a small figure running in the distance.

Salem.

In an effort to slow Pola, he yanked his dagger out of his boot and sent it flying into her hand, pinning her to the grass.

He didn't wait to hear her cry before he dashed toward Salem. That was when he noticed the figure chasing her.

Podak.

Something about the way that Podak looked at her made Cassian's stomach turn. It was more than wanting to catch her.

He looked predatory.

As quick as he could, Cassian drew his gun off his belt and put as many bullets into Podak's back as the weapon would allow.

But he knew that it wouldn't hold him for long.

"Devin! We need to get back!" Cassian called as soon as he caught up with Salem.

"No shit!" he replied as he jumped a good seven feet in the air to deliver a solid left hook to the side of Potek's head.

They were at the border, at least a half-mile away from the city. Much too far for Cassian to make a link with someone. Devin couldn't portal them out and even if he could, the output would take too great a toll on him.

Before another thought could plague him, a portal opened to his left. Cassian immediately jumped away from it. But then he saw the council study, Emori, Cade, and Deianira inside.

He turned, expecting to see Salem jumping through, but she was waiting, watching Devin run toward them in the distance.

"GET IN!" he bellowed after catching her eye.

Her lips flattened and her brows scrunched as she turned away from him to look out for Devin again.

"SALEM!"

Growling, he grabbed her shoulders and pushed her in, watching her tumble into a controlled roll onto the floor of the operations room.

"Devin, come on!" he yelled, turning back.

Devin lifted his knee, then brought a foot down on the ground in front of him.

Potek went flying through the air as the ground shook, but he didn't stay to watch. He sprinted toward the portal.

Cassian stepped through the portal backward, watching as Devin approached.

He was close.

So close.

His hand even made it through.

But so did Pola's.

She grasped Devin's shoulder, yanking him away from the opening.

"Devin!"

As Cassian stepped back through, Podak's body shifted, he started getting to his feet.

Before he even made a step in their direction, a shadow grabbed his ankle, yanking him into the air.

Cassian turned around to find Deianira, feet apart, hands outstretched.

She drew a hand up slowly and pulled it down forcefully.

He turned back just in time to see Podak being swung down to the ground. Hard.

He stopped moving.

Cassian gave his attention back to Pola.

"Not a step," she hissed, an arm around Devin's shoulders, the knife that had been in her hand at his throat. "And just in case you think you're quicker than me, you're not."

"Let him go."

A muffled groan in the room had eyes finding Emori.

She was sweating. She needed to close the portal.

When Devin tried to move, shadows entrapped his arms and legs.

She stepped back, bringing Devin with her. "Tell me where they are."

"You're not going to win this."

She let out a raspy laugh. "Oh, sweetie. If I don't win, nobody does." Her face darkened. "Test me."

Pola brought the knife to Devin's hairline and pressed down as she dragged it down the side of his face.

Devin grunted in pain, squirming against her.

"Let him go!"

"Tell me where they are!"

Step to the right.

Cassian shivered at the voice.

Salem?

Move!

Knowing better than to waste time by asking questions, Cassian discreetly took a step to the right and angled his body away from Pola.

They're too close.

"I'll cut his throat next."

He needed her to move away from Devin.

"Do it," he said.

Pola wasn't quick enough to hide her surprise.

"Excuse me?!" Devin exclaimed, cocking his head back.

Got a shot?

No.

"I said do it. If you think that's gonna get you your damn azraels, you've got another thing coming."

Pola tilted her head, narrowing her eyes. "If you think that your mind games-"

Got it.

BANG!

The side of her face split open as the buckshot tore through her cheek, sending her spinning to the ground.

Cassian ran for Devin, dragging him up and back through the portal.

The second they were through, Emori closed it and fell to her knees.

"Baby..."

Devin ran to her, lifting her up into his arms.

Salem lowered the shotgun and walked back over to the wall to hang it up as Deianira and Cade approached Cassian.

"Are you okay?" his brother asked.

"I'm fine," he gritted out, watching Salem set up to exit the room.

Deianira brought his eyes back to her. "Did you tell her about the trials?"

Salem started toward the door.

"Yeah, can you give me a second?"

Cassian ignored them as they called after him and jogged over to the door just as it went to close.

Salem!

She just kept walking down the hall. So he followed.

Sae!

She still showed no signs of stopping.

Cassian lost it.

Throwing a fist into the wall beside him, he roared.

SALEM!

She whirled on him, eyes flicking to the hole in the wall.

WHAT?!

Cassian was taken aback, to say the least.

What do you want?! she yelled.

He blinked, shaking away his surprise.

Taking a step forward, he seethed. *What the hell were you thinking?!*

She didn't answer. But her eyes practically burned as she glared at him.

He shook his head, not even recognizing her.

You blocked me... he rasped.

You were distracting me...

His jaw dropped. *From getting yourself killed?!*

Her gaze grew even colder.

The same way you're about to? I'm going to get myself killed by conversing with three primas, but you're not by taking on ten of them? Alone?

He pointed a finger at her. *First of all, if you thought I'd let you go into that death match anyway, you're not as smart as I thought you were.*

Her brows dipped.

And second, Salem, you told me that you lied about being the most fit to go. What did you expect me to do?

I expected you to respect my decision to go.

He threw his arms out. *Then, why can't you respect mine?!*

Because it wasn't supposed to be you!

Yes, it was! he yelled down the link. *You knew it was meant to be me and you lied to make the exact same decision I'm making right now! You can't seriously be mad at me for that.*

Her chest heaved as she quieted, but he wasn't done.

You are the only *person around here that has never treated me like I'm some depressed kid that needs a hug, and all of a sudden you're lying for me? Why? You don't think I can do it?*

You're not a number, she argued.

Cassian frowned, confused. *What?*

You are not a number! she yelled. *You have thoughts! And feelings!*

Salem, what are you-

She cut him off. *There are extraneous variables and uncontrollable factors...*

Cassian shook his head. *Salem, you know that if anyone can do it, it's me. Why don't you want to admit that?*

I only lied to protect you, she retorted defensively.

And why do you think I'm going?!

Salem paused, sputtering.

He frowned, taking a breath.

Did she really not know?

That's not your job, she said quietly, firmly.

He narrowed his eyes. *And what makes it your job to protect me?*

Salem looked him dead in the eye, her face scrunched, her hands shaking like she was a bomb about to-

EVERYTHING!

He flinched at the pure rage he heard in her voice as she advanced a step.

Everything makes it my job! I'm a SENTINEL! It's what I was raised to do! It's all I've ever known! But you used my words against me!

She took another firm step forward.

Cassian could only step back.

I only admitted to lying to give you peace of mind, but you TOOK that, and USED it, and now I CAN'T DO MY JOB! she screamed. *Why am I even here if I can't do the one thing that I was taught to do?!*

The second the words stopped, Salem's eyes widened as she brought a hand to her lips, stepping back.

You can't seriously believe that... he whispered, his heart breaking for her despite his own anger.

Salem was antsy all of a sudden.

I don't want to talk about this anymore.

He wasn't having it. *Well, I do. Do you really think that you're only here to protect the people around you?*

I said I don't want to talk about this anymore.

That's too bad, Salem! I do!

She didn't shy away at his tone.

Something in her eyes changed though, like a little bit of life left them.

He recognized it straight away.

She looked just like her old self. And he hated it.

Her face relaxed as she tilted her head.

It is too bad, Cassian. But I'm Deianira's sentinel, not yours. My job is to protect her, not you. So enter the trials or don't. March into that forest and die if you want to. You're none of my concern anymore.

He couldn't move.

He couldn't speak.

Cassian was rooted to his spot. He stayed in the same place a long time after she'd walked away.

Of course, he'd expected pushback, but not like this.

He'd only hoped that she'd let him go, not give up on him altogether.

Chapter Forty-Seven

You're none of my concern anymore.

Salem had never uttered anything so false in her entire life. She had no idea where all the anger came from.

She'd kept her head down her whole life, did what she was told, never complained. But she couldn't keep it in this time. It felt like he was taking away the only thing she had to offer him.

She hated it. Hated the thought that he might die doing something that she was meant to do.

It made her feel useless.

Salem was too focused on her inner tumult to notice the figure that came around the corner.

After nearly running into him, she looked up to see someone who she really didn't want to deal with today.

Finch.

"Oh. Hey, Salem."

After everything that had happened, Salem wasn't in the mood for niceties.

She didn't nod or greet him back. She just waited for him to say whatever it was that he wanted to say.

Finch's eyebrows lowered before he shook it off. He leaned in close.

"Earlier, I heard Eulalia telling Cassian about a possible attack."

Salem did not like the way that he spat out Cassian's name. "I'm the Deputy so if something's going on, I should know about it."

Salem wanted to roll her eyes. Something she'd never even done before.

She typed out a message instead.

> ***QIN:*** *You're the Deputy, Cassian's the Head. If anyone needs to know, it's him, so I can assure you that your involvement is not needed. Do you have any other unnecessary concerns or can I go?*

Finch seemed taken aback by her words.

Salem knew that she could be blunt at times, but she always did her best to come across as polite.

That excluded this conversation.

He narrowed his eyes and tilted his head.

"I take my job very seriously. A lot more seriously than you do apparently, taking time off just to avoid me. Real mature."

Salem was almost amused at how incorrect he was, but also bored by his ability to make everything about himself. She would've loved to correct him, but the current issue was a sensitive one. No one other than those in the High Council were privy to that information.

Finch huffed out a laugh. "Nothing to say? Just as I thought. You know, you have some nerve walking around here like you're the Gods' gift to Terra when-"

In the middle of Finch's rant, Salem realized something.

She might not have been able to explain the circumstances to him, but she didn't have to stand there and let him ridicule her for something that he couldn't even begin to understand. She outranked him, she had no obligation to listen to him.
"-You think you're better than me, is that it? Would you have given me a chance if I abandoned my family for six years and came back with a rodent and a bad attitude?"
With her previous thought in mind, Salem averted her eyes from Finch's mouth and turned. She took a deep breath before she started walking again, away from him.
She couldn't remember the last time she felt so weightless.
If it wasn't for her conversation with Cassian, she might have even been proud of herself, but she didn't think that there was anything that could pull her out of that hole.
So she went home. She didn't know what she'd do when she got there, but she just needed to be alone.

Chapter Forty-Eight

Easel set up and paints in place, Salem took a seat on her little stool and stared at the blank canvas.

Painting.

This was how she'd been spending her time over the past week. Trying things she'd never tried before, cooking different foods, even going out without a reason to.

The more time she spent on these activities, the less time she would have to stress about the current predicament.

She picked up the paintbrush and gently dipped it in the blue pot. Blue was her favorite color so it made sense to start with that.

She jumped right in.

She gently swiped the brush across the canvas a few times before switching to a light shade of pink, folding it in with some yellow. After a while, she swirled together some red and white before adding that into the mix.

Thirty minutes in, Salem abandoned the stool and chose to stand, moving around the canvas to get her angles perfect.

She was on a roll.

When her eyes hadn't left the canvas for a while, she started to wonder how much time had passed.
The lights pulsed.
Her shoulders dropped.
Just when she was beginning to enjoy herself, she got interrupted.
Salem carefully placed the brush down, careful not to get any paint on her floors, and padded over to the door.
Upon opening it, she found no one.
Well, not no one.
A cat.
Echo.
Her tail slapped against the floor as she stared up at Salem.
Salem eased back into the room. She really didn't want to run into Cassian if he came to look for her.
"Go home," she whispered.
As Echo swayed, Salem noticed a small piece of paper stuck in her collar.
After checking the hallways again, she bent down and retrieved it from her. Opening it up, Salem read.

> *I know you don't want to see me right now, but she wants to see you. I'll be in the training room all day if you want to talk.*

He left her on purpose.
Salem wasn't sure if she was pleased or annoyed by the gesture. Despite wanting to keep him out of her mind, she couldn't help the warm feeling that bloomed in her chest at the thought that he was still thinking about her, even when she'd lashed out at him.

As she stepped aside, Echo got the message, standing up and passing her. She ran right up to where Salem had her paints set up.
Salem closed the door and jogged up to her to stop her from making a mess when she noticed that Echo's eyes were fixed on the painting. Her tail stood straight, her head tilted.
Looking back at the painting, Salem frowned as she found what she was staring at.
How hadn't I realized?
The whole time that she was working, she'd been painting him. It was right there, clear as day. His eyes, his mouth, even his short pale hair.
She hadn't even planned it.
Salem took the painting off of the easel and placed it on the floor, facing the wall.
Echo quickly lost interest and walked away, but she called her back.
"Echo." She turned around. "Do you want to go for a walk?"
She doubted that Echo understood what she was saying, but the look of excitement in her eyes told Salem that a walk was a perfect idea.
She set off to grab her boots when movement under the door caught her eye.
A thin envelope slid under the doorframe, halting near her foot.
It had to have been Cassian.
But why wouldn't he have just written whatever he needed to say in the note he left with Echo?
Frowning, she went to pick it up.

"TerraPod," Devin called. "Zoom in," he instructed as the images displayed across the screens in the operations room enlarged.
He indicated the middle one.
"This whole thing? Nanotech," he smiled proudly. "Not even a bullet's getting between those threads. I even doubled up on the chest piece. You know, vital organs and all that good shit."
"How is me wearing this any different from me wearing kevlar?" Cassian asked, trying his best to engage despite his lack of enthusiasm.
The suit looked good.
At the top, it looked like a normal tight black t-shirt, but looking closely, you could see the thick mesh-like pattern on the material. Even the black pants looked like standard issue enforcer uniform, but it was connected to the top by the thick belt in the middle with several holsters and compartments.
It looked practical, comfortable.
He just didn't see why Devin was going all out.
Devin's face lost all of its joy.
He sputtered. "Kev-kevlar?" he exclaimed, his voice reaching a concerningly high pitch. "I show you this piece of art and you're asking about kevlar? It's like asking what's the difference between chocolate and vanilla ice cream?"
Now Cassian was really confused.
"I...like them both?"
Devin scoffed. "Vanilla is the shittiest flavor and you know it!"
Cade put his hands on Devin's shoulders, holding back a laugh. "Okay. Why don't we let Devin finish explaining."

Cassian tamped down his snort. "Yes, please continue."

Devin shot him a glare.

"As I was saying, while you're in this thing, you're bulletproof. That doesn't mean you should try to shoot yourself in the chest at close range," he quickly added. "It won't get through, but the impact will probably send you into cardiac arrest."

"I'll make sure to not do that," he said, nodding.

Devin gave him a bored look before continuing.

"I can remotely monitor and regulate your temperature through the suit." He waved a hand as Cassian raised his in question. "You'll be in the forest until it's over. That could take days and we don't know enough about the weather conditions near Patriam. Better safe than sorry. Also, this only protects you from physical attacks, but as you know, their biggest advantage against you is their power."

"Cassian's pretty powerful too," Cade said.

"So he doesn't want the elixir I produced to temporarily disable their abilities?" Devin drawled.

Cassian looked up. "He wants it. He definitely wants it." Anything to increase his chances.

Devin snorted. "It's still being synthesized, but it'll look like this."

A little black vial showed up on the screen.

"I managed to get a trace of the stuff that Po-squared used to nap us off of the oxygen scrubbers. It's pretty strong but you'll need some way to get it into their system. Eyes, mouth, nose."

"What about through cuts?" Cade asked. "Like if he was to douse his weapon with it."

Devin frowned. "That's actually a good idea." He rolled his eyes. " Fine. I'll get you some coated bullets." He made a quick note on his bracelet. "Weapons are up next."

Devin's eyes flicked to Cassian's before focusing on the screen. "I asked Salem to help me design this one."

Cassian was stunned.

Not in a bad way or a good way.

Just confused.

She didn't want him to go, but she helped Devin design his weapons.

He looked up at the screen.

A battle-axe.

"The handle's made out of a material similar to bamboo that I chemically modified. High tensile strength, lightweight. Obviously, we couldn't pair that with steel for the head because of the weight distribution, so we went with something a little different." He paused for effect. "Fortium."

It looked like any other metal, but it shined like it was alive. Cassian stared closer at the holographic display. He'd never seen anything like it.

"I'd never even heard of it until she suggested it. I've been running tests on it and technically it's not a metal and it's not *not* a metal. Its properties are all over the place. The only one you need to be concerned about though? Anything can sharpen it."

Cade frowned. "Is that a good thing?"

Devin shook his head, exasperated, muttering under his breath, before responding. "The more you use it, the sharper it gets. Every time you wack some shit with that, it comes back better."

Oh.

Cassian took his eyes off the screen and looked at Devin.

"Thank you for all of this. Really."

Devin's head went down as he lost some of the stage presence that was there a second ago.

"Nah, I was just bored, so I thought, why not. You kinda did take my job, so I needed something to fill my time."

Cassian shook his head, rolling his eyes. Even amongst the humor though, Devin needed to understand.

"I mean it. Thank you."

Devin shook it off. "It wasn't all me. As I said, Salem helped me design the axe. And I may have designed the suit, but Cade's the one making it."

Chapter Forty-Nine

Cassian grunted and panted as he swung his arm up to put the pole through the next opening. Left hand ahead, he removed the pole in his right hand and gritted his teeth, straining to hold his weight as he repeated the action, climbing further.

It wasn't just a test of strength. Being able to hold his body weight up on one arm was hard enough, but he had to be precise when trying to place the short pole into the hole above. The holes in the wall were made to fit the poles almost exactly, nothing bigger. So one wrong move and-

"Heads up!"

That's all that was said before a knife hit the wall, right beside his head.

He reflexively released the poles and plunged the twenty-foot drop back to the ground.

Although he had been facing the wall, his back to the entrance, he knew exactly who it was. Only one person in the palace was that insane.

He groaned as he got up and spun, glaring at her.

“Are you out of your fucking mind?!” he asked, panting.

“Yes,” Deianira responded with a sweet smile.

Cassian rubbed a hand over his head. “Seriously, you’ve got to stop. You could’ve hit me.”

Her head cocked back, screwing him. “Don’t insult me. If I wanted you dead, I wouldn’t have said ‘Head’s up’ first, would I?”

He just shook his head, mouth open in disbelief.

Deianira rolled her eyes and proceeded into the room. As she got closer, Cassian noticed something in her hand.

A bottle.

A bottle of whiskey.

His brows furrowed harshly.

Cassian knew that Deianira was a little nutty, but he would’ve never thought that she would put her baby-

“Oh my Gods, would you stop looking at me like that!” She raised the bottle and showed the closed seal. “It’s not for me.”

Phew.

“It’s for you, dumbass,” she declared as she removed her shoes and took a seat on the mat.

Cassian let out a breath and took the spot next to her. “Why?”

She placed the bottle between them. “I don’t know. You haven’t said much about how you feel about this whole trials thing. But I assume you must be nervous.” She laid back on the mat and looked up at the ceiling. “It’s the same one that Cade and I drank the night before the Prima Ball.” Her face broke into a small smile. “We got drunk. We had fun and,” The humor faded. “I said some things...But he didn’t let me get away with it. He made sure that I knew that he’d be sticking around.” She finally met Cassian’s eyes with a laugh. “And he's put up with me for the past seven years so I swear by the whiskey. Drink."

As Cassian reached for the bottle, he thought about Deianira's words.

That did sound like Cade. Sticking around even when people tried to push him away, putting others' needs before his.

He took a swig and let it wash down.

"Damn," Deianira said beside him.

"What?"

She shrugged. "I was kind of hoping you would choke so I could call you a bitch."

Cassian couldn't help but snort. "Me and whiskey are old friends," he said quietly.

Deianira just rolled her eyes humorously.

She inched herself up on her elbows.

"How are you feeling though? About the trials?"

Cassian shrugged. "I don't know. I'm trying not to think about it."

"What does that mean?"

"I just don't want to get in my head. If I keep telling myself that they're stronger and faster, I'm only setting myself up for failure. So, I'm just training. For a random event."

She nodded thoughtfully. "That makes sense." She sat up and dusted off her arms. "Well, if you're already training-"

"No!" he said before she could finish her sentence.

Cassian got up and took several steps away.

Deianira stood too. "Why so boring, Cass?"

He put his hands up. "I refuse."

It wasn't just her safety he was worried about.

It was his.

Not just from her, but Cade too.

She threw her arms up as she tilted her head. "Come on. Three rounds, that's it."

Cassian knew that there wasn't a way to win this. If he fought her, he could potentially hurt the baby, get hurt himself, and then get put in the clinic by Cade. And there was no way to turn her down either. Any second now, Deianira would launch herself at him.

Just when he thought he'd have to make a run for it, she conceded.

"Fine," she huffed. "But you have to drink. It's good luck."

Chapter Fifty

Salem picked the piece of paper up for the twenty-first time today.

No matter how many times she read it, she wasn't satisfied.

So she just read it again.

As the lights pulsed, she flinched.

She never used to have visitors, but now it felt like someone was always outside.

Alarm struck in her mind when the lights didn't stop at three.

It just continued, over and over.

Pulse. Pulse. Pulse. Pulse. Pulse.

She reached under the table and swiftly pulled down the handgun strapped to the bottom, already on her way to the door. When she got there, she put her back to the wall next to the door and rested her hand on the handle.

Three,

Two,

One.

She pushed the door out of the way while stepping out in front of the stranger, gun cocked and aimed at his chest.

Not a stranger.

Cassian.

She lowered the gun and quickly stepped back.

What is he doing here?

"... woah... was hot..."

Salem could barely understand a word he said. His lips were moving so slow and so fast at the same time.

His eyes widened as he brought his hands up.

'Sorry. I'm a little forgetful.'

No, he wasn't.

He was drunk.

Despite all her promises to herself, Salem sighed and stepped aside, letting him in.

First, his brows rose, then his face softened as he started moving his feet.

Just before he entered, he grabbed the back of her neck and dropped a kiss on her forehead.

Salem flinched, surprised by the gesture, but Cassian didn't seem to notice.

As she closed the door, she watched him unsteadily remove his shoes and nudge them to the side, right next to hers.

She finally faced him.

'You're drunk.'

Cassian frowned and shook his head vehemently. *'No.'*

At her straight face, he gave her a droopy smile. *'Yes.'*

Salem almost cracked a smile at his goofy face but managed to keep it down.

'Why did you come here?'

She probably knew why, but it wasn't something she wanted to search for. She wanted him to say it.
His hands moved painfully slowly as his face dropped. *'I missed you.'*
That same warmth bloomed in her chest.
'And you won't talk to me,' he signed, his face falling further, his nose scrunching. *'And tomorrow, I'm gonna do something really fucking scary, you know.'*
Guilt drowned out that feeling of warmth as Salem took in his words.
'You don't have to be happy about it.' Cassian strolled over to the bed and threw himself back on it. *'But it would be nice to have you on my side. I want to be your concern.'*
Her lips parted.
This isn't what she had intended at all.
Salem didn't want him to doubt himself or think that she wasn't on his side. She just wanted him safe.
How didn't he see that?
He closed his eyes and began murmuring to himself.
Echo didn't move from the corner where she lay, but her head popped up as she watched him curiously.
Salem hesitantly approached the bed, dropping the gun on the table, and sat beside him. The second the bed dipped, he startled.
"Woah!" he exclaimed. "...like a ninja."
She shifted closer, staring down at him.
'I am on your side. But that doesn't mean I'm going to support you when I think you're making a bad decision.'
He stared at her for a while before reaching out to touch her face. She stayed still as his hand stroked across her cheek before tracing the edges of her lips.

Can we pretend?

Goosebumps spotted the back of her neck at his voice.

Pretend what?

He sighed, dropping his hand, still gazing deep into her eyes.

Pretend that tomorrow's gonna be a normal day. Just for tonight. His throat bobbed. *Because if I leave like this, Salem... I will die.*

Ice filled her veins at his words. He meant them too. Nothing about the way he looked at her, or his tone, suggested that it was a joke.

Pretend.

That's all he wanted.

Contrary to what others might say, Salem was emotionally intelligent. She could compartmentalize when necessary. On numerous occasions, she'd put her emotions on the back burner to complete a task. So she could do it again to give Cassian this one thing.

Salem leaned back onto her bed and nestled against his chest.

Whatever he'd been drinking had obviously given him the courage to come over and say all of that, but she could still feel the shaky breath that left him as he wrapped his arms around her and pulled her on top of him.

He didn't even do anything, just held her, his nose buried in her neck.

You smell like paint.

Salem tensed against his chest, an explanation on her tongue.

Best fucking paint I ever smelled.

This time, she did smile. She'd never seen him like this.

He wasn't even making sense but she didn't want him to stop talking. Ever.

She sighed, her smile fading as worry started to cloud her mind.

Getting intoxicated wasn't a good idea, she said softly. *It'll put you at an even greater disadvantage.*

He stiffened. *You think I'm at a disadvantage?* he sent quietly.

Salem clenched her eyes shut, scolding herself for her lack of tact.

She tried to reword her comment, leaning up to look down at him.

You're very strong. It just wouldn't be wise to even give them a chance against you.

Apparently, she'd chosen the right words because as his chest deflated, a small smirk poked out.

I am very strong, he sent proudly.

Salem sighed, relieved. *You are.*

His smile widened even further.

I broke Finch's jaw, he slurred merrily.

Her chest bumped with a short laugh. *You did. He needed three healing sessions.*

Cassian couldn't have looked happier and just for a second, she was too.

His eyes caught her lips. *I like it when you smile.*

She tilted her head, warming all over.

Pulling her back down, Cassian laughed softly.

Pretty Salem...

Her heart was too full.

As she melted further, hiding her smile in his chest, she found herself wanting to do something that she'd never done freely before.

Maybe it was because of how at ease she felt but she was sending the words before she could even think about them.

I got a letter.

He looked up at her and tilted his head.

From who?

She took a breath. *My father.*

For a second, he looked surprised, then something unreadable passed over his expression as his eyes locked onto hers.

She brushed it off, continuing. *He said that he was sorry. And that he wants to see me.*

Cassian cleared his throat. *Do you want to see him?*

She had to think about that.

I don't know. I thought that I did. She paused. *I went to the clinic today.*

If anything, he tensed even more. *What did he say?*

She shook her head. *He wasn't there. Mikhael said that he was involved in a brutal mugging and he would be off for a few days.*

His eyes flicked away from her.

I'm not going to go again.

He glanced back up.

Then why did you go today?

I don't know. I thought I'd work it out when I spoke to him. But I don't want to talk to him anymore.

He pulled her closer up on his chest.

You don't have to.

She nodded, readying herself to say her next words. They made her feel the strangest.

But I do want to see my brothers.

Cassian's eyes darkened. *He told you?*

When Salem frowned, he shook his head.

I mean, he told you that he has other kids?

She slowly nodded. *Yes. Two. Their names are Donnie and Aiko.*

Cassian watched her closely. *Are you okay with that?*

Yes. I haven't had siblings before.

And you want to?

Her heart picked up at the thought, but weirdly enough, it wasn't in a bad way.

Her lips kicked up again as she lowered her face into his chest.

I do.

Chapter Fifty-One

Cassian couldn't have woken up in worse condition. His throat was dry, head was pounding, vision was blurry. But for some reason, none of that seemed to bother him. He knew exactly why too.

It wasn't rare that he'd wake up first, but considering the day that Cassian had ahead, he was savoring every moment.

There wasn't an inch of Salem's face that he didn't examine.

Her thick dark lashes, her thin pert nose, her small yet plump lips. He even strained his eyes through his foggy vision to look at each individual hair on her straight brows.

Her face was perfect. Symmetrically perfect.

Cassian wasn't surprised by that. Not that he thought she'd be anything but, but she had the same number of lashes on each eye, her eyebrows were plucked to perfection, even her hairline was flawless.

Everything about it said Salem.

She shifted an inch in his arms.

He wasn't ready for this to be over yet. After all, this might be the last time.

Wrapping an arm around her waist, he hooked the other under her bottom before scooting her upwards on his body, holding her closer.

Salem lifted her head up from his neck and stared deep into his eyes. Her gaze was knowing. It was like she was thinking exactly what he was.

The last time.

As much as he hoped that it wasn't, this could've been their goodbye.

He was going to make it a real one.

Ignoring his pulsing headache and dizziness, he leaned up and gently captured Salem's lips with his.

She responded immediately.

She understood.

This time started slower, more intimately.

He was tugging at her leggings while she was reaching for his shirt, their lips never leaving each other's as their bodies danced together. They were a tangle of limbs until they'd managed to abandon their clothes.

When he tried to roll them over, he was surprised to feel Salem's hand push at his shoulder, pressing him back down to the bed.

Cassian eagerly received her as she leaned back down to kiss him. He took her lips ravenously while his hands worked below, tugging his length to her center. As he brushed the tip against her opening, he was rewarded with her shudder and nip at his lip.

Mouth never leaving hers, he slowly pushed at her hips, guiding her down onto himself with a deep groan. There was no pausing. Not even as she let out a quiet squeal, trying to shift around on him.

The second he bottomed out, he lifted her again and brought her back down, pulling a satisfied moan from Salem's lips.

Again and again, she rose and fell until they established a steady rhythm that had Cassian threatening to finish early.

Pulling her down, he held her hips and rocked her back and forth.

He couldn't take his eyes off her as her head fell back with a blissful gasp.

The last time.

He was going to make it worth it.

Putting a hand on her back, he pulled her against him, eliminating the space between them. Just as Salem readied herself to move, Cassian drew his knees up and thrust upwards.

She bucked on impact, but he didn't stop at one.

With the force of his thrusts, it didn't take long for her to begin to squirm, for her knees to start shaking. As their lips parted and Salem started panting, Cassian didn't speed up or slow down. He just pinned her to his chest and kept his pace, every muscle in his body tensing as her channel tightened around him.

"Cassian..." she cried in his ear as she climaxed.

Good Gods...

That voice.

He almost lost it right then, but he needed to give her more, everything.

Cassian spun around with her in his arms.

Salem limply fell with him as he positioned himself above her.

With one swift thrust, he was back in.

"Ahh..." Salem moaned, putting a hand to his chest.

One more, he groaned.

She didn't remove her hand, but her legs spread wider.

His movements weren't hurried. He moved deep, slow. He wanted to drive her crazy, and by the way she was leaving red marks down his chest, it was working.

"Please..."

He didn't even need to be prompted. He couldn't deny her when, in Salem terms, she was quite literally begging for it.

He pressed closer, chest to chest, his face buried in her neck, as he picked up his pace. He was dangerously close to spilling, but he could feel her legs beginning to tremble again.

Cassian abandoned his rhythm altogether and just gave it to her. His thrusts became harder, faster. He had no idea how he was holding on with the noises she was making in his ear.

Lifting a hand, he brushed her hair away from her eyes and met them.

Again, Sae.

I can't, she cried, as she dragged a hand down his chest, pushing at his pelvis.

You can, he murmured, giving a shallow thrust against the resistance.

Her hand held steady as she squealed, clenching down on him even further.

Cassian had to look away and bite down a groan.

He met her eyes again, his voice firm.

Move your hand, Sae.

Her eyes were squeezed shut as she took a few short breaths and slowly pulled her hand back.

He dropped a soft kiss on her lips. *Good girl...*

Finally free of restrictions, he drove forward as hard as he could.

Salem let out a broken cry as her legs locked around him. But there was nothing that could've been done to slow his crazed pace as he rutted her.

Cassian lowered his head into her neck as she found her release again, letting out a scream that could've been heard all the way in the arena.

That's it, he moaned, shaking as she squeezed him almost painfully.

He drove into her, finally allowing his release to consume him.

Her breaths were strained as she continued crying out, aftershocks sending her hips into a frenzy.

She was wild, untamed, but he kept on until she pushed against his chest again.

He slowed, but didn't stop until he'd wrung out every last drop of bliss from her body.

When she finally stilled, he didn't roll off of her. He just stared at her as she blinked groggily.

His eyes were the first thing she sought out.

They said no words to each other. They didn't have to.

The message was clear.

No more pretending.

It was time to face reality.

Chapter Fifty-Two

This morning had been exactly what Salem was avoiding. She could pretend for a night, that was fine. But falling back into bed with him only to say goodbye hours later?

This was what she didn't want.

She wasn't stupid enough to believe that if she hadn't slept with him, seeing him leave would've been easier, but somehow this felt so much worse.

Their whole exchange after had been awkward, mechanical. She'd told him that she was okay when he had asked, but she was far from it.

She was panicking.

He was slipping right through her fingers and there was nothing she could do about it. It felt like her throat was closing.

Salem startled as a large hand fanned in front of her face.

'Sorry. Are you okay? You look kind of pale.'

Devin.

Salem nodded stiffly, stepping around him as she started up her aimless walk through the palace again. She might have been losing it, but she had no recollection of why she came out, and she never forgot anything.

The thought made her giggle. A perfect memory and she couldn't even remember why she had left her room.

It didn't take long for a hand to tap her shoulder.

Salem turned to Devin again.

'Okay, that wasn't fucking creepy at all. Do I need to call someone for you?'

She straightened her face and shook her head.

Devin eyed her with concern.

'Have you eaten today?'

Salem checked her wrist.

14:51.

She didn't remember making lunch. Or breakfast.

That had her mind spiraling even faster.

Salem's whole life revolved around schedules. Something so instinctive as eating would never usually slip her mind.

'Woah, okay, come with me.'

She didn't even object as Devin took her shoulders and guided her through the palace.

It took a good thirty seconds for her to realize that he'd brought her to the kitchen.

When Devin released her, she just stood there, so he faced her.

'What's going on? I've never seen you like this.'

Salem didn't want to respond so she didn't.

She kind of liked this new thing, doing whatever she wanted.

Devin's head tilted.

'Are you hungry?'

She'd answer that one.

'Yes.'

He let out a relieved breath.

'What do you like? I'm basically the chef at home so put me to work. Anything.'

She didn't even have to think about it. It was just sitting at the forefront of her mind.

'Ham sandwich.'

He blinked.

'I tell you I can make you anything, and you want a ham sandwich?'

'Yes.'

He sighed.

'Whatever, what do you want in it? You can go crazy with the vegetables but I think they only have a couple of sauces,' he signed before walking over to the cupboards.

'Nothing. Just the ham and bread, please.'

Devin stared at her for a long time.

"I fucking give up..." he muttered as he rolled his eyes and reached for the loaf of bread.

Her stomach finally full, Salem could think a bit more clearly. Her heart was still beating a mile a minute, but she could at least identify the root of her anxiety.

'So, do you want to talk about why I ran into Zombie Salem this afternoon?'

Salem shook her head politely.

He sighed and thought about something.

'I don't want to get in between you and Cass, assuming this is about him, but is there anything I can do?'

Salem was already in panic mode so hearing Cassian's name had little effect.

'No. And I'd appreciate it if you didn't tell him about this. He needs to stay focused today.'

Devin narrowed his eyes. For a second, Salem thought he might pry, but he eventually nodded.

'Whatever this problem is, I'm sure it'll be okay.'

She highly doubted that.

He stood still for a moment, his eyes moving as if he was debating something.

He sighed. *'I have a little sister. Well, not little, we're only eleven months apart,'* he signed, smiling down at the floor. He glanced back up. *'When we were in school, I got tossed around a little from time to time and she was always the one fighting my battles.'* He chuckled. *'I didn't exactly help my situation, but I still appreciated it. Whenever I'd get into trouble with another kid and got all down about it, she'd tell me, if you can't do anything about it, then stop worrying, it's out of your hands. But if you can do something about it, then do it. Problem solved, and therefore, nothing to worry about. At first, I thought she was telling me to just deal, to stop whining. But that wasn't it. She was telling me to stand up for myself. To do something about it.'* Devin met her eyes with a soft look. *'So if there's something you want to tell him, something that's bothering you, you tell him. You still can.'*

She hadn't finished processing his words before she nodded and turned away, her eyes burning. But what he said did invoke something in her.

'Thank you,' she told him. And she meant it.

Chapter Fifty-Three

It didn't take a genius to figure out that Salem was acting strange this morning. To be fair, Cassian thought that he must have been acting pretty strange too.

How were you supposed to act on your potential day of death?

There wasn't much that he remembered from the night before, but he did recall asking her to pretend. Asking her to act like today would be a normal day, and to her credit, she did. But that time was up.

What could he expect from her today?

Would she be back to icy? Angry? Sad even?

Cassian wouldn't know.

He'd been in the arena for hours, training up until the last second. Some time to himself seemed perfect too. He knew that these last few hours of training wouldn't do much to help his situation but it was as good a distraction as he could find.

He dropped the medicine ball and fell to the floor in a sweaty heap.

He needed to stop. Any more and he'd end up hurting himself, which was the last thing he needed.

Finally taking a breath, he went over to the sidelines to pick up his bracelet from where he'd abandoned it.

It's not that it restricted his exercise, he just wanted to shut everyone out for a while.

And rightfully so because he was bombarded with messages the second he turned it on.

> ***JACOBS:*** *Where are you? I need to give you a briefing.*
>
> ***JACOBS:*** *Hello?*
>
> ***RIKAR:*** *There's a meeting in the operations room. You're late.*
>
> ***JACOBS:*** *I'm on my way to your room.*
>
> ***ALDEN:*** *Devin needs to talk you through some things before tonight. Where are you?*
>
> ***JACOBS:*** *Nevermind. I'll just track you.*
>
> ***RIKAR:*** *Cassian, are you having second thoughts?*
>
> ***JACOBS:*** *Cass, why the hell is your bracelet off?!*
>
> ***ALDEN:*** *If you've changed your mind, I can go.*

Cassian skimmed over the messages with wide eyes before checking the time.

18:47

Okay, maybe, he shouldn't have taken off his bracelet.

He made haste, shoving his feet into his shoes, picking up his shirt, and throwing his belongings into his bag.

Cassian all but tumbled into the operations room.

Deianira, Cade, and Devin, all spun at his arrival.

"I'm here! I'm doing it," he panted before anyone could speak.

It was silent for a while before Deianira nodded solemnly.

"Take a seat."

He obeyed quickly, but couldn't help but notice something.

Where's Salem?

Devin wasted no time in launching into his briefing.

"Okay. This time, the trials are being held in the Patrias forest on the other side of River Terra. At midnight, Emori will transport you to the treeline where the other combatants will be. We won't be allowed to enter once it starts so we'll be here watching your every move through this."

Devin placed a small box on the table. A box he'd seen before.

"These are clear lenses, similar to the ones you were issued for the research op, but they're only for visuals." His face tightened. "You can only keep 'em in for three days. It's the longest I could do."

Cassian glanced up. "What if I'm there for longer than that?"

Devin responded in a placating tone. "We won't be able to see you, but we'll still be able to talk. We're going to be checking your location and vitals using your bracelet too."

He was nodding, somewhat satisfied.

"The trials don't actually begin once you enter the forest. You're given an hour to get yourself situated, spread out, and when you hear the signal, then you start. A kill before the signal is grounds for elimination."

"And elimination is..." Cassian warily asked.

Devin nodded grimly. "Death."

Cade took the floor before Cassian could let that sink in.

"I used the intel from your research op to put together a list of your opponents. The more you know about them, the better." He looked nervous, which was understandable considering the circumstances. "The pairs joining already know each other well. For example, from the Empaths, you have Sven and Hanson. They're-"

"Wait, Sven?"

Cade nodded. "Yeah." He flicked his eyes to Devin momentarily. "Lia included him in her report."

Cassian took a deep breath. He wasn't sure about the guy, didn't know what to make of him, but a familiar face couldn't hurt.

Cade continued. "So, Sven and Hanson. They're friends and they may seem softer than the rest, but they're not. Good thing for you though, their fathers were killed by Pola and they're out to get her first. They believe that the azraels have been reigning for too long and want their turn." He looked unsure about the next part. "Apparently, they have some ties to the resistance. I'm not saying that you should consider them allies, but try not to take them out if they're doing the work for you."

Devin took over.

"Psionics. Malia and Dana. They're twins and they can... combine their abilities."

Cassian cursed under his breath.

"By channeling each other, they can put a ridiculous range on their damage. My advice? steer clear of them. But if you can't, try to get one while their powers are linked. It'll put a significant strain on the other and make it easier to uh...kill them."

Cassian nodded, his head cloudy.

"Ren and Nari. The seers. They're two of the youngest contestants and are a couple. They're known to be quite sadistic and enjoy torture before the kill. Empathy is something that they do not have the capacity for so don't try to appeal to their humanity. Their only weakness is each other."

While he mulled over that, Cade spoke again.

"They only have one warlock participating this time around. You've already met him."

Who?

"Potek."

This was just getting better and better.

Cassian needed to ask. "Why would he enter against his wife?"

Cade's eyes were sympathetic. "He's not against her. This might have been due to our lack of cooperation, but he's there to protect Pola. He's acting as a shield."

"But only one person can leave."

"Exactly."

Devin expanded. "He's there to keep her safe, and then he'll lay down his life."

Dear Gods...

"Can he even do that?"

Devin shrugged. "There are only three rules and we're breaking the same one. There's nothing we can do about him."

"It gets worse," Cade continued.

How can this possibly get worse?

"Pola and Vor are fighting for the azraels."

Was he supposed to know who that was?

"Vor is her seventeen-year-old son."

What?

"I'm sorry, she's going to kill her own child?"
Devin shrugged. "It was the only way for her to ensure that another azrael wouldn't beat her."
Cassian was still adamant about going, but the reality of it was only starting to dawn on him. This wasn't a game.
Deianira stopped him before his thoughts spiraled.
"With the amount of history between the combatants, I believe that most of them will end up killing each other off. You just have to stay out of the way for them to do that and take out the last few."
That was true. The thought offered him *some* relief.
"But," Tension re-entered Cassian's spine as Cade picked up where she left off. "As the first of the gifted to take part, you will have a target on your back. That may seem like a disadvantage, and it is, but they also don't know your history. They'll underestimate you." He paused, looking for the words. "If you can, stick to your weapons, hold out as long as possible. There's no need to let them know that you're an actual threat."
Fear is the only thing that Cassian should have felt, but he couldn't help the emotion that overwhelmed him at Cade's comment.
An actual threat.
The fact that Cade didn't object to him taking on the task in the first place should have told Cassian how he felt, but hearing those words was everything to him. It felt like his brother was seeing him for the first time.
Cassian nodded, clearing his throat.
Devin clapped his hands together.
"I need you to put the suit on so we can test your mobility and we can go over some hiding spots that Cade found. We've barely even scratched the surface."

Devin wasn't lying when he said that there was much more to discuss. At three hours, Cassian had almost fallen asleep standing up, but he couldn't afford to miss out on this information.

His suit was a lot more comfortable than he'd predicted. It felt like a second skin.

Salem would love something like this.

Cassian's mind had been doing that for hours.

Where was she?

Did she not want to say goodbye?

He flinched as Devin poked his neck from behind.

"Stay still," he tsked. "I need to make sure the chest plate stays in place."

"How will I take it off when I come back?" Cassian said as he rolled his shoulders forward, realizing just how tight the top of his suit was.

"If you come back."

Cassian didn't laugh.

"Gods, it was a joke."

"Not a fucking funny one," he shot back. His nerves were already suffocating him and he didn't need Devin doubting him too.

Devin stepped in front of Cassian.

"Cass..." His eyes were serious. "The only reason I can make a joke like that is because I know you're coming back. When I volunteered myself, I knew it would be a suicide mission. But not for you. You told me I was crazy for suggesting this thing, but here you are, putting it all on the line for us instead." Devin clapped a hand on his back. "You're too stubborn to die so quit whining."

For some reason, out of all the pep talks and words of encouragement that Cassian had been given, these made an impact.

"Okay," he said quietly.

Devin nodded and gave him a hard pat on the shoulder. "Alright. Come on."

Cassian rolled his shoulders back and puffed up his chest as they re-entered the room.

"How does he look?" Devin asked the room.

She's still not here.

Cade looked him up and down. "Let's hope it gets the job done."

"It will," Devin shot back.

She's not coming.

"And we'll see him the whole time?" Cade asked.

"Yep." He tapped on his bracelet and a screen popped up, live footage of the operations room playing, all from Cassian's perspective. "Right here."

Is she that mad?

"This is your pack. I've tried to make it as lightweight as possible." Devin passed over a small black mesh backpack. "You already know to ration the food, but you should know that I sprang for water purifiers over water itself. I don't want to slow you down when there's a stream running right through the forest."

This is it. No goodbye.

"Cass, are you even listening?"

Cassian snapped out of his miserable haze.

"Yeah, sorry. I'm just trying to keep up."

Devin stared between his two eyes. Whatever he saw, he must have misinterpreted because he threw his arms around Cassian. "You're gonna be fine. I promise."

Cassian nodded.

That wasn't where his mind was, but it helped all the same.

The second Devin backed up, Cassian was wrapped in Cade's arms.

Cade didn't say anything, just held him for a while longer than Devin did.

Cassian didn't expect Deianira to partake but found himself being hugged around her large belly next.

She drew back. "Not this," she said, swishing her hand in front of his torso. "This." She tapped the side of his head. Hard.

Cassian snorted as he nodded. He understood her message.

What now? he thought.

Would they call Emori and send him off now?

Salem.

This all felt wrong. She should've been there with him.

Deianira did a double take as she went to step away from Cassian. She narrowed her eyes at him.

"Cassian, have you seen Sa-"

Click.

Cassian would've asked why she stopped, but he was well aware. Mainly because of the shallow breathing behind him.

And the gun pressing into the back of his head.

Chapter Fifty-Four

He didn't move, didn't even dare breathe as his eyes swept over the others. Some of them were looking back at him, some over his shoulder, but not with worry, with confusion.

Cassian thought Devin would've been the first to comment, but it was Deianira.

Closest to him, she took a step to the side, addressing whoever was behind him.

'What are you doing?'

Wait.

She was signing. Why was she signing?

Devin slowly stepped forward, eyes wide. *'Salem, this is not what I meant when I said all that earlier.'*

Salem?

It was Salem?

Ignoring Deianira's worried face, Cassian took a very short step forward and turned as slowly as he could to come face-to-face with her.

She's here.

But she didn't look like she was ready to say goodbye.

Salem fixed her eyes to his. She looked as calm and collected as she always did.

So, why was she holding a gun to his forehead?

Salem, what are you-

You're not going.

While he was delighted to hear her speak a full sentence to him, this was not what he was hoping for.

Salem, we've been over this.

No, Cassian. You've been over this. I never agreed.

Her voice held so much conviction.

Can you at least put the gun down?

No.

You're not gonna shoot me, Sae-

BANG!

Everyone in the room jolted at the bullet that was sent into the ceiling.

"Salem!"

"Fuck!"

"Are you crazy?!" he bellowed.

She brought her aim back to Cassian.

I wouldn't kill you, but I would shoot you. You can't fight with a bullet in each of your kneecaps. If that makes me crazy, then yes, I am.

Cassian had to shake his head to make sure he was hearing right.

She would really go that far?

He sighed and briefly looked away before quickly backhanding her wrist and using his other hand to twist the gun out of her grasp.

Staring into her shocked eyes, he blindly passed the gun to Deianira behind him.

He placed his palms out flat, as if she might go off at any second.
He wasn't sure that she wouldn't.

I have to.

You don't. Her tone was less confident now, more desperate. *I can go.*

He shook his head. *You know I can't let you do that, Sae.*

She was quiet for a while, eyes darting to the others behind him.

Cassian ignored them, his attention was on her.

She looked back at him, face pained.

Please.

His chest clenched. He just couldn't.

Sae, I'm sorry, but-

"Please..."

Cassian's heart threatened to tear into two.

She was speaking, unprompted. She was begging.

Had he not been so focused on her face, Cassian wouldn't have noticed the watery buildup in the corners of her eyes.

Were those... tears?

He couldn't take this. He took a step forward, hands outstretched. Salem backed up a step to match his, tearing the hole in his heart wider.

"Forty-three days ago," she rasped with a slight hitch. "You said that there wasn't anything I could ask that you would say not to. I'm asking you not to go," she said, straightening her spine. "You can't say no."

He did say that.

But his words weren't enough to let him send her into that forest.

Salem wouldn't give up though.

He knew she wouldn't, but he needed to go. He had a whole nation to fight for.

Her, especially.

He'd only started to shake his head when Salem stepped back, feet apart, fists clenched.

Cassian halted.

He wasn't going to fool himself into thinking he could take her. Even if pigs flew, he'd be in too bad a condition to win the trials.

There was no winning.

Okay. I'll stay.

This was her last shot.

If this didn't work, she'd have to fight him and she wasn't sure if she could do that. Shooting him was one thing, but actively trying to harm him was another.

Okay. I'll stay.

Salem sagged as a sob tore free from her throat. She ignored the different versions of confusion in the room as she threw herself at him. He wrapped a large arm around her waist, cradling her head with the other.

It worked.

He's staying.

She was drained, physically and emotionally.

He didn't seem very happy, but she didn't expect him to be.

At least he's safe, she told herself.

She could feel his chest vibrating as she buried her face in his neck, but she didn't care for what he had to say to the others. She had all she needed.

As his words trailed off, he began walking toward the exit.

She didn't object.

Being in that room was the last thing she wanted.

Salem just relaxed in his arms, closing her eyes as he stroked her head and walked her far, far away.

She didn't care where they went, as long as Cassian came with her.

Behind her lids, Salem couldn't help but notice the drastic change in lighting.

It was very bright, blinding almost.

Just as she went to open her eyes, Cassian gave her a gentle pat on the bottom and lowered her to her feet. The moment her boots touched the ground, he took several steps back while she tried to blink her vision clear.

Cassian?

Why was he moving away?

As her vision corrected, the room started to become more familiar.

The white room.

Cassian.

Salem went to march up to him when she ran straight into a slab of glass.

Glass walls.

Cassian, what are you doing?

He winced as he started to back up out of the room.

Out of the assessment room.

I'm sorry.

Salem's eyes doubled in size as she slapped a hand on the glass.

No, no, no, Cassian, don't!

He looked pained. *I'm doing this for you.*

I didn't ask you to! You said you'd stay!

I know I did. You can hate me for it when I get back.

Salem drew back a fist and sent it into the glass. She didn't expect anything to happen, and nothing did. That didn't stop her from doing it again though.

Cassian came running back to the glass, both palms flat against it.

Please don't do that...

Then let me out! she seethed.

You're going to hurt yourself!

SO ARE YOU!

She felt like she was losing her mind. He was actually going. All this time, it didn't feel real, she thought she'd saved him, but he was actually about to do it.

And there was nothing she could do to stop him. There was no other way.

Cassian rubbed a shaky hand over his head.

Salem, I don't know what else to do.

She kicked the glass. *I told you what to do!*

And I said I can't let you do that!

Cassian, let me out of here, right now!

Will you try to stop me?

YES!

Salem.

She could feel something brewing inside of her. Her behavior so far had already stunned her, but she could feel something more coming. Something darker.

She grabbed both sides of her head and curled her fingers to keep from ripping her hair out.

Sae.

She could barely breathe.

Salem, please understand.

NO! she bellowed down the link.

Cassian flinched and grabbed his ear. *Sae-*

No! I won't understand!

He cocked his head back. *Salem-*

STOP IT!

What else am I supposed to do?!

Salem began pacing, shaking her head, mumbling to herself. Her chest was too tight. She'd never felt pain like this before, she couldn't take it.

Why did her heart feel so heavy?

She knew that there was nothing physically wrong with her, so why did it hurt so much?

She faced the glass as it clicked.

This is your fault... she whispered.

What?

She nodded, assuring herself.

This is your fault! she screamed.

What are you-

None of this would've happened if you didn't...

She trailed off, trying to work it out.

When was it?

When exactly did her obsession turn into...

He marched back to the glass. *If I didn't what?!*

Her head flicked back up.

If...if you didn't touch me! she shrieked down the link. *If you didn't kiss me! If you didn't take care of me! If you didn't make me need you!*

His face dropped.

Salem... he breathed.

She wasn't done.

You made me like this! If you just stayed away from me, it wouldn't feel like this!

It looked like it pained him to ask, but he laid a hand on the glass.

Feel like what?

Salem's eyes narrowed into slits.

No.

He didn't get to do this and then question her feelings.

She took a raspy breath and began approaching the wall slowly. Looking up straight into his eyes, she whispered her next words.

I am telling you now...that I will get out.

Cassian's face hardened as she took a step closer.

You can double the measures on this cage, and I will STILL. GET. OUT.

This time, he moved back as she took another staggered step.

I will get out and I will find you, and you will wish I didn't.

She didn't even let him cut in as she felt the link wobble.

SHUT UP! she yelled.

Salem paid his anguished face no mind. He was the one hurting her.

Cassian Alden, if you leave me here...and something happens to you,

He swallowed.

After I've killed the person responsible...I will kill you myself.

As Cassian's eyes widened, she licked the salty tear from the corner of her lip and pinned him with a deathly stare.

Then, she blocked him.

She didn't want to hear anything else he had to say. She couldn't.

His voice had been the only thing she'd heard clearly in years, it was something she cherished. But in the moment, there was nothing she wanted to hear less.
It wasn't long before Cassian was slamming his palm on the other side of the glass, trying to get her attention.
It was no use, it was soundproofed.
Cassian's chest rose as he walked backward toward the door.
He's leaving.
Seeing his retreating figure was almost enough to make her want to reach out again, but she didn't have to. He might not have been able to speak to her, but he was making sure she heard him.
He fixed her with a cold look. *'You might think that I'm doing this for the sake of it...or to rob you of the opportunity, but I say this with absolutely no remorse...'* He took a deep breath. *'If you had said anyone else's name that day, any name but yours, I wouldn't be doing this.'*
His gaze was brutal.
'I thought Devin was out of his fucking mind when he brought this shit up, but now I'm doing it. For you. How do you think I feel about you, Salem?! Do you think this is easy for me?! Do you think this is a game to me?!'
His hands shook with fear, with rage.
Salem couldn't look away.
'Maybe you volunteered yourself out of duty or your incessant need to save everyone around you, but I'm doing it because I love you!'
Her breath caught in her throat.
He went on, his hands frantic, his face pained.
'I know you think I won't make it, but I'm promising you that I will. I swear to the Gods, I'll come back for you. Because I want to live for you, I want to live with you, I want to marry your crazy ass, and I want to buy you a house and learn to cook the shit you like. I want to look after you

every day, and I want to sleep in the same bed with you every night, and I'm going to do everything in my power to make you happy. I will come back because I want to do everything with you, Sae.'

Salem shuddered, trying to silence her sobs as she dragged a hand down the glass.

'So yes, I'm sorry for tricking you, but I'll be damned if I'm sorry for protecting you!'

She watched, frozen, as he backed up the last step out of the door and swiped his bracelet across the panel.

It didn't take more than a second for the door to slide closed, but it took five for Salem to well and truly lose her shit.

To be continued...

Thank You

Thank you so much for reading 'Brother of The King Consort'. I hope you enjoyed reading it as much as I enjoyed writing it. I must apologize for the cliff-hanger but it was too good of an opportunity to pass up. With this in mind, I would like to announce that there will be a third and final book in the QOTD Series by the name 'King of Patriam: Outlaws'. It will be a continuation of Cassian and Salem's story, while also introducing a few new characters to add the found family aspect. To keep updated on its progress and see its release date/promos, check my social media (handles are in my kindle author profile).

See you soon,

- Amizah R

Printed in Great Britain
by Amazon

23361279R00248